THE RATTEN EXPEDITION

THE RATTEN EXPEDITION

DAVID A. HORNUNG

iUniverse®

THE RATTEN EXPEDITION

iUniverse books may be ordered through booksellers or by contacting:

iUniverse
1663 Liberty Drive
Bloomington, IN 47403
www.iuniverse.com
1-800-Authors (1-800-288-4677)

ISBN: 978-1-4917-7476-2 (sc)
ISBN: 978-1-4917-7657-5 (hc)
ISBN: 978-1-4917-7475-5 (e)

Library of Congress Control Number: 2015915795

Print information available on the last page.

iUniverse rev. date: 08/03/2017

The following is a work of fiction. All characters are the author's invention and are not related to any persons alive or dead. Where historic persons are referenced, they were giants one and all.

Annie Marie, PJ, Brady, Portos, and Arimis would like to reassure all readers that no cats were harmed or killed during the writing of this book. Cat food dishes were refilled, along with kibble bowls and water dishes, at regular intervals, although, occasionally, it was necessary to remind the writer that scratching one's family members took precedence over writing.

My thanks and praise to Father Peter Drilling, former rector of Christ the King Seminary (retired) and my source of information on all things Catholic. He is also one of the finest men I have ever known and an outstanding educator.

An additional tip of the hat to Holly, my editor at iUniverse, for all the painstaking corrections and encouragement. Cannot forget Pricilla Mangold my proof reader for this edition. You learn by doing and I learned that a proof reader is very necessary!

CONTENTS

SUMMER IN THE YEAR OF OUR LORD 1869

She heard all the people cheering—something about General Lee meeting with General Grant at Chattanooga to surrender his army. She saw the shadow drift across the cheering scene as one of the giant army airships patrolling the city's harbor approached, its crew yelling themselves hoarse and adding to the din.

None of this mattered to the girl; nothing meant much to her except that she was hungry, so hungry she did not even feel it anymore. She was weak, that she could feel. It was in her mind that she knew instinctively that she needed food. Momma had given her food, but that was a long time ago. Momma had been warm when she held her, but she did not remember being warm; it was a faint memory. She saw soldiers in the streets and knew something about the war being over or almost over or some such, but it meant nothing to her. All she knew was Momma was gone and she needed food.

The policeman heard the cry of the street vendor and saw the little child running toward him. He ducked back around the corner. Showing no visible effort, he snared the child as she turned around the corner where he lay in wait. Once he had the child in his arms, he noted she was female, so skinny it was hard to tell at first. He noted just how thin she was and so weak she could not run very quickly. *Another street urchin,* he thought, *probably turned out by parents who could not feed her.* The girl screamed and then fainted in his grasp.

The street vendor showed up, telling the copper to arrest her for theft, the apple still in her hand.

The copper looked down at the unconscious little girl and told her in an Irish brogue without much feeling, "It will be the workhouse for you, me darlin'." With that, the officer put manacles on the child. He had seen how these urchins could fight when they woke up, the fear coursing through them. He did not need the scratches on his face just because he felt a bit sorry for her.

Later, the girl, having regained her weakened faculties, sat alongside some other criminals in a hard, cold jail cell. At least she had gotten some old bread and water while she awaited her fate; it was like a banquet to her. The door was unlocked, and the turnkey told her to come with him. The girl followed along. However, as soon as they cleared the cell block, she bolted for the doors. She had almost reached her destination and, with it, her freedom, when a rather large, well-dressed man who looked more like a banker than a policeman, seemingly coming from nowhere, grabbed her and picked her up. She clawed and bit like a wildcat, but the man ignored her attempt at freedom.

He set her down and looked at her. "Relax, girl. I am not here to harm you but to take you to a better place. Do you understand?"

The child looked back at him. She knew she could not escape. The man had a firm grip on her arm. His hand felt like the iron shackles the crusher had used when he brought her in.

He continued in a firm but not harsh tone "What is your name, girl?"

The child looked at him. She did not know what to make of this situation. At eleven, she did not have enough experience to process what had happened to her—that and her body was still weak from lack of food, which made it even harder to think. He shook her again as if to show her he was in charge. She realized that she really didn't have much to lose. She looked up at him. "My name is Julia."

Julia tried to make sense of what was happening as the turnkey came up and said, "What do you think, Mr. Anderson? I told you she's a feisty one."

Julia continued to process the scene as the man looked down at her again. And then he spoke to the officer while still looking at her. "Indeed she is. I think she will fit into my school's educational program very well, very well indeed. The usual finder's fee and, of course, you will see all the arrest records are eliminated, Murphy." This last was not said as a question but more of an order.

She saw the turnkey smile. "Indeed, Mr. Anderson. Yes, sir. I understand. She was never here. The city's finest has never heard of a 'Julia'. As always, very nice doing business with you, sir, a fine government representative such as yourself."

Murphy smiled as several greenbacks and gold coins were handed over. What did he care what the man wanted the girl for, although he could guess some men liked them that young—not his sport. But anyhow, it was not his problem anymore—just one less vagrant, hungry street kid for the city to deal with and feed.

The man called Anderson did not care what the copper thought of him. He looked down at the girl saying, "I run a special school for young women such as you. The food is good and plentiful, the course of study quite interesting. I think you will like it."

The girl looked fearful but resigned. She knew that she was going with this man whether or not she wanted to. She asked him in a resigned voice, "What do I call you, sir?"

Julia took in that the man's face softened a bit, and he smiled as he was looking down at her. He said, "You can call me Uncle William. Come along. You have quite a few classes to worry about Julia and I think you will enjoy meeting the other girls."

With that, the two left the police station and stepped out into the city, where people were joyfully celebrating the end of ten years of civil war. They climbed into a carriage and started the trip to the special school Anderson ran. The little girl wondered what her life would be like from then on.

CHAPTER 1

A CALL TO ARMS

It was mid spring, and New York City's weather had been fair so far this year, the year of our Lord 1877. The mud was minimal and what there was of it was mostly a result of the buckets that were emptied out of the windows and doorways—that and the open sewers. The boardwalks at the sides of the streets helped to keep some of the dirt and mud at bay, although they were far from a perfect solution. This was not the best part of the city; indeed, as anyone who was familiar with the city would know, the Five Points in New York, to put it very mildly, was the most disagreeable area of that bustling, sprawling metropolis. The area was run down, although that was a bit of an overstatement, since many of the buildings that formed Five Points had been poorly designed and haphazardly built with decidedly inferior materials so that their current condition differed very little from that of their original state. Broken windows, doors hanging at an angle, and several burned-out shells were visible.

The man stood out as he walked along the street. It was not that he was unusual; if anything, he was rather ordinary. He was only slightly taller than average. His was a trim build, not so odd considering that many folks still engaged in manual labor, in spite of the vast advantages that the thrilling technology of steam allowed. This was especially true when combined with the excellent degree of control that Mr.

Babbage's engines—steam powered, of course, and much smaller and more powerful every day—exerted in an almost magical, wizard-like way. It seemed that each new day brought forward a decade's worth of new inventions and industries, the pace of discovery spurred on by the decade of war and now a decade of uneasy peace. The shipyards had begun building powerful undersea ships, and mighty airships crisscrossed the skies. Even in the cities steam tractors pulled carriages and freight along the streets. Rumors had circulated that men had even exceeded the limits of the atmosphere, far outstripping the rigid airships the army and navy used.

The man's face was handsome, but not, as the ladies would say, one that would sweep a girl off her feet. Still, it was handsome enough that most ladies would, most assuredly, not be embarrassed to be seen on the arm of such a gentleman as they stepped out. The hair that showed from under his hat was dark brunette, with just a sprinkle of gray here and there. His face was cleanly shaven and his complexion gleamed a healthy color. No, he was in appearance a most ordinary sort of gentleman. The only exception was, perhaps, the eyes. They were brown—not so spectacular. It was the way they moved, constantly, as if they were encompassing and evaluating everything and everyone around him, missing nothing.

What truly made this man stand out was that he seemed to be out of context. This was because of his choice of clothes and the firm tread with which he moved along. His clothes were clean and well tailored, definitely those of a proper gentleman. They were not, perhaps, from the best shops—not a dandy then—but of several orders of magnitude better than the attire worn by those around him. This included all others in the adjacent area and, for that matter, several blocks in any direction. This area was home to the great unwashed of New York's society; it was as if here one found the discharge of a human sewer pipe, the dregs of humanity. Their clothes were mismatched and, in some cases, not much more than rags. Even those items that had come off the dead—and in far too many cases they had—were mere rags. Yes indeed, it was, in great part, the man's clothes that caught the eyes of those who were sober enough (or not deep in the embrace of some of the various opiates the residents were so fond of) to notice.

On his head perched a well-made John Bull, not sitting squarely as quite a proper gentleman but with a slight rake to it as an adventurer might affect. His feet moved him firmly along the street. Finally, he carried a cane with a wolf's-head top, although from his pace it would seem to be unneeded and merely a fashion accessory. It seemed odd, that cane, such a thing a dandy might carry. However, this man did not appear to be a dandy but, instead, a solid man whose clothes were fashionable but also functional. If he was a not a dandy, then what would one make of him? His articles of clothing were, without doubt, the accoutrement of a man who used his brain and not the sweat of his brow to make his way in the world, perhaps a banker or a lawyer. This made one wonder what he was doing here, of all the places in the sprawling city that he could have chosen to visit.

The man walked along, seemingly oblivious to what was transpiring around him, except for those eyes, always searching and noting. As he passed a rather dingy and vacant alley, he turned in. Two local residents, not surprisingly, followed him into the alley. As they rounded the corner, their obvious quarry was not to be seen. They rushed forward, only to stop dead in their tracks as a firm baritone behind them asked from a deep and dark doorway, "Looking for something, or should I say, someone?"

The men turned, and the smaller and somewhat grubbier of the two—although that was only relative since neither of the pair smelled sweet and fresh—smiled. The smaller man had a rat-like appearance and pockmarked complexion, while his larger companion looked more like a mongrel dog from the garbage dump. We should note further that on neither of the two could a clean patch of skin be found; that is, if one could stand the smell and get close enough to look. The smaller man replied in a bit of a snarl, "Looking for you, mister. Thought a man of means like yourself would like to make a donation to help the starving poor."

The man looked at them and just, almost imperceptibly, shook his head and said, "And if I don't have such a mind to do so?"

"Well, then, I guess we will just have to persuade you." Taking over from his shorter friend, the taller partner pulled a truncheon from his waistband as he said this. Simultaneously, a knife appeared in the small one's hand as he started to sidestep for a better attack position.

The gentleman smiled slightly, and, with a flick of his right hand, the wolf's-head cane came up toward the knife wielder's throat, its tip suddenly extended as a surgically sharp, eight-inch blade blossomed from it as if by magic.

Meanwhile, the larger of the two was looking down the business end of a four-barrel pepperbox, which—if anyone had been able to ask him and was of a mind to do so—the man would have sworn was constructed of four rather enormous pipe culverts welded together. To others, the barrels would have seemed somewhat less than gargantuan, actually on the small size, but it is a subtle difference in perspective that tends to determine how one forms his or her vivid and immediate impressions.

The would-be muggers suddenly froze in place, giving a look that anyone who has hunted deer at night with a lantern would recognize. They were as still as statues, except for the sweat that blossomed on their grimy faces.

"Why don't I just agree to leave a small donation in the local church's poor box instead?" the gentleman spoke softly, as if this were just a pleasant exchange between old friends.

It seemed to take no time at all before the pair, as if in unison, replied that such a donation would be a fine thing indeed and added that they hadn't meant anything and were truly sorry for any misunderstanding. The man smiled at them and said that he was glad the matter could be resolved in such an amicable fashion. He added that the two could now take their leave, which, to no one's surprise, they did in a most expeditious fashion, disappearing down the alley so fast that one would have expected a whirlwind of paper and dirt to remain swirling in the wake of their hasty departure.

Returning the small but quite lethal gun to its concealed holster, the man pushed on the wolf's left ear. The glistening, razor-sharp blade disappeared as quickly and silently as it had appeared, and the cane was just that again, a simple walking stick such as a proper gentleman would carry, nothing more than a fashion accessory. The man paused only a moment to ensure that the two would-be thugs had, indeed, decided to look for easier pickings, before turning on the heel of his Wellingtons and regaining the street to resume his determined walk toward his destination.

Several more poor and drab but, he thought, delightfully unexciting blocks later, the gentleman turned off the street and headed through a much-mended wooden gate and up a short brick walk to the rectory of Saint Brigit's Roman Catholic church. The building in question was decidedly better than the structures around it, except for the adjacent church itself, although, given the neighborhood, that was indeed faint praise. By this time, it was mid afternoon, and the shadows were beginning to lengthen. As it was still spring, the days were on the short side. However even this early in the year the weather was warm and dry, a perfect day to pay a visit. The wolf's head tapped politely on the solid wooden door.

A sound came from inside and the door opened slightly to allow a wary eye to appear. A stiff, female, Irish voice asked, "What is it you would be wantin'ir?"

The gentleman replied, "It is not, madam, what I want but what the first sergeant wants with me that brings me here."

The voice started to reply and got only as far as, "This is a house of God; there are no soldiers..." before it was cut off by a new voice, one that was far more masculine but gentle. "It is all right, Mrs. Kelly. I know this man. He is a friend, and besides, I doubt if the likes of him would find the contents of our parish poor box worth his efforts should he choose to rob us."

"Well, I never," said the first voice behind the door.

Then the door opened to reveal an older woman in a stiff dress, worn and frayed but mended neatly and quite clean, especially when compared to the rest of the area and its residents.

"Come in, Major. I should not want you standing there in plain sight," said the man, whose cassock and Roman collar made it clear he was a priest, as he opened the door further. "It would not do at all to have anyone reporting to the archbishop that I was having Protestants over to our church. That would not do at all."

As the gentleman stepped into the hall, he surveyed the priest, a slightly built man with a full head of gray hair. The major thought back to the time when he had last seen the man and reflected that his current appearance was hardly what one would imagine as the image of a grizzled First Sergeant of Infantry in Union blue. But then, as it is often said, looks can be deceiving. Underneath the cassock, the major knew from long experience, was a man of tireless energy and unflinching courage, who would fight to preserve the Union or when needed against Satan's evil in defense of his flock.

The housekeeper, as she obviously was, left in a tizzy upon hearing this exchange. "You should forgive Mrs. Kelly. I don't think she approves of me socializing with the wrong sort of people," the father chuckled.

"I quite understand, First Sergeant, or should I say Sergeant Harrigan. Can't let such things get back to Headquarters, can we?"

The priest smiled and replied in a quiet tone, "Major, it's just Father Peter now. The war has been over for a time." What he said was true; the last shots had been fired in 1869 some eight years previous."

The gentleman had the same somewhat vague, haunted look about him as the good father had. "I know it all too well, Peter," he replied. "It seems like several lifetimes ago. As for me, it is now Professor John Morton of the Museum of Natural Sciences." Drawing a breath, Morton continued, "If it had not been for Erickson's steam-powered land monitors and the new airships, we would still be fighting the secession."

"We might not have needed them if that fool Wilkes from the *San Jacinto* had not fired on the *Trent*, killing several officers and men just to haul off Mason and Slidell. There was no way England was going to stay out of the war after that," the priest replied. He continued, "With England's navy attempting to break the blockade and funneling material into the South and her amassing troops on the US-Canadian border so that we had to split our forces, I am amazed that the war *ever* ended!"

"Agreed, Peter," said the Morton. "As I said, if it had not been for Erickson's inventions, both land and sea, the blood would still be draining into the ground like some macabre fertilizer."

The father looked tired for a moment, old memories weighing him down. With a bit of new energy, he brightened. "Where are my manners? We are standing around here as if there were not a camp stool in the parish. Come into the parlor and have a seat," he said.

The two men moved from the small hall into a somewhat run-down but clean and serviceable parlor and took their seats. "Don't mind the furniture; it is all hand-me-downs," said Father Peter.

The professor looked about and said, "Let me guess—from the uptown parishes when they get new."

"Not quite. More like from the poorer parishes, who get it from the better ones, and then they get newer used." He smiled and, with a chuckle, went on. "We have a saying around here that even the church mice have used mouse holes."

John Morton laughed at this bit of church humor. "I have to admit that I was surprised by your request to come here. As you noted, there is little love lost between the various church denominations."

Father Peter looked at his former commander and friend and replied, "Sir, I learned a long time ago, seems like a thousand years or so, that what is most important about a man is whether or not you can count on him when you see the elephant, that first taste of death in combat, not his religion or ethnicity or even the color of his skin. I remember when those darkies from the Second US Colored Troops had the picket at Sharpsburg when the Rebs attacked us. They held the line, not giving an inch until they virtually ceased to exist and gave us the time to form up and meet the attack. If they had cut and run, we would probably have lost the battle and most of the division, but they stayed. They bled most profusely, but they stayed nevertheless. So there are more important things than where a man goes to church on Sunday—as long as he goes." The father finished with a smile.

The professor smiled, somewhat sadly one might say, and thought back. As his eyes became unfocused, it was clear he was seeing another time and place...

The morning was somewhat damp, and the camp was quiet as Captain John Morton walked along. He stopped by the fire and warmed himself, trying to get the dampness out of his bones and the heavy wool of his uniform. After a nod of invitation from his sergeant, he thankfully helped himself to a cup of the coffee that the older sergeant had brewed up.

"Think we will see any action, Captain?" asked the NCO. The sergeant was one of the oldest men in the unit, most of whom were still boys in their teens. It was his age, experience, and steadiness that had given him the three stripes on his arm.

"Not according to the colonel," the officer replied. "There aren't supposed to be any Rebs within fifty miles or so. I just hope the Rebels got the same message."

"Indeed, sir, I would like one quiet day for a change; I really have come to relish them."

"Are the men dug in?" the officer asked.

"Not enough to my liking, but, as you say, the Rebs are not supposed to be here, sir," the sergeant replied.

"Well, get them up and start on the works. The Rebs have hit us where they weren't supposed to be far too many times before," ordered the captain.

It was at that point they heard a crackle of rifle fire.

"Who has the picket?" asked the captain with a sharpness in his tone.

"C Company 2nd US Colored Troops; they are an experienced outfit, and they can fight, sir!"

The captain seemed to be thinking that maybe the shot had been a false alarm when the crackle of rifle fire came again, heavier and far more prolonged this time. "Get the men up, Sergeant. Sounds like the Rebs did not get the same message the colonel did!"

All of a sudden, they heard a sound that wasn't quite artillery fire but similar.

"Bugler, Drummer, sound assembly," the captain yelled. "It looks like we are in for a fight!"

Men were hastily donning uniforms and grabbing weapons. NCOs, in the tradition of thousands of years of warfare, were yelling and cursing, not to mention delivering a few well-placed boots to the backsides of the men who were slow to get ready and fall in. The fighting sounded closer now, but there was still time to take up the prepared positions and grab extra boxes of cartridges. Men stripped the wrappers off the boxes, filled ammo pouches, and shoved any spares into their pockets, along with an extra handful of percussion caps. Ramrods rattled up and down the line as rifles were loaded and rammers returned. Then there was the dreaded waiting, and time seemed to stretch on forever. Each man tensed with every report of those strange, not-quite-cannons sounds going off. The more experienced men were steady, each man at the ready, for most, after six years of war, knew what was coming. For some of the younger recruits, it would be the first time they would see the elephant, and for some among them, their first battle would be their last.

From the woods came a rush, a flash of blue.

"Hold your fire! Those are our troops."

The black troopers ran pell-mell to the Union lines. A burly black sergeant major carrying a white officer ran up and unloaded his burden near the captain.

"What is happening?" asked the captain.

"Sir, Rebs, sir, at least a brigade's worth that we saw. Held them up as long as we could, sir," responded the colored sergeant, gasping for a lungful of air after his burdened sprint.

"Where is the rest of your company, Sergeant Major?" the captain asked, looking at the handful of men with the sergeant major.

"This is all there is, sir. The secess don't take no black men as prisoners; we fell back as slow as we could. I tried to hold it together after the captain took a bullet."

"You held up a brigade that had artillery for at least half an hour with a company?" The captain gasped in shock.

"No, sir, that artillery was ours. Corporal Liman came up with an idea that we tried; worked pretty good too." The sergeant major's voice carried a tone of pride.

"Is the corporal here?" asked the amazed officer.

"Yes, sir. Liman, over here; tell the captain your idea," ordered the black NCO.

A young, lightly colored black man came up and saluted the captain and sergeant smartly. "My blunderbuss, sir." The young man pulled a piece of pipe out of his haversack. He went on, "At least that is what I call it, sir. You know, just like what the old pirates used. Only one shot but at close range. It can cut down the Rebs like a sickle through wheat."

The captain started to ask more about the device but was interrupted by a cry from the line of, "Here they come!"

"Form up what is left of your company, Sergeant, and prepare to plug any gaps in our line," ordered the captain.

"Yes, sir," the big black man responded.

"Prepare, aim, fire!" And the battle was on.

Time itself became amorphous, seemingly speeding up and, some of the time, going in slow motion without rhyme or reason as events happened in different areas of the battlefield. At one point, the Federal line began to waver, but all of a sudden, a phalanx of black troopers rushed in and, fighting like men possessed, reinforced the line.

As the battle progressed, the troops realized they were being flanked, as the company to their side began to fall back. It was at this point the young corporal set up several of his devices on the rapidly thinning blue line. With a scream like soldiers from hell itself, the Rebels charged the flank of the company's position. With a bang like a cannon, the pipe exploded outward; at least twenty rebel troops lay dead or screaming as they died in front of it. As the rest of the devices released their deadly hail more Confederates lay dead or wounded. The black troopers charged the Rebels and, though still heavily outnumbered even after the detonations, pushed the rebels back in disarray, taking advantage of their enemies' shock over the power of the new weapon.

The battle raged for what seemed like hours, although in truth only some thirty-five to forty minutes had passed. Near the end of it, there was an *explosion from an artillery round, and the captain lay stunned and shaken. With a yell, a Confederate soldier charged the fallen man, obviously intent on finishing off a fallen Federal officer.*

Just as his bayonet was about to run the officer through, there was a flash of blue, and the Rebel looked down to see the bloody point of a bayonet sticking out of his own chest. The man in butternut looked surprised and then rolled up his eyes and died then and there. The older sergeant pulled his weapon free of the dead soldier's back and then continued to guard his captain, while the officer slowly shook off the effects of the near miss.

The fighting was savage, but Captain Morton and his soldiers held the line as wave after wave of butternut and gray surged against them. Just as it looked like the company and, with it, its fellows of the regiment,were about to be rolled under in an avalanche of Rebel troops, a bugle call sounded, and hard-charging reinforcements moved in. And almost as quickly as the battle had started, it was over. The men of the company looked around and started to tend the wounded and pile up the dead.

Soon, a brigadier general appeared, unstoppable in his praise for the company and its commander. He said that if they hadn't stopped the Rebs when they did, the regiment's flank and probably the position would have been lost and the rest of the brigade with it! The captain said that his men and the colored troopers, especially Corporal Liman, were the ones deserving of all the praise. The promotions came shortly thereafter; the captain became a major in command of the regiment, although it was so depleted that it was not much more than a battalion in strength, and the company's older sergeant became a first sergeant. As for Corporal Liman and his blunderbuss, the latter were soon to be used more often, and the corporal became a sergeant.

CHAPTER 2

WHERE A PROBLEM IS REVEALED

"I truly am forgetting my manners," said the priest after a long moment. "Care for a drink?"

The parlor came back to the professor's vision as the events of long ago receded into his memory, and his thoughts returned to the here and now. "A little early for that Peter don't you think?" replied Professor Morton.

"Not with what I have to tell you," answered Father Peter. Having said that, he stood and went over to a small secretary and, opening it, removed a cut glass decanter and two glasses. He poured a healthy two fingers into each glass, gave one to the professor, and kept one for himself, and returned to his seat.

Taking a sip, Morton said with a pronounced intake of breath, "Decidedly not altar wine."

Peter looked at him gravely. "No, something stronger for what I have to tell you."

"Before you began your tale, Peter, I would make a small donation to your congregational poor box," Professor Morton said as he took several bills out of his wallet.

"It is the parish, John, but the donations are still very welcome—although I must ask why?"

"Because of a discussion I had with several members of your parish, did you say. Nothing of import, but still, I like to keep my word, even if given under extenuating circumstances," he said, smiling.

"I never question a charitable act for the poor, at least not to the benefactor's face," said Father Peter as he took the money.

The two men sat quietly for a few minutes, each marshaling his own thoughts. The pair warmed themselves before a fireplace lit to ward off the spring chill and reignite their even warmer comradeship.

But as fine as such times were, the moment could not last forever, and after a few short moments, the priest started to speak. "John, I must admit that I have kept track of you—well not just you but most of the survivors of the regiment—as best I could; old habits die hard. After all, I was charged with the administrative paperwork. The good Lord knows how the army loved paperwork, almost as much as Rome itself." The priest chuckled.

"Well, that answers how you managed to find me after all these years. It's not exactly as if I have been bleeding the newspapers' ink supply dry now, is it?"

"Oh you have been in the papers enough, given your various discoveries and field expeditions, if you read though them and then use that to follow you in the various scientific journals," replied Father Peter.

"Now I am surprised; not exactly the bibliography for a man of the cloth. I would have thought following up on scientists working to support Mr. Darwin's discoveries," said the professor.

"On the contrary, I like to keep tabs on the opposition. And if you promise not to tell the bishop or my parishioners, I think God is big enough to handle Mr. Darwin and his theories. After all, he still made the world and all that is in it. The Bible does not say how, and for that matter, what does a day mean to an immortal being who was, is, and will evermore be?" Father Peter said quietly.

"I can see why you do not want me talking to the bishop. You would be drummed out of the Church."

"We call it excommunicated. Your army life is showing through, John." Peter chuckled, an Irish twinkle in his eyes.

"Well, Peter, you have told me the how but not the *why* for the invitation."

"John, I am losing parishioners, and it is very alarming," said Peter.

"In this neighborhood I can't see that as surprising," responded John with a shrug.

"I would normally agree with you, Major, I mean, Professor, but these missing men are different. The men who have vanished were solid men, not the usual barflies and dregs that one finds too many of in the Points. Nor were they the ones who ran with the gangs. The men in question all had families and were stable, men who looked forward to coming home, no matter how poor it was, to see their wife and kids. It wasn't just my parishioners either. I checked with some of the other priests in the area. It is the same story over and over again; men who were the last ones who would desert their families have gone missing. John, I need your help. I've women clutching their children frantically because they've lost their husbands or at least the men in their lives!" This all came out in a rush, almost a torrent of worry from the priest.

"I'm not sure what I can do," said Morton. "What have the police said?"

"The crushers don't worry much about the people in the Points. Disappearances are a good riddance as far as they care. They do precious little for anyone from here." The father spat this out.

The professor looked quietly at his friend. No, Peter was much more than a friend. This man had saved his life during that unexpected battle. He'd later returned the favor. And so it had gone throughout the war, time after time, each one had saved the other. No, the priest was more than a friend, far more indeed. He saw the pain on Peter's face at the thought that someone had hurt the flock God and his Church had entrusted to him, that he was to care for that flock and somehow he was failing in that duty. Duty was a mistress that John Morton understood extremely well. "How can I say no, Peter? I owe you too much. How can one refuse to help his brother, to quote Shakespeare, 'we band of brothers'."

"I do not remember that name from the regiment, John. What unit did he serve in?"

"Don't worry about it, Peter. He was a writer from a long time ago." The major -cum- professor laughed.

"You don't owe me anything, but I thank you for any help you can give, John," Peter said. Deep sadness showed on his face.

"Let us attend, then, to the business at hand. What can you tell me about these missing men?" John's tone of voice was one he himself might not recognize but many a young man would know well. It was the tone he used to quiz students from one of the universities he dealt with. He used it now without thought as he went into problem-solving mode.

"Well, I can only tell you about the men from my own parish. There have been some seven of them over the last three weeks. Two were bothers, but I can see no relationship to the others," Peter replied.

"We have, then, a puzzle. Let us see if we can put the pieces together so we can see what the picture they formed looks like."

The professor kept asking questions for the rest of the afternoon, trying to find some connection between the missing men. They went over the various places of work, churches, and saloons the men had frequented and covered many other aspects of their lives.

"Nothing appears to be clearing this muddy stream up, Peter," said John. "Do you have any information about the men from the other parishes?" he inquired, adding. "I did not realize there were that many churches in this area."

"No, nothing, really, beyond their names, John. The parishes are basically walking distance. Almost no one here has a wagon or horse, so everything is based upon how far one can walk."

"Let us do what we can. At this point, we need to divide up our meager forces. You need to talk to the other families and priests in the area and find out what you can about these other men—where they lived, what they did, anything and everything, just as you did for your own missing sheep."

"Mostly it will be the other priests who I'll talk to. Most of the women work also, so no one is at home. What will you be doing, John?" he inquired.

"I will be going where you can't, Peter," smiled John.

"You mean you will be going to the bawdy houses and saloons," came a shocked voice. "I do have to admit I have had to minister in those myself," added the priest, lifting his eyes up to heaven.

With a smile and a bit of a devilish grin, Morton said, "Those and the various Protestant churches in the area, to see if they have any sheep that have strayed."

"Oh, yes, I forgot there are other denominations in the area. My collar might be a tad too tight not to have thought of that." Peter smiled, shaking his head.

"Till tomorrow then. We can compare notes over coffee, say around four o'clock?"

"Till then, John."

Father Peter and the professor both rose, and the priest escorted his friend to the door.

Early the next morning, dressed in clothing he would expect to be seen in on one of the field expeditions he had been on, on so many occasions, John Morton began his investigations around the Points. A solid morning of walking and talking netted him more missing men and not a lot else; it seemed no one had any idea what was happening to the men. Nor did it seem that anyone was aware of just how many missing persons there were in this area.

After several hours of walking and questioning small, poor churches and hole-in-the-wall saloons with sawdust on the floors and the strong smell of beer in the air seemed to run together. In the afternoon, John looked in on several of the families of the missing men from some of the Protestant churches, assuming Peter would be handling the Catholic ones.

A little after four o'clock in the afternoon found Morton again in front of the parish door. In answer to his knock, Father Peter opened the door. "Come in, John," he said as he led him down the now familiar hall to the parlor. "What have you found?"

"Not much, Peter. There are quite a few men and some women and children missing, but no one has heard anything about them. It was as if they never were," said Morton. "The only connection seems to be that they all went missing either late at night or in the wee hours of the morning, at least if the time was known."

"That is about what I've come up with myself," said Peter. "I have talked to several of the other parish priests, and it is the same story. This morning I had to deal with Mrs. O'Brian. Her oldest son Tommy—he just turned sixteen—has not come home, and she is frantic with worry." The anguish Peter felt was visible in his face.

"Let us share what we have and see what we make of these disappearances so far," said the professor. "Do you have any paper and ink, Peter? I am like most researchers; I think better when I can write up my field notes."

The priest disappeared for a few minutes and then reappeared with paper, ink, pens, a pencil or two, and a small knife to sharpen the pencils and clean the pen. Morton began to write; he recorded the names and dates, the few facts they had about each of the missing people. John compiled a similar list of those he'd learned about, noting names, dates, ages, sex, the time each disappeared and what he or she was doing at the time if known.

Much later, Mrs. Kelly brought in a dinner tray for both men with a very tasty hot stew and fresh, thick dark bread. Off to the side was a pot of coffee, accompanied by a glass of cream and a sugar bowl.

After she left, Morton spoke. "I think your housekeeper is warming to me." He smiled.

"Some, but it is also that she has caught wise to the fact you are trying to help me solve these disappearances," said Peter. "She is one of those in this corner of hell who still cares about others."

The men ate in silence. Finally, Peter went to his cabinet again and came back with two glasses of brandy.

Looking at the pile of notes and lists, Morton sighed. "For the life of me, I can't see any connection between these people. They live in different areas of the Points, work in different locations, go to different churches, have different ethnicities, associate with groups that meet in different saloons; the only thing they seem to have in common is that they are missing." Morton just shook his head in frustration. "There has to be something we are overlooking, Peter—something we are just not seeing!"

As the evening wore on, both men fell asleep in their chairs. Exhaustion was a relentlessly hard taskmaster and it claimed both men.

The next morning, they were awakened by the housekeeper bringing in a breakfast meal, along with another huge pot of coffee.

"I see why you want to hang on to her, Peter," said the professor as he helped himself to the coffee and then, more slowly, savored the wonderful tastes of the breakfast. "She is a gem."

"That she is indeed, John; that she is," agreed the priest.

As the men ate breakfast, they decided to go back to knocking on doors and trying to piece the puzzle together.

"Till later then, Peter," said Morton as he took his leave.

"Till later, John," responded Peter as they went their separate ways.

Towards the end of the day, the men met again and again started to add to the pile of data they had mined, hoping to find something that would tie the missing persons together.

"Nothing, Peter," said Morton in frustration.

"Nor I, John. There is nothing here except that they are gone," growled Peter, running his hands through his thinning, gray hair.

John nodded in agreement. "Let us see if we can track their movements before they went missing. Do you have a map of the area?"

"Indeed, John. Hold on." Peter fetched a map from his desk.

"Let us assume the missing people were going where their families thought they were going. All right, let's start with your parish's men, shall we?" said the professor.

"O'Reilly left his home about five thirty in the morning, here," said Peter, pointing at the map, "and went to work at the boatyard here." He pointed to another location.

"Except this time he never showed up at the yard," said Morton. "You know the area better than I do. What route would he most likely have taken, Peter"?

"Most likely through here and then here." The priest traced a route on the map. "The next man—another O'Reilly, although no relation to the first—started at the tenement where his family lives and was on his way to the slaughterhouse there." Again, he pointed to the map.

"And how would he have gone?" said Morton. Now, the priest drew a different line on the map.

Together, the two went down the list of the first seventeen missing people. Fifteen of them had probable routes that crossed in a one-block area. "Peter, I think we have found our missing link, if we assume that these other two disappeared from some other cause," said Morton. "What is in this area, Peter?"

"There are some unused building, and if I remember right, there were some tunnels that were started for sewers and the underground train tunnels, but they never progressed very far. There was something not right about them, weak soil or some such. But I never heard any more," said the priest.

"Whoever is taking the missing people, for the most part, must be operating in this area and in the early morning hours," said Morton. "I know some of the women work also, and the children might have gone through there in the evening to fetch beer or drugs for their parents."

"I think we need to take a look there," said the priest, almost in a snarl.

"Agreed," said John.

CHAPTER 3
_____

A Savage Encounter

arkness still prevailed, as the sun had yet to rise in the early spring morning hours. The two men, plus several others, met at the rectory.

"I see you brought some help," said the professor.

"Likewise you too, John," said Peter. He introduced five rough men, all of whom were stevedores and worked on the city's docks. They had the muscular appearance of prizefighters. He told Morton that they were all relatives of the missing parishioners.

In the same vein, Morton introduced the four men he had brought with him as fellows he had used on several of the museum's expeditions. They were all solidly built, although not quite as big as the men Peter had recruited. All the men were armed, Peter's with knives and clubs. Morton's men carried knives and .45-caliber revolvers. Morton himself carried a Winchester lever-action rifle, and a .45-caliber revolver was visible in a cross-draw holster. Several of the men carried lanterns.

"Let's be off then," said Morton. "Be careful and watchful, as we have no idea what we are up against," he added.

"Wouldn't be the first time," said one of Morton's men.

"Aye or the first donnybrook we've been in," replied one of Peter's men in a heavily Irish accented English.

They set out on their way. Peter led the procession since he was familiar with the area; he felt as if he were back in the army and his unit was probing for a weakness in the enemy lines. He seemed to conduct the search without thought, as if it were instinctive or born of many years of experience. The men following his lead were quiet, each man alone in his thoughts and each man with his senses as keen as they could be.

One block from the questionable area they stopped. Peter, seemingly without any problem, let John take command, as had been the case during the war. John, in turn, took the command as if he too had reverted to his army days, the smoothness of his leadership born of many years of training and too many battles. John quietly directed the men to pair off, one of Peter's men with and one of his own men.

Following his instructions, the pairs spread out around the block in question so that they had it under close observation. Yet they had moved so quietly that no one in the area was the wiser as to their presence. After about half an hour of observation during which they detected no movement, one of the parishioners walked slowly forward, as if on his way to work. The evening was as still as could be, or as still as it ever was in New York, the silence broken only by ships' horns, the chuffing of locomotives from the rail yards, and the banging of train cars. The men were straining to hear or see anything happening in that deserted block, where all that could be seen were several abandoned, single-story wooden buildings that had enclosed the start of the tunneling, long since boarded up.

The parishioner had gone about halfway down the block when a flurry came from one of the tunnel head buildings. The men who had held back saw a flash of movement. Whatever the moving blurs were, they were fast and gray in the limited starlight. The unknown creatures pounced upon the man, and blood flew. The remaining watchers came forward in a rush, falling on the attackers. Knives and clubs lunged and swung, curses flew, and animal-like growls filled the air, only to be met by gunfire. More forms came from the abandoned building, several of them leaping toward Morton. Only this time, they were met with a blast of powder and a hail of shotgun pellets from a very short, double-barreled shotgun Father Peter had produced from under his jacket. The fight was fierce and bloody. The attackers were incredibly fast and savage. In the end, teeth and claws were no match for edged steel and shot—but not by much. Most of the men had at least some wounds.

Morton looked at his friend and comrade with a bit of shock. Father Peter just shrugged and said, matter-of-factly, "I thought it might be more useful than an aspergil and holy water."

"Indeed," replied Morton.

Whatever had happened, it was over for now. As if to give proof to the deadliness of the situation at hand, two of the parishioners were dead, and one of Morton's men badly injured and dying, along with another of Peter's people. The wounds were sickening; both of the dead had their faces and throats ripped apart, while the wounded had deep bite marks with large portions of flesh missing. One of the wounded had lost his arm from the elbow down.

As the priest began to bind up the wounded and give last rites to the dead, Morton took one of the lanterns to examine their attackers. Only one was left. The others had seemingly vanished, most probably dragged off by the others of their kind. None of the men, no matter how tough, were inclined to follow the creatures and finish them off. Even those not injured were exhausted and badly shaken from the brief but furious fight.

John went over to examine the one remaining enemy corpse. Looking down at the thing in the light of the lantern, Morton's mouth gaped open. To say he was astonished at what he saw would, to be frank, be putting it decidedly mildly. The creature, for it was most certainly not a man, was vaguely humanoid and would have stood about five feet tall. It was bipedal with two arms and two legs, but that was where the resemblance to a man stopped. The creature was gray like a rat, with wicked-looking teeth and three-fingered hands that ended in sharp claws. Its eyes were larger than a man's, most probably for increased night vision, thought Morton. It wore no clothes but was covered with coarse, short fur, except for a short, bare tail.

As Morton was finishing up his initial field exam, Father Peter came up. "By all the saints above and the Holy Virgin, what is that thing!" he exclaimed in a horrified voice.

"That does seem to be the question of the hour, does it not, Peter?" Morton replied. "I am going to have to get this, whatever this is, back to the museum so I can do a proper study."

"What for, so you can write a scientific paper, John? No, this abomination has to be destroyed!" Peter cried out, almost bordering on hysteria.

"Peter, no," said John, grabbing his friend by the shoulders and looking him square in the eyes. "We have to study it. We must know what we are dealing with so we can fight it! You don't believe these are the only ones in New York, do you?"

Peter looked dazed for a minute, almost as if Morton had slapped him. Then, as if by the hand of some illusionist, the priest disappeared, and the veteran first sergeant appeared, "John, forgive me. You are right. We will need all the intelligence we can get on the capabilities of the enemy, for certainly these things are the enemies of man. Such a thing could have only been sent by Satan himself."

"Thank you, Peter. I knew you would not fail to see the danger," Morton said, almost as if in prayer. "How are the men, Peter?" he asked.

"Several dead—I gave them the last rites—and several more badly wounded, not to mention almost all had at least some minor injuries. I did what I could for them. My dear God, they were fast, faster than butternut cavalry and worse than the Rebs for sure, even without that scream of theirs."

"Everyone, listen up. We need to get away from this place. We will need a wagon of some type to handle the dead and wounded," commanded Morton.

"I know the priest at the local parish. He is a seminary classmate of mine. I'll get a wagon," said Peter as he hurried away.

John spoke in an authoritative tone to one of the men he had brought and who was miraculously unharmed. "Johnson, get me something to cover up the attacker."

A piece of canvas was secured, and the body wrapped and covered.

Soon, they heard the clatter of wagon wheels, combined with the clip-clop of hooves as Peter came around the corner leading a pony pulling a small wagon.

"Good work, Peter," said John.

"Oh yes, but I was astonished to find out that my old classmate knew such colorful and somewhat less-than-sacred language for a priest at this hour," Peter said with a sigh, as if he was trying to take his mind off what had occurred and what they had found.

The men loaded the wagon with their dead and injured companions, weapons, and lanterns and, finally, the body of the attacker wrapped in the canvas. Shortly thereafter, they dropped the injured parishioners off at a barber's shop to be sewn up as best the barber could manage.

Peter looked at John. "He was a medical orderly in the war. He has done many good things here, for we have no real doctors in this area."

"Well, if he served in the war, at least he had plenty of practice," noted John.

"That and the gang wars here," said Peter with what was obviously a heavy heart.

The rest of the parishioners were let off at the church. Morton's injured man was dropped at a hospital, which was only slightly out of the way. Finally, the wagon with the strange attacker stopped behind the uptown location of the museum at a rear loading door of the castle-like structure. Morton removed a key from his pocket and opened the door. Soon he had a light and he and Peter manhandled the body off the wagon and onto a cart from the museum.

John turned to his friend, "Peter, return the wagon and say nothing about this to anyone. Just spread the word for people to stay away from the area. We don't know what this is, but we do not want a panic or a mob on our hands. We must keep this under wraps until we have more information."

"I understand, John. The folks in the Points are poor and not well educated. Most remember stories of the various fae and fairy folk from the old country, so it is far too easy to frighten them anyhow. There is no need to start wild rumors, and we definitely need to know more about the enemy," replied Peter. "I will caution my people not to say anything too," he added.

Morton looked at his friend with sad eyes. "Peter, I am sorry about your people. Based on what we saw tonight, the speed and savagery of these creatures, I doubt we will find any of the missing ones among the living."

"Your man too, John. I will say a prayer for him."

"He was not much of a churchgoing man, Peter, but it certainly cannot hurt. Thank you. Perhaps say a prayer or two for the rest of us too, for I fear we may need it," Morton added quietly.

Morton disappeared into the museum while Peter left with the wagon. A museum guard locked the door after the unlikely pair. Morton was well known, but a priest? That was different, not to mention that most of the museum staff did not bring in specimens in the predawn darkness wrapped in a bloody canvas. The quiet guard noted the strange burden the wagon had discharged and read the name on its side.

The morning light was just beginning to rouse the great city. Its inhabitants had slept through the events of the night and had taken no collective notice. The few who had heard the gunfire wisely chose to ignore it.

CHAPTER 4

A Most Interesting Discovery And Meeting, To Be Sure

Morton worked in his laboratory all morning. While most of his work centered on fossils, his lab was also well equipped, with an autopsy table to do work on much fresher specimens. In truth, on several occasions, he had been enlisted to assist the police with an especially unusual case or when some sort of animal was involved. His apron was covered in blood and gore, and still he worked on. He finally removed the blood-spattered apron and collapsed on the cot he kept in his adjacent office, tired beyond caring. His sleep was fitful and far from pleasant, his unconscious mind reliving the past hours' horrors. He was stiff when he finally awoke, his mouth dry, and he was hungry. He was shocked to find, when he looked at the clock, he had been unconscious for nearly ten hours. He looked out the window, and the fading spring daylight confirmed what the clock told him.

Arising from his cot, he stretched a bit to work out some of the kinks. He went over to the sink, got a drink, and splashed some water on his face. Luckily, because of the attached lab, he had running water in his office-cum-emergency bedroom. He donned some clean garments kept in the office for the same reasons he had the cot in there; it was not the first time he had pulled late hours on a research project.

Finally he felt better. Ignoring the hunger in his gut, he went back into the lab. He stopped dead in his tracks when he saw a man in the uniform of a U.S. Army colonel staring at the body on the table. He noted the Medical Corps insignia on the man's uniform.

"I see you finally woke up, Major," said the strange officer.

John unflinchingly and slowly studied the officer and then replied, "I see you let yourself in, Colonel …?"

"Anderson," the man replied. "Let me introduce my associate, Miss Julia Verolli," he added, nodding at the corner behind the door.

Morton quickly looked over his shoulder, only to glance at what he believed to be a short and delightfully curved and very attractive, dark-haired young lady in her late teens, with just a slightly dusky hue to her features. He noted these details only in passing, though, as his attention was most decidedly focused on the very deadly-looking, short-barreled, not-at-all-cute Colt revolver she was pointing directly at him.

"Pleased, at least I hope I am, to meet you, Miss Verolli. And it is professor, not major," said Morton.

"Please, call me Julia. After all, we have been properly introduced, sir," she said, smiling, while all the time the deadly colt never wavered. Instead, it continued pointing directly at Morton's stomach.

"Sorry to say, Major Morton, but it is Major. Your commission has been reactivated, and you are now in the United States Army, not the New York State Militia," so spoke a smiling Colonel Anderson.

"The war is over, Colonel. I mustered out," growled Morton.

"Really there must be some mix-up in the paperwork. You know army paperwork. We can try and get it straightened out, but of course you will have to wait in Elmira Stockade while we do that." Again that same pleasant smile came from Colonel Anderson as he made this rather simple and yet threatening statement.

"My, what a wonderful bedside manner you have, doctor. I trust Miss Verolli's is better," replied Morton, none too happy with the way the conversation was going.

"I would not know. A gentleman, which I am by act of congress, never discusses such things," retorted Anderson with the same imperturbable smile.

A bit of a rather unladylike snort sounded behind Morton, and Miss Verolli said, "How pleasant an experience it would be of course would depend on the gentleman in question and my mission in particular."

"Let me guess," quipped the major (at least major for now). "You finished bottom of your class in finishing school."

The lady in question had started to reply when she was cut off by the colonel, who was no longer smiling. "Please, you two, we have urgent business to attend to. Where did you find the Ratten and what were the circumstances?"

"The what did you call it?" Morton asked in an incredulous voice.

The officer looked at him squarely. "We called it a Ratten after its parentage, a most disagreeable side effect to some government research that was being conducted," he replied.

"I was beginning to think that it was some kind of rodent, even though I could scarcely believe the result of my examination. I suppose it would be impolite of me, or at least a breach of military protocol to ask a superior officer, a side effect of *what* research?" Morton asked with a straight face.

"Perhaps later, after you have answered my questions, Major. Where and under what circumstances did you find the Ratten? And how many did you see?" By now, no trace of Anderson's earlier smile remained.

Morton's answer was cut off by the sounds of a scuffle from the outer office. A somewhat smaller man in colorful civilian attire, topped off with a fine, dark brown bowler hat, knocked on the door and spoke to the officer. "We have the other one, sir."

"Thank you, Corporal. Please show him in."

Without further hesitation, Father Peter was thrust into the laboratory, sputtering and obviously highly agitated.

"Peter, seems as if I just saw you. Let me introduce you to our new friends," said the now reluctantly reactivated major quite smoothly. "Father Peter Harrigan, this is Colonel Anderson, U.S. Army and, if the insignia is to be believed, Medical Corps. The young lady with the strictly-business-looking Colt is Miss Julia Verolli."

At this, Miss Verolli executed a ladylike curtsy. Still, the pistol never wavered, a most impressive feat indeed.

Father Peter smiled. "Must have been an interesting finishing school you attended, miss."

"A very fine school indeed, Father. And I graduated with honors, top of my class, Major, I will have you know." This last was spoken politely but, at the same time, with a note of disdain.

"Tricky to pull a movement like that part off, do you not think, Peter?" asked the major.

"I take it I missed part of the previous conversation," replied Peter dryly.

Anderson resumed his smile and simply said, "Now that I have your attention, gentlemen, I trust the young lady can put her ordinance back into her bag. After all, gentlemen such as yourselves most certainly would not want such a fine young woman to strain herself, would you?"

Morton smiled and replied, "Especially not if the strain would lead to muscle tremors, say in her hands, like her trigger finger. I would never think of it, would you, Peter?"

Father Peter, smiling his best pastoral smile, told the assembled group that, indeed, he would not want to cause such a fine young lady any such potential distress. As if it had never been there, the small gun had its hammer let down and cylinder rotated to rest on an empty chamber before it disappeared into the young woman's muff, and she stood there, appearing for all the world like a young and innocent school girl.

"Now shall we return to the matter at hand, Major?" said the officer with some stiffness.

"Major?" said Father Peter. "I was not aware, John, you had gone back into the army."

Morton looked at his friend and, with what most people would not by any means call a smile, simply remarked, "Neither was I, Peter, neither was I—until just *very* recently; there was apparently some problem with my discharge orders."

"As for you, Father, or should I say, First Sergeant, my superiors will talk to Archbishop McCloskey so that you can have a bit of a temporary parish, so to speak," said the colonel.

Both Morton and, as he could see from the look on his friend's face, were less than happy at the turn events were taking. Both had been quite content being out of the army and enjoying, respectively, a life of scientific research and being a simple parish priest. Morton realized, however, that in this poker game, he didn't have openers, let alone a winning hand—not to mention the fact that he was aware that Anderson had at least a queen behind him, with a Colt in her muff. As this thought was in his head, he also mulled over that he was not alone. His friend was also in the game, whether or not he wanted to be.

Having considered all the options available, John drew a breath and began to tell the colonel and his story of what had happened so far. At various points in John's narrative, Peter added several details relating to the dates of disappearances of the missing people.

Peter, like his former commander, was aware that the man in front of them held all the high cards. As a former soldier, Peter was no stranger to games of chance himself.

As the two men finished their story, Anderson looked at them. "Very good. That was clever tracing the missing men's trails. Our people were at a loss as to where to begin. The Pinkertons, at times, are not the best." Focusing on Morton, he continued, "What has your dissection found so far, Major?"

Morton spoke, somewhat haltingly at first but more rapidly as he continued with his notes on the autopsy. Without thinking about it, he dropped into his best lecturer manner as if in front of a group of students or fellow scientists. "If it were not for the large size of the creature and the fact that it walked, at times upright especially during the attack—although I admit things were somewhat confused in the heat of the battle and memories are rather fragmentary—I would say, based on the internal organs and external features, this creature was some sort of a rat."

"Indeed, Major. We call it a Ratten," replied Anderson.

"So you said," Morton quickly replied and then added quite firmly, "All right, you admittedly and quite literally have us here at gunpoint. I demand to know what we are dealing with since you seem to be familiar with this, Ratten, did you call it."

Anderson looked at him as if weighing a decision in his mind. Should he tell Morton and Harrigan the story? Or should they be simply disposed of now that he had all the information the pair possessed? Without betraying any of the emotion that he had, if indeed he had any at all, he began to speak. "As you are both aware, the Federal government was beginning to scrape the bottom of the barrel for new recruits; with the Rebels resupplied by the Redcoats on the northern border, there were simply not enough men for the war or, if it came to the Brits, wars that we were having to fight. Add in the draft riots and backlash against taking the blacks into the army, and things were getting dicey indeed."

"What about the steam-powered land monitors that Erikson developed?" interjected Father Peter.

"They were still in development, along with the rigid armed airships; no one knew for sure if they would even work, let alone turn the tide of battle," responded Anderson. "We were looking for something else, a new supply of soldiers; that was the reasoning that gave rise to the Amsterdam Project."

"You mean our own government created these godforsaken monsters!" exclaimed Peter.

"The times were desperate, priest! Desperate men take desperate chances and are willing to play God if their despair is great enough. And our situation, for sure, was most desperate!" Anderson's volume rose in response to the obvious criticism that Father Peter had implied, as if volume alone could justify the dead thing on the autopsy table. Drawing in a deep breath and letting it out, Anderson continued in a more controlled fashion. "We searched out the best people we could find to help us improve the men we had—make them bigger and stronger, able to do far more with less sleep."

Morton looked at Anderson with a look of what some might call pity on his face. "So you used volunteers to try to make some super soldiers."

Anderson looked at him directly, as if he had found steel to put into his spine. "No, not volunteers but men condemned to death for various offenses, such as desertion, murder, pillage or rape—men who were completely expendable."

"Dear God, how could you do that? Is that what became of them?" whispered Peter, motioning to the cadaver on the table.

"No," snarled Anderson. "The original men died. There were no further experiments. The project itself was pretty much a complete failure. It was for nothing those men all died. The professor and Chen's work did not produce a single viable soldier," said Anderson.

"So where did these creatures come from? And who did this?" asked Morton.

Anderson again seemed to be deciding something when Julia, who had almost been forgotten about—a true measure of how stunning the developments had been —spoke from behind them. "William, they know too much now for it to make any difference if they hear the rest of the story."

Anderson looked as if he were weighing her words. Then he spoke, "You are, as usual, insufferably right, Julia." He looked Morton in the eye and continued his dissertation. "Professor Wilfred Ulrich of Stuttgart was brought in. He had been working on formulas to stimulate growth in horses for the German Army with some success. He was not the only one, of course. We found a Chinese herbalist named Chen Sun, as inscrutable as they come. Neither one was making much success until they started to work together; then it was like magic. There were all sorts of formulas that seemed to verge on the miracle we were looking for, but none were quite it. The human test subjects grew, but the side effects were lethal; some were so strong and uncontrollable we had to shoot them before they could do any damage."

Father Peter looked as if he wanted to vomit. He forced himself to look at Anderson. "How could you do that to men? Such an abomination! Do you even have a soul?"

Anderson was almost snarling when he responded to the priest. "Do not judge me, Father. The war was almost lost, the Union was going to dissolve. Ruin faced the nation. My project was a chance to save the nation. The men we used as test subjects were cowards, thieves, murderers, and rapists all; we did what we had to do!"

Morton interrupted, putting his hand on his friend's shoulder to calm him and then looking at Anderson. "Go on with the story. What happened then? How did *this*"—he gestured to the table—"come about?"

Anderson took in a deep breath, let it out slowly as if to steady himself, and then went on. "When the first land monitor was christened and went into battle, its Gatlings and cannon breaching the Confederate lines that had withstood horrendously costly assaults at Petersburg, the Rebels could not match it with their limited industrial base, and the tide began to turn on land. Meanwhile, with the new steam-powered lighter-than-airships to scout for the navy and the new sea-going, double-turreted monitors, we were able to hold the Royal Navy at bay on the sea so that we could again enforce the blockade and cut off the Rebs' supplies. Granted, the Royal Navy has its own versions now, but it took them several years to catch up. By then, the war was virtually over. The decision was made to close down the project, or at the least reduce it substantially to a mere small research office. Indeed there had been many who had never wanted it to begin with. Finally, about a year ago, it was decided to close it down completely."

"How enlightened," quipped Peter.

Morton looked at his friend to quiet him and nodded at Anderson to continue.

Anderson went on as if he had not heard the priest. "Ulrich and Chen were upset that their work would not be going forward. They had become obsessed with the project, almost as if they were madmen; then again, after everything that has happened, perhaps they were. They disappeared. We could find no trace of them or their research. They were gone as if they never were, as if they'd vanished into thin air—at least almost."

"Let me speculate. They left behind these Ratten as you called them," said Morton.

Anderson looked slightly haunted but went on. "Actually they were apparently a bit of side research we had no knowledge of. The pair had managed to have their laboratory moved to an isolated, abandoned warehouse so it could be kept secret, I must admit, with inadequate supervision. My fault. When it was ordered that the research be completely ended, the Ratten were discovered in their warehouse/lab. They escaped—or to put it more lightly, were released by some kind of timer the pair had set upon their departure. When my men went in to secure the building, the Ratten got out into the city, but not before killing and eating a score of men. We knew they had escaped but had no idea where to look for them. We had men, both undercover military and the Pinks looking for them, but nothing." Anderson drew a breath. "We could not let knowledge of the project get out into the public. They had to be dealt with and quickly, since there was too great a chance that, not to put too fine a point on it, they could breed like rats."

"How did you find out about us?" asked Peter. "I certainly told no one."

"Let me guess," said Morton, "informers to keep an eye out for unusual happenings."

"Indeed, Major; in this case, one of your museum's guards—very reliable chap," confirmed Anderson. "Do not be too surprised. We have men all over the city, and your guards are not all that well-paid. We received the word that a mysterious body had been brought in, in the dead of night, by several men, men covered in blood including a priest and a distinguished member of the museum staff. Julia was assigned to look into it."

"A most resourceful young woman," said Morton while finally taking a far too brief moment to appreciate the young woman's delightful aspects.

"Indeed, Major. As I was saying, once Julia had confirmed that you had indeed found one of the Ratten, I had my men take up positions while some of the Pinkertons backtracked your movements, which lead us to Father Harrigan," Anderson concluded.

Peter looked somewhat confused. "How did they find me?"

Anderson smiled. "The wagon you brought the creature to the museum on had the name of the parish you it borrowed from. A talk with the monsignor gave us your name, Father."

"So now you know how and where we found them." Morton looked at Anderson and, shifting his eyes slightly to his friend, asked the obvious question, "What happens to us?"

"A valid question, Major, for both you and the sergeant. What indeed. The fact is, from what you told me, there are more than just the one. And as you both must realize by now, these creatures are extremely dangerous, far worse than their smaller cousins, especially if they can breed anywhere near as fast. These creatures pose a threat to the entire city, if not the country," said Anderson. "As you must realize, we cannot let word of this get out, or there would be widespread panic."

"Not to mention revulsion at the government," noted Peter.

"That too, Sergeant. As you know, the government is shaky after the attempt on President Grant's life, although he is recovering, thanks be to God. But the South is still simmering and ready to boil over at anytime, especially with Her Majesty's government continuously fanning the flames. The damn Brits will not let go! To top it off, Mexico is still in a state of brutal civil war, with the French hanging on, so much so that the entire Southwest is in a state of turmoil. Neither the French nor the Mexican Rebels can control the Apaches, so they can raid across the border into Arizona and Texas!" replied Anderson. "Gentlemen, we need this ended, and it has to be ended quickly and quietly. So far there is only the one colony, or rat's nest, that we know of. Do I have any volunteers?"

Morton and Harrigan looked at each other, and an unvoiced communication, such as happens with men who have trusted each other with their lives in desperate circumstances, passed between them. "We will do it, sir," said Morton. "We will need supplies and additional men."

"Very good. I will leave you two with Julia to work out the details. Report to me when the mission is over. She knows the address."

Before either of the two men could voice an objection against working with a female on so hazardous an undertaking, Anderson had walked out the door.

John and Peter looked at each other and then at Julia, who smiled sweetly and said, "What do you boys think, poison gas or explosives?"

The pair looked at each other again and, even more so than before, wondered exactly what they had gotten themselves into.

Morton was the first to shake off his surprise, and he looked at the woman in front of him. "I think gas and firearms. We will have to check to see if we got them all, and that would be impossible if we blew up the nest or hive or rat hole or whatever we call it."

"Oh I suppose," responded the young lady in a rather wistful tone. "It's just that I do so love explosives."

Father Peter shook his head in total astonishment and finally just settled for making the sign of the Cross. Then he squared his shoulders as if he were back in a blue uniform instead of his cassock. Still, he wanted to know more about this "finishing school" of Julia's.

"Let's make some plans and a list, shall we, gentlemen?"

Sometime later the trio departed the museum, each with his or her appointed tasks and a list of things to procure. Then as time allowed, each would get some rest before the night's action began.

While it did not occur to either of the men, since time immemorial, experienced soldiers have seemed possessed of the ability to grab sleep whenever a chance presented itself, almost as a reflex. It had been so since a unit of Greek Hoplites was camped outside the walls of Troy. It would appear that both the major and the sergeant fell back into their military life with little or no trouble; each managed to take a nap.

CHAPTER 5

DRAWING A QUEEN CAN CHANGE YOUR HAND

It was late afternoon when the two men met again. The meeting place was a vacant storefront just down the street from the entrance to the abandoned tunnel construction buildings the Ratten had attacked from. The mild weather had turned gray, and a light rain had begun to fall.

As Peter and Morton waited, a wagon driven by Julia pulled up. She set the brake, tied off the team, and climbed down. The men were somewhat taken aback by her appearance. Julia wore a duster over pants and a shirt, and heavy boots, and her black hair was tied back instead of piled on her head in the latest fashion. Both of the men had seen women dressed as men before in certain circumstances. Morton's experiences in the western wilderness had informed him that some places simply did not agree with lace and petticoats, and Peter had seen women in his parish working alongside the men. Still, it was disconcerting, if not shocking, to see this finishing school girl in the middle o f New York City dressed as if for work.

Julia looked at the pair, and then politely suggested they both shut their respective mouths. Or did they plan to stand there staring all night long?

John recovered first and, by way of reply, said, "Why are you dressed that way?"

She just looked at him with no attempt to hide her annoyance. "You certainly do not expect a lady to go through tunnels in a fine dress, do you, Major?"

"I do not expect a lady to go into tunnels at all, especially ones filled with dangerous predators," replied the major with a snort.

"Major, I am trained in the use of the gas bombs and various other pieces of equipment, and you are not, nor, dare I say, is the father. We are not handing out communion hosts, you know."

Both Peter and John looked stunned at this exchange, but the priest took over from his suffering ex-commander, "Really, Miss Verolli, I hardly think this attack is a task suitable for a young woman! You can show us, and we will take it from there."

"Father, with all due respect, I do not have the time to teach you all you need to know and be able to perform the mission as needed. I am going, and that is the end of it. Now, if you would be so kind as to help me unload the wagon, we can get ready." That being said, Julia started toward the back of the wagon.

Morton shook his head. "I think we just met our Waterloo, Peter."

"Waterloo," replied Peter. "Is that somewhere near Elmira?"

"Close enough to see it," said Morton somewhat exasperated. "Let us see what else our fair maiden has in store for us, shall we?"

As Morton and Peter started walking toward the rear of the wagon, several shapes appeared out of the rain and fog. With no hesitation, Morton's hand held a Colt single-action army revolver.

"At ease, Major. These men are under my command," barked Julia. "I believe I told you we would need more firepower during our planning session, did I not?"

"Indeed you did, Miss Verolli," agreed Peter before John could make a reply. "I am hardly in a position to complain, but could you hold down the surprises for a while, or at least until we are done here? My nerves are not as young as they once were."

"My apologies, Father. And please call me Julia. Miss Verolli sounds so formal, and we are, after all, planning to attack an enemy position together, are we not?"

"Julia then, and trust me, you do not have to remind me about the operation," replied Peter.

As the extra men who would be accompanying the trio into the tunnels began to unload the wagon, Julia introduced them one at a time. All were former soldiers, experienced veterans, even though they wore civilian attire. They were four in number. The only one Peter and John recognized was the shorter man who Anderson had referred to as corporal when he'd delivered Peter into John's laboratory. There was little talk among them, as if they were used to working together. *A trained unit then,* surmised Morton.

In this assumption, he was proven correct. In the brief words exchanged with and between the new men, he found that they had served with D Company 2nd U.S. Sharpshooters, more commonly referred to as Berdan's Sharpshooters. *Indeed,* Morton thought, *not just good men excellent men.*

The first items off the wagon were pistols, again Colt's newest single-action army revolvers in .45-caliber, along with holsters and ammunition. Next came rifles and shotguns. The rifles were lever-action, repeating carbines manufactured by Winchester Arms; these were also chambered in the .45 Long Colt. This was a handy feature in that one did not have to separate one's ammunition since either weapon would handle the same cartridge. Next, several of the men were issued repeating lever-action shotguns in twelve gauge, along with the appropriate ammunition and belt pouches to hold spare rounds. Finally, Bowie knives and several axes were handed out.

Miss Verolli holstered what had been a long-barreled Colt .36-caliber revolver. She explained that the pistol had been modified by one of the sharpshooters to handle a metallic .38-caliber round for faster reloading. Julia explained, with some seeming embarrassment, that the .45 had a bit too much kick for her—not that she could not handle it of course, but it did make her slow on the second shot.

Father Peter just nodded his gray head in agreement, mumbling, "Of course, never know when you might need that second shot."

After this not immodest arsenal was distributed, several more items came out. Julia held up what looked like some kind of lantern. "This is a new lime-light lantern, which projects an intense beam of light," she explained. "It uses the same principal as the newest stage lighting, but it has been miniaturized and made portable; it is so bright it may disorientate the Ratten."

"How long is it good for?" asked Morton.

"Several hours. However, if you throw over this valve and arm it so"—she demonstrated—"whatever gas remains will detonate in about thirty seconds."

"How charming, a lantern that turns into a bomb. Every parish should have one," said Peter with a sick smile.

"Thank you, Father. I cannot take credit for the lantern itself. That was the work of a classmate of mine, but the idea for the bomb portion was my contribution. I think it makes the lantern ever so much handier. Do you not agree?" said Julia quite demurely.

Father Peter, looking pained, just nodded. Once again, he found himself wondering about Julia's finishing school, and once again he settled for making the Sign of the Cross—something he had been doing a lot of lately, at least far more than usual, even for a Roman Catholic priest.

Next, Julia began to remove several strange objects; they looked as if they were made of rubber or a tar-impregnated canvas with pieces of glass embedded in them were it would cover the eyes. "These, gentlemen, are protective coverings for you that remove the gas from the air you breathe." She smiled sweetly.

Both Morton and Peter looked befuddled.

Julia had a former sharpshooter don one of the coverings. "As you can see, the device seals out the gas while the unit removes it as you breath, thus allowing you to move in the contaminated aetheric."

"I can see where breathing would most decidedly be a good thing," agreed Morton.

"Indeed, Major," Julia said with a note of disdain, looking very much as if she was happily contemplating the major not breathing. As she continued, she handed a covering to Father Peter, who looked somewhat skeptical at the whole idea.

With a gentleness much in evidence, Julia began to take out of the wagon some metal and glass containers that were about the size of a milk bottle. "These, gentlemen, are the gas ordinances that will do the job on the Ratten."

Both Morton and Father Peter looked at the devices. The gas grenades certainly looked harmless and innocuous enough, and they murmured words to that effect.

Julia looked up from her work and said, "Gentlemen, I must assure you that these are hardly harmless. These devices, when properly activated, release a deadly gas, a mixture of chlorine and carbon monoxide. They should terminate the Ratten without any problems."

"If you say so, Julia," replied Morton as he surveyed all the weaponry they would be carrying.

Julia replied as if she was reading his mind or at least the expression on his face which was actually fairly easy, since he had made no pretense of hiding his doubts. "Insurance, Major; after all, as the instructors taught us at school, a young lady must be prepared for whatever eventuality occurs. Do you not agree, Father?" She directed this last to the poor, suffering, Father Peter.

"Oh, indeed, Julia. Who am I to argue with your school's faculty? I am but a simple parish priest," replied Peter.

"Oh hardly so simple, Father. I have seen your war record and the numerous decorations and mentions in dispatches," Julia replied.

Peter looked surprised. He had put his whole heart and soul into his clerical duties, so much so that, most of the time, he had blocked out the horrors of the war. By way of bringing the subject to a close, he merely replied, "Those things were in another life and a long time ago, Julia, so long ago."

Julia simply nodded and went back to her work preparing the devices for use. Shortly thereafter, everything was ready for the assault. Morton assumed command and had each man and the lady check their weapons for use. Julia double-checked that each one had his protective aetheric freshener properly fitted and sealed. Finally, Julia handed out the gas dispersion devices to the men, and they proceeded to the entrance to the Ratten nest.

Morton, again seeming to take command of the unit, detailed two of the men to keep a rear guard for any possible returning Ratten, as, based upon their investigation and experience, the creatures were nocturnal. Additionally, the two were to keep stray civilians out of the danger area.

Then the group lit their lanterns; the amount of light stunned both Peter and Morton. It was as if the sun itself was shining in the deserted building. Morton's attention wavered for just an instant, as he found himself wishing he'd had one of Julia's portable illumination devices available on his last expedition. With a firm internal command to himself, he got back to the business at hand and began searching the interior of the building with the beam of his light.

It seemed as if everyone was holding his or her breath when, suddenly, the stillness was shattered by a double thunderclap and flashes of light. One of the sharpshooters had rapidly fired his rifle twice, and two of the Ratten who had been trying to shield their eyes from the sudden, intense light, stopped caring anymore as their heads exploded. The large .45-caliber bullets tore through them, and a thick, red spray of brains and blood with chunks of gray matter in it hit the wall and floor near them. John was relieved to have such men backing him up. The shooter, Bill, had fired before he could even draw a bead on the first target.

The rest of the team continued probing; they found nothing but the opening of a tunnel in the floor.

The group advanced and carefully looked into the tunnel, only to see several sets of eyes and a ghost of gray fur moving. Several of the men, including Morton and Peter, opened fire into the tunnel. Suddenly, a voice was telling them to hold their fire, and next, one of Julia's devices bounced down the tunnel. With a slight pop, the device started to emit a pale, yellowish gas that quickly filled the space.

They saw several of the Ratten fall, writhing in obvious pain. Even though the creatures were utterly hostile and vermin, Peter could not stand the sight and dispatched them with well-placed shots from his new shotgun. The group proceeded down the tunnel. Every twenty or so feet, Julia took another gas device and tossed it ahead of them.

Behind them, the group heard a fuselage of shots and then silence.

Morton quickly, with a muffled command, told Peter to go and check. Then he turned and signaled the group to continue the advance. The men and Julia continued, stepping carefully over dead Ratten bodies. In several side chambers, they found the remains of the missing people. There were no survivors to worry about. All, along with what Morton and the others thought to be various animals such as dogs and small farm stock that many families in the Points kept, had been more or less consumed by the Ratten. The carnage was total and sickening. Several of the group would have loved to take off their fresheners and vomit, but Julia warned them sternly that to do so would be a death sentence.

They heard a sound behind them, and before any of them could shoot, they noted the beam of light as Father Peter rejoined the rest. Speaking to John and Julia, he reported that several of the Ratten pack had returned but that the two men left to guard the entrance had ensured they would be no bother to anyone ever again.

Reaching the end of the tunnel felt somewhat anticlimactic. All the Ratten were dead, and not so much as a whisker twitched. Julia's gas dispersion devices had done their work with grim and complete efficiency. Multiple bodies lay slumped in various positions—each seemingly had died in pain, gasping for breath—both in the main part of the abandoned tunnel and in several side chambers the creatures had carved out. Even though they were monsters, Morton felt sick at how they had died.

Steeling himself, he looked around, checking the bodies. "I need to remove several of these bodies and get them back to the museum for study," he said.

"Why on earth would you need to do that?" said Julia and Peter, almost simultaneously.

Morton looked at them through the built-in glasses of the freshener. "These two," he said, pointing at two of the gray bodies, each about four and a half feet long and with notable swelling in the mid region and prominent nipples, "are or were pregnant females. We need to know if these things breed true or not."

"Very well, Major, I see your reasoning," replied Julia as she detailed the two remaining soldiers to drag the two bodies in question down the tunnel to the entrance.

As they began to retrace their steps, Father Peter asked about the human remains.

Morton looked at his friend and slowly shook his head. "Peter, there is not even enough left to identify them. The best you can do is say a prayer and leave the rest up to God. I am sure He can handle it. After all, he took care of the butcher's bill both sides racked up in war."

Peter looked pained through the glasses but nodded his head. He turned back to the desecrated bodies and began to pray, his head bowed. His shoulders sagged as if under a great weight, which indeed they were, even if it were an unseen one. When he finished, the group continued up to the entrance.

When they were back in the building, Julia told the others it was safe to remove their protective fresheners. They all took in a deep breath, as if it were a sip of the finest champagne that France had to offer, for nothing had ever smelled as sweet.

Julia instructed them to turn off their lanterns and then, collecting them, began to throw them down the tunnel as far as she could. The last one she armed, and as she threw it down the tunnel after the others, she admonished the group to leave the premises.

Just as they cleared the building's doorway, a seismic shudder and a blast knocked them flat.

As they regained their feet, Julia seemed quite radiant. "Oh that worked much better than Genevieve or I had expected," she exclaimed. "Quite satisfactory, don't you think, gentlemen?"

The professor and the priest looked at her and then at each other. Morton shook his head, and the put-upon father made the Sign of the Cross, again.

CHAPTER 6

THE QUICKSAND GETS DEEPER

The bodies were loaded into the wagon, and the extra men disappeared into the night just as they had appeared earlier. With Father Peter handling the team, the three, plus two corpses, made their way back to the museum. Morton left to locate a handcart. In the meantime, Father Peter pulled the two dead Ratten to the back of the wagon while Julia held a lantern for him. Peter seemed relieved that it was a standard lantern and not one of the special exploding models that Julia seemed so enchanted with.

Morton returned with the handcart, and the pair loaded the two Ratten onto it. Again Julia held the lantern for them.

"I shall see you tomorrow morning, Major, to hear the results of your autopsy," said Julia lightly, as if making a date for tea with a friend.

Morton looked tired and replied, "Julia, I think after all we have been through tonight, you can call me John. And make it later. I need some sleep; it has been a rather tiring night."

"Indeed, John, then until tomorrow afternoon, say for tea?" Without waiting for an answer, she turned to Peter and asked in a young girl's voice, "Father can I trouble you to escort me to my lodging? After all, one never knows what one will find in the city after dark."

"No trouble. I would be happy to. I just hope the archbishop doesn't find out I was out with a young lady after dark." The last part Peter said under his breath.

"You may count, most assuredly, on my discretion, Father," said Julia in a conspiratorial tone and a sparkle in her eyes. Peter just rolled his eyes.

Morton pushed the cart into the museum as the wagon pulled out. Ironically, by chance, the same museum guard who had been there several nights ago locked the door behind him.

After Morton had deposited the two bodies in his laboratory, he locked the laboratory door as he left and, with the last dregs of his energy, returned to his lodgings. Without further adieu, he fell on his bed and was soundly within the embrace of Morpheus within seconds; his only concession to undressing were his weapons, boots, jacket, and hat.

The next morning, John's valet found him still sleeping and was somewhat shocked at the sight. It was not the first time he had seen his employer come home from a field expedition in a state of exhaustion; however, where the professor had been on said expedition in the city was quite beyond him.

John woke up to the noise of his valet, after a surprisingly good night's sleep given the previous day's events. After a shave, bath, and other gentlemanly necessities were finished, he completed dressing for the day. As a last but by no means insignificant thing, he partook of a fine breakfast with extra coffee, black, strong, and with extra sugar.

John Morton found himself, if not a new man, then at least a renewed man and able to engage in whatever the day might bring—for example, Ratten autopsies. Thus attired in fresh clothing and with a washed and well-kempt appearance, he proceeded to the museum and, more specifically, his office and laboratory.

After removing his jacket, he again donned his heavy apron and gloves, picked up a scalpel, and firmly set to work. He worked slowly and carefully as he tried to understand as much as possible from each slice of the scalpel or weight of the organs in question on the scale. Each organ removed was placed in a jar of formaldehyde to preserve it.

Some hours later, he was just completing his examination of the second body when there was a polite knock at his door.

Morton covered the bodies, and telling whoever it was to be patient, he removed the apron, wiped his hands, and opened the door to find Julia standing there looking very lovely indeed. Morton realized that this was the first chance he'd really had to do a proper inspection of the lady.

"I hope I measure up to your expectations, John." Julia smiled up at him.

Morton realized he must look like a bounder, a cad, or at the very least a lovesick schoolboy and rather hastily ushered her in.

Julia again smiled at him and said, "I really do not mind. I very much appreciate being appreciated by a handsome gentleman."

Morton finally recovered from his embarrassment and offered a chair and asked if he could get her anything.

Again putting him at ease, she answered, "Yes you can, tea, but after we are done here and in a proper setting. Thank you." Her warm brown eyes seemed to pull Morton into their depths.

"Indeed it would be both an honor and a pleasure, Julia. But as you said, first to the business at hand," said Morton, trying to get his head back to thinking straight. *What is it about this woman?* he thought. He had been out with ladies before, although not ones who blew things up or handled a Colt with such ease and grace. As he showed her into the office and adjoining laboratory, he continued trying to figure out what was going on with him.

"John, what have you found out?" said Julia with an attitude that sounded as if she were discussing the latest young lady's hat styles from Paris instead of two sliced up monsters on the examining tables. She bent over the corpses to gain a better look.

Morton began his dissertation. "The females are not much different from the male I examined the other night. Smaller of course, they average about four and a half feet tall and weigh about ninety-five pounds. The teeth and claws were every bit as formidable—nasty bit of work there. That, however, is not the interesting part; these"—he picked up a jar with an embryo in it—"are much more interesting and a far nastier surprise." The jar in his hand held a Ratten fetus, and there were seven jars in all. The remains of the eighth fetus were in small, dissected pieces in a tray on the examining table. Morton continued, "There were actually eight, four from each female. I have no idea if that is standard or just random luck. But this much I can tell you—they are breeding true; these creatures, if they had been birthed, would have grown up to be just like their parents, no question."

"Then let us hope we got the entire nest and that we got it in time before they spread and created other nests. I would hate to think what such creatures could do among the city's back alleys and dark places. The police are not equipped to deal with this sort of thing. If nothing else, it would certainly plunge real estate prices and send the market into fits."

Morton looked grave. "Indeed, the police are generally not equipped with poison gas and exploding lanterns," he agreed. "Given the timeline Anderson gave us and based upon my autopsies, these offspring take somewhat longer to reproduce than those of their smaller cousins, so I think we may have gotten them all. However, it would be best if your Mr. Anderson kept his informants on the payroll for a while, just to be sure."

"I shall file a report with Colonel Anderson, but not until after we have that tea." She picked up her gloves and offered the major her arm.

The couple left the museum and headed for a small nearby restaurant John knew.

Several weeks passed with no further contact from either Anderson or Julia. Professor John Morton was beginning to feel as if the whole incident with the Ratten had been just a bad dream, except for the part about tea and, for himself, coffee. The Tea had been extended to dinner with Julia Verolli; that part had a distinctly pleasant tinge to it. John had discovered that indeed she was every bit as intelligent as she was pretty. No, cancel that; she was beautiful, not just pretty, and perhaps even more intelligent.

To be perfectly honest with himself, she was a bit intimidating; a gentleman was used to the idea that females should be not only gentle and fair but useful in a household kind of way. Most men were not comfortable with the idea that a woman should be scientifically literate and—how to put it?—quite deadly. She had taken his well-ordered world and turned it inside out and upside down while shaking out all the pockets too. That, he thought, should just about cover how he felt about Miss Julia Verolli except every time he thought about her, he found himself smiling; damn women!

He had known women before and in more than just platonic ways; she was not the most beautiful but she was so lovely and just so nice to talk to.

Morton shook his head, trying to clear it. It was time to put Julia behind him and get back to his research and teaching. Besides, he thought, he had not heard from her since the dinner after the incident.

John went into his office and laboratory suite and started to go through the mail that had arrived over the weekend, this being a sunny, however cool, Monday morning.

He was soon busy at his work and looked up in response to a knock at the door, somewhat surprised to note that several hours had passed. *I must be getting over that infernal woman*, he thought.

With a brief, "Come in," the door opened to admit young Simon Thompkins, one of the curator's aids, with a message that, as soon as he could make it, the curator would be pleased to see him in his office.

He thanked the lad. He finished up the letter he was writing and, donning his coat, he prepared to go upstairs to the curator's office. It would never do to keep the high potentate, or at least that was Morton's secret title for Dr. Chesterfield, waiting; after all, he did sign the pay vouchers.

The curator's office was located two floors above Morton's basement world. He was wondering what would have brought the summons. It was rare that he was called to the inner sanctum since, as a senior researcher, he was given quite a bit of discretion as to his projects and research. He only hoped he was not going to have to explain the whole Ratten affair, especially since he had been sworn to secrecy about the whole thing. Morton was quite sure that the less the world knew about the creatures that had lived in those tunnels, the better off all would be.

Morton arrived and checked himself in the mirror just outside the office—jacket and tie matching. In fact, he thought he looked the perfect picture of a proper researcher at the museum. He went into the outer office, where he was greeted by Thompkins again, now back in his routine role as Dr. Chesterfield's personal secretary. With a smile, Thompkins told him to go in; the curator was expecting him.

John gave a polite knock and entered Chesterfield's office. The curator looked up and smiled—no didn't just smile, but *smiled*, a big, beaming smile. Morton suddenly got nervous. The old military instincts—never, ever volunteer—kicked in, as if being awakened after the short slumber of only a few weeks. "Morton," said Chesterfield with the same smile, "how are you today, my boy? John, how did you do it?"

Morton was completely befuddled. But, always prepared, he did not let it show, simply replying, "Well, you know, sir, always working on something—irons in the fire, etcetera." As he was saying this, he was wondering as fast as a human mind could what the devil the curator was talking about.

"John, you are way too modest; to arrange funding for an entire major research expedition by yourself, and from a new donor as well, is really quite astounding. And, I might add, very impressive, very impressive indeed!" Dr. Chesterfield beamed, slapping John on the back.

Morton kept the smile on his face while his mind raced, and he started to get the strong feeling of his stomach falling, as if in one of the new elevator cars; this situation was most disconcerting. However disconcerted he may have been, the professor managed to mask all these sensations and say simply, "Well, sir, I was not sure that the funding would come through, so I did not say anything. You know, I did not want to get anyone's hopes up, sir. I have to ask how you found out," he said, verbally scrambling to find out what was going on. Morton realized that he had that same upside down, inside out feeling he had felt only several weeks earlier with a very specific young lady.

"Why, John, the Anderson foundation contacted me just last evening at the club," replied Chesterfield.

"At your club, sir," said Morton, still trying to find all the pieces of the puzzle so he could start putting them together.

"Why, yes, John. Mr. Anderson himself made my acquaintance. He is apparently applying for membership in the club. Oh I do hope the committee approves of him. Quite an outstanding chap. But I suppose you know that already. In fact I plan to sponsor his membership application; truly splendid fellow. Anyway, he told me how impressed the foundation selection board was with your proposal about the research on primitive fossil life forms in the western territories. He told me confidentially, you understand, that it was one of the best they had ever seen." With this, the curator patted John on the back again.

"Well, sir, I congratulate you. You certainly have the better of me; I did not even know, although I had hoped"—*at least I think I did*, thought Morton—"that the foundation had approved it," replied Morton with a forced smile, wondering what he was involved in now.

Changing his tone somewhat, Chesterfield went on. "I suppose I should admonish you though, John; you really do not have the authority to hire new museum staff without my approval. However, since Mr. Anderson told me the foundation will be covering additional staffing because of the extent of the expedition—and he did mention a young lady he thought would be a significant asset—I suppose we can let it go just this once. Mind you, do not let it happen again. I am still the curator," Chesterfield harrumphed.

"Absolutely, sir! Never again. It was just that the foundation made such a very strong recommendation," Morton said quickly, hoping to salve the curator's wounded pride.

"Oh, it's all right, John. I had the chance to meet the young lady in question this morning. Between us, I can see why you would hire her. Not only is she well schooled and quite the typist, but she"— Chesterfield looked around to see no one was listening—"she does substantially improve the decor in the office."

By now, Morton was sure his stomach was in total free fall off what seemed like a very tall building indeed. He just smiled and nodded in agreement. Morton, following the sick feeling he was getting, said, "I take it you like the Mediterranean look in women, sir?"

"Well, I try not to be restrictive or judgmental about these things, but I must say she is quite uptown, as the saying goes," Chesterfield replied, quite pleased with himself at finding use for this bit of the latest in fad phrases.

Given this last reply, Morton was very certain who his new secretary was.

"John," the curator said, changing subjects, "I must say I was surprised to get a letter from the archbishop just yesterday, asking if we had any expeditions heading out West. Apparently, he is hoping to send a priest out to the territories to inspect some of the mission work the archdiocese is doing, hoping to hitch a ride so to speak. I know it is most unusual. I am not sure if I approve—you know, allegiance to Rome, papist, and all that. I am not sure if they are true Americans." The curator was almost babbling as he continued. "I know it would be asking a lot and I have, I mean to say, I have never pried, but could I prevail upon you to help out here? After all, papist or not, the archbishop does seem to have a lot of connections with Tammany Hall." This last came out almost like a plea, not at all what Dr. Chesterfield normally sounded like.

John just looked at the curator and smiled. At least this smile was not as forced as those up to this point had been; he had a strong feeling about just who the bishop's envoy would be. Morton replied, "Sir, it is not a problem. Even though I am a staunch Evangelical, I served with quite a few Catholics in the war and still call many of them my friends."

The curator looked relieved. "Well, I guess that makes up for that minor hiring indiscretion, doesn't it?" he said. He added, after a moment, "To be honest, John, I think I should advise you to rethink. I mean, taking a young lady, especially an unmarried young lady of such delicacy and sensitivities on a field expedition to the untamed western territories—I'm not sure if it's quite the thing to do. I mean, it could be dangerous. No telling what could happen."

Morton smiled, a bit weakly, and said, "Trust me, sir, from what I know of this young lady, it really should not be a problem." Under his breath, John mumbled, "I just hope the territories can handle her."

The rest of the time in the curator's office was somewhat anticlimactic, with coffee, some rather nice pastries, and one of Dr. Chesterfield's imported Cuban cigars to finish things up. During this pleasant interlude, Morton tried to face the fact that, somehow, he was not done with the Ratten business. Had more nests been found? What indeed was going on?

CHAPTER 7

THE GENTLEMEN AND THE LADY PARTAKE OF A FINE LUNCHEON

Morton reached his office just about the same time he managed to get enough equilibrium back so that his stomach stopped its free fall. As he approached the door to his office, he heard a faint mechanical noise and, seizing the knob, was shocked to find the door unlocked. He double-checked his pocket to see that the office key was still there; it was. Opening the door, he went in, only to find that an additional desk had been moved into the office and Julia was sitting at it typing away on one of the new typewriters, looking as efficient as a secretary could be. Morton was stunned, and his face showed as much.

"Oh, there you are, Professor Morton. I was wondering when you would return," said Julia brightly as if appearing in a man's locked office was the most natural thing in the world for a young lady to do. She smiled even more, if that were possible, and continued, "I have been working on typing up your old field notes."

Morton shut the door and with a completely bewildered expression on his face, said, "How did you get into my office? The door was locked."

Julia, still smiling, replied simply, "That nice Mr. Thompkins let me in when I explained how you had not remembered to give me a key for the office yet. He is such a nice young man. Why he even arranged to have an extra desk brought in for me to work on."

"A nice young man? Don't you mean a nice young boy? Julia, given his youth and lack of experience, your manipulation of the boy seems to be almost child molesting!" Morton was shocked to find himself angry with young Thompkins, although he was not sure why.

"Professor, now you must not be hard on him; he was just trying to help your new office assistant after all. Really, he is a sweet lad," Julia said in her best, helpless-little-girl voice.

This act might have worked with those members of the museum staff who had not seen her in action, especially the look of pure joy on her face after setting off a truly thunderous explosion. Morton, however, was not among that number, having seen the aforesaid lighting up of her face. Lowering his voice, he said, "Exactly what is going on, Miss Verolli? Please do not give me the innocent act either, Miss Bernhardt."

Looking decidedly less innocent, Julia looked at him and hissed, "Major, keep your voice down! As far as everyone else around here knows, I am your new field assistant and secretary. And, by the way, they are all atwitter at you, a single gentleman, hiring a young unmarried female, no less, to fill the position. They are given to understand that my placement was based upon the glowing recommendation of Mr. Anderson of the wealthy, philanthropic Anderson Foundation." She looked around and continued, "There are further complications to be dealt with and your country needs your help! Is that clear, Major?"

Morton looked stunned and just nodded. "Why it is truly, perfectly clear, Miss Verolli. What choice do I have? Your recommendations were just glowing, and the curator himself even seems quite impressed."

"Why thank you, sir, and please tell Dr. Chesterfield that I am honored by his kind words." Julia smiled, reverting back to innocent young secretary mode. She continued, "By the way, Professor, Mr. Anderson sent a note asking if you would have lunch with him at the club today; the club managers were kind enough to extend provisional privileges to him based on his application and the curator's recommendation. He also mentioned that he would appreciate it if I came, since he thought it important that notes be kept for the record of the expedition."

While Morton was digesting this bit of news, she continued, "I would not want anyone to talk, sir. I know how the gossipmongers can start their tongues wagging, so I took the liberty of asking your friend Father Peter Harrigan to join us. Not only is he going to be joining us on the expedition as the archbishop's representative, but I felt, and I hope you don't think me too presumptuous, sir, that he could act as a chaperone today?"

Morton just smiled and nodded. He had fought too many battles during the war and almost as many skirmishes with the other museum staff for funding and resource allocations not to realize that he was being completely outmaneuvered. There were times when a true gentleman could only surrender and, hopefully, do it with grace and style. He looked at her and simply said, "My dear Miss Verolli, I am looking forward to escorting you to lunch. Shall we get ready to leave then?"

The weather was clear again but the temperature continued to be a little on the cool side even as the day moved along. Morton had offered to pay for a hackney coach, but Julia said that they had the time so why not enjoy such a beautiful day? Then the two of them had walked the several blocks to the club. They were still in the lobby, Morton removing his coat after helping Julia to remove her cape, when Father Peter arrived.

Morton approached the head valet asking if Mr. Anderson had arrived and informing the man that they were expected. The valet was quite taken aback at this group. While he certainly had no trouble showing Morton in, Julia and the good father were another matter. This, after all, was a gentlemen's club, and young ladies were, therefore, not allowed, not to mention Catholics, especially a priest! It took all of Morton's powers of persuasion to explain that the young lady was his secretary and that Mr. Anderson, of the very wealthy Anderson Foundation, wanted minutes kept of their meeting and that Father Peter was a personal representative of the archbishop, who, as John whispered in the man's ear quite confidentially, had the ear of Tammany Hall. All the explanation and a small monetary gratuity just to ease the man's obvious agitation at the breach of propriety gained the party's entrance. During the extended discussion, the two persons in question had appeared to be enjoying the exchange between Morton and the valet.

Morton, after finally winning the little skirmish, looked at his companions and noted, "I could have used some timely assistance back there."

"Ah, John, you seemed to have it all under control; bless you, lad," said Father Peter with an Irish twinkle in his eye.

"As your secretary, sir, I thought it would be above my station to interfere," Julie replied, all the while looking as innocent as a schoolgirl.

Morton snorted at both of these helpful statements and was going to retort when the valet showed up to escort them to Mr. Anderson's private dining salon. Turning to follow, the trio was soon seated with Anderson at a rather elegantly laid table.

Of the four of them, poor Father Peter looked the most out of place as he sat there admiring the place setting. John looked at his friend and inquired if there was a problem. Peter looked up and said, "Sorry. I am just not used to eating on china that does not have chips or cracks and where all the pieces match. It is quite a delightful experience."

Anderson laughed and said, "Wait till you taste the food; it is quite extraordinary. The club has one of the finest chefs in all of New York."

Peter looked at him. "I did not say I eat poorly," he replied. "Mrs. Kelly, our housekeeper, is a splendid cook. It is simply that I have never eaten with such fancy finery. Nevertheless, I am prepared to enjoy the meal and thank you for it."

Anderson was slightly taken aback but recovered quickly and replied, "Point taken, Father. Please do enjoy. I am afraid field-cooked meals will not be of this caliber."

The meal was served, and it was everything Anderson had promised. Soon the dishes were cleared. Then Anderson and Morton settled back with brandy and cigars, while Father Peter enjoyed his pipe with some wine. Julia settled for some fine tea and no tobacco for her; proper ladies never indulged in such a vile habit—most distasteful. The room was quiet and the door closed when, finally, Anderson called the meeting to order.

"I want you both to know that the government is very appreciative of the work you two did in the recent affair," started out Anderson.

"Somehow I sense a *but* coming. Is there is another problem, Colonel?" queried Father Peter in his gentle voice.

Anderson looked somewhat annoyed at the priest but continued. "Not *another* problem," he clarified, "but—we think—more of the same problem, so to speak. The Pinkertons picked up the trail of Ulrich and Chen in Chicago but lost it again further west." Anderson paused for a breather and, looking at the professor and the priest, went on. "We think, based on some rumors that have surfaced, that the pair has continued the experiments. You can only imagine what this could lead to, this duet of monster makers with a grudge against the country for shutting down their work. An army of the Ratten appearing in a major city, with the death and destruction that would accompany them. Hundreds or thousands dead before the government could react. Panic and fear sweeping the streets. The potential results, gentlemen, are too horrible to contemplate."

Morton looked back at Anderson with a steady glare. "That and the good folk of the country finding out that their own government started this demonic research; I can only imagine how that would play out."

"I will not debate the point with you, Major," growled Anderson. "But as you say, the good folk could rise up. There would be panic and anarchy on top of the problems a plague of Ratten would cause. We are talking the darkest anarchy, gentlemen. The country needs calm so soon after the war. With the British still bristling and snarling at our borders, we cannot afford another upheaval of this proportion. Either or both the British and the French might take that as a chance to increase their territory in North America. We could see more war.

"Gentlemen, I need—no, the country needs—a team to go after this pair, to eliminate them if possible or at least stop them! Even more importantly, that team must remove the threat of the Ratten before it becomes public knowledge."

Morton and Peter looked at each other, and finally, John Morton turned to Anderson and answered the challenge. "We do not approve of what you and yours have done, sir. But you are correct in that this must be stopped and the quieter the better. The resultant upheaval could well tear the country apart as shaky as it still is; so we are in."

Peter added, "And may God help us."

The rest of the discussions were somewhat technical insofar as the details of what was available to them. In actuality, other than maintaining the secrecy of the nature of the assignment, literally the full gamut of the government's resources was theirs.

After the meeting, John secured a hackney coach for Julia and told her to go back to the museum to keep up appearances while he had some business to discuss with Father Peter.

After she left, he turned to his friend and asked him, "Peter, you told me when this whole business started that you kept tabs on the various members of our unit. Have you keep them for any of the other units we were involved with?"

Peter seemed surprised but responded, "Well, yes, some; not all of them, John. What, or should I say who, are you looking for?"

"Remember the day at Sharpsburg when the 2nd U.S. Colored Troops held the picket line?"

"Not something you would forget, Major." Peter dropped back into to his former life without even a second thought. "If it had not been for their bravery and sacrifice, I doubt very much we would be standing here talking about it."

"All too true, Peter," responded Morton. "We would be acting as fertilizer in a field somewhere. But it is those men I was referring to; more specifically, do you remember Corporal Liman and his blunderbuss?"

"Oh, I remember him well enough. He became a sergeant, and that device of his helped the war effort," replied the priest. "I do keep tabs on some of them, if not all of them. I would have to check my records at the parish rectory though. Why are you interested in him?"

"Let us just say that, before this business is over, I have a strong premonition that we could use someone with a deft hand with tools and a talent for tinkering. I think that Mr. Liman may just fill the bill nicely that and we already know he is not a man to run when he sees the elephant. And I strongly suspect that he can be counted on even if the elephant looks like a large rat instead of a man wearing gray or butternut," responded Morton in a hushed tone.

Peter looked at his friend and former commander and nodded. "Indeed, sir," he said just as quietly. "I think you are more than probably right. Let us return to the parish, and I will check my records."

With that, the two men turned and started off in the direction of the Five Points and Father Peter's records.

"John, I do not know how you did all this, but to have a special set of train cars outfitted for your expedition. Why that is truly unbelievable," said Dr. Chesterfield, who stood in the doorway to Morton's office, or more specifically, the office he now shared with Julia. "Why I have never heard of such a thing! You must know it will set the whole scientific world abuzz with envy. This is certainly going to help the museum's reputation, to say the least. You know, everything has been so focused on the future. The newspapers and monthlies are all worked up about the steam technology advances, to say nothing of the amazing power of the Babbage engine. But with this type of major expedition, my God, John, you are going to put natural history back on the front pages of all the newspapers!" At this point, the curator stopped to take a breath, which gave Morton a chance to get in a word.

"Well, sir, as you are aware, the Anderson Foundation is most supportive of my research and expects success. They back it up by making sure that my staff and I have all the tools and resources that may be needed," he said, matching the curator's excitement as best he could. "But just remember that success is *expected*; Mr. Anderson does not seem to be the type of a man who brooks failure."

"Well, that much is certainly clear. But a whole train? My God, John, that is absolutely outstanding!" continued Dr. Chesterfield, with barely time to take more than a single breath.

Morton kept trying to calm him. "Curator, it is hardly a whole train. There is a Pullman car for myself and several key assistances, which includes a small kitchen and a parlor-cum-office for Miss Verolli to keep her records; a modified baggage car remodeled into laboratory space with room for specimen storage; and a bunk car for some workers, with more extra storage space. Really, that's only three cars, not a whole train." Morton was pleased to see that he was, just barely, getting the curator off the ceiling and his feet touching the floor.

"I suppose you're right, John. But it is still quite the thing," Dr. Chesterfield conceded. "I don't suppose there is any chance of getting a tour, is there? I mean, it is quite a feather in the museum's cap, so to speak."

"Sir, that would be a little difficult, since it is being fitted out for us at Mr. Anderson's private works in Albany. However, I am certain that Miss Verolli can arrange for some photographs and sketches made for the museum's records and to be released to the newspapers," Morton replied, trying to deflect the curator's interest. It would, after all, be hard to explain why a scientific expedition needed a Gatling gun, along with enough other small armaments, ammunition and explosives to overthrow a small country.

Dr. Chesterfield looked a little crestfallen, but he perked up when Julia smiled at him and told him how she would make the photographs and sketches a priority. She also said that she would try her very level best to keep the museum informed, via letter and telegraph, of the expedition's whereabouts and discoveries so that he could keep the public informed. Why it would be almost as if all of New York were with them on what should prove to be a most exciting journey of discovery. By this time, Julia had moved over to the curator and smiled at him, looking up at him with what could only be described as worshipful eyes.

Chesterfield was a happy man and left beaming. He retreated down the hall with a bounce in his step. Morton and Julia could hear him going down the hall toward the stairwell back to his office, whistling a happy tune. Both breathed a sigh of relief.

Julia looked at Morton. "I can understand why you did not want him to see the train and equipment. But what made you pick Albany, when the train is being fitted out in Harlem?" she asked.

Morton smiled and answered, "The curator hates budget battles, and going to Albany reminds him of the state legislature, so it is one of his least favorite places on earth."

Julia cocked her head quizzically, prompting Morton to continue. "The New York Legislature is one of the most dysfunctional bodies on the planet. Besides, we are passing though Albany on our way to Buffalo."

Julia looked surprised and asked, "Why Buffalo?"

Morton responded with a smile, "Why to see if we can recruit our next team member for this deadly game, Miss Verolli, the Jack of Spades. At least I hope we can."

CHAPTER 8

SHUFFLE OFF TO BUFFALO

he cars were attached to a northbound passenger train in the city, and with little notice or fanfare, the travelers began their journey, first northward, crossing over the Hudson River near Albany, and then almost straight westward along the New York Central's water level route toward Buffalo. Along the way, Father Peter and Julia had some time to talk, which gave them a welcome opportunity to get to know each other better; their relationship had, thus far, been built on limited encounters as compared to the one Julia and John Morton had started to form in their shared office.

Julia was interested in Peter's pilgrimage from tradesman to soldier and then on to priest. Peter told her how he had come to meet a certain young captain during the war and of the times they had shared and the moments in which they'd saved each other's lives. He went on to tell Julia how, by the end of the war, he had enough of the killing and seeing men maimed for the rest of their lives and of the women and children caught up in the horrors of war. He said he felt that he needed to atone for all this and made the decision to become a priest, as he put it, "To try to heal the wounds of mankind." He also talked about his time in the seminary and of his studies. He finished with what it was like to be a parish priest in a small and very poor parish.

Father Peter, on the other hand, learned little enough about Julia. She was quite reluctant to talk about her previous work for Anderson— "classified you know." What he did manage to find out was that Julia had been a starving orphan who had been picked up for petty theft when she was about eleven years old. But somehow, instead of going to an orphanage or a workhouse, she'd wound up being trained and educated at a very exclusive finishing school for young ladies. It was a most interesting school to say the least, since it taught not only fine arts such as music, dance, and literature, but also some quite questionable subjects, including seduction, weaponry, cryptography, armed and unarmed combat, and poisons. She said little, but Peter managed to figure out that this particular school tended to admit children in similar circumstances to Julia's, that is, females who were alone and had no one to miss them.

It became obvious to Peter that Anderson, or men like him, felt that having a highly versatile, attractive, and deadly young lady around was an asset. It was obvious that Julia loved Uncle William, as she called him in private, although not as a lover but almost like a father figure or favorite uncle. Peter felt sorry for her in a way. It was obvious that a man like Anderson did not care about young ladies like Julia, outside of what they could do for him. These women were to him, an asset to be used.

Near Syracuse, they were laying over while the cars of their little expedition's train were switched onto a new train for the final leg to Buffalo. It was quiet for a time while the engine had uncoupled and moved down the line where it had spotted its tender, which was being coaled and the tank topped off with water for the final section of the first part of the journey.

Morton was pleased that Anderson had provided, among other useful items, an exceptionally excellent cook, who did an unquestionably fine trout with almonds. The dinner was consumed with delight, all agreeing that it was indeed an excellent meal. Morton also thought that Julia looked lovely in a somewhat daringly cut dark blue dress that showed off her figure superbly. Over a fine white wine, the discussion turned again to the mission. Julia again asked why they had to stop in Buffalo and who this new team member that John had mentioned.

Morton looked at her as he savored the fine white wine that had been served with dinner. "We are in route to the West to track down Ulrich and Chen and, furthermore, to end whatever evil they have already done and stop what evil they have planned, Julia."

"I am aware of that, Major, but what does all that have to do with Buffalo? Nothing in the reports referred to that city," responded Julia tartly. "You both realize that time is of the essence in this matter." She directed her gaze at both Morton and Peter. "I assume you saw the notes from the Pinkertons in Chicago."

At this point, Father Peter answered, "Julia, we are going to Buffalo since that is the last known whereabouts of an old army comrade of ours, specifically Sergeant Isaiah Liman. We may need him, since we have no idea at this point what that pair have been able to create."

Julia looked surprised and not a little put out. "We have men, and I can get more if we need them," she retorted. "I believe with Corporal Tinsman and his men, we already have enough soldiers."

"Julia, you misunderstand. We are not going to recruit line infantry. That is not to say Corporal Tinsman and his men are among the finest one could wish for to watch your flank or back. This particular Liman is Isaiah Liman, the gentleman who saved our lives and those of many others at Sharpsburg with a little invention of his he called a blunderbuss," Morton said, taking over from Peter.

"I have heard of him. We studied the use of the blunderbuss in school," said Julia, looking interested. She grew animated. "I did not know you knew the inventor himself!" She took on the air of a young lady about to meet a famous actor or vocalist. She sounded rather smitten.

Most certainly a further unspoken comment on the rather interesting curriculum of the schooling she received, thought Father Peter.

"I hope we can get him to join us," continued Morton. "Isaiah is a true genius and a steady man in a tight spot. Considering what we may be up against, I thought it might be prudent to have a man who was handy with tools and mechanisms—not that you are not, Julia," he added quickly, seeing the look on her face. "But coming up with an idea, such as your exploding lanterns, is different from actually building a working prototype."

Julia looked slightly mollified and responded, "Well, I agree having an extra set of hands at the workbench would be useful. I am not saying that I am not, you understand, but I do agree that sometimes an extra set of hands is highly useful." This last was spoken while her nose lifted slightly in the air, and then she added, her air of excitement having returned, "I must admit, I have always wanted to meet Mr. Liman ever since seeing his device in action during one of our class's laboratory sessions."

Father Peter looked bemused, having already gotten wise to Julia's education, and dryly noted, "Must have been an interesting laboratory. I can only wonder about the cooking classes."

Julia beamed, totally missing the priest's dry humor. "Oh they were quite complicated—you know, how much poison to add to make someone sick but not kill them and how to hide the various flavors so the intended dose not realize what he or she is ingesting. I do say it was one of my harder classes."

At this, the poor, put-upon priest only rolled his eyes and once again made the Sign of the Cross.

Sensing the conversation drifting in a totally different direction than was prudent, Morton interrupted the exchange. "There is one other factor in his favor," said Morton. "Isaiah will be able to go places and dig up information that would be unobtainable to us. Would you not agree, Peter?"

Peter nodded and smiled in agreement.

It was a short time later, just after the two men had lit their cigar and pipe respectively, that they felt the thud and heard the squeal as the cars were coupled. Several tobacco puffs later, they heard the air brakes being pumped up and the conductor shout, "All aboard." The engine whistle shrieked and the bell started to clang, and the team felt the thud of the slack being taken out of the couplers. The wheels began to squeak, and they felt the gentle rocking as the train began to move. The team was again on its way to Buffalo and a meeting with an old comrade.

At about ten in the morning, the cars of the expedition were uncoupled from the train, and a short transfer took place. The train was switched to a secluded siding at Buffalo Central's new Upper Terrace Street Station. The three principals left the train under the watchful eyes of the corporal and his men. They walked over to the station to secure transport.

Julia indicated that she wished to do some shopping, since the major and Father Peter did not know the exact whereabouts of their friend and she did not want to miss the chance to arrange for some more supplies they might need on the mission. Besides, she had heard rumors of a truly fabulous millinery shop in the downtown area. As the gentlemen might appreciate, such an opportunity simply could not be squandered. Whether or not the gentlemen in question could appreciate this fact was open to question; nonetheless, Julia was soon passing out of sight in a carriage, leaving the gentlemen to wonder about such an opportunity indeed.

Morton and Peter split up to track down the whereabouts of Sergeant Liman. Morton headed downtown to various newspaper offices, while Peter went to check with the diocesan office for a start. Peter told John that, while he doubted that Isaiah was Catholic, that did not mean that someone at the office might not do business with a highly talented tinker. Besides, he did have to present the archbishop's compliments to the local bishop. Thus, the three dispersed into Buffalo, having agreed to meet for lunch later in the day.

It was later in the afternoon when Peter and John met at the Tift Hotel's restaurant near Main and Mohawk, not far from the train station. Peter spoke first. "I hope you have more to report than I do, John; no one in the church knows much about him, except that he is an inventor."

Morton shook his head in resignation. "I am afraid, Peter, that I have come up as empty-handed as you. The newspapermen in this town are a closemouthed lot. It is as if they are all afraid you are trying to scoop their story."

At this point, Julia was escorted by a smiling young waiter, who seemed to be quite taken with Julia's comely appearance, to the table. After she was seated and the three had ordered, Julia asked what success they had had in tracking down their quarry.

Morton looked grim as he related the news that both he and Peter had come up with very little in the way of information.

As he finished, the same young waiter brought their luncheon selections and rather fussed over Julia.

As he left, Morton said in a low voice, "Julia, I think it would be best if you turned down the flame. I am not sure if that poor young lad can take it."

Julia demurely smiled. "Oh, I think he can take it." Smiling an even bigger and brighter smile, she asked simply, "Would you gentlemen care to hear how my shopping went this morning?"

Peter looked at her and, putting on his best pastoral face, said, "Not that your choice of headgear is not of interest, but we still have to find and, hopefully recruit Isaiah."

"Really, Father, I am hurt if you think I was only shopping for a new hat, although I did find the most delicious one in a lovely blue. I really think I look so good in blue, do you not agree?"

Both Morton and Peter agreed that indeed she looked exquisite in blue. Or *almost any other color*, thought Morton. But they really did have to get back to the business at hand.

Julia smiled at this and cheerfully continued, "I am glad you agree on that at least. But as I was saying, hats were not the only thing on my shopping list."

Both Morton and Peter tensed, waiting for a soliloquy on dresses and other such female interests, only to be shocked when Julia said, "Well, as I was saying, I found a most delightful chemist's shop for some additional items that any well-prepared research expedition would need and a lovely clockmaker's shop for some more mechanical parts. You never can have enough, you know.

"You know it is wonderful how tinkerers form a close-knit community. Why it was just amazing that the fellows at the shop happened to be well acquainted with your friend, Mr. Liman," she added innocently, as if discussing the weather.

Peter and Morton looked at each other sheepishly, realizing that Julia had trumped them again. Both men were silently kicking themselves not to have thought of that approach. They tried to put balm on their wounded male pride by way of another drink.

Morton, admitting defeat, shook his head and, with a nod to Julia, asked quietly, "Truly, Miss Verolli, you have bested us seemingly without even trying. Pray tell, where did your sources say we could find Mr. Liman?"

"Oh, I thought you would never ask," responded Julia sweetly in her best little-Miss-Innocent, schoolgirl voice.

Morton and Peter both looked somewhat more than annoyed, and Julia decided that perhaps their poor male pride could not handle any more teasing. She answered John's question. "Mr. Liman has a small shop down on Fourth Street near the county jail. He apparently designs and builds clockworks and other various devices."

CHAPTER 9

IN WHICH A JOKER IS PULLED
AND DISCARDED

Lunch was soon completed and their bill paid. It was only a short while later that their carriage pulled up in front of a small shop on Fourth Street. The sign over the shop said simply, "I. Liman Clockworks and Mechanicals."

"This must be it," said Morton dryly as he stepped down and onto the sidewalk. He turned and helped Julia down, grasping her about the waist. He could feel the slimness of her body and its warmth through her blouse and corset. He was breathing somewhat more deeply than he had been.

"Why thank you, Professor," Julia said, using his civilian title, as any proper museum secretary would when they were in public, and attempting to look somewhat helpless.

The good father joined them on the sidewalk, breaking the spell Julia seemed to weave over John—a spell young ladies have cast over gentlemen throughout human history. Morton tipped the driver and gave him an extra coin to wait for them. Thus, the three turned and proceeded to the shop's door. As Morton held open the door for Julia, they could hear raised voices in the shop.

"Mr. Benton, you owe me for the clockwork toy for your daughter; you cannot just leave. Sir, I will call the police!" said a voice.

A second voice replied, "Go ahead, you two-bit nigger! Who do you think they will believe? You or an upstanding white man like myself?" This was followed by laughter and the sounds of a man walking toward the door.

"Excuse me, sir, I was just leaving," said a portly, pasty-faced man dressed in a waistcoat and puff tie.

Morton did not move. He merely looked down at the man and spoke quietly. "If I understand correctly, you somehow forgot to pay the proprietor."

The man looked flustered. He raised the cane in his hand as if to strike Morton and rapidly spit out, "Sir, let me pass. I owe this nigger nothing. Now again, sir, let me pass."

Morton merely stood there, not moving and simply looking down at the pasty-faced man.

The man started in again. "Sir, let me pass. I don't know what you think you overheard, but I cannot believe you would take the word of this darkie over me, a white man." The man pulled himself up to his full height, which was just about level with the bottom of Morton's chin, and seemed to shake with fury.

Morton continued looking down at him and quietly spoke. "What you seem to be asking, if I understand you correctly, is whether I would take the word of some obviously white piece of trash like you, who would cheat a man out of the reward for his labor, over the word of a man who fought for his country, kept a steady head, and by his genius, helped to end the rebellion. If it had not been for him and his comrades' sacrifice, my friend here and I", he gestured to Peter, "would probably not be alive to be having this conversation with you. Is that what you are asking?" Morton tipped his head, and his face seemed to get visibly darker with barely repressed anger.

The pasty-faced man seemed to shrink in upon himself and become paler, if that was possible. He looked as if he had seen a ghost, or perhaps more accurately, a demon—a very large, very angry, very nasty demon, who would come from your deepest, darkest nightmares and bite your head off for a snack. "Well, perhaps I was mistaken," he said, his voice trembling. "I do believe I may have forgotten to pay my bill. How kind of you to remind me, sir."

"Trust me. It was no problem, sir," responded Morton, gesturing to the back of the shop, from whence a middle-aged, light-skinned black man appeared.

The newcomer looked surprised at the appearance and the exchange, which he had clearly heard.

The small, pasty-faced man almost threw a wad of greenbacks at the proprietor and, clutching his package, scurried past Morton as if the devil himself was giving chase. The door slammed shut, the little bell on it ringing wildly. Isaiah picked up the money and looked up at the three people in his shop. "Do I know you gentlemen and miss?" he asked, slightly wary of the white folks.

"It has been a while, sir," said Morton in a gentle voice. "Perhaps if I was in a Union officer's uniform and the good father here in that of a Union sergeant, we would be more familiar."

"That and if my hair was a wee bit darker and I didn't have quite so many wrinkles," added Father Peter with a slight bit of a sigh.

Julia smiled and curtsied and simply said, "I, sir, have not had the pleasure."

Isaiah Liman looked at the two men, and then a flash of recognition came into his face. "You were that captain at Sharpsburg, when the Rebs hit our picket," he said in a rush. He looked at Peter and said, "Sorry I don't rightly remember you, Reverend. I hope you will forgive me, but as I remember the day, it was a somewhat busy morning."

Father Peter smiled and put out his hand, grasping Liman's enthusiastically. "Do not worry about it, son," he exclaimed. "You and your fellows saved us all. You held the line better than any outfit could be expected to do. It is we who owe you. Oh," he added, "one small matter; it's Father, not Reverend."

Morton smiled and said, "John Morton of the Museum of Natural History in New York and my secretary, Miss Julia Verolli." He motioned toward Julia. "Isaiah, is there anywhere we can talk, ah privately," finished Morton.

Isaiah looked at Morton for a moment, stepped around the trio, and went to the door. He locked it and put a *Closed for Lunch* sign in the window. Coming back, he motioned the three of them on and said simply, "Please follow me."

He led the three of them back past the counter and then through a door to what was obviously his work area, for it was cluttered with various piping, valves, gears, springs, screws and fasteners, plus all sorts of other mechanical components. On the bench itself they noted plans and sketches, along with partially built mechanical devices. To the side were several finished items, such as a steam-powered laundry washer and a device that seemed to be used for cleaning floors. Julia seemed very interested and wanted to stop to look, but Morton eased her along. Finally, they passed through a second door into what were obviously his living quarters. Isaiah put a few new pieces of coal and a bit of small wood to help the coal catch into his stove. Finishing that task, he filled a kettle from the sink and put it on to boil.

When he finished this, he turned, sat down, and said simply, "Tea will be up in a while. I hope you like it. My wife loved it. She never did much like coffee, and I guess I picked up the taste from her."

Peter looked at the man, who now seemed smaller and deflated after this last bit of talk. "You said she *did* love it, Isaiah. What happened?" he asked softly, as if he was in the confessional.

Isaiah took a breath and looked up at the priest and tried to smile. When at last he spoke, it was if he was whispering and in a voice that was a hundred miles away. "Not much to say really. She died nigh on to two years ago. She died in childbirth, and it was our first. The baby didn't make it either. I lost my whole world in one afternoon. No, there is not much more to say."

The three looked at the man who had lost so much. Finally Peter said, "I am sure they are with God, son. I know that seems little comfort, but it is the best I can offer." Peter reached out and put his old hands on the man's and squeezed them, trying to bring comfort where there was so much pain.

Isaiah looked up and seemed to bring himself back to the here and now from the place and time he had just been. "Well, I better get the tea ready," he said. "My Ruth would never forgive me if I did not show good manners under our roof." With that, he arose and began setting out some cups and saucers, mismatched but clean like the ones Father Peter was used to.

With the tea in the cups, he smiled and said, "I guess it ain't right to burden you folks with my losses. I'm sorry."

John looked at him, his eyes bright with sincerity. "It is no trouble," he said. "And I can vouch for the good father. He has a very absorbent shoulder if you need to cry some." He picked up the tea, took a sip, smiled, and said, "Your wife would be proud of you. The tea is excellent."

"Indeed, Mr. Liman, it is quite refreshing," Julia agreed. "I really haven't had a decent cup of tea for quite some time. Certain members of the museum staff much prefer coffee to tea, so one is forced to brew coffee every day." This she injected with just a touch of distain, much to Morton's surprise. "I am truly sorry to hear of your loss," she added. "You must have loved her very much."

Father Peter took up the conversation. "Indeed it is like I am back in the rectory at Saint Bridget's. Mrs. Kelly, my housekeeper, does brew up a fine cup of tea in the afternoon." At this Peter got a wistful smile on his face, as if wishing for a simpler time and life, which, needless to say, he was.

Isaiah looked happy, especially when Morton said that his wife would be proud of him. Finally he asked, "I am curious. Why are you here? My shop is somewhat far from Manhattan, and I find it a little hard to believe you just stopped in for a cup of tea."

Morton looked thoughtful for a moment and finally said, "You are right of course. Isaiah, we are not here for tea, although it is much appreciated. The truth of the matter is we need your help; we need a man of your talents."

Isaiah looked surprised. His body language and voice changed suddenly. "What white folks need a darky for? You got cotton to pick in Manhattan?" By now he was almost snarling, the acidly bitter memory of his wife and child's death so fresh in his mind. "I ain't nobody's house nigger or stable boy!"

Morton looked shocked at this outburst. He shook his head. "No. As I said, we need a man of your talents and abilities to counter a threat to the nation, a most serious threat."

Isaiah looked somewhat mollified, but still raging, he replied, "I worked on a plantation for the first fourteen years of my life as property before I escaped. The only good thing was the overseer took a shine to me and taught me how to read. Guess he wanted a son after his own boy drowned. After I escaped, I shoveled out stables while I learned a trade from the town blacksmith. After that I studied on my own while I stood by my nation for six long years in the war and bled for it! In gratitude from the nation, when Ruth was in labor, the hospital did not take in black people. So I watched my wife and child die! Do you think I give a damn about the country?"

Father Peter looked at the man so filled with righteous rage and spoke quietly. "Mr. Liman, Isaiah, there is no way to make up for what you lost. There is no way to say sorry that would enough. But it does not change the fact that your help is needed to counter a threat that could destroy the country."

Liman was getting up steam to reply when Julia said, with some force, "We can just reactivate his military service, John."

Isaiah looked stunned at this outburst. Whether it was the implied threat of being recalled to the army or the fact that a woman, especially the man's own secretary, would speak to him in this manner no one could say, even Isaiah himself.

Morton shook his head and replied forcefully, "No, Julia, I will not press-gang a man into service. That is Anderson's way, not mine. I want men who are willing to do what must be done, not men forced into servitude. I was in a war to end that."

Peter, seeing the tension building, broke in. "Julia, John is right. Isaiah has already paid a high price—truly his measure in full. We can only ask him to help." Turning slightly, he faced Isaiah squarely, and when he spoke, he looked directly into the younger man's eyes. "Isaiah, the danger the country is facing is not just to white Americans but to all people, including the black ones. The men we are trying to stop have created hideous monsters. We saw firsthand the results of their carnage back in the city." At this point, Peter looked somewhat sick as he recalled the scenes in the tunnel. He went on, "All are in need of your help, including your own kind. We cannot ask you for your help to save those who would turn your wife and child away when their help was needed, but would your Ruth have wanted you to turn your back on young black children who may never get a chance to grow up if these monsters are not stopped?"

At this last, Isaiah looked from Father Peter to Morton and in a quieter voice said, "Ruth loved children. We were so excited to be having one of our own. She would help out all the women in the area, no matter who they were or what color, or anything else for that matter, with their children. No, I guess she would not be very proud if I turned my back on helping children." He took a deep breath at this, looked around again at the unlikely trio gathered in his shop, and finally asked, "So what is this problem that you need my help with?"

Morton began the explanation about the research and how the Ratten had been created, with both Father Peter and Julia adding in their parts. Finally, as the afternoon wore on and the teacups had been refilled several times, Morton finished the story up to that point.

Isaiah just shook his head. "Our own government did this—created these monsters that have attacked our own people? I just cannot believe it."

Julia said, echoing Anderson's refrain, "It was the war, and the government was desperate. The goal was never to create the Ratten but to help our own men."

Isaiah looked directly at her. When he spoke, it was again with barely repressed fury. "You mean the government was trying to create a new race of slaves don't you? Someone to drive forward under the whip, 'yes, master, I will go kill them Rebel sons of a bitch for you, master, yes, sir'!"

"It was not supposed to be that way. I don't know. Maybe it was. I was not there, but the Ratten, that the government had no part of," replied Julia.

"Oh, I feel so much better already. If President Lincoln had not died at the theater of a heart attack in sixty-eight and was still alive, I would send him a thank you note for sure, missy." The sarcasm and vitriol literally dripped off Isaiah's tongue.

"Isaiah," said Morton, "Peter and I felt the same way about this, this abomination. You have to believe that. We were not happy, but if you saw the remains of the men, women, and children that these creatures tore apart and fed on as we did, well, it simply does not matter much how we feel about it. It just matters that they be stopped!" Morton looked the man straight in the face. "We need your help. You are one of the best tinkers in the country, a wizard with clockworks and gears. Please believe me, I know these things do not discriminate between young and old, white and black, or men and women."

Isaiah looked at Morton. "You said I had a choice didn't you, sir? You were not going to force me. Is that not right?"

Morton kept his gaze steady and returned Isaiah's look. "That is right. This is a volunteer mission, Sergeant. No one is being forced."

"Then in that case, sir, I done my share of war for this country. You can deal me out," responded Isaiah with bitterness dripping off his words.

Julia started to say something, but Morton cut her off. "No, Julia, I told you that was Anderson's way, not mine or Peter's." He looked at Isaiah and said, "We are sorry to have bothered you, Sergeant. I hope you find whatever it is you are looking for, and I am sorry to hear about your wife and child. Thank you for your time and the tea."

The three stood up, retraced their steps through the building, and left the small home and shop. Outside, the three found their carriage and returned in silence to the rail siding and their waiting railroad cars—each wondering if any new reports on the Ratten had come in and whether their efforts were too late to make a difference.

CHAPTER 10

WHAT HAVE WE HERE?

Dinner that night was a quiet affair. Even an excellent cut of beef done to perfection and a fine Madera wine to wash it down did not improve the mood. Morton was talking with Peter. "I had really hoped to recruit Sergeant Liman; the man is a true genius with clockwork and mechanicals. Some of the ideas he had were amazing. I saw designs for improved underwater working gear and improvements for the army's air fleet, not to mention farm and household ideas."

Peter replied with the same dejected tone, "True, John, but after his loss, I cannot really blame him. And he's right; he paid in full—fourteen years as a slave and six more years of hell in the war. The man's heart is heavy and full of bitterness. If there were more time for him to heal, then maybe. But as it is, I don't see much hope of recruiting him." Peter left off with a sigh and a shake of his head. "All we can do is pray for him and for his peace."

John nodded. "That's all true, Peter. But the fact of the matter is, we need someone who can do what he does. Don't be upset, Julia. I know you have the imagination and creativity for the ideas, but that's different from Isaiah's talents at the workbench. The man is a true virtual virtuoso with gears and his tools."

Julia looked up. "I understand what you mean, John. The brief chance I had to look around the man's workshop truly was amazing. He had ideas in progress I had never thought of; that idea for a small high-pressure tank for air to help men trapped in sinking ships was genius. I must admit that, even with the lanterns, it was my idea but Genève's artistry that created them. You are right. He would have been a most useful asset to the team. But what's done is done. Do you two know of anyone else?"

Father Peter sat for a minute, his face looking almost as if you could see him going through pages of notes in his head. When he finally spoke, his speech was slow, as if it were being played on one of the new recording devices whose spring was just about exhausted. "Not really. Oh I know some good men but none whose abilities are at the level of Isaiah's. He is indeed one of a kind, unless we can recruit Edison or Tesla, which I doubt—not that I can imagine Anderson would let us try."

John stood up and donning his hat and picking up his trusty cane, said simply, "Neither can I. Perhaps a walk will help clear my head." With that, he turned and walked toward the end of the car.

The sun had gone down, and evening was starting to darken the skies when Morton left the train. He was walked as if his feet were disconnected from his brain, but in reality, they were taking him into the Canal District. There, the Erie Canal terminated and met the Buffalo River and Lake Erie. The district there was a maze of feeder canals with their docks and wharfs, further connected by cobblestone streets and railroad tracks. Huge warehouses with their freight companies and monstrous grain elevators loomed like giant mountains in the dark, and finally he came to the Great Lakes freighter docks. These engines of commerce were supported by a huge number of bars, saloons, bordellos, eateries, and shops. These serviced the various groups that peopled the docks—lake seaman, stevedores, canal boatmen and hoggies (the lads who led the horse or mule teams that pulled the canal boats), teamsters, and dockworkers—all of whom hated the other groups, not to mention saloon owners, gamblers, whores, ruffians, thieves and cutthroats. These groups were very fair-minded and preyed on all the rest in a totally nonpartisan manner. This area was among the vilest places on earth. It was as if, unconsciously, he realized that a bit of action might clear his mind. As he walked, his mind poured over the events of the day. He was trying to figure out how he could have handled the matter better. He was annoyed that Liman had refused to join them. Still he realized it wasn't Peter, Julia, or himself who were at fault; it was society that had hurt the man so badly, perhaps even more than the slave master's lash had.

Even with so much to think about. The part of his mind that had been honed by years of warfare and field expeditions in dangerous territory where Indians and criminal gangs still rampaged, many holdovers from the war itself, was still alert to anything that could be a threat. It was thus that, when he heard a high-pitched cry, he stopped, and all of his senses were immediately on full alert. He heard the cry again, coming from an alley just ahead. It was an animal cry of pain, and it was followed by harsh laughter and a guttural growl. "Quiet, bitch, and we will all give you some fine white meat." More coarse laughter sounded out.

Morton moved forward, more carefully now, his pepperbox already in his hand; he'd switched the cane over to his left. He eased himself around the corner and peered at a group of four young men holding down a young girl—no, she was more like a child. Her filthy dress had already been torn and ripped, exposing her black body. The girl, though pinned to the ground, struggled in her attackers' grasps. The leader, the biggest one, seemed to get annoyed with her and backhanded her, knocking her senseless. He stood up and began to untie the rope that he used in place of a belt to hold up his trousers. The teenager was smiling, while saying to his mates, "I'm first, and then the rest of you can enjoy yourselves."

At this point, Morton spoke up from behind the group. He had moved forward, but so intent had they been on the hapless child that they had not noticed his stealthy approach. "I have a much better idea. Why don't you lads run along and find someone your own age to play with." His voice was cold, hard, and flat; there was no warmth or forgiveness in the words he spoke.

It at once became apparent that these lads would never become good card players, as they completely misjudged their opponent. The big one turned on hearing the voice, losing his balance and tripping over his own pants, which were now down around his knees. The others let go of the girl, and all turned to face him. The girl was too stunned from the blow to move. It was obvious that, between the physical damage and fear, she was losing consciousness. The leader, as he obviously was, struggled to get to his feet around his tangled pants and said, "I got a better idea, mister. I think you owe me and my friends here the contents of your pockets for disturbing our fun. After all, we was just gettin' to the good part."

Morton just smiled, as a hungry wolf might be said to smile. "I don't think so, trash. Why not see if you can take it." Some part of Morton wanted this chance to take revenge on a world that had thrust him into the hell of this assignment and drawn him back into the army after so many years of war, a world that had denied him Isaiah's needed services. Morton needed to find a lightning rod for the anger that was building up in him, and these four nasty, useless lumps would do nicely.

The leader had finally gotten to his feet with his pants secured. He pulled a straight razor out and, with a smoothness born of practice, flicked it open. The gang started to advance on Morton. John did not hesitate; the leader screamed as three of the four bullets of the pepperbox struck home, two shattering the arm that held the razor and the third taking him in the gut. The last one whined away in the night. He lurched away, holding his arm and trying to hold his stomach at the same time. John only briefly noted that the leader was out of the fight, as his attention was on one of the gang who was trying to move in. This time, the cane flicked up, and the ganger looked down to see his intestines starting to fall out; the eight-inch blade had suddenly appeared at the end of the cane and, in a smooth arc, sliced open his stomach. His gaze was short-lived as his eyes looked up at Morton, and then they were the empty eyes of a dead man, and he collapsed to the ground.

The two remaining toughs looked at each other and then at Morton, still with that wolf's smile on his face to match his cane. His eyes looked as if they belonged to some dark and deadly mythological monster. The pair wheeled and ran, as if their lives depended on getting as far away as they could as quickly as they could, which was true. Morton was still looking for blood as an antidote to the rage that consumed him.

As soon as the remaining toughs disappeared, Morton seemed to come back to his senses, leaving the combat mode that had momentarily consumed him. Quickly, the eight-inch blade retracted as he opened the breach of the small pepperbox and reloaded it for action, in case the thugs had gone for reinforcements. He then moved forward and checked the pile of blood and intestines in the alley, as it hardly resembled a man anymore. At least this one would not bother anyone again; he was a dead as could be, just like all those Morton had seen in the war.

Finally, after he had ensured the immediate area was safe, or as safe as could be in this part of Buffalo's Canal District, Morton went over to the girl. Checking her, he found she was alive but unconscious. Morton stripped off his jacket, picked the child up, and wrapped her in it. Then, holding the little girl in his arms, he made his way back toward the station area and the train.

A short time later, he saw the welcoming lights of the train. As he approached, he called out to Peter and Julia. It was Corporal Tinsman who responded first. *The men must be standing a guard mount even in the city*, Morton realized. *Very good men indeed.* By that time, Peter and Julia had appeared on the car platform. Julia was the first to speak. "My God, John, what happened?"

"Some of the local toughs tried to take advantage of this child; I persuaded them to change their plans for the evening, at least one of them permanently," replied Morton, handing the girl up to Peter.

Julia, looking down at the child, was shocked at how young she was. "Oh my God, the poor thing cannot be more than ten years old," she said in a rush. "Peter, quickly, put her in my compartment while I get some supplies."

With that Julia, Peter, and the girl disappeared into the car.

Tinsman looked at Morton. "Whereabouts did it happen, sir?" he said simply as if asking a man on picket what he had seen.

John gave him directions. With that, the corporal called another of his men, all three of whom were now up and dressed and, Morton noted, armed. Thereafter, Tinsman and one of the other men left to, as he put it, police up the area. Tinsman told the other two to keep an eye on the train.

Finally, shaking a bit as the adrenalin-fueled effects of the deadly battle wore off and the aftereffects took hold, Morton inhaled deeply to steady himself and then climbed up the steps. He was still shaking slightly as he let himself into the car. When he passed through the door, he could hear Julia's voice alternately barking instructions to a very worried and concerned Father Peter, who was in the corridor, and saying soothing things to the child, almost singing a lullaby to sooth to the young victim. Morton looked at his friend and, with a nod of his head, indicated Julia's compartment in an unspoken question.

The good father answered in a hushed voice, "I think the child is all right, but Julia tossed me out like five-day-old fish. It's no wonder she took the disguise as your secretary. The only person I know who can be more dictatorial is Mrs. Kelly."

Morton smiled weakly and spoke quietly to his friend. "Peter, I don't know about you, but if the sergeant major is done issuing orders, I could use a brandy. Would you care to join me?" Peter simply stepped aside and motioned with his hand, and the two men went into the parlor of the car, whereupon John collapsed in a heap into a chair and Peter retrieved a decanter and two glasses. After the brandy was poured, John explained the events of his evening stroll. Peter just sat and listened quietly, as if hearing the confession of a troubled parishioner at Saint Brigit's.

The next morning, John, Peter, and Julia were partaking of a delicious breakfast in their car. It was a subdued occasion, though. Not only did they have the young girl to worry about—Julia had said it would be best if the local police were kept out of it since that might lead to questions it would be better not to have to answer—they still had no idea who to get to fill the hole in their team that Isaiah's refusal had left.

John looked at Julia. "You look as if you didn't get much sleep last night. How is our new passenger doing?"

"How kind of you to note my lack of sleep, Major," Julie replied, giving him a cross look.

Morton looked sheepish. "Sorry," he said, "that didn't come out the way it was meant. I know you were looking after the girl till late, Julia."

Father Peter tried to hide a small smile at his friend's firm step in the proverbial cow pie.

"It's alright, John. I'm just tired is all." Julia went on, "Physically, she is not too badly hurt as far as I can tell. She's weak and beaten up some, but I do believe she will be fine with some food and rest. Speaking of food, please pass the biscuits, would you?"

It was during this exchange that they heard a wagon pull up, along with some cursing and clanking.

Julia, looking somewhat surprised, said simply, "Whatever can that be? I have ordered nothing!"

Morton smiled as he heard Peter mumble under his breath, "What? Not another half a ton of explosives or perhaps a Nordenfelt to add to the Gatling gun!"

"Really, Father, a gentleman does not mention a young lady's purchases in public," chided Julia in a huff.

"Perhaps we should investigate," replied Morton, bringing his companions back to the matter at hand. He stood up, simultaneously checking his freshly cleaned and oiled pepperbox. He was followed by both Julia and Peter. As the trio moved to the door, they heard some yelling between the sharpshooter detail and someone else. Morton picked up his pace and was soon passing through the door at the end of the car. As he stood on the car platform, his gaze lit upon a most unlikely spectacle.

Isaiah stood arguing with Corporal Tinsman and one of his men about putting his belongings on the train. As the two were nose to nose, John thought it prudent if he intervened. "Corporal, if you would please stand down. Sergeant Liman, what brings you here this morning?"

"You still got that tinker's position open, Captain?" asked Liman.

Morton smiled and replied, "Well, we have had some promising candidates, but yes, it is still open, Isaiah. Corporal Tinsman, Sergeant Liman will be joining our party, so please give him a hand."

Julia, who by now had also appeared on the platform, looked at the groaning wagon, and with the perfect air of a competent secretary, said, "Perhaps I had better arrange for an additional car, Professor."

Morton looked at her and then back to the wagon Isaiah had arrived with and smiled, saying, "Indeed, Miss Verolli, that would seem to be an excellent idea."

As the dustup settled down, Tinsman grinned and shook Isaiah's hand. "They did not say anything about another recruit, Sergeant," he said simply. "No offense meant by it."

"None taken, Corporal. If you will give me a hand, we can move the wagon over and unhitch poor old Sampson here. He done been straining himself to get this here wagon over to the station."

With that, the two men headed toward the wagon.

"Mr. Liman," Julia called after them, "if you will, we have breakfast and coffee in here. Would you join us?"

Isaiah looked up at Julia and replied, "Any tea, Miss Julia?"

"I do believe we have some tea on board, sir," she said in a cheerful voice. "I will have Cook put on the kettle."

CHAPTER 11

WHERE THE JACK OF SPADES IS DRAWN

A short time later, the four were seated around the table, said table now set for that number. The unloading was waiting for another baggage car to be switched onto the train. Morton started the conversation. "I am indeed happy, no make that very happy, to have you here, Isaiah, so do not take this the wrong way. But what changed your mind?"

Isaiah looked at them each in turn and said quietly, "After you all left, I just sat there looking around the house and shop. I realized that— oh hell—I realized that there was nothing there for me since Ruth and the baby died except an empty space where my joy should be. I cannot leave Ruth's spirit to be ashamed of me now, can I? Not to mention the thought of some other child not being allowed to grow up. What do I call you, sir, Captain?"

John released his breath. "It was Major by the time the war ended, but John will do just fine, Isaiah. Welcome to the team." Morton clasped his hand and shook it one man to another.

"Isaiah, what is it that you have in the wagon?" asked Julia, her curiosity obvious.

Isaiah looked at her, clearly relishing the hot biscuit and jam he'd tucked into. "Well, Miss Julia, Major, like I said, I thought after you all left that there was not much of a life I had there. It all seemed pretty empty after Ruth and the baby died. I figured might as well pack up and be done with it. So I did."

Snagging another biscuit, he liberally smeared it with jam, took another drink of tea, and continued speaking as he ate. "I didn't have much in the way of personal things, just some clothes, a Bible, a sketch of Ruth, and a crib I had started for the baby. I left that for the Watkes family down the street—nice folks with a child on the way. Funny, some can't seem to stop having kids; others can't even have one." This last seemed to start taking him away to a different place and time. But with a shake of his head, he drew himself back to the present and went on. "I left most of the machines I had finished for my customers to pick up. They were for far less lethal pursuits than what you folks have in mind—not much call for heavy artillery in the city. The rest is tools and designs, plus whatever parts and pieces I had in the shop. There is nothing here for me now, so I figured I might as well clean out what was useful and get started on a new life. Past one ain't been none too good, now has it."

Father Peter looked at him with kind eyes. "Isaiah," he said softly, "we certainly can't promise that life will be better with us. But you are welcome here, and such as it is, at least it will be different. Hopefully, it will be a time to rebuild and try to put to rest what was taken from you."

Julia smiled and said, "You must tell me about Ruth sometime. She must have been an extraordinary woman. I would like to know more about her."

Isaiah swallowed a mouthful of jam and biscuit. "She was that indeed," he said. "Thank you, miss."

Julia, putting on her business face, spoke more to the point. "So, what did you bring us?"

Isaiah smiled, and as he was about to answer, they heard the chuffing and bell clanging of a steam locomotive and then felt the bump of a car being coupled up. Julia looked pleased, and with a delightful smile like a child on Christmas morning, exclaimed, "I think the corporal has secured our additional car. Mr. Liman, would you care to unpack and show me what you have added to our rather modest expedition supplies?"

Isaiah grinned and, wiping the jam from his face, finished his tea in a single gulp. "Why, Miss Julia, I would be delighted," he said. "Mostly, I have brought you a complete tinkerer's shop so I can fabricate whatever we will need. However, if we can, there is a siding near where my shop was. I have some heavy equipment that would not fit in the wagon that might be of some help."

Julia smiled. "Just talk to Mr. Tinsman, and I am sure he can arrange for a pickup."

With that, the two of them excused themselves and left for the front of the train to supervise the unloading of Isaiah's now portable workshop and storeroom.

Peter looked at John sitting there and slight shake of his head said, "Three train cars and now another—that's modest? I should hate to see our Julia when she packs for serious traveling. Where would we put the field artillery?" With a shake of his head and a look of bewilderment as was usual around Julia, he added asking, "So where to now, John?"

Before John could answer, they heard Julia tell Isaiah that she had to check on their latest passenger.

Seconds later, Isaiah stormed back into the parlor, hands balled into fists. Getting in Morton's he yelled, "You didn't tell me about keeping children to molest, Major, *sir!*"

Before John could even get a word out, Peter was at Isaiah's side. "Isaiah, you anger is righteous indeed but quite misplaced," he said, trying to calm the man.

"What you talkin' about, Priest?" screamed Isaiah, froth forming on his mouth.

Peter explained what had happened the night before and how John had saved the little girl. As he told the tale, the black man seemed to deflate. After Peter finished, he hung his head and sheepishly said, "I'm sorry, Major. I guess when I saw the bruises on the girl, I just done blowed the pop valve clean off; it hurt, sir. The baby, Ruth's and mine, see, was a girl." He was, by this, time crying openly.

Morton just put his hand out and, taking Isaiah's, he said, "No problem, Sergeant. I would not want a man in my unit who did not take offense at a child being hurt. Now, enough of this behavior. I believe you and Julia have a wagon to unload and stores to pack." Morton smiled and Isaiah smiled back, wiping the tears away with the back of his hand.

"What about the men you said was hurtin' that girl," said Isaiah through clenched teeth.

Father Peter interrupted John before he could answer. "Two of them will not be bothering any more little girls, gentlemen. Corporal Tinsman told me they found the one you shot, John. He only made it around the corner and into an alley. They policed up the area; it will be just two more corpses when they clean the canal next spring."

Isaiah looked satisfied, if not relieved, and turned back to Julia, who had overheard the exchange. She smiled at him and said quietly, "You were going to show me your wares, sir."

After the two left the car, Morton returned his friend's smile and replied, "In answer to your previous question Peter, to paraphrase Mr. Greely, go west, old priest, go west."

Peter and John were starting to discuss where the train should head next when they heard a sound from Julia's compartment. Getting up, they moved down the car to check. Knocking gently at the door, John opened it slowly, only to be met by a high scream. He tried to talk to the girl, but she was in such a state that she, in all probability, did not even register the sound of his voice or the words he spoke. Morton was a good enough tactician to know when a strategic retreat was called for and reinforcements were needed. He hastily backed out of the compartment, sliding the door closed behind him. He sent Father Peter to fetch Julia.

Shortly thereafter, both Julia and Isaiah came into the car and stood outside the door. Julia gently moved Morton aside and said, "Let me try."

With that, she opened the door and stepped into the compartment. The young girl just stared at her as if struck dumb, her eyes the size of saucers. Julia tried to calm the girl, but she was shaking so badly that even Julia's soft voice and tender touch did nothing to help. It was as if she were deaf.

Julia was looking helplessly around, wondering what to try next, when Isaiah stuck his head in. The child looked at him and said, "Poppa," almost as if saying a prayer. "You said you would come back." Suddenly, she stiffened and, burying her face in the pillow, screeched, "You're not Poppa. Poppa is dead; he died." With that, she wailed all the harder.

Isaiah motioned Julia out and went to sit beside the bed. He just sat there stroking the girl's shoulder and making quieting sounds to her. Finally, after a time, the crying started to slow down, and the little girl gasped for breath. "Tell me about it," said Isaiah. "Tell me about your family." He continued, "Ain't no one gonna hurt you, girl. That's it—just cry it on out."

Finally, the girl sobbed slowed, she grabbed a lung full of air and looked up at Isaiah. Wiping at her eyes with the back of her hand, she just asked, "What do you want, mister? Do you want me to pleasure you?" The voice sounded a hundred miles away. Isaiah knew that voice, for he had heard it every time he talked about Ruth and the baby. The pitch was different, but the distance was the same.

Isaiah cried inside and just continued to stroke the girl's shoulder. As softly as he could, he replied, "No, missy, you don't have to pleasure me nor any man, 'lessen you want to, not now, not ever."

The young, frightened girl looked at him and just sniffled through her tears.

"Although it would give me pleasure if you would tell me your name," Isaiah added. "It's kind of hard to keep calling you little girl."

She looked up at him again, and timidly, almost fearfully, she replied, "It is Sarah, sir. My name is Sarah."

Isaiah felt a lump form in his throat. He looked down at the child and simply said, "Sarah, that is a beautiful name. My daughter was going to be Sarah. My wife, Ruth, loved that name."

The little girl was silent, and then after a moment, she asked, "What happened to Sarah, sir—I mean your Sarah?"

Isaiah closed his eyes for a moment then opened them. Tears ran down his face as he told the child, "She died, Sarah, along with Ruth. She died at birth. I don't rightly have anyone now; they both gone. What about you? Where are your parents?"

Sarah looked away from him "They gone, sir. Poppa died in a fight some time ago, and Momma died—I think it was two months ago—of the fever."

"Do you have anyone, Sarah?" Isaiah asked gently. "Aunt or uncle, sisters?"

"No, sir, it's just me. I don't got no one. I been living on the streets, runnin' and hidin'." The little girl's voice was not much more than a whisper now, as if the crying and answers so far had sucked all the air out of her. "You're not going to leave me, sir!" she said suddenly, her voice almost a shriek, as if it came from a drowning person crying for help to the distant shore.

"No, little Sarah, I ain't gonna leave you," Isaiah said. "You just rest now. My friend, Miss Julia, she will fix you up something to eat. Would you like that?"

"Yes, sir, it has been a while since I had anything to eat except some scraps." Sarah smiled tentatively at Isaiah.

Julia, who had been listening at the door, came into the compartment and smiled. Sarah clutched the covers up to her chin, eyes darting back and forth between Julia and Isaiah.

"Well, young lady, then I think it is time overdue for some breakfast," Julia said with some humor in her voice, "You just wait, and we shall go and get some." Then, motioning to Isaiah, she shooed him out with an, "Excuse me, sir, but there are certain things ladies must have some privacy for."

With that, the three men were together again in the corridor. Isaiah looked up at Morton. "I can't be leaving her, Major. That girl needs me."

"Isaiah, be reasonable," Morton replied. "We must find an orphanage for the child. We cannot take her with us. Or did you forget that this mission will probably be very dangerous? The men we are after are both brilliant and extremely dangerous, not to mention their monstrous creation. It is no place for a child."

"Isaiah, is it that she needs you? Or do you need her?" asked Father Peter quietly.

Isaiah looked resolute and replied, "Maybe that, or maybe both, Father. But it doesn't change the fact that I cannot leave her. Maybe it is just that I have lost too much already, but I will not leave her!" This last was said in a voice that allowed for no discussion.

Morton looked exasperated, but it was at this point that Julia opened the compartment door and said simply, "What are you three doing standing around blocking the way?"

The three gentlemen started individually to reply, but she just shooed them out of the way and down to the parlor and then motioned Sarah to follow her. The little girl was wrapped in a blanket. Her clothes, such as what was left of them after the gang had tried to tear them off her, had been little more than rags to begin with and now were just strips of cloth. "Well, first a good breakfast, and then we will go on from there," said Julia. With a sharp look at the men, she continued, "And you three can just make yourselves useful or at least find somewhere else to lay about."

Father Peter just smiled. "Gentlemen," he said, "I do believe Miss Verolli has pulled rank on us."

Morton and Isaiah both looked like privates being addressed by a sergeant and, saying, "Excuse me," departed for other parts of the train.

It was just a little later in the day when Julia told Isaiah that Sarah was in their compartment and sleeping. She told him to tell Morton that she had some shopping to do and would be back later. It was all Isaiah could do to stammer out a hasty, "Yes, Miss Julia," before Julia was climbing into a carriage and disappearing toward Main Street and Buffalo's shops and stores.

In this, she was lucky, since Buffalo was one of the major cities in the country and, between Main Street and other venues, was a shopper's delight.

When Isaiah conveyed the message, he, Morton, and Peter, along with Tinsman and his men, just stood around scratching their heads and wondering what was going on.

Several hours later, Julia returned with a huge array of parcels and boxes so that the carriage was filled to overflowing. Julia alighted and, in the time-honored way of all good sergeants throughout history, began organizing a bucket brigade, only instead of putting out a fire, the men were passing boxes and packages up to the train and down to Julia's, and now Sarah's compartment too. When done, the men still had no idea what was going on. But they were happy, for whatever it was seemed to be done for now. The fire brigade, having finished their work, found themselves dismissed by Julia, who retreated into her compartment with Sarah.

It was time for dinner, and Morton noted that five places had been set. The men all gathered and were just sitting down when the now double-occupancy compartment door opened up, and Julia, followed by a freshly scrubbed Sarah in a simple blue dress and shoes, appeared. Although Sarah still had some of the bruises she'd received from the gang, the men sat there, stunned at the transformation—until Julia harrumphed rather loudly and they scrambled to their feet.

Julia looked down at Sarah and spoke with a proper Bostonian accent. "Remember, Sarah, a gentleman—or gentlemen, in this case—always stands up when a lady enters the room, although occasionally they may need to be reminded."

Sarah went over to the table and started to pull out a chair. Julia tapped her on the shoulder. "Dear girl, that is simply not done. A gentleman always helps a lady to be seated," she said with a sharp look at Isaiah and then Morton.

As Morton pulled out the chair for Julia and Isaiah pulled out the chair for Sarah, the ladies were seated, and dinner began, with Father Peter saying grace.

Morton wondered exactly how they had gotten into this predicament. It was obvious that not only Isaiah had taken to Sarah; something had happened between Julia and Sarah. This mission had just taken on a whole new level of problems.

CHAPTER 12

ON A TRAIN BOUND FOR THE WEST

Somewhere in Pennsylvania, just over the border between New York and the Keystone State, on the train heading west, the four adults sat around the table in their coach, having finished dinner. Earlier Sarah had said good night to Father Peter and Morton and, rather impulsively, hugged Isaiah. Julia had escorted her to their compartment and, having made sure she was asleep, returned to the parlor. The train was attached to a slow drag freight train heading to Cleveland, and it would be going through the night. The expedition's cars had become too great a weight to be hauled by a fast passenger train without overloading the engine, or at least slowing it enough to ruin the railroad's schedule. They could feel the tug of the engine and hear the miles going by in the steady clack of the rail joints and the sound of the distant whistle warning of the multiple grade crossings they passed.

After the table had been cleared, Morton opened the conversation by asking Julia if they had received any word from Anderson about their quarry.

Julia generally replied that, indeed, they had some leads but that these were varied and of a confusing nature. Morton said, "I really did not expect any better; the Pinks love to provide information, even if it is not the best or most accurate. The government should have learned that in the war. So what do we have?"

Julia excused herself for a minute and shortly returned with a folder full of letters and telegrams. "This is what I have received so far," she said. "It seems to indicate that Ulrich and Chen are somewhere in the western territories or possibly Northern Mexico."

"How can we miss with such detailed information as that," grumbled Father Peter.

"Indeed. Should be as easy as brewing a cup of tea," chimed in Isaiah, who was beginning to feel more at home as part of the team.

Morton privately agreed with them, but they still had a mission to accomplish. "All right, Julia. Give us the reports slowly so we can digest them," he said. "We will have to see if there are any we can reject or discard so we can try to track this pair of monsters down."

The men slowly listened and made comments as Julia slowly read through the reports. Many made little or no sense. Some, such as fires or attacks on ranches or wagon trains, could be discarded as Indian attacks or natural causes. On further reading, they determined that several, depicting some bank robberies and warehouse burglaries, could lead to their quarry but in all likelihood were the work of criminal gangs. Additional reports were of a curious nature that might indeed bear further investigation. One or two in particular were of definite interest, such as a report from a sheriff about a strange animal.

They all agreed that the pair would want to be somewhere near a city so they could obtain supplies for their Ratten experiments. In addition to the aforesaid reports, Anderson had supplied sketches of the pair, along with a great deal of background material on both men. As far as was known, both Ulrich and Chen were city men with no known experience living in the wilderness. Ulrich had been a highly acclaimed professor of pharmacy in Stuttgart, Germany. Notes, though, from when he was recruited for the original project said he had no sense of morality. Chen had come to the attention of the American ambassador in Peking. He was, for the most part, quiet and well known in Chinese medical circles. On the other hand, one note suggested he had a rather large sexual appetite especially for white women and could be easily bribed.

When the meeting was winding down, Morton summed up the information they had so far. "It would appear that our quarry is somewhere in the western territories, probably near the Dakotas. I sincerely hope to learn more from the Pinkertons when we stop in Chicago. That's where we have the last definite sighting of the pair, and it's fairly recent. Also, Julia, please wire ahead when we stop next for water to obtain as many of the western newspapers as possible. We may catch a bit of luck with some obscure news story. Also, wire Anderson to forward any such reports from Federal marshals, land agents and military units, along with any Indian agents. The pair may be working near a reservation, since there is less law enforcement presence in those areas. We also need to figure out how these two are surviving; it's not as if they can sell the Ratten. After that, we can reassess and figure out the next logical locale and we can arrange for our cars to be attached to a train heading out that way."

The meeting adjourned, and the participants headed to their respective compartments.

The next morning, Father Peter was alone in the parlor when he heard a door slide open, and shortly thereafter Julia and Sarah joined him at the table. He helped the ladies to be seated and said grace again. Julia was speaking to him when Sarah piped up, "Are you her father?"

Peter looked surprised for a moment. He tried to think of a reply to her question without embarrassing her. Finally he smiled and simply said, "No, Sarah, I am not Julia's father. Father is an honorific, such as Mr. Morton is called professor or Isaiah is Mr. Liman. I am a Roman Catholic priest, and that's how we are referred to, just as a Protestant minister might be called Reverend." He stopped there, not wanting to bring denominational differences in. Peter knew the girl had been through enough without getting into that ugly catfight.

Sarah looked confused and looked up at Julia for some sort of guidance. Julia just looked down at her and said, "It's all right. Father

Peter is just like a minister back in Buffalo." She too wanted to avoid a deep theology session at the breakfast table. She changed the subject by asking Peter, "Where are the major and Mr. Liman this morning?"

Peter smiled and replied, "No doubt sleeping in, with all that happened yesterday. The *professor*," he said, emphasizing the title so to remind Julia that indeed little pitchers have big ears, "had more than a little excitement yesterday, and Isaiah is tired out from the packing and unpacking, I expect."

Julia started to reply when Morton appeared and looked like a man seeking coffee with the desperation of a Knight of the Round Table questing for the Holy Grail. After securing himself a cup, he said hello to the ladies and the good father. Then he sat back, finished his coffee, and had soon done serious damage to a heaping helping of what proved to be an excellent breakfast. At last, seeming to be satisfied and fortified, he poured a second cup of coffee while his dishes were cleared.

Morton sipped his second cup slowly and cleared his throat while looking at Sarah over the rim of his cup. Sarah looked somewhat downcast, as if the attention Morton was paying her was scary—which in all truth, it was to her. He was obviously trying to find the right words to address her. Taking another sip of coffee, he finally plunged in. "Sarah, how would you like for us to find you a place to stay? I am not sure a scientific expedition to the untamed West is a proper place for young girl? I know Father Peter could find a nice convent somewhere along our route. Would you like that, Sarah?"

The little girl sat there looking scared and trying to hold back the tears that obviously wanted to come out, "Sir, Major Professor, sir, I would really like to stay here. I don't have no folks, and I don't—what is a convent anyhow? I just don't want to be left, sir." This last part came out with a strain, as if the poor girl was going to lose control. She went on in a rush, "Besides, Major Professor, sir, Isaiah, Mr. Liman, sir, he don't have nobody either. And I could take care of him, sir." Her tone had a plaintive air about it now—it contained fear and the desire to cry, mixed with hope.

It was at this point Isaiah came into the room wanting breakfast. He looked around and saw Sarah, her little face filled with fear, and asked, "What is going on here?" The tension in his words was obvious.

Morton blew out his breath and shrugged and, with a laugh, told him, "I think you are being adopted, Isaiah." Both Father Peter and Julia joined him in laughing, while Sarah looked as worried as could be.

Isaiah looked like a man who was very confused, but the group just motioned for him to sit down and have some breakfast.

Morton finally recovered enough to start talking again. "Sarah," he addressed her, trying to look most severe and professorial, "first of all, it is just professor. Major was my old title in the army."

"Yes, sir, Professor, sir," squeaked the little girl, hope beginning to build up slowly in her.

"Now second, young lady, I do not intent to have any slackers on my expedition. Is that clear?" Morton continued in his best lecture tone.

"Yes, sir. I'll work hard, sir, if you let me stay." Sarah gulped.

"All right. We will try it for now, however since you will be part of the expedition you will also be representing the museum and as such there is a certain level of professionalism demanded, is that clear, young lady?"

Again, Sarah affirmed that she understood, although she looked confused. She was not exactly sure what professionalism meant. Isaiah was watching closely, making sure that Morton was not planning to abuse the obviously scared girl.

"Very well then. You will start by helping Miss Julia prepare articles for the newspapers back home, even though they will just be about our travels to the", he hesitated a second, searching for the right phase, "research area." She will also be cataloging items we find; you will assist her with that as well. Additionally, she will be receiving many newspapers and looking for information that may help us in our", again that hesitation a minute to find the right word, "research."

"Yes, sir," replied Sarah, obviously overjoyed. Then the scared little girl was back in force! She was trembling as she blurted out, "I don't know much about words and letters, sir. We were traveling up North and trying to find a place to stay. Momma, she taught me a little, but there wasn't much time. And Papa died, and then Momma died."

Julia took over, "Obviously then, lessons will be a part of your job, along with proper deportment."

Sarah looked up a Julia almost in awe. "You gonna teach me letters, Miss Julia, and how to be a porter?"

Julia laughed and smiled down at her. "Yes and no. I am going to teach you how to read and write, but deportment is how to behave like a proper lady, not about being a porter."

Sarah was beaming.

Morton took back over. "You can wipe that smile off your face, young lady. That is not all. I will be teaching you mathematics and natural science, while the good father will be teaching you Latin. Is that clear?"

Sarah gulped again. "Yes, sir." She was obviously beginning to be a little overwhelmed.

Morton looked at her again. "And finally, Mr. Liman will be teaching you mechanicals, on top of which, since you volunteered, you are charged with taking care of him." With that Morton sat back and poured another cup of coffee. "Still think you want to join the expedition?"

Sarah's face looked like that of a child who had just found out about Christmas. She gasped. "Yes, sir!"

Julia said, "All right. Lessons begin soon. You can help Cook clear away the dishes. And then, little missy, report for duty."

Sarah jumped up and started to clear the dishes. Isaiah looked at the rest of the team, and in his face, they could see the heartfelt 'thank you'.

Morton wondered if he had done the right thing. He also liked Sarah and did not want to see her hurt in what was probably going to be a very dangerous mission.

CHAPTER 13

IN CHICAGO, A DINNER

uring a layover in Toledo for fuel and water, Julia went to the telegraph office. Soon, the message was being received in New York. Just as she boarded the train, the engineer took up the coupler slack, jostling her somewhat and dislodging her bonnet. Straightening her hat, she proceeded through the end door and down to the parlor, where she had left Sarah working diligently on her letters. Sarah looked up and smiled as Julia returned. It was obvious to the entire team that the little girl had taken to Julia like a big sister. Sarah clearly wanted to please Julia more than almost anything. That fell behind only one thing, taking care of Isaiah, which, now that the professor had made it part of her official duties, she seemed to think of as a sacred trust.

As Julia sat down, Sarah asked her, "Did you send the telegram, Miss Julia? It must be a lot of work being a secretary. You need to know how to do so many things." More than a hint of hero, or more accurately heroine, worship was evident in the small voice.

Julia simply smiled at the girl. Perhaps it was the fact that Julia had no known kin, no ties to her past before the day she was caught and turned over to Anderson, other than a last name sewn into the clothes she'd had on that day. Or perhaps it was motherly instincts. Whatever the case, she had bonded with Sarah just as deeply as the little girl had with her. "Well, yes. I indeed sent the telegram. By the time we get to

Chicago, we should have our own engine for the train." *Although, how we'll catch anyone or anything if we keep getting attached to these oh-so-slow drag and peddler freight trains, I don't know,* she added to herself. It was bad enough that they really had no idea where their quarry might be, but the longer it was taking to get to Chicago, the colder the trail was getting. "As to knowing so many things," she continued out loud. "Yes, there are a lot, especially if you work for a scientist like the professor. How are the Latin lessons with Father Peter coming? You will be needing a lot of Latin if you are going to help me; the professor uses a lot of Latin, you know."

Sarah looked a little worried. "I'm not so sure. It is very complicated, but Father Peter does make it kinda fun. He showed me how some English words came from Latin just by the sounds. He was helping me with the reading a bit too. Still, it's pretty confusing, ma'am."

Julia tried to look stern at her young charge, but it was not working too well and said, "Young lady, it is not *kinda* but *kind of* and not *ma'am* but *madam*. Are we clear?"

Sarah looked downcast, as if she had let Julia down, and squeaked, "Yes ma'am, I mean madam."

Feeling that was enough of a long face, Julia smiled and said, "All right, let me see how you are doing copying your letters."

Sarah held up her paper and waited to see what Julia would say.

Julia, looking very serious, said, "Very good, quite a bit of improvement. But try to work on getting the letters to flow a bit more, all right? And just what happened here?" she added, indicating a rather long tail on a letter.

Julia had been surprised to find that Sarah actually knew more "letters," as she put it, then they had been led to believe. Julia did not think she was hiding anything; she just had no self-confidence. And after even a few days with her, Julia had learned that Sarah was highly intelligent.

Sarah looked up. "I didn't mean to. The train jumped," she said in a plaintive voice.

Julia laughed. "Oh I know. I almost lost my bonnet, so I think we can ignore that, all right." She smiled at Sarah as if they were sharing a joke between them.

The little girl beamed and went back to work with a look of deep concentration on her small face, while Julia began working on yet another article, covering the preparations for the expedition and the planning that had to go into it to be sent back to the curator at the Museum. *Must keep up appearance*, she thought. She had already done some pieces on the researchers and their backgrounds, although her own had been heavily altered. It would be more than a stretch for any readers to believe a museum or any other kind of secretary was the explosives expert. Isaiah got that accolade.

It was just then that John Morton walked into the parlor. He looked at the two of them and asked how things were going. Julia said that she had taken the liberty of arranging for their own engine so that their progress would not be so impaired. Additionally, she informed him that she had requested the various reports and newspapers that the professor had requested for his research. Morton then asked Sarah how her lessons were coming, for he too had fallen under the child's spell.

Sarah smiled shyly at him, for in truth he seemed quite intimidating to her, and held up her paper. She added, "I kept working while Miss Julia sent the telegraph all the way to New York City." She sounded as if the notion of sending a telegraph message so far was the most amazing thing she had ever heard of; in truth, given her limited life circumstances, it may well have been.

Morton smiled. "Very good, Sarah," he said, "and also to you, Miss Verolli. Julia, are you sure that the budget can handle our own engine?" John gulped and looked slightly pale at this point.

"Oh absolutely, sir. Why, Mr. Anderson said to spare no expense to facilitate your research, none whatsoever, sir. I also took the liberty of setting up an appointment with the local Pinkerton representative as you mentioned you thought they might have some idea as to the location of the research objects you were interested in."

Morton just nodded and wondered what he could do on a real research expedition with Julia's help, expertise, and total flare for logistics.

Julia looked at her small watch, which she wore as a broach, and said firmly to Sarah, "I believe, young missy, that you are supposed to be forward for your tinkering lesson with Mr. Liman."

Sarah looked at her, obviously torn; she wanted to stay with Julia, but she also loved spending time with Isaiah. Recently, she was starting to slip and call him Poppa. No one corrected her, especially not Isaiah. He had said to Father Peter that maybe Sarah and he needed each other, for it was amazing how one little girl could fill such a big hole in his heart and spread a balm on his soul.

Julia looked firm and Sarah put her pencils and paper away as if they were state secrets. She headed down the passageway and into the compartment she still shared with Julia. She then changed her dress for some more rugged clothes; after all, a lady did not work in a tinker's shop in her good dress; it just was not done. At least that is what Miss Julia said, which made it the law. Soon thereafter, she disappeared out the door and headed toward the car now holding Isaiah's new "shop on wheels," as he put it.

The next several days passed in much the same way, the miles being slowly eaten up by the turning wheels of various freight trains as they drew steadily nearer to Chicago.

It was midmorning several days later when they finally arrived in Chicago. However, several hours had elapsed by the time Corporal Tinsman had arranged for a switcher to make a short hop to one of the several passenger stations in Chicago. The train was finally spotted on a coach track with a steam line hooked up for heat and for the kitchen. By this time, it was late afternoon. Morton made a few inquiries at the station and when he returned he went to talk to Julia.

Julia was by herself in the parlor working on yet another article for the museum. Sarah was with Father Peter for her Latin lesson and Isaiah was forward in his shop on wheels. Morton cleared his throat and rather hesitatingly asked Julia, "I know time is of the essence, but still, it is somewhat late in the day to visit the Pinkerton offices or do much other research. So I was wondering if you would care to go to the theater tonight. They are doing one of the new musicals. I thought it would make a nice change of pace."

Julia raised an eyebrow at Morton and thought for just a minute before she replied, "Why, Professor John Morton, what would your colleagues at the museum think if they knew you were asking your single female secretary out without a chaperone? How scandalous, sir!"

Morton smiled and said, "Well, to the best of my knowledge, none of them are in Chicago, and a gentleman never discusses these things, does he?"

Julia batted her eyes. Finally, she said, "Well, I am a quiet and shy young lady, but I suppose that one can be daring once in a while. So the answer is yes, John Morton, I would love to go out this evening, but only if you tempt me with dinner too."

John looked happy as he left to reserve tickets and a table.

Later on, Julia was getting ready for her evening with Morton when Sarah came in from her lessons with Father Peter. Sarah looked at her and was speechless, which indeed was something to marvel at, as she'd turned into quite the talkative little girl since having joined the expedition and gotten over her initial shock. Finally, she asked, "Are you going out, Miss Julia?"

Julia smiled. "Yes I am," she replied. "Professor Morton has asked me to dinner. I hope you approve." This last she said with a conspiratorial wink in Sarah's direction.

Sarah, still a little nervous about her new family, spoke in a whispper, "You are coming back, aren't you?"

Julia laughed and hugged her. "Yes, silly, but after your bedtime. I asked Father Peter to hear your prayers, and Isaiah will tuck you in. And you best be asleep by the time I return."

Though Sarah looked relieved, a little worry remained, her lingering uncertainty about these new people in her life obvious. She looked seriously at Julia. "Miss Julia, do you really promise to come back?" she said.

Julia held the little girl at arm's length, smiling, she said, "Cross my heart, Sarah."

Sarah looked relieved but said, "All right, but be careful. Cities are dangerous places, especially after dark you know."

"Yes, madam. You do not have to worry. The professor will protect me. Do you think that will be safe enough?" asked Julia, trying to look very serious.

"Well, I guess so, but still be careful, I—" Sarah started to cry. "I could not stand to lose you, Miss Julia!"

"I promise we will come back to the train right after the theater," said Julia.

"I thought you said dinner?" Sarah's concern had now clearly returned.

"John, the professor asked me to dinner and a musical. Is that all right?" replied Julia.

"Well, all right, but you are coming back right after the musical, right? What's a musical?" asked Sarah, as if verifying her sister's activities were of the right sort.

"I will tell you about it in the morning, young lady. And yes, we will come right back to the train. I promise. Now I have to finish getting ready for my evening with the professor. I would not do at all to disappoint one's employer, now would it? Would you give me a hand with these bows?"

Sarah beamed and began helping Julia with her dress, obviously delighted that she could be trusted with such an important job.

Later, Julia and John bid the others a good evening and left for dinner. John was already breathing somewhat heavily, as Julia had picked the same dark blue dress that not only showed off her figure but, as noted, had that somewhat daringly low-cut neckline. Her glossy black hair was done up and a beautiful onyx necklace and matching earrings drew attention to her neckline. John commented on how lovely she looked.

Julia laughed and told him, "You, sir, would not believe the inquisition I had to go through to get permission to go out with you. A mother superior at a convent school could be no worse than Sarah."

John laughed, imagining the scene, and said, "Well, in that case, I better have you home on time. Or we will not be allowed out again."

They both laughed.

Dinner was all that could be hoped for, and John thought the food was good too. He had all his attention on Julia; it was hard to believe that such a beautiful and delightful young woman could be so dangerous when necessary. They talked of pleasantries over dinner, lest anyone overhear their conversation. John told her how he had been a small college professor when the war broke out. He had joined in late 1862, when it had become obvious to all that the war would not be the short, quick affair the newspapers had all predicted.

Julia said she would have thought he would have gone in earlier; after all, he seemed the adventuresome type. John told her shyly that he did not enjoy the killing and that, while he considered the Union's and President Lincoln's cause to be noble, the truth was, he had not wanted to go into the army. However, when Britain sided with the Confederacy, he'd known he had to do his duty. Julia did not tell him of the conversation she'd had with Father Peter but let John tell the story of how the sergeant had saved his life. She also noted that he left out the times that he had saved Peter's life, as if he did not want to puff himself up—*not only handsome but modest and noble. Actually*, she thought, *very handsome and*, smiling at the thought, she secretly told herself, *very sexy.*

John saw the smile play about her face and inquired what he had said that was so amusing. Julia laughed and said that she was thinking about Father Peter as a grisly sergeant; it was so hard to picture. John bought this white lie and went on with his story of how, after the war, he had done some very early research with Othniel Marsh, who'd recommended him to the museum. He told her how the curator had seemed to find his tales of derring-do on his trips to the Dakota badlands and the Central and South American jungles more newsworthy than his discoveries, much to John's embarrassment. However it had provided him a chance to continue his research. He told her that Dr. Chesterfield loved the coverage the museum got in the papers about brave men facing hardship and danger, having to deal with uncivilized peoples to advance mankind's store of scientific knowledge. "Sometimes I feel like I am a character in one of Ned Buntline's dime novels," he confessed.

Julia thought that very amusing and laughed in a very ladylike way. Keeping up her smile, she asked him in a whispered tone, "For a man who is not an adventurer, how then, sir, do you explain your oh-so-fancy and quite deadly cane? And I should also question that nasty little pepperbox you carry."

John was surprised, but replied honestly, "Julia, I said I did not enjoy killing. But there is some truth to what Dr. Chesterfield has had written about some of my explorations. There were some nasty scrapes, and I am a reasonably quick study. One has to adapt to the times and circumstances. I only hope I can adapt fast enough for this mission—before there is a horror unleashed." John changed the subject rather abruptly and asked, "How did you know about my cane?" His surprise at her knowledge was clear in the tone of the question.

"Well, sir, I recognize the workmanship; after all, I am in the business," said Julia demurely, as if she were discussing a secretary's selection of typewriters instead of a concealed and very deadly weapon.

John continued, trying to change the subject. He told her how impressed he was with her ability to organize all their logistics and that he thought it would be truly wonderful to have her on a real research expedition and that her perfume was just so lovely. John quickly shook his head, as he realized that he had spoken without thinking or, in reality, spoken what he was thinking, and quickly turned red with embarrassment.

Julia laughed even more at John's predicament. "Thank you, fine sir," she said simply. "I have been complimented but never for my ability to organize a train and supplies before. And I am very glad you like the scent, sir." She smiled again, and before long, dinner was over, and they headed over to the theater to see the musical.

Julia enjoyed herself very much. She could not seem to remember when she'd ever gone out with a very nice gentleman just for the enjoyment of his company and not as part of some assignment for William Anderson. It wasn't, of course, that she would not do things for Anderson. But John was very nice, and not having to immediately worry about how to dispose of a body or open a safe or which papers to steal, but just to walk arm in arm with a nice man and be a young girl for a change was, in truth, a most wonderful treat.

All too soon, the show was over, and the pair walked back to the station and the waiting train. John stopped and, with a thudding heart, turned to kiss Julia. She started to respond but just as suddenly pushed him away.

John looked confused and then turned red with shame. "Julia, I don't know what came over me. You must think me a cad to try and take advantage of you ... to try and take advantage of my position," he stammered.

Julia looked up at him. He was so tall. "John, it's not what you think. I wanted you to kiss me, but we have a mission that has to come first! It is bad business when teammates are more than that. It just, it complicate things." Julia was telling the truth. She had wanted Morton to kiss her and more; she was starting to have true feelings for him. She was enough of a trained agent, however, to know that giving into these desires would lead to problems. She reached up and touched John's face and added quite firmly, "Besides, John Morton, if I thought you were a cad or some such, I would not be here looking up at you. I would be lifting my skirt and stepping over you, as you would be in a heap at my feet."

Morton looked stunned, and then his shock morphed into sheepishness.

Oh God, Julia thought, *why does he have to look like such a young boy? Was it not hard enough when she'd had to push him away just now?*

"You're right of course, Julia. I just forgot myself. Can you forgive me?" asked Morton as he straightened up.

"John, I just told you I wanted it too, but the mission has to come first. Maybe there will be time afterward, if you still have any interest," replied Julia.

A few more quiet words passed between the two, and then they went into the train.

Julia pulled the compartment door closed, and a sleepy little voice said, "You came back, just like you promised."

Julia went over to Sarah's bunk, stroked her forehead and said lovingly, "You are suppose to be asleep, young lady, not waiting up for me." With that, she kissed the little girl and began to get ready for bed herself, thinking what it might be like to have a normal life with a museum research professor as her husband.

Just after she had climbed into bed she sensed a small body approaching and made room as Sarah climbed into her bed and cuddled close as if to make sure Julia would be there in the morning. It was in that position that they both fell fast asleep.

CHAPTER 14

IN CHICAGO THE NEXT MORNING

reakfast was in progress when John arrived in the dining car. Father Peter and Isaiah were cheerfully working on a significant reduction in the number of pancakes stacked in a pile when he sat down. As he placed his own pile of pancakes on a plate, both men looked at him with raised eyebrows. He had just started to say that he'd had a most wonderful evening with Julia the night before when the lady in question arrived, along with Sarah.

The gentlemen stood as the ladies were seated, and breakfast recommenced. Sarah was brimming with questions about going out to dinner and what a musical was. She especially looked at Morton, as if to make sure that nothing had happened to Miss Julia. John thought back to Julia's comment about an inquisition by a mother superior and realized that, even as the good Protestant he was, he was most assuredly beginning to understand the true depth of fear that comment could cause.

It was at this point that Father Peter jumped in and rescued his former commander, just as he had done in the war. Only in this case, the assailant was alive at the end of the rescue. "John, I thought you would like to know that our newest member seems to have a flair for languages. Her Latin lessons are coming along nicely."

Sarah beamed at the compliment and seemed to forget about the evening before.

Morton, sensing a chance to extricate himself from the interrogation he was being put through, simply replied, "Very good, Peter. She also seems to have a flair for mathematics."

If possible, Sarah's smile got even bigger.

Morton continued, if for no other reason than to keep Sarah's mind off last night's activities, "What is everyone planning today as far as our research goes?"

Isaiah replied while adding sugar to his tea, "I thought I might visit some of the various tinkerers in the area to see if there is any word on what anyone is working on", he fumbled for a moment as he searched for the words to keep the reason for his investigations from Sarah, "in terms of fabricating research equipment." With that, he took a sip of his tea and looked like a man who has seen heaven; the tea was, as far as he was concerned, the best he had ever had.

Father Peter was next to respond to John's question. "I must present the archbishop's compliments to the bishop of Chicago and perhaps see what the local church news is." This was obviously Peter's way of saying he would check to see if any of the local parishes had had any problems of a mysterious nature. Since Chicago had been the last confirmed sighting of the pair of renegade scientists, the father and the others wanted to spread their net as wide as possible. Even though John and Isaiah's inquiries promised better results, asking at the churches could not hurt, and Peter, like the rest, had a cover story to maintain.

Julia said simply, "Sarah and I have to pick up the papers and reports you had me request, sir. I believe that they are being held at the local federal magistrate's office downtown for you. After that, we will be here reviewing them. What about you, Professor?" She used his title instead of his name so as not to remind Sarah that she and John had been out last night.

John looked at his team and simply replied, "I will be meeting with the local Pinkerton representative to ascertain what information they have on our research subjects."

Each of the adults was trying very hard to ensure that Sarah was unaware of the true nature of the expedition.

After breakfast, Sarah had to change out of her pants and heavy top, since a lady did not go out to government offices in rugged work clothes like the ones she'd dressed in to work with Isaiah; it was just not done. Miss Julia said so, so that was that. She emerged in her proper attire, a white blouse, a gray skirt, and matching jacket. Her feet were in patent leather shoes. She had put on a simple straw hat with a flower on it and white gloves and stood before Julia as one would a soldier upon a parade ground ready for inspection. Once Julia had inspected her charge and nodded her approval, the two were off.

Morton watched them leave, looking at Julia as she climbed into the waiting carriage. Peter came up beside him and simply noted, "I take it you find our Julia interesting."

"Indeed, Peter, indeed. However, as she reminded me last night, there is a mission to complete first before we can explore other interests." Morton sighed and, turning, retrieved his hat and cane. Then he himself exited the train and headed for the local Pinkerton office.

Sometime later, Morton found himself being ushered into the office of a Mr. John Thorton, the local senior agent in charge of the Chicago Pinkerton operations. He introduced himself and showed Thorton the letter from Anderson authorizing him to act on the government's behalf.

Thorton opened his safe and pulled out a series of files to show to Morton. Looking seriously at Morton, he said, "I do not know what these two did, but they are dangerous, Mr. Morton. They put two of my best men in the hospital. What are they up to?"

Morton shook his head. "I wish I could tell you, but I am afraid I am not at liberty to do so. What happened to your men, Mr. Thorton?"

Thorton looked put out. "I don't know. All we can get out of them is some crazy story about monsters. It is a miracle they both lived. They suffered from smoke inhalation and burns, and they were the worse for it. However what is even worse, mind you they were both steady dependable men, now the pair are confined to the asylum, crazy with fear of these horrible monsters they swear they saw."

Morton looked grave and asked Thorton, "Did the men describe the monsters at all?"

Thorton sat back as if slapped. "Are you trying to make fun of my men?" he demanded. "These were good men, I will have you know, Morton!"

Morton shook his head. "No, Mr. Thorton," he replied, "I am not making fun of your men. The two men we are looking for have been known to modify various animals to frighten people so as to hide their illegal doings. We believe they may have used some drugs to induce hallucinations in their victims. I thought if you could enlighten me, it might fit the pattern we have seen before so that my team and I can be sure we are on the right trail. Believe me, absolutely no disrespect was meant in any way."

Thorton looked at Morton as if he were trying to judge the man, and seeming to finally decide, he replied, "Very well, Professor. The best we could get out of the men was that the creatures that attacked them were some sort of giant rat, although I do not have any idea what you could use to trick people into believing in such creatures."

Morton looked thoughtful. In order to gain the man's confidence some more, he said, "Sir, from what we know of these men, the drugs they use are quite potent. It would not take much for your men to be terrified. Stronger men have had their minds turned inside out." He went one to ask Thorton to give him the rest of the details as far as his firm understood them.

Thorton looked back at Morton, seeming again to be sizing the man up. Finally, he snorted and started to speak. "We were on the lookout for the pair as we had been instructed. A man with a German accent in the area was not much to go on. Many immigrants from Europe pass through Chicago. However a Chinaman, now that was different. We got word from some of our informants that a pair of men matching the description had been seen along the river docks. We canvassed the area looking for them, trying to pick up the trail. I will tell you it was none too easy, the Chinaman, Chen Sun his name was, kept a pretty low profile. Must have realized how much he stood out—not a big

Oriental community hereabouts. Anyhow, we were told, expenses be damned, find them at whatever the cost. So we kept spreading the net and the money around till we got lucky again. Several of the ladies of the evening let our men know that a certain Oriental gentleman seemed to have an appetite for young white women, if you follow me?"

Morton said simply, "I was in the army for seven, almost eight, years during the war, sir. I follow you right enough."

Thorton nodded and kept on with his tale. "We found the pair living at a warehouse. The building had been leased to a Herr Mouser, rent paid first of the month in cash. The owner did not mind the pair keeping their business a secret; there were no problems, and he liked the cash aspect. Much less paperwork, you understand. We watched them for two weeks, trying to see what they were up to. The German seemed to do all the legwork. Chen stayed pretty much inside and out of the public eye. We would not have even known he was there except for the nightingales, and I ain't talkin' the feathery kind either."

Morton indicated he should continue.

Thorton picked up his story. "After two weeks, we decided to see if we could figure out what the two were up to, so my men decided to have a little look-see. They went inside and were attacked. We do not know if it was deliberate or accidental, but the warehouse soon was on fire. Personally, I think those slime bags set it afire deliberately. Both of my men were badly burned. We managed to speak to them before they went to the hospital. That's when they first talked about the monsters, claiming to have seen them up close and personal. I went to the hospital myself several times after that but their story never changed."

Morton thought for a few minutes as he digested the information he had just received. Then he asked, "Did you find anything in the remains of the warehouse?"

Thorton looked at him in a funny way. "We found some corpses and remains in what had been jail-like cages. Not much was left; everything was burned just about beyond recognition. But the remains looked like they might have been some kind of dog or something. Whatever they were, they were big. I feel sorry for whatever they were, monsters or not; lousy way to go—burned to death while trapped in a cage."

Morton again paused to digest what he had just heard and then asked, "Do you know what happened to Ulrich and Chen?"

"Well, Mr. Morton, we traced them to the docks again. It seems they had been running some kind of a market for drugs. They found a ready market; the men loved it—made you work like a horse, get all kinds of extra pay, except after a while, it had the slight drawback of making you madder than hell itself. The men who used it would attack anyone for no reason. It seems our pair escaped before the madness became common knowledge."

"Everything you've told me sounds just like the men we are after," said Morton. "What happened then?"

Thorton was obviously uneasy. "They disappeared. Seems they lost most of whatever they were working on in the warehouse, but they also seemed to have plenty of cash from the drug sales. The last we could trace them, they supposedly hopped a steamboat up river and then disappeared a town or two later downriver. Our best guess is that they headed west toward the railheads. The men there will pay for a drug like that. There would be big money to be made and no questions to be asked. One other thing—my men did manage to find out some of the materials the two had been purchasing before they went missing. I hope that helps."

Morton looked down and spoke slowly. "That leaves a lot of country to hide in. Well, thank you for your time, Mr. Thorton. I hope sincerely that your men recover."

Morton took copies of the reports the Pinkerton agents had filed, including copies of Ulrich's invoices, and left, heading back to the train. Morton realized that the drug Thorton had referenced matched the drugs the pair had been working on for the army, the drugs that had previously been abandoned when the same dark side effect, the uncontrollable rage of those who'd been taking it for a time, had come to light.

By way of his return route, Morton checked with several of the railroads in Chicago to see if he could find out where the largest area of construction was. It seemed their lead had narrowed based upon the time they spent in Chicago, he thought. At least, Morton told himself, the haystack the needle was lost in had gotten smaller.

Father Peter had left just after Morton and made his way to the bishop's chancellery. Presenting himself, he talked with various staff members and renewed some old contacts from seminary. He was sipping coffee when he spotted an old friend, Father Gabriel. "Gabe," Peter greeted his old friend, "how are you doing?"

Gabe looked up and smiled, for he had not seen Peter in well over three years. "Peter, what are you doing here? I thought you were back east in the city, leading the quiet life of a small parish priest?"

Peter fumbled about for a little while, using the cover story of how he was traveling with a scientific research group while he inspected several mission projects the archdiocese had funded. He was not all that sure his old friend bought the story. Gabe was looking at him quizzically.

Finally, Peter, thinking quickly, told him that, with the archbishop's blessing, he was assisting the government in tracking down some counterfeiters who had set up a shop in his parish so he was somewhat familiar with them and their habits. Very hush-hush, so don't tell anyone. Gabe seemed to buy this story and wondered at how exciting it would be to work with the Department of the Treasury, or so it seemed to a quiet priest from the Midwest.

Gabe did admit, however, that he had some excitement of his own. Peter looked up, interested, and urged him to go on. Gabe told Peter about how some of his parishioners had been recruited to help manage some animal experiments but had been scared off when they started seeing monsters. Gabe told Peter, "I started a temperance group in the parish. I am firmly convinced that the only giant rats around were the ones you see through the bottom of a whiskey shot glass or a beer mug."

Peter agreed that Gabe was right about the horrors of demon rum and John Barleycorn. Peter managed to get some more details about these drunken visions out of Gabe before he left for the train and his chance to report to John and Julia. The information was not much, but at least it did seem to confirm that the pair had been active in Chicago.

Isaiah spent the morning going from place to place, talking and more so listening to the various tinkerers, chemists, and suppliers in town. He learned that quite a bit of activity was going on in and around Chicago as far as inventors and tinkers went. Plenty of new designs for farm equipment, not to mention steam ship applications for the Great Lakes trade, were in the making. However, he didn't learn much on the pair in question.

Isaiah was in a chemical and medical supply house when he overheard the proprietor talking about how it was a shame that the Chinaman had left, him being such a good customer and all. Not only did he buy a lot but paid cash on the barrelhead too. Indeed a shame to lose such a fine and steady customer. Isaiah talked to the old Negro cleaning man and found out the Chinaman had bought all kinds of equipment to make drugs. Dobkins, that was the old fellow's name, added that, with all the work he'd done helping to pack it up so nothing broke, the man had hardly tipped him at all. "Treated me like dirt, he did. Course he didn't do any more for the white boys," Dobkins added. Apparently, Chen did not discriminate. "Treated us all like we was dirt."

Isaiah followed up and asked some of the others. He bought some bottles of rum and a couple of Tennessee whiskey, which seemed to help lubricate the conversation quite a bit. He found out where the supply house had been delivering the materials. The one fellow who seemed to appreciate the rum more than the others told him confidentially that the other fellows were having some fun at his expense. The warehouse they delivered to had burned down, but he knew which boat the Chinaman and his friend, a white guy—"he talked with an accent like one of them Dutchman"—had hired him to take some of their goods to. They didn't say, it but it had been obvious that they were gettin' ready to light out, quick like. The fellow figured they were probably behind in their rent.

Isaiah gave him an extra bottle and some food money and left for the docks to check on the riverboat schedule.

CHAPTER 15

JULIA AND SARAH'S TALE

Julia and Sarah had a quiet start to their morning errands, which included going downtown. Sarah was not used to riding in a carriage. Mostly, she had to worry about not being run over by wagons back in Buffalo's Canal District. But ladies rode in carriages, according to what Miss Julia said. Therefore, they rode all the way to the foot of the business district, which made for a most pleasant trip for Sarah.

When they arrived, the two ladies climbed out so they could ride on a trolley car. It was there that a man in a blue uniform tried to grab Sarah and make her ride in the back, away from Miss Julia. Sarah was more than a little scared; however, Miss Julia smiled at the man, a conductor she called him, and explained to him that it was all right.

The man insisted and this time grabbed Sarah. All of a sudden, Julia reached forward, seized the man's wrist, and twisted it slightly; all of a sudden, the conductor was on his knees crying in pain. Sarah backed up when she saw the look in Miss Julia's eyes, like those of a dangerous animal, and heard the man crying out in pain some more. Fearfully, she grabbed at Miss Julia's skirt and said, "Please, Miss Julia, don't hurt him anymore. I don't mind. I will ride in the back of the trolley. Please don't hurt him no more."

Julia looked at Sarah and shuddered. Then she took a deep breath and let the man go, her face returning to the look of a simple young secretary. She said to the man, "I am sorry, sir. It is just we are on official museum business, and you startled me."

The conductor, probably not wanting to admit he had just been manhandled by a mere five-foot tall, ninety-nine pound, young female, said, as he climbed to his feet, that it was all right but the little black girl still had to ride in the back of the car.

Julia looked at Sarah, smiled, and then said, "All right, we shall both ride in the back." She took Sarah's hand, and the pair proceeded to the rear of the trolley and found a seat. Sarah looked up at her somewhat fearfully. The woman who'd become angry with the conductor was a side of Julia she had never seen before, and it was most certainly a side that Julia had never wanted her to see.

Julia looked a little nervous and put her arm around Sarah. "I am sorry if I scared you, Sarah." She spoke quietly. "It is just that, well, when he grabbed at you, I guess I panicked a little." Wetting her lips, she went on, "You see, when I was growing up, I never knew my parents or any of my family. I was raised on the streets like you were after your mother died. I, well, until I went to the finishing school, I never really had any family. And I guess if you don't mind, I tend to think of you as a little sister, and I, well, I did not want anyone hurting my family. I just could not stand it if he had hurt you!" This last was blurted out in a most un-Julia-like way, thought Sarah.

Julia saw Sarah look up at her and smile. She felt the little girl try to get closer to her, as if she was trying to remove the fear she saw in Julia's face. "It is all right, Miss Julia," she said. "He did not hurt me, and I love you too."

What Sarah did not understand was that Julia was not afraid of the conductor. She had killed and disposed of much bigger and much more dangerous men than him. She was afraid Sarah would find out about her and what she was. She was afraid that Sarah would be scared of her so much she would not want her in her life and that terrified Julia. That kind of fear was something she had never felt before and she was trying her best to deal with it while not letting on to Sarah how she felt.

The rest of the ride they sat quietly in the back of the trolley and enjoyed the ride. Sarah marveled at all the tall buildings and busy streets.

Julia and Sarah went into the courthouse to pick up the professor's various government reports and a variety of newspapers that Julia and her team hoped would yield some reference to the pair. Sarah was quite amazed at the amount of paper they had to carry. It was a tough job being a secretary to a scientist like the professor, but she would carry her share and not let Miss Julia down. Her very own big sister. Julia, in turn vowed to herself that she would never let Sarah, her little sister, down.

Sarah was a little dismayed when Julia had to stop at a police station. She had to wait on a bench and watch the professor's papers while Miss Julia went to talk to a man called the captain. As she sat on the bench in the hall, she was worried that Miss Julia was going to make trouble for the conductor or, worse yet, try to find an orphanage for her.

Soon, Miss Julia came back and said they could leave and return to the train. Sarah asked what they were doing there. Julia smiled and said she was just checking on some facilities the professor might need on the way home—you know, to store some of his specimens. Sarah was relieved that their stop did not have anything to do with finding an orphanage. Then she thought about it and wondered what a specimen was.

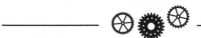

The team met back at the train and, over lunch, began to compare their various findings. Sarah was told by Miss Julia that she had to take a nap; after all, it had been a very busy morning. Sarah started to protest, but Miss Julia gave her a I-will-not-brook-any-nonsense-young-lady look, and Sarah dutifully trotted down the corridor to the compartment they shared. This seemed like the simplest way of getting Sarah out of hearing range for a while.

John opened the proceedings by telling what he had found out at the Pinkerton office, filling the others in on how their quarry was raising funds for their research with their drug operation.

Peter confirmed the story, telling everyone what his school friend Gabe had told him about the men in his parish and the pair of men who were creating monsters.

As it was, it was Isaiah who supplied the missing piece. He had been able to track the fleeing pair to a riverboat named the *Nancy B*. Luckily, the boat was in port, and Isaiah had been able to talk to some of the crew. They told him that the pair had gotten off three stops down and were heard talking about the Great Northern Railroad and how it was being built as fast tracks could be laid.

Morton was in good cheer. It seemed as if they had a solid lead, although there were several areas of construction that the pair could have gotten off to. At least as far as they could determine, none of the Ratten were loose in Chicago.

Julia confirmed that the local police had had no unusual reports of monsters on the loose. Apparently all the creatures had died in the warehouse fire. She theorized that the pair must have been surprised by the secret visit of the Pinkerton agents and not had a chance to release their creations in the city in order to create chaos and cover their tracks. They were all glad to hear that. They had enough problems with the case without needing to hunt down more of the vile beasts in Chicago.

Morton said they'd have the train head out toward the railhead, noting perhaps they'd get lucky and find something in the mountain of reports and newspapers that Julia and Sarah had returned with.

The group broke up, and Isaiah went to check on Sarah's nap and tell her to get ready for her tinkering lesson. After that, he went forward to his workshop on wheels. In passing through the bunk car, he let Corporal Tinsman know where they would be heading so he could make arrangements. The engine already had sand in the sand dome, a full load of coal and the water tank topped off in the tender. It would just take a while to fire the boiler and raise steam. Of course, the corporal had to tell the engineer and, in turn, the conductor had to get their train orders from the railroad dispatcher, for it would really not do to meet another train going the opposite way on a one-track line.

On board the train, Peter, John, and Julia sat around the parlor looking at various U.S. Government reports for a wide variety of agencies and a plethora of newspapers, hoping to find some article about unusual occurrences that might give them another lead. Isaiah and Sarah were forward in Isaiah's workshop for Sarah's mechanicals lesson.

John was searching through some newspapers from the southwest hoping to find a lead on the whereabouts of the two men they were after, just in case their information was wrong. Julia looked at papers from the Northwest. After several hours of reading about cattle rustling, claim jumping, and other assorted goings-on neither was any nearer to finding a lead.

At least their search had been through news and, as such, somewhat interesting. Father Peter, as if in an act of penance for some perceived sin, had been valiantly poring through numerous government reports from various agencies. He had spread before him papers headed Army, Navy, Life-Saving Service, Lighthouse Service, Federal Marshall Service, and every government agency in between, including the Department of the Interior and the U.S. Postal Service.

All of a sudden, Peter sat up and asked, "Where exactly are we headed?"

John looked up in surprise. "We're heading for Saint Paul via the Rock Island Railroad," he replied. "It seemed as good a direction as any based upon the information Isaiah got about the pair heading toward the railhead for the Great Northern. Why? Have you found something?"

Peter looked anxuiys. "It may be nothing but there is a report here from an Indian agent on a reservation in the Dakota Territory that may be related to our quarry."

John held out his hand for the report, while Julia slid closer to John so she could read it over his shoulder:

To: Bureau Indian Affairs, Washington, D.C.

From: Rock Face Reservation, Dakota Territory

Subject: Unrest Among Tribes

Request immediate assistance from US Army to ensure tribe does not jump reservation. Indians acting increasingly agitated. There is much chatter among the tribal members about an evil manitou (Indian evil spirit) that has created monsters to destroy them because they have let the white man into their ancestral lands.

Believe this may be the result of dissident elements in the tribe or possible whites who are looking to foment trouble so they can claim Indian lands. Also unable to rule out possible British involvement. British forces active along border in Canada.

Request assistance of US Army, including cavalry and infantry. Additionally, request US Marshal to investigate if white involvement. Should Indians leave reservation, have insufficient forces on hand to contain them. Situation explosive.

Sheppard, Thomas J. Agent Rock Face Reservation

John and Julia both looked up at Peter. Julia was first to speak. "It seems we are headed to the Dakota Territory, gentlemen. Although I am surprised; they only had a bit over three weeks' lead on us."

John looked at her and replied, "It certainly fits. The railroad is building near the reservation, and they could have stocked their supplies up in Saint Paul. This area is out in the wilds, but things may have gotten too hot for them in the cities. For sure everyone seems to know the railroad is paying big money for men who can put track down in a hurry. It is especially so with the British on the border. The Federal government wants to be able to shift troops quickly should the need arise."

Julia nodded. "We can move faster if we use one of the army's airships, John."

John shook his head in reply. "No, Julia, we do not want to spook our quarry. For the life of me, I don't see how arriving in a eight hundred-foot airship with U.S. Army emblazoned on its side is exactly subtle. Besides which, we may need the extra equipment on the train. Also, the ships are still in short supply and are used mostly for patrolling the more remote areas of the border. I do not think the army would be happy to share. We may need to persuade them to do so later, so let's keep that ace up our sleeve for now."

"All right, John," she replied. "Remember, though, these two are fast movers. They have slipped through our fingers before."

"True, Julia, but as far as we can determine, they do not know we are on their trail. So far, they have been reacting to local law or the Pinkertons. Remember, after all, we are just a museum research expedition, all in all, really rather harmless." Morton gave her a small smile.

CHAPTER 16

WHAT HARM CAN A DAY IN SAINT PAUL CAUSE?

The train continued on, dropping Isaiah and Father Peter in Saint Paul to check and see if they could find any information on whether or not Ulrich and Chen Sun had stopped there. This seemed like a strong possibility since it would have been the last major city before the Dakotas and the railhead. Before they left the train, Julia noted she'd also be stopping to send another telegram to Anderson, telling the pair that it might help. Both were a little quizzical as to what aid further communication at this point could provide, but left, promising to rejoin as soon as possible.

Peter and Isaiah began to investigate. Isaiah was somewhat surprised to find that the atmosphere in the shops was much the same as he'd encountered in Buffalo, skepticism at his color, until he started to talk. Then it was like the tide coming in; the love of invention and tinkering kicked in, and all of sudden it was like he was a long-lost relative. Several said there had been some Germans through the area, but no one remembered a Chinaman. He spent the best part of the afternoon talking to the tinker community but without uncovering any real information. It seemed as if there were plenty of Germans in town, along with the Scandinavians who made up the bulk of the population. Next, he was onto the various suppliers in town.

Isaiah had been in and out of several shops just chatting up folks when he got to what would prove to be his last stop. The proprietor was obviously a man who had no use for men of Isaiah's color. The man started in by berating him. Isaiah took this while still trying to get any information out him. The next thing he knew, the man was outside calling for the police. It was shortly thereafter that Isaiah found himself in a paddy wagon in irons.

While Isaiah was making the round of shops and suppliers, Father Peter was following required church protocol. As usual, he needed to stop in to the local bishop's office to pay his respects and present greeting from the New York archbishop; mission or not, he was still a man of the cloth. Since he was there, he also snooped around to see if any strange goings-on had been noted in any of the parishes.

Father Peter was coming up pretty empty-handed; absolutely nothing out of the ordinary seemed to be happening in the parishes. This was not, however, necessarily meaningful information in a mostly Lutheran town. He did use some connections to talk to members of the local police, but that was equally unpromising. It seemed as if most of the members of the Saint Paul Police Department were hard-nosed, solid Lutherans, hardly the kind of folks who would open up to a Catholic priest, no matter who recommended him. The flames of Europe's Reformation wars seemed to be still burning here; he was getting nowhere at what seemed a breakneck pace. He was just leaving the police station when a paddy wagon started to unload and he saw Isaiah being pulled out in irons.

Going back in the station, he heard the desk sergeant asking what the charges were. The officer replied that the darky had been making a lot of fuss and bothering a couple of proprietors of some shops. The officer told the sergeant that the man claimed to be a tinker and was just trying to find a lead on some work, 'as if any darky could be that smart'. They both laughed at that one.

That is when the desk sergeant saw Peter again. "What do you want, papist? I told you before we got no information for you here."

Peter put on his most benign face and smiled at the officer. "Well, you seem to have arrested one of my parishioners." He gestured at Isaiah. "I am just trying to help the poor fellow."

It was a short time later that Peter and Isaiah found themselves in a somewhat-less-than-nice guest room at the same police station, shackled together. Peter looked at Isaiah. "The next time I say that," he said, "please, try to look a little more Catholic, would you!"

Isaiah just snorted at the father's attempt at humor and then said, "I don't know how we are going to get out of this, on top of which, I did not find a damn thing out about the pair of them. This day is not going any too well."

The pair spent the night in custody, and both were somewhat surprised the next morning when they were taken into the police station captain's office. The captain had the officers remove the shackles from Isaiah and asked the pair to sit down. "I need to apologize, but you could have identified yourself," he said to Isaiah, who sat there looking stunned.

Isaiah, still trying to figure out what was going on, simply replied, "If it is all right, could you have the irons taken off the father?"

"Is he working with you, Agent Liman?" asked the captain a little nervously.

Isaiah, still trying to figure out what was going on, replied simply, "Yes, yes indeed, Captain. He is one of our best."

The captain looked a little confused. "The telegram we got from Washington simply said that you were working on a counterfeiting case, Mr. Liman. We would have never made you for a treasury agent. How long have they been hiring Negroes?"

Father Peter, starting to catch on to where this was going and what the nature of the telegram Julia have had sent must have been, piped up. "There is some confusion, Captain. Actually I am not with the Treasury Department. I am, in fact, a priest. However, the men in question had set up operations in my parish back in New York, and I had met them in the course of my ministry. So the Treasury Department asked the archbishop to, uh, borrow my services to help assist in their capture. Is that not right, Agent Liman?"

Isaiah quickly picked up where Peter had left off. "Absolutely, Father. You see, Captain, the father here is the only one to have gotten a good look at them. He is absolutely vital to their capture. As to your other question, I am actually one of the first black agents the treasury has trained. It seems they needed someone who could work undercover. Who notices someone like me? Now, I really have to ask you to keep this quiet. These men are very slippery, and we have been tracking them over a large part of the country, just missing them at several turns. They are a most cagey pair, sir."

"Well, Agent Liman, you can rest assured on the discretion of the Saint Paul Police Department. Is there any help you need?" he added, obviously not wanting to get on the wrong side of a Federal agent, even if he was a darky.

"Well, actually, we could use some assistance," replied Isaiah, willing to use whatever advantage he could find. "The men in question lost a lot of their equipment in Chicago in a fire. They only just managed to elude capture by the Pinkertons. We think they may have been trying to restock their equipment and supplies here in Saint Paul or Minneapolis. Any information you might have or could find would be most helpful."

The captain looked at the pair and said, "Well, I am happy do a little checking. I have some contacts across the river. I will see what I can find out. What are we looking for?"

Father Peter and Isaiah gave the captain copies of the description of Ulrich and Chen Sun that Anderson had supplied to John at the start of the affair. This was coupled with some ideas of the type of equipment they might be purchasing, based on the list of supplies they had been buying in Chicago which the Pinkertons had provided. The pair promised the captain to return later.

Deciding not to push their luck, Father Peter and Isaiah decided that leaving the police station was at the top of their list of things to do.

Breakfast was the next order of business on that list; the cuisine in the police station had not been the best.

As soon as they got out of the police station, Isaiah turned to Father Peter with a simple, "What was that all about?"

Peter smiled and, chuckling, related to Isaiah how he had told Julia about the story he had given his friend Gabriel to explain what he was doing so far outside of his parish, not to mention the Diocese. When he had finished, he told Isaiah, "It seems our Julia has now made it an official cover story. Congratulations, Special Treasury Agent Liman."

Isaiah shook his head and was at a total loss for a retort. Finally he settled for saying, "Let's get breakfast; seems I worked up an appetite being chained up to you all night."

With that, the two made for the nearest restaurant that would serve both blacks and Catholics in a lily-white Lutheran town.

Several hours later, the two were back at the police station getting the information that had so far eluded them. The German and the Chinaman had been in town and had, indeed, stocked up on equipment and supplies. They were last seen having their purchases loaded into a drover's caboose and having it attached to a freight heading toward the Great Northern's westernmost railhead.

The pair thanked the captain for all the assistance that the Saint Paul Police Department had given them, noting that, to be sure this aid would figure prominently in Agent Liman's reports back to Washington.

Isaiah and Peter wasted no time in sending a coded telegram off to the town where Morton and Julia had arranged for a stopover and to wait for reports. Before they reached the door of the telegraph office, the key was clacking again. The telegraph operator yelled for them to wait. They looked at each other in surprise.

Peter simply stated, "Our Julia must have been waiting for us."

Paying the operator, the pair left the telegraph office to find a quiet place to decode and read the reply. When deciphered, it read simply:

Proceed Fort Savage, transportation arranged for Lt. Colonel Harrigan and his aide, Sergeant Liman.

"Who are we impersonating now?" wondered Isaiah out loud.

After obtaining a pair of fast horses at a livery stable, the pair left for Fort Savage just outside of Saint Paul. Father Peter and Isaiah both were none too happy about this, as they remarked to each other that they had both been in the infantry, not the cavalry. However, speed was of the essence; they needed to get on with the mission. Besides, Isaiah desperately wanted to see if Sarah was all right. The little girl was now firmly in Isaiah's heart.

The miles sped by, and early the next day, the fort appeared in the distance.

The fort occupied a large, sprawling area. But it was mostly empty, except for several mooring towers and a medium-sized stockade, with most of the buildings safely inside the walls. The fort was dominated by a large landing field for army airships, hence the towers; however, only one was currently docked. As the two rode up, more than happy to be leaving the cavalry, they could see on the side of the airship the words "U.S. Army" and, under that, "USAS Congress." The Congress was one of the smaller, earlier model ships built during the last two years of the war. She was about 650 feet long and just under 100 feet in diameter. They could also see the multiple barrels of two .45-caliber Gatling guns poking out of her control gondola. Her class of ship had proved the key to holding the British navy at bay. Since it could search vast areas of the ocean, before the Royal Navy could land supplies, she and her sisters could alert the powerful U.S. Navy where to concentrate. While some of the ships remained under control of the navy, most had been transferred to the army. Now they were used primarily to patrol the huge border between Canada and the United States where there was far too much border and nowhere near enough troops.

As they approached, a sentry detail stopped them, demanding to know who they were.

Father Peter spoke up. "Lieutenant Colonel Harrigan and my aide, Sergeant Liman, here to obtain transportation."

The corporal of the guard looked at their civilian attire, noted their lack of proper identification, and ordered them to dismount slowly and carefully. They were almost strip-searched and then marched under a heavy and unsmiling guard detail to the commanding officer's office, where they were shown in.

The post commander, a full colonel, looked at them, and in a less-than-welcoming voice, said, "Just who the hell are you two?"

Peter introduced himself and his aide and asked that they be given transportation.

The colonel replied, "Why are you two out of uniform? And just what is going on here? I have held up a patrol for two days by order of the War Department in Washington in order to give you every assistance. I have Brits on the border and red skins ready to go on the warpath! Just what makes you so special, *Lieutenant* Colonel," demanded the colonel, emphasizing the lieutenant.

Peter tried to look his military officer best, at least how he remembered it from his days in the army as a sergeant, and standing ramrod straight, he replied, "Sir, my aide and I have been chasing two British spies who Washington thinks have been trying to inflame the tribes here in the area and in parts of the east. We are working undercover as a priest and a tinker, trying to pick up their trail. As you can imagine, with all that is going on, time is of the essence."

The colonel looked hard at them for a minute, but, faced with a very stern directive emanating directly from the War Department in Washington, he had little choice but to accept their story. Without any trace of a smile or any other emotion, other than perhaps severe annoyance, he briskly told them, "Get aboard. The Congress lifts within the hour."

As the pair walked to the airship, Isaiah whispered to his friend, "Undercover as a priest and tinker. That was original."

Peter whispered back, "Well, I was trying to come up with something to explain our dress, and I was not about to claim you as a parishioner again."

Before long, the pair was seated in the Congress's control car, slung under the ship's body. This comprised the lower level of habitable space, except for the two Gatling gun stations below. It was hardly a luxurious setting. As noted, the ships had been rushed into service and had seen few upgrades since the war. No walnut or brass here, just plain steel and dark green paint. The captain gave the order as he stood behind the helmsman, the trimsman off to his right and the engine telegraph to his left. Behind him, a plot table was covered with maps and navigation equipment.

Soon, the ship was lifting off. The ship's captain, who was indeed a captain by his bars, tried to make them comfortable. "Colonel, do you have any idea where exactly we are headed?" he asked as he stood by his chart table.

Peter replied by giving the name of the town where they had sent the telegram. The captain looked down at his charts and, picking up a pair of dividers and a ruler, did some brief calculations on a pad obviously there for that purpose. Looking up, he said, "Barring any problems, we should have you there by early tomorrow. I hope that that will be satisfactory."

Peter assured the officer that it would be excellent.

Peter was somewhat nervous, till Isaiah told him the ship used helium for lift and that gas was nonflammable.

Since Peter and Isaiah had been riding through the night to get to the fort, they were both utterly exhausted. They found a corner of the car, curled up, and did their level best to grab some sleep. The Congress ate up the miles through the night. The sound of the wind across the hull and that of the rhythmic throbbing of the ship's engines and steady hissing steam almost seemed like a lullaby to the two men, although in truth they were so bone tired from their all-night ride, the post's brass band marching through at full volume would not have sounded much different.

CHAPTER 17

NOT ALL PLANS GO THE WAY THEY SHOULD

By morning, the two, while somewhat stiff, were at least rested and ate a filling if somewhat plain breakfast, courtesy of the ship's crew. Isaiah asked if he might see the ship, explaining that, being undercover as a tinker, he wanted to get a feel for their transport. In truth, he was fascinated by the huge cells that stored the lifting gas and the compact steam engine that powered her flight.

All too soon he was being recalled to the control car, where the captain was addressing the lieutenant colonel. "Sir, we do not have a ground crew, so we will have to let you down in the landing basket. There's not too much crosswind, so it should be a fairly stable drop. I will try to get you as low as possible; there's a clearing coming up."

Father Peter, or in this case Lieutenant Colonel Harrigan, swallowed and, forcing a smile, said, "That will be fine, Captain. Do you see any sign of the railroad or a train?"

Grabbing a speaking tube, the captain spoke into it and then listened for an answer. He turned and spoke once more to his undercover passenger. "Colonel, yes we spotted a passenger train on a siding about a mile away to the east. I do not want to get too close, sir, for fear of the sparks from her stack. This clearing is about as close as I can safely get you and your aide."

"I thought the gas you used for lift is nonflammable?" asked Peter.

The captain replied, "Indeed, sir, but most of our hull is lightweight waterproof silk to save weight, except for the area around the ship's funnel, which is asbestos. The silk is flammable, sir."

Peter replied evenly, "Understood, Captain. That will be fine. I and my aide thank you for a pleasant ride and the generous hospitality." The words were uttered by a somewhat green Father Peter.

Shortly thereafter the Congress came to a hover about a hundred feet off the ground. Peter and Isaiah climbed into the landing basket and began their descent to the ground. Isaiah was fascinated and he surveyed the scene around them, while Father Peter was huddled in the bottom of the basket, praying nonstop all the way down. After two minutes, or as it felt to Peter, two hours, the basket reached the earth with a slight thump. Isaiah helped Peter to his feet, and the two of them jumped over the side. For his part, Peter was truly overjoyed to be on terra firma again.

Isaiah was more than a bit bemused at the scene that Peter's case of nerves had caused. The pair waved up at the airship's crew, and the basket disappeared up into the belly of the gondola. The Congress began to move slowly off to her planned patrol route.

Peter and Isaiah started off in the direction of the rail siding holding the train. They had not gone far when they heard John's voice calling out to them from a distance.

Isaiah replied, and before he could go another ten feet, a bolt of calico and small child hit him, almost knocking him down. "Poppa, where have you been? And are you all right? And how did you get here? And what was that cloud?" All this came tumbling out of Sarah, seemingly without her taking a breath.

Isaiah picked the little girl up and held her and then kissed her on the top of her brow. "One question at a time, young missy," he laughed. "I told you Father Peter and I were staying behind in Saint Paul to check on a few things for the professor's research and that we would meet up with you later. And now it is later, and we are here, all right?"

Sarah's eyes were looking at Isaiah, but remembering her manners—Miss Julia always said a lady is known by her manners—she said hello to Father Peter too.

Isaiah put Sarah down and said to her, "Girl, you starting to put on some weight, growing up before my very eyes."

Sarah beamed up at him. He took her hand, and the three of them started to walk toward Morton and the train.

"As to what the cloud was and how Peter and I got here," Isaiah told the excited little girl holding his hand tightly, "we were riding in a United States Army airship, and this is where they were able to drop us. Does that answer your questions?"

By this time, they'd reached John, and the three men shook hands. Any more than that was impossible to wedge in with all Sarah's questions.

Far from being satisfied with Isaiah's explanation, Sarah was, if anything, more full of questions—How did it fly? How high did it go? What was it like? And just about everything else.

Isaiah laughed and slowly began to answer her questions. So busy was he answering Sarah's seemingly endless series of inquires that he was actually surprised when the train was suddenly there before him.

All of a sudden the door to the platform flew open and Julia came flying out. Seeing the group, she appeared very relieved. "Sarah, there you are. I have been looking everywhere for you." Julia let out a deep breath.

"Miss Julia, Poppa is back!" she cried.

"Young lady, have I not told you that you should not run off by yourself?" Julia sounded both cross and relieved at the same time, a mixture only a big sister can truly do justice to.

Sarah looked crestfallen, as if she had hurt Julia, and said, "I am sorry, Miss Julia, but I heard the professor saying that it might be them when he saw the cloud, I mean airship, and I just got so excited that I ran after him. It was Poppa, I mean Mr. Isaiah, and Father Peter." She looked for a minute as if she wanted to cry.

Julia looked at her, and the highly trained, mission-hardened agent wilted. "Well, if you were with the professor," she said, "but do not let it happen again, young lady."

"Yes, madam," said the small voice. It then went on, "But he and Father Peter were flying, Miss Julia, in an airship." And a very happy little girl was back.

Julia smiled and said to both Father Peter and Isaiah, "I am glad to see you both back safe and sound. Certain members of the expedition have been very worried about you both and one in particular. How was Saint Paul and what did you find out?"

Peter answered since Isaiah was busy holding Sarah. "An interesting town. We were not having much luck, but thanks to some timely help from, of all places, the Treasury Department, we did manage to get a solid lead on some potential research, uh, sites. Also we were able to get a ride from the army. However, is there anything decent to eat; airship rations are not the best?"

Sarah, hearing this, looked up at Isaiah with a frown on her face. "They didn't feed you proper?" The clear upset in her voice confirmed her deeply held suspicion that someone had to take care of Isaiah, and she was just the young lady to do it. Dragging him into the parlor, she had him sit down while she went to find Cook and make sure he was properly fed, oh, and Father Peter too. Miss Julia, after all, said one had to remember one's manners; that was a very important thing for a lady to remember!

Isaiah looked somewhat amused at Sarah's fussing and his was very much the face of a man who loved his daughter, for that, pretty obviously to everyone, was how he thought and cared about her. He looked at Peter and commented, "I wonder if I will be let out to play by myself anymore."

Peter just shook his head smiled. "Remember the morning after John brought her aboard he told you, *you were being adopted?*" With that, he started in on the rather tasty looking sandwiches that Sarah had just returned with for both him and Isaiah. "Still, son, you could do a whole lot worse for family. Enjoy it now, for in all too soon a time, some young fellow will be wanting to take her away from you."

Isaiah looked shocked for a minute and then smiled. "I expect you're right, Peter. Still, it is nice to have a family again." This last was muffled around bites of sandwich, which in truth was very good.

John interrupted their lunch and said, "When you two are done, I need to speak to you up in the shop car about some modifications to some of our research equipment." This was, of course, a simple dodge to throw Sarah off about the real mission.

Sarah beamed, and Morton looked at her. "I believe you have lessons with Miss Julia, young lady."

Sarah looked somewhat annoyed, since it was obvious to her that Isaiah could not manage by himself without her checking on him, but the professor was the boss. Besides, she thought, how much trouble could he get into only a few cars away? Still, she hugged him and made him promise to tell her all about his adventures in Saint Paul and on the airship ride over dinner.

When the three men were clear of Sarah, Peter and Isaiah filled John in on what they had found out. After unrolling and studying the maps in the shop car, they figured that the drover's caboose would be at a small junction point about another fifteen miles down the rail line. Morton said, "I think we are still on solid ground if we go forward and lay over at the junction. So far as we know, the pair is not on to us yet; we are just scientists being backed by a wealthy industrialist back east. We may be able to end this. We will know more when we get closer and have a look at our quarry's den."

Isaiah looked a little nervous. "What about Sarah, Major?"

"I think Julia can handle Sarah while we move on Ulrich and Chen. This, gentlemen, is our best chance. We can pull in at dusk. I will alert Corporal Tinsman and his men. We need to hit them hard and fast."

Some distance away, farther down the line, two men packed their horses' saddlebags with large sums of cash and a few provisions. They smiled at each other and left their railroad car. Who cared what happened to it? Its purpose was served, and it was time to leave for more promising endeavors that they already had well underway.

John had assembled the team for a planning session. Of course the first thing that did not go according to John's basic plan was that Julia was *not* staying behind to watch Sarah. "Absolutely not, John Morton. I am a trained agent and I am going!"

Isaiah was none too happy about this. "Who is going to watch Sarah? It's not like she can go with us!"

"Sarah will be sleeping and Father Peter can watch her, Isaiah," replied Julia in a very tough Special-Agent-Julia voice. "Our best chance is that they are in the caboose. Now we need to hit the car from both ends and watch the sides. These drover cabooses have loading doors on both sides, since they act as both a caboose and a coach-and-baggage car. Since there are only seven of us, we'll put one on each side to watch the baggage doors and two at each platform end. The seventh person can keep an eye out from the top of our tender; it should give him a good view of the area." Julia had been sketching out an attack plan on a piece of paper in the parlor.

Morton looked a little less than happy with this and said, "All right, you can stay on the tender while we move in. Once it's clear, you can come down and take a look, all right?"

"No, John, it is not all right," replied Julia. "Bill is the best marksman in the group." She was referring to one of Tinsman's former sharpshooters. "He will watch from the tender. I will go in with you, while Isaiah and Tinsman go in from the other end of the car. John and Sam will watch the two side doors."

Morton was beginning to fume and started to say something when Julia simply said, "Major, I need to talk to you outside." Morton started to reply when Julia cut him off with a hard and simple, "Now, Major!"

John had no choice but to follow if he wanted to say anything more to Julia, as she was striding to the end of the car and its door onto the platform.

As the door closed behind the pair they were alone on the car's platform, where John grabbed her arm and started to say, "Julia, be reasonable. This is very dangerous." He got no further then that when, after some quick and nasty moves by Julia, he was on his knees with a rather wicked-looking blade at his throat and an "Oof" escaping his lips.

Julia looked down at him and steeled herself. "I told you, John, it was bad business when teammates became more than that! I am not some innocent little schoolgirl you need to protect. I am instead a very highly trained agent who can handle herself, thank you very much, Professor John Morton. Besides, I make a much smaller target then some tall, gawky gent like yourself. Am I clear, Major!" She added a bit of extra pressure to John's arm by way of making her point.

John grunted out in pain. "You have made your point, Miss Verolli, very clearly. We will do it your way."

Julia looked relieved and the blade suddenly disappeared. The pain in John's arm joint subsided considerably. Rising in a slightly shaken manner to his feet, he looked down at her and repeated, "You are right, nothing more than teammates." With that, he turned and entered the car.

Julia looked at his back and, wiping a tear from her eye with the back of her hand, exhaled. She straightened her spine and followed him in.

John looked around the war council and said, "Julia convinced me she was right. Bill, check out one of the Sharp's Falling Blocks, the one with the scope. Make sure it is sighted in before we move the train up. Right now we should be far enough away so that any shot will not carry to the railhead and spook them."

With that, the last few details were gone over and the meeting broke up. Julia remained behind and just looked at the door John had just gone through. She was so deep in her thoughts that she did not realize Father Peter had not left with the rest of the group and was, in fact, standing right behind her. "What? The tough-as-nails secret agent being human?" said Peter.

Julia whirled around. "What are you talking about, Father?"

"Julia," continued Peter, "I have married enough young couples to see it in their faces when they care about each other. John may not know it, but you rather fancy our professor."

Julia sighed. "You cannot tell him, Peter. This mission is critical. These two have to be stopped, and that has to take precedence over my feelings for John." She added in a much harsher tone of voice, "Is that clear!" With that, Julia turned away again and started walking toward the end of the car and the rest of the train.

Peter looked sadly at Julia's retreating back and simply replied, "Perfectly, Julia, but I still know you care."

Julia hesitated only a split second and then resumed walking.

Later, as the train was in motion and dinner was being served. Sarah was complaining about being sleepy at the dinner table and Julia helped her to their compartment. The others could hear Sarah saying that she wanted to see the railhead. And what was a railhead? Julia hushed her and told her she could see it in the morning. Shortly thereafter, Julia returned to the parlor.

"Sarah will be sound asleep till morning," she said to the group.

"You drugged her!" Isaiah was alarmed.

"A very mild sleeping potion. Trust me, it will not harm her, Isaiah." Julia wet her lips and continued, "You are not the only one who cares about her, sir." She said this last in a tone that was anything but the voice of a trained, steel-hardened agent. Julia looked down the corridor to the compartment and blinked, as she seemingly changed before their eyes and once more was a very dangerous young lady.

CHAPTER 18

THE ASSAULT

T he team felt the train coming to a stop and heard the squeal of brakes and, finally, the hiss as the air system released and some steam vented. "We should prepare," said Morton. He sent Tinsman and one of his men to check the location of the drover's caboose while the rest of the team double-checked their weapons. Julia disappeared into a separate compartment to change. When she reappeared, her hair was tied back and she was wearing a black top and pants, her feet were in sturdy boots. Several knives, including a pair of finely balanced throwing knives, were at her shoulder, and her short-barreled .38-caliber Colt was on her right hip. The young lady from the fine young lady's academy was gone, and a very dangerous-looking doppelganger had replaced her.

Morton was stunned. This was Julia as he had never seen her, not even that night in the Points when they had gone after the Ratten nest. This woman was obviously very, no make that extremely, dangerous, and Morton was more than a little shocked.

Julia looked at him and said, "John, you can close your mouth. We need to get ready."

John closed aforesaid mouth with an audible snap and had started to reply when Tinsman came in. John looked as if he wanted to say something but merely turned to the corporal and asked him what the situation was.

Tinsman looked at Julia and smiled as if he were satisfied with the team's quality, and, addressing both of them, said, "Boss lady, sir, the caboose is about a hundred yards up the line. There are some cars around it, so there's plenty of cover for us to move in close. I did not see any light in it. I don't know if it means anything, but the gandy dancer's camp seems in a bit of an uproar, sir."

Julia looked confused. "Who"?

Morton briefly glanced at Julia and informed her, "He means the railroad crew. That is what they call the men who lay the track because they make it look almost like a dance." Morton looked back at the corporal and asked, "Do you know if it has anything to do with our quarry, Corporal?"

"Not as far as I could tell, sir, but I did not check it out too closely. I figured the less anyone noticed us the better, sir."

"You were right; it is probably better. All right, you all know the plan. Let's move out."

Isaiah turned to Peter. "You gonna be all right watching Sarah?"

Peter looked at his friend and said, "I am hurt you even asked," and smiled at him. Then he picked up the new repeating-lever action shotgun and bandoleer of extra shells Julia had insisted he carry instead of the old, trusty double barrel he had brought.

The team moved out the door and quietly began to advance on the caboose that was their target, a true den of evil. Soon the team was in position.

At a single whistle from Morton, the group moved forward. The two end doors went flying open to reveal a fully stocked laboratory on one end and a small sleeping compartment on the other. However, both were empty of humans. Julia told the team, "John, you and Sam keep a lookout while Isaiah and I look around for anything that may be of help." With that, she and Isaiah began to look for notebooks and anything else that may help them in their search for the pair.

Soon they heard a shout from outside, "Major, we got company!" one of the former sharpshooters yelled.

Morton looked up and saw an angry mob approaching them. As it got closer, the mob looked more like a pack of rabid wild animals, with men tearing at each other and moving toward the caboose. Morton made a quick decision. "Everybody out! Let's go!"

Julia started to protest when John picked her up bodily and threw her over his shoulder as he ran for the end of the caboose, away from the approaching mob. The team regrouped and watched in horror as what had once been men began to literally tear the car apart with their bare hands, heedless of the damage they were doing to themselves. As pieces of the car fell on them, the men partially crushed still went on with their demolition. Part of the mob saw the team and started toward them. By this time John had set a spitfire-mad Julia down and turned her around so she could see for herself what was happening.

The team began to retreat toward their train, but the mob, if it could even be called that, for it was more like a seething mass of tormented beasts, kept moving toward them. Finally, they began to fire their weapons, at first hesitatingly trying unsuccessfully to scare the men off. The mob seemed to ignore the storm of lead death coming at them. Finally, the team was firing as rapidly as possible. They watched as men with obviously fatal wounds kept coming forward, as if unable to do else, crawling or dragging themselves forward.

The team was back to the train when Father Peter appeared on the platform of the workshop car and leaned out. He fired over their heads with the shotgun blasting men to bloody bits as fast as he could work the action and reload.

Soon it was over. The carnage was all around them, and several of the men finished off the survivors of the mob. The entire team was shaken and retreated into the car to reload in case the horror was not yet over. Morton rallied his men and sent them to guard, while he and Julia went to check on the gandy dancer's camp.

They were sickened at the sight they saw. No one from the camp had survived the events of the night. It was obvious to both of them that Great Northern would not be building much up from the railhead anytime soon.

Julia looked at John. "My God, John, this is a nightmare!"

John could only nod gently in reply, fearing that if he nodded too hard he would start to heave.

"Julia, did you and Isaiah find anything that would explain this?" John just kept looking around, as pale as a man could be. He felt as if he was visiting hell itself. "Julia, even in the war, it was not like this. These men were literally torn apart by each other!" John was visibly shaken.

"John, I don't know," replied Julia, obviously trying not to vomet. "We got some of their notebooks. Maybe something in them can explain this. Oh God!" Julia, the highly trained, tough agent, doubled over and began to retch.

Beside her, Morton looked pretty queasy and green himself.

Stepping over to Julia, John helped her stand up straight and simply said, "Let's get back. There's nothing more we can do and for sure nothing more to be learned from the caboose." The car in question was burning now; a spark or a broken lantern must have touched off the conflagration. The various chemicals had spread over the wooden car, and grease from all the wheel's journal boxes' packing added to the fuel. It was obvious that, by morning, it would be nothing but a pile of ash and cooling melted metal.

They walked back to the train. John helped Julia up, with Father Peter there to pull. He turned, and motioning to one of Tinsman's troopers to help him, he picked up two more-or-less intact corpses, and they put them in the laboratory car. John told Tinsman to have the train backed down to the previous location; from there they'd telegraph in a report.

Soon the train was in motion, and John went back to the parlor car, where, like the others, he poured himself a brandy. Sitting down he started to shake.

"John," a soft voice came from beside him. "Thank you." It was Julia, obviously as shaken as any of the men.

John looked at her. "Sorry I had to rescue a very highly trained agent, but it seemed like a good idea at the time." This he said with a weak smile.

"I am not sorry; John Morton, but just as a teammate," whispered Julia as she bent over and kissed him lightly on the cheek.

John just smiled and went back to his brandy as the train backed down the rail line.

After John recovered his composure, he went forward to examine the bodies of the two men they'd loaded into the laboratory car. John bent to his grisly task with an intensity that surprised even him. Meanwhile, Julia began to look at the few notebooks and papers she and Isaiah had recovered.

Isaiah peeked in on Sarah, who as far as he could tell, had blissfully slept through the entire episode. He was sorry he had snapped at Julia and wanted to thank her for sparing his daughter the sight of that butcher's shop; no, it had been more like a slaughterhouse. Even the aftermath of Sharpsburg had not been that bad; the men out here had been completely out of their heads. What could have done that?

After a while, Julia looked up and heard a soft murmuring. Wondering what it was, she followed the sound to Father Peter's compartment. As she listened, she heard the old priest praying and crying at the same time. Knocking, she opened his door and saw Peter kneeling at the side of his bunk. Julia went over to him and, as gently as she could, lifted his head up. "Peter, what is it?" she softly said to him, in the same voice she had used on Sarah when she first came on board.

"God, oh my God, Julia, I killed those men. How can I be a priest, a man of God and kill my fellow men? I am supposed to save them, child. What have I done! That was supposed to be behind me when I left the army." Peter was openly crying now. His face was crumpled in deep pain.

Julia looked at him for a moment. Then she knelt down and helped him up. "Peter, you did what had to be done. Those were not men anymore; you did not see what John and I did in the camp. Oh, Peter, let your heart be at ease. They were not men anymore."

Julia guided Peter to the parlor, and when she had him sitting down, she got him a brandy from the sideboard. Then she just sat beside him and held him, rocking him, and speaking softly, trying to calm him as one would a small child. Peter just kept sobbing. They were like that when Morton came in.

He looked shaken and even more so when he saw Peter and Julia, who was still singing almost a lullaby to him.

Peter looked up and saw John, and he cried, "Oh, John, how will I ever atone? What penance can I do for what I did tonight?"

"Peter, rest easy, old friend. You did not kill anyone. Those what had been formerly men were already dead or near enough anyhow, so there was no difference," said Morton quietly.

Peter looked at him as if he were mad. "John, what are you saying? What do you mean? I shot those men."

John looked at his old friend and then at Julia. "Peter, I just finished an autopsy on two of the men from the mob. They would have been dead in another twenty minutes or so—half an hour at most. Their brains were so swollen up that their eyes were being pushed out of their sockets. The poor creatures, for they were not men anymore than the Ratten are rats, those creatures were mad with pain and probably desire for the drug that Ulrich and Chen sold them."

Peter looking stunned stared at his friend, and as the meaning of John's words took shape in his mind, he looked like a man on death row who had just received a pardon. "They were already dying?"

Morton nodded. "Peter, you did them a mercy. They must have been in the agonies of Dante's Inferno itself. I cannot even imagine the pain they were in; it would have made the surgeons' amputations back in the war look like removing a small splinter in comparison."

Julia looked up at John while she still tried to comfort Peter. "John, what did you just say about their brains swelling?"

John looked at her. "Indeed, in both men their heads almost exploded when I opened the skulls."

"Wait here," she said to the pair as she went to retrieve the notebook she had been looking at when she'd heard Peter's prayers. "My German

149

is a little rusty, but it makes sense now." She was holding the notebook and began to explain. "This is a little crude, but basically it says that prolonged exposure to the drug causes an irreversible madness and hostility. It says the subjects will go mad trying to get more of the drug but that, after awhile, the drug has no further effect, and they just go berserk and die."

John looked as if he'd found out he had been cheated at poker. "Bad timing. We missed them due to bad timing. That is why they were not in the caboose or at the camp. They must have seen the telltale signs and taken off just before the railroad workers turned into monsters!"

Peter looked as shaken as if he had found out there was no God. "All the saints in heaven, they knew what that stuff would do, and still, they sold it to those poor men; what kind of abominations are these two? They make the Ratten themselves look angelic!" Peter was in a manic state.

Julia went to Peter's side and began to calm the older priest again.

Morton looked at his old Friend "If you still think you need penance, Peter, then we need to stop them before there are more scenes like this."

Peter just looked at John and stroked Julia's hand that was on his shoulder. "Amen, John, amen to that."

CHAPTER 19

OVER THE RESERVATION

At the last junction point where the telegraph lines ended, the team sent a coded report to Anderson, then they began to decide their next move. Julia was the first to speak. "John, I think your guess was right about why those monsters were not there." The men looked up at her. "I have been reading the last of the few journals and records we were able to recover. They had a pretty good idea of how long men could take the drug before the final effects came on—that and there were some signs in the victims that they must have seen. I am guessing they figured it was time to hightail it before what we saw last night happened. Based upon some more of the notes, I would estimate they would have had no more than a day or two's warning that the end was near."

Peter was obviously still suffering more than the rest of the team "We missed those monsters by just a hair's breadth. I only can pray to God we can stop them before they cause this curse to fall on anyone else!"

"We will do our best, Peter; I only hope it is enough," said John, putting his hand on his friend's arm. "All right, anyone have any ideas on where to look next? It is a pretty good guess that Julia is right and the pair made off well ahead of our attack and with plenty of greenbacks to finance them. It's no wonder they left all their equipment there at the railhead."

Isaiah spoke up. "It would have been too hard to move by wagon, and since they had plenty of money, they could easily rebuild if they had their research. The question is, where did they light out for?"

Peter suddenly shook his head. "Of course! It's obvious."

The team looked at him.

"Do you remember the report from the Indian agent about monsters on the reservation?"

John and Julia both went for the map of the territory; John was slightly quicker than Julia. "The reservation isn't too far from here. They might have been experimenting there. They probably felt that there would be less law enforcement on the reservation."

An expression crossed Julia's face that suggested she had had an epiphany. "I think, gentlemen, we may have made a mistaken assumption. Isaiah, do you still have that list detailing equipment and supplies the Saint Paul Police Department think the two purchased?"

"Just a minute and I will fetch it." Isaiah got up and went down to his compartment.

On returning, he gave Julia several sheets of paper and said, "Right here."

Julia looked at the list and then handed it back to Isaiah with a raised eyebrow. He looked at it for several minutes, and suddenly he, too, wore an ah-ha expression.

Morton, obviously wondering what was going on, finally piped up. "All right, you two. What is it?"

Julia looked at John and Peter and said, "The caboose was not the main laboratory. It would have been almost impossible to get all this equipment and supplies in there. According to this list, they had really stocked up; no wonder they needed their own car to carry it all. From the brief opportunity we had to look when we raided the caboose, we saw only enough equipment and supplies to manufacture the drugs they sold to the gandy dancers. Most of the stuff on this list wasn't there. Ipso facto, that was not their laboratory; it was just enough of a laboratory to generate their cash flow."

Isaiah picked up. "They must have set up a new main laboratory, especially if they were working on the Ratten Project. It would have been impossible to hide those things from the railroad crew if they had them anywhere near the camp. Since they would have had to go back and forth to do their research and run their drug business, I am guessing I know where the real laboratory is—either on or near the reservation."

Morton looked at the map. "That is still a huge chunk of territory to search. The reservation is huge! I have no idea how we will ever find them."

Peter, who until then had just been listening in, spoke up. "Excuse me, Professor John Morton! I expect a better attitude from the man who found the Ratten nest with nothing more than some paper, pencils, and questions, when the entire United States government had come up empty-handed." Peter sounded a whole lot more like a first sergeant on a drill field with new recruits than a priest at that point.

John looked up and half saluted his friend. "Yes, Father First Sergeant," he replied.

Julia tried to suppress a laugh and lost.

Morton looked at her and said, "Lose the smile, Agent Verolli. I could use some help."

Julia shook her head and began to clear a space to start work when there was a small sleepy voice behind them. "I'm hungry." Sarah appeared from Julia's and her compartment down the corridor, still yawning.

Quickly, the meeting broke up.

After lunch Sarah remained disappointed. She could not get over the fact that she'd slept through a chance to see a railhead—not that she was sure what it was, but a lady obviously needed to know these things, at least if she was going to be like her big sister, who seemed to know everything. As Sarah and Isaiah left for his workshop, he was assuring her there would be other sights to see.

John, Peter, and Julia began to look at a map of the territory to try to figure out where the two men could have set up their research. John stretched a bit and looked at the two of them. "Well, we seem to have it down to about three areas that they could possibly have used. All are near enough to the rail line so they could have offloaded their equipment and supplies and moved them by wagon or packhorse without too much trouble and not too near any known villages. But that still leaves a lot of ground to cover. We will need an army to cover all that ground looking for a trace of them. It's going to take time!" John was mad that the two had escaped again.

Julia said, "I had best send for reinforcements. It may make things on the reservation even worse with all the troops we will need."

Peter squared his shoulders, made the Sign of the Cross, and spoke up. "I hate to say this, but I have an idea how we can cover much of the ground and, hopefully, not stir up the Indians anymore then they are already."

John and Julia both looked at him rather expectantly.

Finally Peter spoke again. "The Congress—when Isaiah and I rode in her, we could see quite a bit of territory. If we had some decent field glasses, we might be able to spot something from her. Since the government uses the ships to patrol the border, it wouldn't seem so strange to see one near the reservation, given the unrest."

Julia was the first to speak up. "Peter, that is brilliant! I can wire Washington, and she can pick us up." She noted the look that crossed Peter's face at that point. "Peter, what is the matter? You do not look very happy for someone who just came up with such a brilliant idea."

Peter looked at Julia and replied rather weakly, "I am afraid that myself and airships are not on the greatest of terms; it is really just a terrible way to travel. I am not at all convinced that man was meant to fly with the birds."

John patted him on the back. "It's all right, Peter. Someone will have to watch Sarah. Isaiah and I can make the flight."'

This brought a loud harrumph from Julia. "Excuse me, I am the trained agent, remember, Professor?"

John looked at her and, without meaning to, smiled and sighed just a little. "Julia, I did not forget. And if I wanted to take over the airship and have the crew done away with, you would be my first choice. However, that is not the objective. Both Isaiah and I have had far more experience in scouting for military signs in the wilderness then you have, and I am a trained scientist used to looking for small things that do not belong. Are we clear, Miss Verolli?"

Julia looked a little put out, but she knew John was right. "All right, sir, but you are not to take any action until we can get enough people into position. No heroics, John Morton." Crossing her arms over her chest, she tried to look stern.

"Yes, madam, no heroics. Believe me, Julia, after the Points and last night, I am taking no chances with these two. After what we've seen, I am starting to believe deeply in a faith called devout cowardice." John impulsively kissed her and turned away.

After he was out of earshot, Peter looked at Julia. "It will be all right, lass. He is no coward, but he most definitely has a healthy respect for what we are up against—that and he wants to come back to you, you know."

Julia tried to straighten her spine even more than it already was and look tough. But she instead she said to Peter, although she was looking at the door John had gone out of, "He'd better come back, and in one piece if he knows what is good for him."

Peter just smiled and, as usual when dealing with Julia, rolled his eyes, although this time for a change, he did not feel the need to make the Sign of the Cross. With that, Julia went forward to send the telegram that would recall the Congress.

It took several days plus several hours for the Congress to meet them. Isaiah was explaining to Sarah that, no, little girls could not ride in army airships and that, yes, he would be careful. Sarah was obviously less than amused. She was not at all sure that riding in airships was a safe way to travel, and if it *was* safe, why couldn't she go along? This went back and forth several times, until Bill, who was on sentry, yelled that he had spotted the airship. Sarah turned and disappeared into the galley.

Isaiah said to Morton, "Guess she's mad at me."

John just smiled at his teammate as they got ready to leave.

They had climbed down off the train and were moving a safe distance away to a nearby clearing for the landing basket when there was a cry behind them, and Sarah was running after them with a basket. "Poppa, here. I remembered that they did not feed you any too good before, so I had Cook make up some sandwiches. I helped." Sarah looked up at Isaiah, who took the basket and then handed it to John.

Isaiah picked Sarah up and said, "I love you. Now you take care and do what Father Peter and Miss Julia say. I will be back before you know."

"I love you too, Poppa. Please come back." Sarah smiled at Isaiah and hugged him back.

"Back to the train now, young lady."

With that, John and Isaiah continued their walk to the clearing and waited for the landing basket.

John looked at Isaiah. "It's good to have someone to come back to, I guess."

"Oh and you do not, sir? I seen the way you look at Miss Julia," replied Isaiah.

"As she had reminded me, we are just teammates—at least for now," John said in a downcast way.

"Pity you don't have eyes in the back of your head, Major, sir. That gal cares about you too, you know; she just don't want to admit it," said Isaiah.

Further conversation was shut off by the arrival of the landing basket.

The two men climbed into the basket and waved up at the crewmen manning the winch. As they started to ascend, and the surrounding countryside opened up before him from the view of a bird, John Morton felt a spark of excitement. *This is truly amazing*, he thought.

Before long, the basket came to reside in the belly of the Congress, and they were welcomed aboard. A corporal escorted them to the bridge where the captain was waiting for them.

"Welcome aboard, gentlemen. What is so important that we have been pulled off our patrol twice now?" said the ship's captain, who recognized Isaiah as the lieutenant colonel's aide from several days ago.

Morton offered his hand, which the officer refused, obviously irritated at his ship being used as some form of carriage service. "I am sorry we had to divert you, your crew, and ship Captain, but the matter is of the utmost urgency. We need to find some men who are stirring up more trouble than you can imagine, and we need to do it quickly. Captain, I am not at liberty to tell you more, but the matter is that serious, and the men we are after that dangerous—not only here but to the nation as a whole." Morton did not retract his hand but kept looking the young officer in the eye.

Finally, the officer, with a nod, reached out and took Morton's hand. "Very well, if it is so important that the Department of the Army and the War Department say that my ship is under your command, then who am I to argue?"

Morton smiled and replied, "It is your ship, sir. You are in command, but we do need to do some reconnaissance, if you would be so kind. I believe you have already met Sergeant Liman, and I am Major John Morton."

The officer smiled and said, "All right, where are we going? And what are we looking for?"

John pulled out the map of the territory he and Julia had worked on. They stepped over to the airship's chart table. He unfolded it and showed the captain the areas they needed to cover.

The Captain, looking at it, said, "We can cover those with no problems, but since there is no moon tonight or the next several nights. That will mean observing only during the day so we will be several days scouting these areas. Our timing will also depend on the head winds; it has been blowing a bit of late. Any problems with that?"

Isaiah smiled and said, "I hope the sandwiches my daughter packed will hold out."

The captain looked up and replied, "Sergeant, we have more than enough rations on board for the flight."

Isaiah laughed and said, "I know that, Captain, but my daughter is ten and fusses over me enough for sure."

The captain looked a little confused. "What about her mother, your wife?"

"Dead, sir. We don't have nobody but each other now," Isaiah said quietly.

The captain smiled and said softly, "I am sorry, and I understand, Sergeant."

Then the captain began giving orders, and the two men felt the engines begin to increase revolutions and the Congress began to pick up speed as she heeled slightly and came to a new course.

"What are we looking for, gentlemen?" asked the captain again.

John looked thoughtful for a minute and finally replied, "Captain, I know this will sound strange, but we are looking for a hidden laboratory with giant rats."

The captain looked up in shock. "Major, misusing a U.S. Army airship is a serious matter; if you are trying to pull off some bit of tomfoolery, then I am not amused!"

John again looked the man square in the eye "This is no prank, Captain! The men we are after are vicious killers. If you do not believe me, I suggest we take a short detour and fly over the Great Northern's railhead so you can see some of their work—and just a sideline at that. As to the rats, that is highly classified information, and not a word is to leak out or you and your entire crew will be patrolling the arctic wastes over the Alaskan Territory. Am I clear!"

The officer's head came up as if he had been slapped. He looked at Morton and then gave another order to change course once again.

About an hour later, a squeal sounded from one of the voice pipes. The captain went over and listened. "All right, Major, the railhead is just ahead. Let's go forward to the observation station and see what we shall see, sir."

The captain led John and Isaiah out of the control cabin and forward through the great ship. As the three men looked over the ship's railing at the very front of the great airship, they could see the camp. John offered the Captain a telescope he and Isaiah had brought with them. The captain replied curtly, "Major Morton, we are fully supplied," and pulled over a pair of heavy, high-powered binoculars that were mounted on a swiveling bracket in the forward lookout station so they could be handled more easily.

As he trained his gaze at the sight below them, they could all hear him gasp. "My God, what happened down there?" His voice was cut off by the sound of him retching over the side of the ship. Even in the war, as a young officer, the captain had never encountered anything quite like this.

"The men we are after sold some of the workers a drug they made which allowed each one of them to work like a full crew. The one slight drawback to the drug is that it drove them into a murderous fury after prolonged use; there is no known antidote. What you are looking at down there is the result. There must be some scent associated with the drug. It looks like not even the scavengers have touched the remains. My people and I barely escaped with our lives. There were no survivors from the railroad crew." Morton helped the captain stand up and continued. "Do not feel too badly. Most us had the same reaction when it was all over."

Morton's thought turned to the dead for a moment. The Great Northern would be sending in a new crew soon once it had been too long since they'd heard word from the crew below. *I hope that the remains of the men get a decent burial*, he thought. The men had not asked for what happened to them.

Isaiah pulled a small flask from inside his jacket and offered it to the captain. "For medicinal use only," he said. "I figure this most definitely counts, sir."

"Dear God, I cannot believe what I saw," the young officer gasped. "You say this was just a sideline to what they were working on and not the real evil?" The captain took a healthy pull from Isaiah's flask before returning it to him with a simple, "Thank you, Sergeant."

Morton looked at the young officer. "Indeed, Captain, I am sorry you had to see that, but you have to understand just how badly we need the use of your ship. We have to find these men and deal with them!" Morton continued to look at the young officer to make sure he not only recovered, but understood the gravity of the situation.

The captain took a deep breath and, recovering, said, "Gentlemen, the services of the Congress and her crew are at your disposal. Let's return to the control cabin."

After saying that, the captain led John and Isaiah back along the catwalks through the great ship to the control cabin, and there he began to plot a new course. Once he'd given the new orders, the ship again began a slow turn, and the crew could feel the engine noise and vibration increase slightly.

"Gentlemen, please make yourselves comfortable. We have about three hours before the first area comes up. I will let you know." The captain turned and went to stand behind the helmsman and near the elevatorman and engine control telegraph.

Morton and Isaiah sat down and began to enjoy the idea of flight. The view was quite unlike anything Morton had ever seen before. Isaiah had seen some, but in truth, both Father Peter and he had been so exhausted from their all-night ride that they'd slept most of the way back to the train. So he too was enjoying himself immensely as he took in the world below him from this new vantage point.

Almost like a blessing, both were able to forget for a little while the mission they were on and enjoy this new sensation.

However, as it is said, all good things must come to an end. A young private showed up to give them the captain's compliments and let them know they were coming up on the first suspect area, if they would follow him to the Captain.

They made their way back into the control cabin. "I hope you are enjoying the ride, gentlemen. We are coming up on your first target area. How do you want to proceed?" The captain looked at them in deference.

Morton looked at Isaiah and then at the captain. "I would like to go in as low as reasonable and as slow as possible, sir, so we can scan the area as completely as we can, looking for signs without spooking our quarry, if they are indeed down there."

The captain looked thoughtful for a moment. "All right, we shall pass southwest to northeast. That should give you the best light without any glare on the glasses so you have the best visibility. This is not the first time we have been on a scouting mission, you know."

Both John and Isaiah looked a little sheepish, and John nodded to the captain. "Thank you, sir. I yield to your expertise. We thought we might have been the ones who came up with the idea." And he laughed a bit at himself.

The two men went forward to the bow and took up their stations, looking intently at the ground for any sign of their quarry. The great ship made a very complete coverage of the area, going over it from several directions. But the men detected no sign of any laboratory, or for that matter, much of anything except virgin forest. Soon, one of the ship's crew answered a squeal from the voice pipe, and turning, he told Morton and Isaiah that the captain wanted to know how to proceed.

Morton looked at the man for a moment and, with a sigh, told him to tell the captain to proceed on to the next site. They had come up with a dry hole. With that, they turned the lookout back over to the airship's regular crew and retraced their steps back to the control car. They found the captain standing at his usual station behind the helmsman.

The captain looked up when they entered. "It will take us awhile. We are picking up some headwind. I plan to reduce speed and try to come in at first light. I don't see any reason to go over it at night; with little moon tonight and some cloud cover, I doubt we would see anything."

Morton agreed with the captain's assessment. The next thing, they were seated and eating a rather plain ship's ration of cornmeal and crackers; at least the coffee was hot and strong. Morton leaned over to Isaiah and whispered, "I see now why Sarah packed us some sandwiches; must be nice to have someone to care about you."

Isaiah smiled and whispered back, "What is the matter, Major, you don't think Julia can make a decent sandwich?" Since he was supposed to be Morton's aide, he used his rank in front of the crew.

Morton snorted, "I told you, Julia has made it very clear we are just teammates, at least for the duration of the mission."

Isaiah looked at him and, lowering his voice, said, "John the mission is not going to last forever."

Morton thought about what Isaiah had said and about the knife Julia had held at his throat back before the attack on the caboose. He did not want to think about that because then he would have to face the fact that maybe Julia was not interested in him, a dull museum professor. And he had found that, as dangerous, bullheaded, and exasperating as she was and against every shred of common sense he had, he was very much falling in love with Miss Julia Verolli.

The two slept through the night although Morton less so as he was dreaming about Julia and wondering what it would be like to have a beautiful, trained, and very dangerous agent for a wife. He kept coming back to one question: How could such a person be interested in sharing a dull museum professor's life?

CHAPTER 20

INTO ANOTHER RAT'S NEST

The sky was just beginning to brighten and the lingering clouds to leave when John and Isaiah were awakened to get some more of the filling but dull rations. Morton thought that, even if airship travel was exciting and marvelous, he really did miss Cook's idea of breakfast fare.

They met the captain in the control cabin. Both Morton and Isaiah were beginning to wonder if the man ever slept. "We will be coming up on site number two in about fifteen minutes, gentlemen," said the officer, who looked fresh as a daisy, much to both Morton's and Isaiah's amazement. "I assume you want the same search pattern?"

"If you please, sir. Sergeant Liman and I will go forward with your permission, sir." Morton saluted the young officer.

The captain returned the salute and merely replied, "Gentlemen." With that he turned back to his duties and Morton and Isaiah set out on the long trip along the catwalk, past the great cells of lifting gas, forward to the bow observation station.

The great ship flew over the area in its slow and deliberate search pattern, and still there was no sign of the rogue laboratory whatsoever— no structures or movement, not even a tent, let alone any tracks.

Morton and Isaiah made their way back to the control car. Morton looked at the captain. "Let's hope the next area has something of interest."

Several hours later, the pair made the trip forward once more. This location was the same they saw nothing but virgin forest.

They returned to the control cabin, and the captain just said, "I am sorry, gentlemen. Is there anywhere else you would like to try?"

Morton shook his head sadly. "Not your fault, Captain. You and your ship and crew have given us every cooperation and showed us every courtesy, and we thank you for it. I am afraid we are out of places to look, so if you would be so kind, please take us back to our train."

With that, the Congress gently took a new heading.

About ten minutes after they had changed course, the voice pipe squealed, and the captain went over to answer it.

They could hear him reply. "Very good, Jones, keep an eye out. Helm, prepare to come about new course one five three, engines at one half. Trimsman, take us down to three five zero feet. Gentlemen, by way of courtesy I think you might want to go forward to the bow observation station."

Morton and Isaiah took off at a dead run for the front of the ship. Once there, they met Air Shipman Jones, who pointed, telling them where to look. The hillside below had a small cave in it. But more interesting were the innumerable tracks around it—unlike anything Isaiah had seen before.

After studying through the powerful binoculars, Morton looked up and said to his friend, "Jackpot. Those are rat tracks; they're huge but definitely rat tracks! Lucky for us, these are city boys. They didn't even try to hide the cave entrance or sweep the tracks."

Isaiah just smiled, a very unpleasant smile; it was time for some payback. With that, the two returned to the control cabin.

The captain said, "What now, gentlemen?"

"Can you show us the location on the map?" Morton directed.

"Indeed, sir. We are just about here." He pointed at a spot on the map.

"Then we need to get out of here. I do not want to spook them before we can get into position to attack, Captain. You and your men have done a great service to the country." Morton began to roll up the map. "Please head for our train best speed, if you would, sir."

The Congress began another turn, and Isaiah could hear the engines speed up and feel the huge ship began to climb, while John continued speaking to the captain.

It was late in the day by the time the Congress lowered John and Isaiah to the ground via her landing basket. Immediately, the pair made for the train, waiting about three-quarters of a mile away. Climbing aboard, John immediately told Tinsman to get up steam; they were moving. Sarah was there waiting for Isaiah, who picked her up and hugged her very tightly and, by way of hello, told her, "Those were the best sandwiches. The airships rations have not improved a bit since the last time I was on board."

Sarah beamed and hugged Isaiah back. She heard the whistle she asked, "Are we going somewhere?"

Isaiah looked at the little girl who was becoming his daughter in all but blood, deciding how to reply, "Yes, Sarah, we are moving so that we can check out a possible research site that the professor and I saw from the airship."

Sarah's face lit up. "Can I go see it too?"

"Well, first we have to make sure it is safe. Then we will see, okay?" Isaiah said, trying to sound calm and not wanting to scare Sarah. "For now, you will have to stay with Father Peter."

Sarah looked crestfallen, but Isaiah looked firm. Understanding there were some things her father would not budge on, she nodded an okay.

Meanwhile John was talking to Julia and Peter out of Sarah's hearing. "It's them all right! Not exactly where we thought. They must have found the cave and decided the extra distance was worth it to have the shelter. If we move fast, we can be there by first light. Hopefully, the Ratten will have gone underground for the day. Peter, I need you to stay with Cook and the engine crew to guard the train and keep her ready."

Peter looked at his old friend and replied squarely, "John, I would rather go with you. Those men and their horror have to be stopped! However, I have to admit you're right. I am the oldest and slowest, but as long as I don't have to run far, I can still stand guard with the best of them."

"Thank you, Peter. There is no one I know who I would rather have guarding my back door." Morton put his arm on Peter's shoulder. Turning to Julia, he said, "Julia, do you have the materials to make more of your gas?"

Julia smiled demurely and said, "Why, sir, a good secretary anticipates her employer's needs, didn't you know? How much to you think we will require?"

John considered the question for a minute. "Better have as much as you can make, Julia. There is no way to be sure how deep the cave is from the air, and someone—I cannot remember who—said I was not to go down there alone."

Julia looked at him. "Just teammates, John. I will get to work. I hope Isaiah can help me."

It was at that moment that Isaiah showed up. "Peter, will you—." Peter looked up and cut him off. "She will be as safe as I can keep her, Isaiah."

The black man looked relieved.

"All right, we all have work to do. Let's get busy," Morton told his team.

The meeting broke up, each going to prepare as best he or she could for the upcoming battle.

Sarah was a more than a little nervous when she went into the compartment she shared with Miss Julia; Julia was there getting dressed. But the garments she donned weren't anything Sarah had seen before. She was all in black, with boots on. She had knives and guns everywhere. "Miss Julia, what is going on?" this came out in a very scared little whisper "Why do you have all those weapons?"

Julia tried to think of something to tell Sarah. She had almost forgotten the little girl in the rush to get ready. "Well, Sarah, I am going out with the professor and Isaiah to the site, and it may be dangerous. So I have to be ready. You know, just in case."

Sarah was now very scared. "Please take care of Poppa for me. And you be careful too. I don't have nobody else." Tears formed in her eyes.

Julia looked at her. "It is not *nobody*; it is *anyone* else, young lady. And I will watch over your father, all right? Now I need you to be brave. Do you understand?" Julia tried her best to give Sarah a reassuring smile and hug.

Sarah nodded, but it was clear she was scared.

"Now Father Peter will be in charge, and you do what he says," Julia said firmly. "I need you to stay here until we are gone. I promise, we will all be back."

Julia left the compartment; her heart was breaking—not at the thought of what lay ahead but because she had to lie to Sarah. A big sister should not have to lie to her little sister. She straightened up and said to herself, *Yeah, hard-as-nails, tough secret agent!* Then she started through the train.

As the team gathered in what was the professor's laboratory car, each member silent checked and rechecked his or her weapons. Julia was in her black outfit, and Morton and Isaiah wore various shades of gray and brown, while Tinsman and the three sharpshooters were in their green sharpshooter uniforms from the war. There was a hiss of declining air pressure from the brake system, and then they heard the engine let off excess steam, and finally, with a squeal from the brakes on the wheels, they felt the train slow to a stop.

Tinsman threw open the baggage door to a dim predawn twilight. While the rest of the team finished their preparations, Isaiah said he had to go forward for something. The five men and one woman climbed down and began to unload various supplies and munitions. They heard the baggage door on Isaiah's shop car open, and suddenly a ramp dropped down. They all looked up in surprise as a steam-propelled vehicle started down the ramp.

"I thought this might be a good time to test my new steam-powered assault wagon," Isaiah said, surveying the others. "It's not as heavily armored as Erikson's, but it is faster and more nimble."

The five people looked at the steaming beast in amazement. It had six iron wheels, each about four feet in diameter, with iron and wood sides. A smoking steam boiler stood near the back, while Isaiah sat in a seat with numerous control levers and pedals.

Julia was the first to recover her voice. "Where did you … How did you … What!" Julia was sputtering in a most un-Julia voice.

"Step aboard. It has to beat walking. I know; I served a while in the infantry," responded Isaiah with a big grin. "In answer to what I think was your question, Miss Verolli, the wagon been something I've been working on for a while. You remember back in Buffalo I told you I had some heavy equipment to load. Well, this is it. It was after we had a ride in the Congress that I was able to put the finishing touches on it. Those engines in that ship were fine pieces of workmanship and design. Yes, madam, I do say." Isaiah sounded like a man in love as he described the engines.

As the team moved the pile of equipment over to the steam wagon, as Isaiah referred to his invention, he asked several of the sharpshooters to give him a hand with the final touch. The men climbed aboard, and together they pulled the cover off the Gatling gun that had been in their inventory and mounted it on the back of the wagon. Isaiah went back and hooked up a pipe and hose to the modified gun.

"Another idea I got off the Congress," he explained, "a little extra firepower, although I must modestly submit, I think I have improved on it a bit, yes sir. We now have a steam-powered Gatling gun. Just point it, open the valve, and feed it. I give you the latest advances of modern technology, a steam-powered rat smasher." Isaiah beamed at the team.

Morton looked up at his friend, "I wondered what was up in the mail compartment under the tarp. I hope this is up to your usual standards, Sergeant Liman. Our lives may depend on it."

Isaiah looked at John as he resumed his place at the front of the wagon. "Count on it, sir. Bill if you would be so kind as to keep stoking the boiler every now and again, we can go. Based on the map, we should have more than enough coal and water for the round trip."

With that, Isaiah pulled down a pair of goggles, everyone else grabbed a handhold, and the vehicle took off, leaving the train growing smaller in the distance.

Through the train's windows, two sets of eyes watched the giant contraption leave. Peter said a prayer to keep his friends safe and to stop the evil that was about in the land. While he was praying, Sarah watched and cried, hoping that her father and sister, her whole family, would come back to her.

The team made good time through the terrain. The moon, somewhat fuller, shone brightly. The sky was clear, so the starlight added to the light, this allowed Isaiah to drive slowly but steadily through the night. Although the steam wagon was a vast improvement, it was not perfect; in several spots the team had to get out and push. In two steep spots, they had to tie several ropes to the front of the wagon and use the axle hubs on the powered wheels as capstans to pull the wagon up the hills. Still, Morton and the sharpshooters had to agree that it beat walking by a country mile. Julia, who had never served in the infantry, was not as sure as her male compatriots; the wagon had very little in the way of springs so that she was bounced around quite a bit. By the time they had gone several miles, she was glad she did not have her dress and bustle on as she thought she might have been bounced right out of the steam wagon.

About a mile from the cave entrance Morton had Isaiah stop the wagon. The sun was just beginning to come above the horizon. The men and Julia got out and deployed in a skirmish line, moving forward almost like ghosts in the dim light, halting and listening every few steps. Each man and the woman understood that the team's only advantage was surprise. They knew that, if the Ratten saw them coming, all their firepower might not be enough to ensure that they would not all wind up dead.

They covered the last few yards by crawling, each one taking up a position so that the cave mouth was covered from every possible angle. John watched for a while as the sun went higher in the sky. He motioned to two of the men to move forward with him. They stopped about fifty yards from the opening and donned Julia's protective masks and then resumed their stealthy advance. They had gone about halfway to the mouth of the cave when they saw movement near its mouth. They froze as one of the Ratten looked out, almost as if it were a sentry. They waited for what seemed an eternity, but the Ratten did not move.

Morton realized that, sooner or later, the Ratten would spot them; the only choice was to attack. He took the gas bottle and tossed it from the prone position he was in. Before the bottle reached the mouth of the cave, two more were in the air, as both of the sharpshooters had released the first of their bottles. The bottles broke and they could see the gas began to spread. The Ratten choked and keeled over but not before emitting a piercing shriek.

Morton and the two men were up on their feet and surging forward, throwing more of the bottles into the cave mouth and down as far as they could. They could hear the Ratten shrieking and spears with sharp flintheads thudding into the ground around them. Morton was surprised, since before, the Ratten had only their teeth and claws with which to defend themselves—or attack. As they finished throwing the last of the gas bottles into the cave, they loosed a volley of shots into the darkness.

Morton and the two men pulled back a bit and took out the lanterns Julia had issued them. Lighting the special lanterns, they started forward. They heard a shout from behind, and Julia, in one of the masks, was trotting toward them. Suddenly there was a fuselage of shots, and Julia clutched her side as she was knocked down. Luck was with her at least on one account; even though she hit the ground hard, none of the bottles of gas broke. But she wasn't moving.

All of a sudden, the other two sharpshooters on the ridge were firing as fast as they could. The shots slammed into the hillside around the cave mouth. From their positions, the sharpshooters had seen hoards of Ratten charging from the backside of the hill. It would seem the pair of rogue scientists had managed to create a small army; at least forty or fifty of the creatures came into view. The team's fire was less effective than they'd expected, since the Ratten were throwing a seemingly endless supply of spears at them, and ducking and dodging was a necessity.

Ripping off their masks, as they had not even gotten close to the cave entrance, Morton and the two men who'd moved forward with him ran for cover as more spears and rock pummeled the ground around them. Morton made a direct line for Julia. It was there that he stood protectively over her, firing his Winchester as fast as he could and then switching to the Colt.

Suddenly they heard the almost continuous booming roar of the Gatling; Isaiah, in the steam wagon, had pulled up. As quickly as possible, Isaiah had jumped to the back to work the gun. He fed magazines of ammunition into the gun as rapidly as he could. Morton pulled off his pack and grabbed a rocket out of it. Jamming the tail into the ground, he lit the fuse at its end with the flash from his pistol, and with a *whisssh*, it took off, and there was a bright, red explosion in the air. He was back firing and reloading even before the rocket exploded. Meanwhile, the Ratten still came on.

Julia started to regain consciousness; she felt the pain in her side, and her head felt like it had exploded. She could barely see as she tried to open her eyes; there was a red mist over them. It was hard to make sense of what she saw. There was John standing over her firing and then swinging his rifle as the Ratten closed in. The last thing she remembered was that it was getting very dark, and there was a loud and terrible, prolonged thunder. She thought regretfully that she would never know what it was like to be married to a dull museum professor before the darkness took her.

CHAPTER 21

WHERE SARAH LEARNS THE TRUTH

etween the Gatling on the steam wagon and the two from the Congress, which John had signaled in, the men finally managed to halt the Ratten attack. Two of the sharpshooters were injured, and Julia was badly hurt. She was bleeding profusely from a cut on her head where she had hit a rock in her fall, and Morton did not understand why no blood was coming from the wound in her side. He knew she had been hit because of the damage to her blouse, and he could see some red through the torn fabric. However, a quick check confirmed that she was still alive. John was no doctor, though, and knew she would be better cared for on the airship.

Morton took stock. Three members of his small team were out of the fight because the Ratten had reached the team's skirmish line. Above, the Congress made another pass, and he heard sporadic bursts from her two guns. After finishing her search for remaining Ratten, the great ship came to a hover over them. The basket was lowered, and Morton, Isaiah, and the two remaining sharpshooters placed the injured into the basket as gently as they could. The basket was soon winched up, and it disappeared from view as it was taken aboard the Congress. Before long, the ship turned and began heading for the train. John thought of Julia and ached to go with her, but he knew where his duty lay.

Morton and the two remaining sharpshooters put their masks back on, while Isaiah kept watch with the Gatling on the ridge. Entering, the trio found that this nest was bigger than the one in New York had been; indeed, it was at least three times the size of the nest in the Points. A series of tunnels led to smaller caves, branching out from the main cavern. And as they studied the layout, the men soon realized what had happened. Several of the tunnels had been carved out recently and seemed to lead to spots just below the surface of the hill, behind and to the sides of the tunnel mouth. When the gas landed, some of the Ratten must have busted through these emergency escape tunnels and then launched a counterattack.

Worse yet, a second natural cave entrance on the reverse side had been well camouflaged. Tracks showed where horses and supplies had been kept. Ulrich and Chen must have gone out the back entrance and escaped but not before getting off the shot that had wounded Julia. Morton was beside himself with both fury and worry. All he could think of was how small and broken Julia had looked lying unconscious, blood covering her face, in the bottom of the landing basket. Morton was furious with himself; he had badly underestimated the pair. Ulrich and Chen had not forgotten to hide the cave entrance but had deliberately left it clear as day, so anyone trailing them would not bother to look at the rest of the area more closely for any hidden entrances. And he had done exactly what they'd expected and wanted!

The men loaded two of the Ratten bodies onto the back of the wagon for autopsies later. After searching for anything that might help them pick up the trail of the two men or anything that may have had any bearing on the research the two had been conducting, they set charges. John stood beside the steam wagon as the blast shook the ground and the cave collapsed in on itself. He looked up at Isaiah and said, "We may as well head back; there's nothing more for us here."

Tinsman added, "That and before the Indians spot us and get riled up anymore then they are, sir. Any Indian would have to be long dead not to have noticed something going on here."

The remaining men climbed up, and Isaiah, once more at the controls, began to feed steam to the engine. Isaiah got the wagon turned, and the four remaining team members headed back toward the train. With only three pairs of hands, all belonging to men who were now exhausted, to help over the rough patches, the return trip took a lot longer than had the trip to the caves. To add to the workload, it had started to rain, creating muddy patches that made the going all that more difficult.

Julia was in and out of consciousness and remembered the sound of voices and a wind and trembling noise before she blacked out again, wondering which way she was headed. When next she awoke, she was in her bunk with an anguished Sarah looking down at her and holding a cool compress on her head. Julia tried very hard to form words, but all that came out was a bit of croak.

Sarah looked startled and then ran to the door crying "Father Peter, it's Miss Julia. She's awake!"

Julia, overhearing this, thought very groggily that it was, perhaps, somewhat more than a bit of an overstatement. She really had to have a strong talk with Sarah about exaggerating so much.

Before long, Peter was there looking down at her. "Easy lass, you gave us quite a scare. You took a nasty fall and banged your head on a rock, not to mention a pretty bad bruising on your side."

"Wha, what happened?" said Julia. She felt like she had a mouth full of cotton. "Where are the others? How are John and Isaiah?"

"Here, lass, first some water; just a sip now," Peter told her as he put a glass to her lips. "Seems as best I could piece together from Bill and Sam, not that they are in very good shape themselves, you took a bullet and were knocked down. I know I should not mention this, but those are some interesting undergarments you have, Julia. That corset of yours stopped the bullet; otherwise, I would have been giving you the last rites."

"I thought for sure I would be seeing the face of God. All I remember is John standing over me and a stream of Ratten pouring toward us. Then the world went dark and there was this horrible thunder," mumbled Julia. "And how did you know about my corset, standard issue for female agents?" With this last, Julia fell back into the arms of Morpheus.

Father Peter just sighed and said to himself, *Well, somebody had to get you stitched up, lass.*

John, Isaiah, and the two remaining sharpshooters arrived back at the train much later. Morton told them to put the two Ratten bodies in the laboratory car. Meanwhile, Isaiah began to load and secure the steam wagon. While this was going on, John raced to check on Julia and the other two men. Father Peter told him that Sam would be all right in about a week, but Bill was not going to be on active duty for quite a while.

John looked at him in obvious distress.

"Son, she will be all right. She was banged up, but she will need some rest. Sarah is watching over her. Go on. You can see her now, but be gentle. She took quite a knock on the head. Besides, if you don't go to her, you will not be of much use to anyone." Father Peter waved John off with a sigh and a blessing.

John opened the door to the compartment and saw Julia unconscious in her bed, with Sarah by her bedside fast asleep in a chair.

He stepped in, and in a flash, Sarah was awake. "Poppa?" she asked.

"Isaiah is fine, but I think he wants to see you more than anything right now."

Sarah glanced at Julia as if reluctant to leave her side.

John nodded. "It's all right, Sarah. I will watch over Julia. Go on now."

Sarah scampered out of the compartment and headed forward to find Isaiah.

John sat down and stared at Julia. He was still wondering if a woman like this could find a quiet, not to say dull museum professor of any interest when he saw her eyes flutter open. "Hello there, tough special agent," he said trying to keep his tone light.

Julia looked at him and, in a very groggy voice, replied, "Not so tough, I fear, John. I hurt all over. What happened? You were there standing over me firing, and then everything went dark, and there was thunder. I thought I was dying, and I did not think I would ever get to see you again." Julia was crying now.

John smiled down at her and very gently stroked her head on the side that did not have the gash in it. "I thought you were dead. I saw the shot hit you, and you went down like a rag doll a child had tossed away. I was so scared. Julia Verolli, I love you, and I could not stand to lose you."

Julia looked up and stroked his cheek and, in a still very groggy voice, said, "I would tell you to kiss me, you tall, silly man, but right now, I think it would hurt too much. What, ouch, what happened?"

John wiped a tear away. "Simple. The reason it got dark was because I fired a rocket to signal the Congress. She came in at full power, and her hull was blocking the sun. The thunder was the sound of her engines and Gatling guns firing—that and Isaiah's steam Gatling. The captain of the Congress wants to know if he can borrow Isaiah to work on his ship." John smiled at this last bit, trying to cheer Julia up.

Julia tried to sit up a little and winced in pain. John gave her some more water. "Here. Settle down. You are out of this fight for a while, young lady. I still cannot understand why you are not dead. That bullet took you square in the side."

Julia smiled weakly at him and, in a barely coherent way, replied, "My corset, standard agency issue for female agents—the boning is reinforced with a fine steel mesh, knife proof. Bullet must have been mostly spent. The corset took most of the blow, but I am going to be bruised for a while. My side really hurts. John Morton, what were you doing trying to do saving me? You should have gone after Ulrich and Chen. You silly, stupid male." And then a very groggy Julia said, "I love you, you tall, stupid man," and passed back out again.

John smiled down at her and said, more to himself, "I was saving the life of a highly trained special, very special agent. It seemed like a good idea at the time."

Before long, Peter stuck his head into the compartment. John stepped over, and they stepped into the corridor so that they would not disturb Julia.

"John, get some rest yourself. You look like a man who has been on a long three-day tear around my parish." Peter spoke quietly but with firm authority.

John was so tired he found himself trying to decide where Peter had gotten that tone of voice—from the army or the seminary. With a start, he realized that, if he was thinking like that, he indeed was tired.

He'd started to protest that someone had to watch Julia when Peter put his hand on John's arm. "Get some rest. I will keep an eye on the fair maid until our pint-sized answer to Clara Barton comes back from checking on her father. *Now go!*" He said the last bit in his best parade ground drill instructor voice.

Following that command, John staggered to his compartment and fell into the bed, just able to take his boots off and undo his various weapons. Sleep was upon him like a dense, dark fog moving in from the ocean over the city's Battery Park. It seemed that, just seconds after his head hit the pillow, he was unconscious.

Sarah returned to Julia's and her compartment to find Father Peter sitting in the chair reading a book with one eye and watching Julia with the other. "Poppa is all right," she told Peter in a quiet voice. "Father Peter, what is going on? I did not know science was so dangerous." She spoke this last in a very small, scared, and confused voice. She had been caring for Julia. Now the sight of, not to mention the smell of rotten eggs coming from the dirt-like grit of the burnt black powder that covered Isaiah from head to foot was quite disconcerting and, to her ten-year-old mind, terrifying.

Peter looked at her steadily for a moment. "When Julia wakes up, I think you should ask her, all right? Sarah, it is something that has to be between the two of you."

Sarah just nodded at Father Peter. When he got up, she took the seat he'd vacated as he left their compartment to check on the condition of the other injured men.

When Julia awoke, it was dark out. She realized several things all at once. Her head still hurt, but it was clearer now and her side felt as if someone had tried to stave it in with a thick piece of cordwood. Sarah was sleeping in the chair. And, finally, she had to pee. Taking stock of all these things, she decided that having to go to the bathroom was probably what had woke her up.

Julia managed to sit up with some effort, which woke Sarah, who jumped up to help her. With a prodigious amount of effort between the two of them, she managed to make it to the commode. It was at that point that a somewhat disheveled John Morton decided to open the door rather than knock, in case Julia was still sleeping. In a flash, Sarah was there barring the way with her small arms folded over her chest. She looked up at Morton and said quite forcefully, "Excuse me, sir. There are some things a lady needs privacy for." She slid the door shut with a firm thump in Morton's rather surprised face.

Julia started to laugh at this but decided that was a bad idea, since it made her side hurt worse, so she just smiled and, looking at Sarah, said, "Thank you, Sarah. Impossible man, really quite rude."

Sarah looked at her and said in a small, shy voice, "Do you love him?"

Julia swallowed and looked sad. "Yes, Sarah, I so love him, but I can't tell him that now. We need to finish our work first."

Sarah helped Julia back to the bed so she could sit down and then brought her some water in a basin and a cloth so she could clean herself up a bit. Sarah and Peter had cleaned most of the blood and dirt from the wound on the side of her head where she had hit a rock when she was knocked down, but still, it felt good to wipe herself down.

As she finished up, she said to Sarah, "Thank you for taking care of me, Sarah. It is nice to know someone cares. And if I may say so, you handled Professor Morton quite well." She tried to smile again and wound up wincing in pain.

Sarah looked at her very seriously. "Miss Julia, what is going on? You were hurt very badly, along with Mr. Bill and Mr. Sam. And Poppa was covered with gun smoke. I could smell it. I know I don't know much, but I don't think secretaries get beaten up or shot at."

Julia looked at her. "Who told you I was shot? I just fell."

Sarah looked downcast. "Miss Julia, I heard Father Peter talking to Cook when Cook brought some hot water to clean up your cut. He said you had been shot. I had to help him get your clothes off so he could check where he thought the bullet hit you. He thought you were going to die. I heard him saying prayers in Latin. I do not know what he meant by the extreme unction exactly, but it did not sound good the way he said it." She looked at Julia, and her face carried the expression of a child who somehow knows when an adult is not telling the truth.

Julia took a deep breath and winced again—punishment, she thought, for lying to Sarah. She started in by taking hold of Sarah's small hands in hers. "Sarah, I have not been totally honest with you, and I hope you can forgive me. I have never had a sister before or really any family, so I do not have a lot of practice at how to treat them. I do not want to lose you; you have to believe that!"

Sarah looked at Julia. Sarah saw in Julia's face that she was scared. She was frightened too, for she loved Julia, who had become like a big sister to her, and she did not want to lose her either.

Julia took a sip of water and went on. "I am the professor's secretary in a way but not really. I work for the government, and we have been trying to catch a pair of very bad men who could hurt the entire country. So I have been playing the part of John's, the professor's, secretary, as a cover to help me catch them."

Sarah gave her a confused, frightened look. The scared little girl of several weeks ago was back in full force. "Poppa and the professor and Father Peter, do they know? And what about me? How do I fit in?"

"Oh, Sarah." Julia sighed. "Yes, they know. We are part of a special team brought together to catch these men. I helped to recruit the professor and Father Peter. They in turn recruited Isaiah, your father. Mr. Tinsman and his men work for me. You were not supposed to be here. That is why the professor wanted you to go to a convent. He thought it would be too dangerous for you, and he did not want to take a chance on you getting hurt. Do you remember how the professor saved you from a gang who were hurting you? Do you remember that?"

"A little," whispered Sarah, as in truth that night was something she had been trying very hard to forget. "So I do not belong?"

Julia was trying her best not to hurt Sarah anymore. "Not the way you mean, Sarah. We were trying to keep this all a secret from you; none of us wanted you to be hurt. You see, now you do belong. Isaiah told me once that he was amazed at how one little girl could fill the hole in his heart. He was broken inside, Sarah; the loss of his wife and child tore him up so bad, and that loss broke his heart." Julia thought back to her first meeting with Isaiah and the pain and rage she had seen in the man. Putting that memory aside, she smiled at Sarah and went on. "You filled that hole in his heart and helped so much to mend it. Sarah, you helped to make him whole again. Oh Sarah, he loves you so much. I cannot even begin to describe how much he cares about you and your safety is everything to him. He told the professor that, if he made you leave, he would leave with you."

Sarah looked up at Julia. "And what about you, Miss Julia?"

"Young lady, were you not paying attention? I told you I never had a family till I got a little sister. Remember in the trolley in Chicago when the conductor grabbed you, and you thought I was afraid that he had hurt you?"

Sarah nodded.

"That is not what I was afraid of, Sarah. I knew you were all right. I was afraid that you would be scared of me when I hurt him. I just reacted without thinking because he had tried to take you away. I was afraid you would not want me in your life anymore. That scared me so much I could have cried; like I said, I never had a family before you!" Julia started to cry.

Sarah just digested this all for a minute. Then the little girl stood, went over, and sat next to Julia on the bed. She put her arm around her big sister and hugged her. Julia winced again, and Sarah looked scared that she had hurt her. Julia just hugged her back and said, "Best feeling in the world."

Julia sniffled a little and, changing the subject, said, "Do you think I could get away with just a robe for dinner? I am not sure I can get dressed yet, and I am quite hungry."

Sarah looked up her big sister and said, "I do not think that proper gentlemen would be upset."

Julia smiled and decided that her little sister Sarah's lessons in deportment were coming along nicely.

CHAPTER 22

WHAT HAVE WE HERE?
STILL, MORE QUESTIONS

It was only a short while later that a still wobbly Julia, with help from Sarah, made her way to the parlor where Father Peter was taking a break from tending to the injured men. Sitting down, Julia asked Sarah to bring her something to eat, something soft and easy to chew. When Sarah went through the door, Julia looked at Father Peter and was trying to find the right words to start with.

When Peter looked at Julia, he saw her quite visible mental discomfort. "Being human again, Julia?" Peter said, smiling.

Julia turned red, and Peter, being the man of God he was, took pity on her. "Julia, it is all right. I have a very poor parish, and many have been the times I've had to perform a baptism while I also helped with the baby's delivery. Several times, I've had to give last rites to a girl in one of the houses of ill repute after a 'gentleman caller,' as they put it, tried to kill her or just decided to beat her up. It is all right, lass. I had to see how badly you were hit, on top of which, you were having a tough time breathing due to some swelling, as it was. So the corset had to come off."

Julia, if anything, turned a slightly brighter shade of red. "Thank you, Father Peter. I would not want to tempt a man of the cloth, especially one as good as you."

Peter smiled at her again. "I have to say, I think John will be most impressed, after you two are properly married, of course."

Julia was now somewhat shocked. "Father Peter, how could you …" she sputtered. Then Julia went on, "I do not have time to be married, Father. The mission has to come first."

"The mission will not last forever, and I told you, Julia, I have married enough couples to see how they look at each other, even if you do it behind John's back. And furthermore, Julia, just because a man is on a diet does not mean he can't appreciate a fine meal, even if he can't taste it. Now, young lady, I have wounded men to attend to."

With that, Peter got up and left to go forward to the bunk car to check on Sam and Bill. As he left the car, he had a small, devilish Irish smile on his face and a bit of an almost cheerful bounce in his step. He firmly promised himself to do penance. But for once, it was really quite satisfying to leave Julia sputtering for a change.

Sarah returned to find Julia sitting by herself and, from the confused look on her face, seemingly unsure whether to be shocked or laugh at her own foolishness and unable to decide.

After John Morton had a door slid firmly shut in his face, having been bullied by a ten-year-old girl, he decided that maybe he should would work on something that would not fight back and headed forward to his laboratory to look at the two Ratten bodies they had recovered. On the way, he met Isaiah, who himself had just woken up. He had gotten to sleep somewhat later than John because he had to make sure the steam assault wagon was secure and the boiler fire out.

"What's happening, sir?" Isaiah asked. The tone of the words made it clear they were spoken by a man in need of a large amount of caffeine.

John smiled at him. "Your daughter, sir, is learning far too much from Julia. She just threw me out of their compartment and slammed the door in my face telling me, 'There are some things a lady needs privacy for.'" This last he said in a high-pitched, little girl voice.

Isaiah looked shocked for a moment and then laughed, a big smile crossing his face. "That's my girl," he said. "I don't know about you, Major, but I need some tea. Care to join me?"

"Later Isaiah. I want to look at those bodies we brought back. I have a very bad feeling about this last nest," Morton replied.

The two men went in opposite directions, Morton forward to the laboratory and Isaiah back to the parlor.

When John got into the laboratory car, he turned up the gaslights, donned an apron, hoisted one of the bodies up onto an autopsy table, and began work. He cut, removed, weighed, probed, and notated. If anyone had been there to hear, they would have heard him muttering and his sharp intakes of breath when he discovered the improved grasping ability of the front paws of this latest batch of Ratten and then the increase in their brain size. After he was finished with both corpses, he studied some of weapons the creatures had used against them, which he'd picked up along with the bodies. This was accomplished with more muttering and scribbling of notes. He cleaned up and wrote some more notes with a worried expression on his face. As finished as he could be in his laboratory space, he collected the notebooks he and the sharpshooters had found when they'd searched the cavern prior to blowing it up. Satisfied, he had done as much as he was able to do, he turned down the lights and headed back to the main car.

As John approached the parlor he saw Julia and Sarah just starting to come up the corridor. Julia was still a little wobbly and Sarah was helping her. John, at the sight of Julia being upright, thought she looked beautiful and went forward to help her. "Julia, can I help?" he offered with a big smile on his face.

Julia just cocked an eyebrow at him and said, "We can manage, Professor."

John was, needless to say, somewhat shook up at this rather cold greeting. "Julia, is anything wrong? I mean, I love you, and you said you loved me."

"John Morton, I never said that. And if I did, I was probably delusional from hitting my head. It is not as if I am some school girl that you can impress you know." Julia was trying to sound very tough.

John looked totally forlorn. "Oh, I guess you were out of it then. But if you do not mind, Miss Verolli, we have some research notes to be translated." John was not aware that Julia had told Sarah the truth about everything, so he held back on what he had found during the autopsies. "I will leave them in the parlor for you."

Julia looked at them and, without thinking, said, "I will look at them now you tall, silly man." John did a double take, and Julia, realizing what she had let slip out, tried to cover. "I meant, I will look at them right now, Professor."

John continued on to the parlor and smiled once his back was to Julia and Sarah.

Julia, with Sarah's help, got turned around and went back to the parlor. She looked at John, saying, "And do not get any ideas, Professor John Morton, just because I am not properly dressed. It is just that my side still hurts very badly, and there is still some swelling. I could not wear anything too tight."

As if to underscore her big sister's warning, Sarah sat there, keeping an eye on Morton, much like the watch a trained attack dog might keep and looking equally ferocious.

John, however, did note that Julia's robe has slipped a little when she sat, to reveal an extremely nice leg. "My dear, Miss Verolli, what kind of a man do you think I am? Are you suggesting I would try to take advantage of a young woman in your state, especially my unmarried secretary? After all, what would my colleagues at the museum think, not to mention my family?" John secured a cup of coffee, returned to his seat, and began to sip his beverage in a quite proper museum professor manner.

Julia looked at him and replied, "Just so we understand each other, sir. Teammates—is that clear, sir! Now about those notes and journals you found."

Morton looked a little worried and glanced down at Sarah.

"John, she knows everything," Julia said. "I couldn't lie to her anymore. Besides, as she noted, secretaries don't typically get shot or beat up."

Sarah looked up at Morton then, and this time the message in her eyes was clear—you'd better take care of my sister or else.

Morton looked a little surprised. "Well, at the rate things are going, she was going to figure out something other than scientific research was going on sooner or later," he finally said. "However, Sarah, what I have to tell Julia is somewhat complicated, so I think it's best you try to get some sleep." Morton reached down to ruffle her hair a little.

Sarah looked at Julia, and Julia said, "It's all right, Sarah. The professor is right, and you do need some sleep. You have been very busy taking care of me, after all, just like a real sister would—maybe even better. He will be a gentleman enough to help me back to our compartment."

Sarah obviously wanted to stay with Julia, but even she had to admit she was pretty tired. So she gently hugged Julia, said good night to Morton, and went down the corridor to their sleeping compartment, but not before giving John one more warning glance.

John found himself wondering which one he should be more scared of, Julia or Sarah.

After Sarah left, John turned to Julia. "First, how are you doing Julia? And second, Miss Julia Verolli, I do not care what you say. I still love you!"

Julia returned the stare. "John, I told you, if you are still interested after the mission is over, then we can talk about our, your, feelings. As to my condition, my head still hurts, and my side is none too happy, but I can function after a fashion. So where are these books and journals?"

John handed over what they had found. He looked at her. "We have a problem. These were not the same creatures we found in New York."

Julia's head snapped up, which sent a bolt of pain through it, which in turn caused her to take a sharp breath. Calming her breathing and slowly getting her eyes to focus again, she looked up at John. "What do you mean, not the same? I saw them. They were Ratten."

"Julia, I have examined the bodies of two of them, along with the weapons they were using and other evidence from the cave. I also remembered their fighting tactics from the Points. These creatures are much more advanced. Additionally, the nest was far more complex and sophisticated than the one in New York. The ones back in the city were basically just large rats, teeth and claws their weapons; these creatures were toolmakers and users. The spears and other weapons and tools I found were made by hand, not bought for them by Ulrich and Chen. The city Ratten just attacked like rats do, coming straight out of the nest in a pack. This nest had sentries and had planned escape tunnels and extra passages that were well hidden. The autopsies I performed showed that this bunch has larger, more complex brains, and the front paws are more hand-like. That means they can make, grasp, and use tools, Julia, not to mention weapons. On top of that, Ulrich and Chen must have been controlling them somehow, as they were in the nest too. Otherwise, why were they not attacked? Julia, this problem is getting much worse; these creatures are evolving, just like Mr. Darwin's theory."

Julia looked absolutely shocked. "Dear God, John, where is this going? Let me take a look, but would you please get me some tea first please? I am still a bit wobbly to try and get it for myself."

John put his hand on her cheek and touched her face lightly. "Your wish is my command, Miss Verolli." With that, he disappeared into the kitchen and shortly returned with a pot of tea, china, and fixings for Julia and a thick sandwich for himself.

Julia just sat there while he was out of the room and touched her face where John had touched it and thought, *tall, silly man.*

John set down Julia's tea and reclaimed his coffee and sandwich while Julia's tea was steeping. Julia stopped wasting time and began to look at the notebooks. Several hours later, she looked up. It was during this period of relative silence that Isaiah and Father Peter showed up to claim some food for themselves. John quickly filled them in on his autopsy discoveries, along with what he had found in the cave system. All the while, Julia kept looking though the research journals.

"John, it looks as if you were right," Julia said, pausing in her labor. "If I understand this correctly, these two have made enormous strides in breeding the Ratten. The ones we found and destroyed were far superior to the ones in their initial experiments. They talk about how the 'Rat Troopers'—that's how they're now referring to them—are progressing nicely, more dexterity and intelligence. However, we do have a problem.

Some of the notations are in Chinese, which unfortunately, I do not read."

Peter made the Sign of the Cross. "Dear Lord in heaven. Do they think that they are God to be breeding such creatures as these?"

John answered Peter. "These men are mad for power indeed, not to mention revenge for having their project shut down. We have no idea what we are up against." John then turned to Julia. "Do the parts of the journals you can read give us any idea where they may be headed next? I had the Congress over fly the area to look for a trail, but the crew couldn't find anything; the forest was too heavy to see anything from the air. That coupled with the recent rainstorm—meaning any tracks we might have found if we were to look on foot will have been washed away—makes our task difficult, not to mention that we need to try to avoid the Indians. I wish we had been able to go after them, but we were down to almost half strength with three of us out of the fight. It was all we could do to check the cave and, to the best extent we could, make sure none of the Ratten had escaped. Not to mention that, as an assault vehicle, Isaiah's wagon is excellent, but it wouldn't be the best at tracking men on horses across wooded country, city boys or not."

Julia looked up. "So far, nothing, John, although I haven't finished going through them. I understand why they got away. You did the right thing. But it will make catching them much harder since now they know we're on to them. I will keep looking, but it will have to be in the morning. I'm afraid I'm still feeling the effects of that rock I hit. Sir, would you be kind enough to escort me to my compartment? I am still a bit wobbly."

John smiled at her. "If I might offer my arm, dear lady. What knight errant would refuse such a request from a damsel in distress?" With that, John stood up and offered Julia a hand getting to her feet.

When she had obtained an upright position, she and John walked slowly down the corridor to the compartment she shared with Sarah. John looked down at her. "Julia, I know for now it is just teammates, but as it was pointed out to me recently, the mission will not last forever. Be assured, Miss Verolli, I will still be interested, that is if you would be interested in a dull museum professor?"

Julia looked up at him and softly replied, "Dull, sir? I thought you told me that your scientific adventures read like one of Mr. Buntline's dime novels. How dull can that be? You really are a tall, silly man." With a soft kiss on the cheek, she was gone, and the compartment door slid shut.

I really am getting to dislike this door! thought John.

CHAPTER 23

THE PROFESSOR GETS AN UNEXPECTED SURPRISE

he team spent a quiet night and reassembled at breakfast the next morning. Julia looked somewhat better, although the part of her head that had hit the rock was still black and blue. She had at least had managed to dress in a blouse and loose skirt. While she navigated on her own Sarah was nearby, just in case she needed someone to steady her.

The gentlemen all stood as the two ladies arrived. Sarah double-checked on Isaiah, to be sure no aftereffects of the fight at the cave lingered. Isaiah was seemingly embarrassed and warmed by this attention at the same time. Finally, everyone was seated and breakfast served.

John opened the conversation by asking Julia how she felt. She nodded not too vigorously and said, "The headache is down to proper proportions and my side hurts somewhat less. Overall, I would say I am on the mend. I should really take the time to send a thank you note to the agency's dressmaker. From what Father Peter tells me, he almost had to give me the last rites, so I shall not complain about a few pains and some bruising to my side."

John smiled at her, as did the others.

Julia continued, "How are Bill and Sam?"

Peter replied, "Sam should be all right by the end of the week; some deep scratches, but it looks as if there is no infection. Bill is a different matter. I have talked to Tinsman, and we agree he should be sent east as soon as possible for recovery and rest. He is out of this fight."

There was quiet around the table at this news, for both men were well liked and trustworthy. John said, "We can connect farther back down the line at Tall Pine Junction. He can catch a train there and start heading back. Is he all right to travel by himself? I should not like to lose anyone else. Losing Bill Welsh brings down our available manpower considerably as is."

Peter assured them all that, while Bill was hurt, he could handle himself with a crutch and should be able to travel by himself; in fact, when Peter had brought the subject of sending him back east, Bill had gotten somewhat indignant, not even wanting to be, as he put it, 'invalided home.' "He will be all right," Peter said. "The man is a fighter. But I think he will be riding a desk for quite a while before he is allowed out in the field again."

Everyone was relieved to hear this.

"Julia, any more luck with the journals as to a lead on our quarry's possible destination?" John asked.

Julia looked around. "Frankly, not much, John. I cannot find any clue about where they might have headed. Of course, the notes contain a large segment I cannot read. I am assuming Chen wrote it and that it's in Chinese. We need someone we can trust who can translate the rest of the journals for us. Any ideas?"

Peter looked thoughtful. "There is a large Chinese community on the West Coast, brought in to work on the railroad. We may be able to find someone there. Otherwise, we would have to go all the way back to New York or Washington to find someone. There might be someone in Chicago, but he or she would have to be investigated before we could hand the journals over; the whole process would take more time than traveling the extra distance. I wish I could help more, but I only speak a little of the language and understand none of the writing."

"Where on earth did you learn Chinese, Peter?" Julia said in shock.

"When I was at the seminary, my roommate had been on a mission trip to China and picked up quite a bit of the language," Peter replied. "I helped him with learning Latin, and he taught me some Chinese, sort of a trade. I didn't learn the reading or writing, but at least I learned enough to speak a little."

John looked at Peter. "Peter, that bit of knowledge definitely makes you the most logical person for the job. Do you think you could take the journals to the West Coast? No offense, old friend, but if it comes to a fight ..."

Peter looked around and replied, "I know, John, I am the oldest and the most expendable. I do not see my heading to the West Coast as a problem. I can make connections and take the Union Pacific westward."

Julia spoke up. "Never expendable, Father Peter; the most trusted with such delicate information." She smiled at him. "The Congress might have trouble with the Rockies, but if not, it would be that much faster."

Peter's face started to turn a slightly greenish color. "I hate to wear out my welcome, after the captain and crew have done so much for us," he said. "Besides, as John noted, we are supposed to be keeping a discreet facade up. And the truth is, I hate flying. So let's keep the Congress or any other airship out of it for just now."

Julia gave in gracefully. "Very well, Father, no airships for now."

Peter seemed to breathe a sigh of relief and continued. "What do you have planned in the meantime? I mean there are no leads to go on at this point."

Julia smiled a rather enigmatic smile. "I rather have a surprise for a member of our team," she said, sneaking a shy look at Morton.

Peter nodded. "I will ride along with Bill as far as I can," he said. "I assume you can make the arrangements for tickets."

"That should prove to be no problem, Father Peter," Julia assured him. "I will also make arrangements for you to meet with the bishop out there. If you need it, your officer's commission is still active."

Peter looked thoughtful. "When I was in the army, I wondered what it would be like to be an officer. So far, between hard, all-night, cross-country rides and having to ride in an airship with poor rations, I think I was, on the whole, much happier as a sergeant then a light colonel. From what I can see, the whole idea of being an officer is much overrated!"

The rest of the team smiled and laughed quietly at this observation.

As breakfast finished, everyone felt the engine take up the slack and heard the steady chuffing of the boiler forcing a draft through the firebox, the hissing as the pressure built up so that soon the air brakes were being released, and finally the huffing of the pistons and creak of the cars as they picked up speed. And then the whistle screeched as they headed for Tall Pine Junction.

John tried to badger Julia about this surprise, but she just laughed at him and said, "If I tell you, it will not be a surprise sir."

Several hours later at the junction, Julia, John, and the others said good-bye to Peter and Bill. Bill looked disappointed at being forced to leave, but both Tinsman and Julia were firm. Peter would ride with him back to Saint Paul and then head south to pick up the Union Pacific then west to California. During the farewells, their train was restocked with provisions and ammunition, which included the necessary material for Julia's gas bombs. In the meantime, the tender had a fresh load of coal, and the water tank was topped off.

Before long, they pulled out of the junction, heading generally west into the Dakota badlands. Several days later, after following various rail lines, the train pulled into a small whistle-stop where their train took a siding. Julia had still not told John where they were going or what was going on and would only smile enigmatically when he asked.

The next morning, Isaiah, and Sarah with him for a change, was unloading the steam wagon. On this occasion, the Gatling was left behind and was being serviced by Tinsman and the other two sharpshooters.

Sarah came to find Julia and told her, "Poppa says to tell you the wagon is ready and he has a full head of steam up." Beaming, Sarah continued, "He is teaching me all about it." The little girl whispered in Julia's ear, "Poppa says a tinkerer's daughter needs to know these things."

Julia returned her smile and hugged her. She then told her, "Well, I am sure that your papa is right. It is good to have family, is it not, Sarah?"

The two hugged each other again, this time with a bit more gusto, since Julia's injuries had some finally healing up to do. Her head at least was back to normal the bruising faded except for a small scar on the side of her head where she had gashed it on a rock.

As Sarah returned to the front of the train to find her father, Julia collared John and told him they were going for a ride and to pack a bag since they would be gone for a couple of days.

Morton was still in the dark as to where they were going or what was going on. But for a change, he was relaxed. After all, they had not heard from Peter yet, and there was nothing more he could do on the case. He, in the manner of troops from the beginning of time, had managed to catch up on his sleep and even enjoy a bit of reading. Julia thoughtfully, had several of his favorite scientific publications shipped in with the usual collection of newspapers and government reports they continued combing through, hoping to pick up something on Ulrich and Chen. These last items had produced no leads whatsoever. So with his mind clear and body rested, he was surprised when he and Julia joined Isaiah and Sarah at the front of the train where the Steam Wagon puffed gently ready to take them where ever Julia had her surprise waiting. Sarah climbed up and seated herself next to her poppa, as she referred to Isaiah, in the driver's seat, with Isaiah showing her the various gauges and controls.

Isaiah beamed down at them over the top of Sarah's head and said politely, "Gentle lady and good sir, would you please climb aboard. We are ready to roll."

After throwing their bags up, John helped Julia up and then climbed aboard the wagon. As the two passengers settled down, Isaiah and

Sarah both donned goggles. Isaiah motioned to Sarah and Sarah let out the steam valve a bit. The wagon started out slowly but steadily gained speed till they were moving at a brisk fifteen miles per hour. As Julia had noted on her first ride aboard Isaiah's wagon, the contraption had little in the way of springs. But thoughtfully, Sarah had secured some pillows for her and John's section of the wagon, so she had at least a minimum of protection from the dips, holes, and bumps of the Dakota badlands.

This seemingly breakneck pace went on for several hours, with John doing the honors of feeding the boiler regularly with a scoop of coal, till the wagon topped a rise, and Isaiah pulled to a stop.

Julia smiled. John could not believe it. There before him in a dry valley was a camp setup with men excavating and digging for fossils. He just sat there with his mouth open and finally looked at Julia and stammered, "Wh?"

Julia laughed. "Really, sir, do you not recognize your own excavation and dig site? John, the expedition had to have something to show the curator. It simply would not do to let my employer come back empty-handed, now would it! Why what kind of secretary would Dr. Chesterfield think I am?"

John was like a child on Christmas morning. Isaiah had Sarah open the steam valve again slowly, and the wagon began the final part of the journey to the base camp.

John looked at Julia "How did you do all this? And who are these men?"

Julia smiled. "These fine young men are students from some of the finest schools, who jumped at a chance for a paid trip to the badlands to work with the famous John Morton of the Museum of Natural Sciences. They have been somewhat disappointed not to meet you so far, but they understand that you have been scouting other sites for future research. I imagine they will be overwhelmed to meet you, sir. I just hope they can get over their shock at you bringing your unmarried, young female secretary and the even younger daughter of your tinker to the untamed west, to a dig site no less. How totally scandalous, sir."

The wagon rolled to a stop again, and the four climbed out. Sarah and Isaiah stayed to secure the wagon and make sure the boiler was properly out and everything was just right.

John and Julia went forward to meet the dig foreman, a fellow named Theodore Armstrong. They found him at the main tent. Ted, as he was called, was a big man, taller than Morton and seemingly twice as wide, with no hint of fat. His face was like dark tanned leather, and it was obvious that he had spent most of his life in the open.

Ted greeted the professor and his secretary warmly. As John and he shook hands, John's hand seemly disappeared in Armstrong's huge paw. John felt a renewal of kinship with the man, rough hewn as he was; Ted had been a foreman on one of John's previous digs. Ted was introduced to Julia and was, as most men were, mesmerized by her beauty, even in the plain-looking pants, blouse, and work boots she had chosen to wear to the dig site and her long, shiny black hair tied back into a ponytail.

Isaiah and Sarah showed up, John introduced the project's tinker and Sarah as Julia's assistant archivist. Sarah beamed at this, as now she had an official title on the expedition.

John and Ted left the headquarters tent, and Isaiah followed, while Julia and Sarah went over to the storage tent to see what had been found so far. Sarah looked up at Julia. "Now we have to make records of all these … what did you call them?"

Julia looked down at her. "Specimens, and you better remember that word, young lady. After all, we are not here to catalog *what- do- you- call- thems*." She was trying to look serious but laughing just the same.

Sarah laughed. "Yes, madam. A good assistant archivist needs to know these things," she said primly.

As they entered the tent, and both Julia and Sarah were more than a little overwhelmed.

"There are a lot of them, Miss Julia! We have to catalog all of these, and some of them are huge." She was looking at a fossil that was some six or seven feet in length. Looking more closely at some of the fossils, she saw the tags. She smiled. "Now I understand why you told me a secretary to a man like the professor needs to know Latin," she said.

These names are in Latin, just like Father Peter is teaching me." Her smile broadened.

Julia smiled down at her, "Just like I said, young lady."

Sarah returned Julia's smile with a sneaky one of her own. "And what about professor's wives? Do they need to know Latin?"

Julia turned red. "That is a question for later, young lady, if John, I mean the professor, is still interested."

Sarah looked at Julia, now being quite serious "Poppa told me the professor is really in love with you, Miss Julia. I think Poppa is right. He really cares about you."

Julia looked down at her little sister and, with a sigh, replied, "Sarah, we have to get the mission finished first; a lot can happen on a mission. That is why I cannot allow myself to think about afterward now. But you are right; I hope he still cares after all this is done. But you cannot tell him I said that; sister's oath?"

Sarah looked a little downcast but said, "Sister's oath."

Julia hugged her and then said, "Well, shall we see what records we already have and what we need to work on, then? Oh dear, where to begin."

CHAPTER 24

THE DIG SITE

Julia and Sarah looked around the tent at the huge number of artifacts and specimens, trying to figure out where to even start. Just then the tent flap opened and a young man came in. He was rather startled to see two females in the tent, especially since one was very pretty and one was young and black. The young man piped up. "Excuse me, but who are you? And what are you doing among these specimens?"

They both looked at the young man. Smiling, Julia held out her hand. "Hello, my name is Julia Verolli. I am Professor Morton's secretary and the expedition's archivist, and this is my assistant, Sarah. And you are, sir?"

The young man stammered for a moment and said, "Hello, Miss Verolli and Miss Sarah. My name is William, but everyone calls me Will, Will Timonds. I am very glad to meet you. I have been trying to keep up with the cataloging and have not had very much time on the dig itself. I hope I have done a good enough job for you. Did Professor Morton accompany you two? Is the professor really as tough as Ted makes him out to be?" He sort of whispered the last question.

Julia smiled, as did Sarah. "Mr. Timonds, you surely do not think two young ladies would travel the untamed west by themselves, I mean without any escort, do you?" replied Julia, trying to act shocked, as would be expected from a simple secretary. "Yes, the professor is here, and Sarah's father is our tinker. As to your second question, young man, I think you will find the professor is a joy to work with. He is very kind, and as long as you are trying your best, he will help you. But he best not catch you slacking off, right Sarah?"

Sarah looked at Will and tried to sound very grown up and imitate the professor. "I will not have any slackers on my expedition."

Julia tried to look serious at this and not laugh.

Will smiled at this, and somewhat flustered at being in the presence of two females, since the dig had been open now for over a month and he was beginning to think that girls were a figment of his imagination, simply stammered, "Can I get you anything, some water or anything?"

Julia and Sarah smiled, and Julia said, "No we are fine. But perhaps you can show us both what you have been doing and how everything is set up."

By the time he had finished showing them his corner of the dig site—that being the records and specimens that had been collected so far, along with how they were to be recorded—Will seemed to have enjoyed the time he'd spent with the two females. He was obviously somewhat tongue-tied around Julia and impressed with Sarah, for it was clear that Father Peter had taught her more Latin than Julia had guessed. Julia remembered how Peter said she had a flare for languages. She'd thought at the time it was just a way to rescue John and herself from Sarah's inquisition about their night out in Chicago, but it quickly became obvious that it was much more than that. It also became clear that Sarah's time with the professor had not been wasted. While she did not know the details, she had a sound grasp of the basics. Will seemed to be taken with Sarah the same way the team had been.

Will looked at his pocket watch then looked at both girls and said, "Cookie should have lunch up. It's not fancy, but it is plentiful, and you can work up an appetite on a dig site. Would you like me to show you the mess tent?"

Sarah looked up at Julia. "Do we want to eat there if it is such a mess?"

Julia laughed and said to Sarah, "No, silly, that's what they call the dining area. Mess is another word for food; it's not that the tent is a mess. Yes, Mr. Timonds, if you would be so kind, please lead the way."

Sarah, much relieved, replied, "Oh, okay. I better check on Poppa. He can forget to eat if he is on a project." Looking up at Julia, she whispered, trying to sound very grown up, "You know how men are."

Julia smiled down at her and, with a hug, whispered back, "Trust me, as you get older, it gets worse. Silly creatures actually, but nice to have around."

They both actually giggled at this, leaving poor Will to wonder what was going on. Julia smiled inwardly, thinking that it was the most wondrous thing to have a sister you could giggle with, almost like champagne bubbles that went up your nose—maybe even better!

At the mess tent the two girls caught up with the professor and Isaiah, who had been inspecting the dig site and meeting the crew. As Julia had told him, there were some fourteen young men from various colleges and schools who were working diligently away exploring the site, each one seemingly awestruck at the chance to finally meet the famous Professor John Morton. John was more than a little amused and not a little embarrassed by all the attention, while Isaiah had been, for the most part, warmly welcomed. Isaiah had already made several suggestions that would ease the burden without sacrificing any scientific discoveries. Needless to say, Julia was most warmly welcomed, as the rest of the lads were like Will in that they had almost forgotten what a female looked like after over a month in the badlands.

Sarah went right to work checking Isaiah's plate to make sure he had a proper meal. John smiled at this until he caught Julia giving his plate the same once-over. Wiping the smile off his face, he looked at her. "I hope it meets with your approval, Miss Verolli."

Julia smiled in return. "I just want to make sure my employer is properly fed, sir; that is all. After all, a secretary's work is never done. I should not want to be forced to inform Dr. Chesterfield of your collapse from malnutrition, sir."

The next few weeks flew by. Julia got to watch John in his natural habitat as it were. He was constantly moving around showing some of the lads techniques to improve their work, lavishing praise on them when they did good work, and making sure they got the proper recognition for the various discoveries. Julia thought he was a most marvelous teacher and researcher. Also a tireless worker, he was generally the first person on the dig site in the morning, except for possibly Ted, and would sit with Isaiah and Ted in the evening planning the next day's activities.

One day, he saved one of the student researchers. He caught the young man working near a small, brush-covered, ditch-like fold in the ground. John pulled him back and very carefully, using a stick, began to move the brush when a rattlesnake struck. John stopped all work and had an impromptu lecture on watching your surroundings and being careful. He explained that snakes like to sleep in the shade during the hottest part of the day.

Because John was willing to share his knowledge, showed that he cared about the people working for him and because he made sure that the lads got the proper credit for their respective work instead of taking all the glory for himself, as some senior researchers were known to do, the young men liked and respected him greatly. By the end of several weeks, Julia could see that the gaggle of young men would clearly follow him anywhere, including hell itself if John said he thought there were fossils to be found there. The young men seemed to worship him, almost as if he were a god, or demigod, at least.

Julie was impressed, but in one way, she was disappointed. John spent so much time on the dig that they had very little time together alone.

However, it is probably for the best, she thought. *No point in getting tongues wagging.*

Julia and Sarah were kept busy cataloging and keeping up with the field notes. Julia was very pleased to find that Sarah was a hard and diligent worker. Sarah was very careful and made sure that the newest finds were placed separately so that they could be cataloged, along with the exact location where they had been found. Sarah was quite firm in the storage tent, and woe to the young man who was careless when placing a specimen other than where she had directed. She spent many hours learning the proper names of the various finds and making sure they were correctly notated. She also seemed to become the camp mascot, as she had an infectious joy and smile.

Julia and Sarah had a tent to themselves and had no trouble falling asleep in the evening. Julia told Sarah that she could not have done everything if Sara had not been there, and said she was very proud of her little sister. While Sarah was working, Julia, in addition to overseeing the cataloging, also had to write articles for Dr. Chesterfield. She counted herself lucky in that one of the lads, a young man named Paul who was going to Harvard, was a very fine sketch artist. She asked John if she could borrow him for a bit and so was able to send several illustrations back to New York for the newspapers, thus helping to keep up their cover story.

Isaiah kept coming up with various small specialist tools that helped the lads in their work. He also developed an interest in the dig, and when nothing else was on his portable tinkerer's bench, he helped with the excavation. It turned out that he was a big help to Morton, since as a trained tinkerer, he seemed to have a good eye, almost instinctive, for which bone went where and how things fitted together. This proved to be an invaluable aid in sorting out the finds.

However all good things must come to an end, and so it was with this scientifically idyllic time. It ended rather abruptly when Sam came over the same ridge they had arrived over four weeks before.

Sam rode into camp and joined Julia, John, Isaiah, and Sarah in the mess tent for lunch. He was carrying with him a telegram that had arrived from Father Peter. Morton explained to the other members of the dig that Peter, an old friend of his from his army days, had joined the expedition as a representative from the archbishop but had gone on ahead.

While the weeks at the site had been a wonderful time, John's thoughts were forced to turn back to the reason for the mission. He could only wonder what atrocious advances Chen and Ulrich had made, given the time that had passed since the team had lost their trail.

When Julia and Sara arrived, John took them aside. He sent Sarah to get lunches for Julia and herself, and the three looked at the telegram. It was short and simple but, at the same time, momentous in its importance. It read:

> To: Professor John Morton, Dakota Territories
>
> From: Father Peter Harrigan
>
> Please proceed to Los Angeles with all speed. Believe I have vital information and possible sighting on research subject of special interest to you. Bring team. Will fill in details upon your arrival.

The team looked at one another.

John spoke up. "Well, I guess this had to end sometime. Isaiah, how soon can you have the steam wagon ready for travel? Julia, can you turn the cataloging back over to Timonds?"

Julia was the first to respond, "That is no problem, John. Sarah has been meticulous in her work, it will just be breaking the news to Will. I think he enjoys digging much more than cataloging."

Isaiah nodded. "No problem, Professor. It will take a little while for the boiler to come up and get everything ready, say two hours or so." He looked hesitant and it was obvious something was bothering him. "John, Julia, what am I going to do about Sarah? I don't want to leave her behind, but I'm sure the train—and where it's headed—will be the best for her."

Sarah had come up behind the group very quietly. "Poppa," she said sternly, "I do not intend to be left behind. Someone has to take care of you and keep an eye on Miss Julia!" This last was obviously a reference to her attack-doglike guardianship of Julia's honor around a certain professor of questionable morals.

Isaiah looked surprised and turned around to see his daughter standing there. "And just how long have you been listening in on our conversation, young missy?"

Sarah looked at her father. "Long enough to know that you could be in danger, and I cannot let you go off by yourself!" As she said this she flew into Isaiah's arms and hugged him fiercely, crying.

John spoke up. "I am not sure a camp in the middle of nowhere is much better, Isaiah, than the train, and at least we will have Peter to keep an eye on her."

Julia just smiled at the man and little girl and thought about John and how it would be a wonderful thing to have someone to care about you like she did about Isaiah. Not that she could not take care of herself, mind you, but still, it would be nice.

Isaiah held Sarah at arm's length and said, "All right. Let's see what you remember about operating the steam wagon."

Sarah smiled, and dried her eyes, and beaming, said, "I remember, Poppa." With that, she bounced off toward the wagon.

Julia called out to her, "After lunch, silly. We do not need to miss lunch with all the handsome young gentlemen, do we?"

Sarah giggled again and came running back to Julia.

"Besides," Julia added, "we have to break the news to Will, and you have to show him where you left off with the cataloging."

Sarah sighed and replied, "You're right, but I hope he can keep it straight." By this time, Sarah had taken quite the proprietary interest in her, as she thought of it, storage tent.

Julia smiled down and said, "We can only hope, Sarah." She lowered her voice to a whisper. "You know how men are."

Sarah giggled some more.

Julia continued in her regular voice, "Now let us find Will and give him the bad news."

John and Isaiah were left wondering what all the giggling was about, but in the manner of men over uncounted ages, decided it was a female thing and left it at that.

Lunch was a quiet affair. The lads were disappointed to find out that the professor and the rest were leaving to go check out a new potential fossil bed. But they understood.

Young Will seemed the most disappointed. For one, he knew he had to go back to being an archivist. In addition, because he had spent part of his time working with both Julia and Sarah, he had developed a bit of a crush on Julia and a real genuine liking for Sarah. He told Sarah that, in a way, she reminded him of his own kid sister back home in Connecticut.

Sarah and Julia took time to fill Will in on what they had been doing and Julia also asked him to send in some reports to Dr. Chesterfield to keep the museum updated on the dig site. While Julia was doing this last, Sarah went off to help Isaiah get the steam wagon ready for the trip. By one o'clock they were ready to take their leave of the site.

As the wagon pulled away from the site, Julia looked at John and said, "You look sorry to be heading after Ulrich and Chen. I mean, it sounds as if Peter has found the first solid lead we have had in quite some time."

John replied, looking back at the site now disappearing over the rise, "Yes and no, Julia. I want to bring those two down and put a stop to their evil, but I really did love being on a dig again—making the discoveries, filling in some of the blank pages in mankind's knowledge. It is exciting forcing the earth to give up her secrets. I guess that sounds silly to a highly trained secret agent like yourself; your life is one of thrilling adventure, is it not?"

"I enjoyed myself, John," Julia said, her gaze and tone sincere. "It was all new to me. And having the chance to work with Sarah was wonderful; she is an amazing little girl, John. In truth, I would have been hard put to manage without her. I also got a chance to watch you at work, John Morton, and that was very enjoyable too, sir."

John smiled and leaned forward to kiss her. "Sir, you best not in case Sarah is watching. You might not survive the attack." She laughed. "Besides, just teammates, John."

John looked at her as they bounced around in the back of the wagon. "Till the mission is over, Miss Verolli, only till then."

Julia, after several hours of being jostled around in the steam wagon, was more than happy to return to the rail siding. The cushions that Sarah had put in the steam wagon served to only partially reduce the jarring she had received from their travels, and she was looking forward to a chance to really clean up, as camp life had not had any luxuries. While being able to see John in his habitat was most enjoyable, she decided that so too was being a clean female dressed as such.

As Sarah and Isaiah began the process of loading the steam wagon and making sure it was secure, John went forward to talk to Tinsman and the engine crew to figure the best route to Father Peter. The journey would not be done quickly, since it involved some backtracking. But that could not be helped.

It took several hours to fire up the cold boiler to bring the engine back to steaming life. And then the team again tasted the tang of the coal smoke, felt the thud of the coupler slack being taken up and the familiar chuffing, and heard the bell clang and the whistle's loud defiant roar. Their home on wheels had begun its next phase of the journey.

Dinner that evening was a delight. Julia and Sarah had each had a chance to bathe and dress up. Julia was a bit shocked at how much of the Dakota Territories they had brought back with them, based on the amount of dirt in the bottom of the tub by the time they finished getting themselves clean.

Sarah asked Julia as they were bathing and dressing what it was like to be at a real school like Julia had been in. Julia told Sarah about some of her schooling, although she edited out some of the more dangerous and more fun but nasty parts. For her part, Sarah was fascinated at the idea of learning how to dance and cook. Julia told her that she should not be afraid that she was not getting a proper education, since most young ladies did not get a chance to study sciences or Latin, not to mention go out in the field and catalog fossils. And most especially, most young ladies did not get the chance to eat dinner with over a dozen handsome young gentlemen every night. Sarah just giggled.

The girls arrived for dinner, and both John and Isaiah were very pleased, although in different ways. Sarah, under Julia's tutelage, was developing into a young lady, and Isaiah remembered Peter's comment on how he should enjoy her now for before all too soon some young gentleman would want to steal her away. John looked at Julia and again wondered what a woman like her could see in a dull museum professor, for she looked very beautiful in a simple green dress.

CHAPTER 25

ON THE TRAIL AGAIN

ife began to settle into a routine as the days and miles passed. As the train traveled on, the scenery began to change, from the browns of the badlands to Minnesota's dark green and brown forests and then, as their route took them southward, to light brown and golden prairies and later to the gray green foothills and the darker grays of the mountains. Julia was still busy preparing news releases for Dr. Chesterfield every day and helping Sarah with her lessons. She and John spent hours reviewing reports and newspapers that they picked up along the way. Sarah, when she was not studying with Julia or the professor, spent her time forward learning about all things mechanical from Isaiah. By this time, Sarah's reading skills had progressed and had markedly improved, so that she was not just reading the newspapers but trying to make sense of the stories contained therein. Meals were shared affairs and a bit more relaxed, since Sarah was privy to the real reason behind the expedition.

The team was further delayed when they found that several of the passes through the Sierra Nevadas were blocked due to early snow storms and they had to detour to a far more southern route. By the time the train was turning north again, they were happy to leave the heat and drab colors of the southern desert and the rails of the Atchison,

Topeka, and Santa Fe Railway behind. They would now be approaching Los Angeles from the south.

Several weeks had elapsed from the start of their journey when the train pulled into a small town just south of their destination. John, hearing the change in the engine and application of the air brakes and then feeling the change in momentum, looked up and said, "I wonder why we are stopping."

Julia, who had been reading various government reports, replied, "Coal and water no doubt."

"No, Julia, we just took on both at the last stop when we had to wait in the hole for the southbound passenger train," replied John.

John got up and was walking toward the door when it opened and a smiling Father Peter came in.

Julia jumped up and rushed forward to give him a hug. "Father Peter, we did not expect to see you until we pulled into Los Angeles. Why are you here?" asked a smiling Julia.

John shook his friend's hand and smiled. "Peter, it is good to see you. Sorry it took so long to arrive, but we ran into a number of problems, not the least of which were those unseasonably early snows. We had to detour. But of course you knew that from our telegram," added John.

Peter smiled, but before he could get out a reply, the door opened again and Isaiah, Sarah, and the sharpshooters came in. Father Peter's return to the rest of the team was welcomed with a great deal of warmth and joy. Sarah ran to hug him and told him that she was now the official assistant archivist and had aided Miss Julia at the dig site, helping to catalog all the specimens. Julia added that she indeed had and that she had made excellent use of her Latin.

The team settled down, and coffee and tea were served. Father Peter began to fill them in on what he had discovered. "I was lucky in that I spoke a little Chinese, although as I told you, it was pretty rusty. Luckily I was able to find out from the local Chinese community which residents could read Chinese; many, like our own folks, do not read or write. Between my rusty, fragmentary Chinese and their fragmentary broken English, we were able to communicate, sort of. Anyway it would seem that our quarry was here. They found a ready band of henchman in the local tongs."

"The what?" Isaiah asked.

"Tongs, Peter replied. "Chinese gangs, just like the Irish ones in the Points back in New York, Isaiah—vicious and cruel too, make no mistake, and greedy. With the cash from their sales of the work drug to the railroad crew, Ulrich and Chen had enough to ensure the cooperation of the tongs. I hate to say it as a proud Irishman, but they could give some lessons to the gangs in the Points on running criminal operations. There is a small Chinese Christian community here, so I was able to make some contacts. I hate to say this too, but some of the local priests have been none too welcoming. I guess prejudice can exist even under a Roman collar. Those that were opened minded minded, at least more so then some of the local clergy, made me feel welcome and were happy to help. Nice folks once you get to know them. Good Christians."

"Peter," said John, "about Ulrich and Chen?"

"Sorry, John, I guess I tend to wander off the main point of my homily a bit," said Peter with a sigh. "My being here was dumb luck; but it seems the pair wound up here. They have been seen at irregular intervals around town. From what I could piece together from some fragments of conversation they had with some of the locals who sold them more supplies, they must have stopped in San Francisco to restock their equipment. They are a cagey pair. They must have been prepared for an attack and kept their cash assets ready to move when they were on the reservation. I sent word to the U.S. marshal in San Francisco to check on them. I invoked your name, Julia. I hope you don't mind?"

"Absolutely not. I have no problem with that at all, Peter. What were you able to find out?" Julie smiled.

"The word I got back from the marshal was that the two had bought enough to fill a railroad box car before they headed down here," said Peter.

Isaiah looked a bit confused. "I wonder why they came down here."

Peter looked at what was now one of his best friends. "I can only guess at that. Chen needed more of his Chinese herbs to continue their evil work. Most of the journal entries in Chinese were about the various effects of those herbs. Also, just a thought, John, they were making strides in their research and breeding program. The Ratten at the cave were quite advanced in both intelligence and tool-using ability compared to the ones back in the Points. The journals seemed to indicate that they thought they could go much further and significantly increase the intelligence of the creatures. One passage, however, seemed to indicate they'd had some sort of a control problem. What the problem was specifically wasn't too clear though.

"To get back to your question, Isaiah," the father continued, "I've been thinking about that. Los Angeles has enough of a population to have what they need, but it's much smaller and much less traffic comes in and out of it than San Francisco. While it would be easier to hide out and blend in in San Francisco, Los Angeles would be an easier spot from which to keep an eye out for strangers. Ulrich and Chen have to be aware now that they're wanted men, even without wanted posters up. A U.S. Army airship with Gatling guns blazing perhaps was not quite subtle enough, and its arrival may have tipped them off." Peter noted this with a small smile. "The Federal government has a smaller presence here than farther north by the bay. Los Angeles is pretty much a small, sleepy town compared to San Francisco—no marshal or even a close military post—so you could be pretty invisible, especially if the tongs were helping you."

"Makes sense," said John. "But that still leaves the major problem. Where are they? And more to the point, where is their lab and their ill-born prodigy?"

Peter looked at his friends and teammates. "I don't think they've gone far. From what we know of them, they prefer at least some civilization—Chicago, Saint Paul, and even the railhead. As we were told, they are city boys. I cannot be sure, but I think I saw Chen at one of the local establishments run by the tongs. At least I think it was him, never having laid eyes on him and with only Anderson's drawing to go by. Anyhow, I talked to some of my contacts and found out that the man I think was him has been coming into town at irregular intervals for entertainment and supplies."

Julia perked up at this "Is there any chance we can follow him?"

"Well, first we have to find him in town. It seems he is wily—always uses different routes and suppliers, although those are somewhat limited. Still, I think it's more than we could cover," responded Peter. "That brings me to why I had to meet you here. As you can guess, I do not exactly blend in in the Chinese community. And as I said, Chen seems to have made contact with the tongs so that I fear my cover may have been pierced. I thought it better to meet you here, which is far enough outside of the town so that I was probably not followed."

"Good thinking, Peter," said John. "How can we approach this? We have to get a lead on these two."

Julia looked at Sarah and said, "Young lady, I think you need a nap."

Sarah looked somewhat annoyed at this, but naptime had become the shared signal between Julia and Sarah that it was time for some "grown up talk." Sarah got up and excused herself. She hugged Father Peter again and left for the compartment she shared with Julia.

As soon as the door slid shut, Julia looked at Peter. "Peter, when you said entertainment, am I to assume you were not talking about musicals?"

Peter swallowed but replied bravely. "No, Julia. As you no doubt remember from our investigations in Chicago, our Mr. Chen seems to prefer white ladies and is willing to pay for their, uh, attention and affections, if you follow me. He seems to have built up a bit of a reputation in the area among a certain type of young women. Lucky for him, the tongs have extended their enterprise to include women of all races—very democratic and open-minded of them."

Julia nodded. "I follow you, Peter. John, this may be our chance to get a lead on them. If I go in alone, I could possible obtain employment in the establishment of one of his, suppliers, shall we say?"

Morton looked stricken. "No, Julia, it would be far too dangerous for you to go alone!"

Julia smiled. "Why, John Morton, are you worried that it is too dangerous or too daring. I believe I can handle the assignment."

John looked quite uncomfortable. "Julia, I really do not think that it would be proper for you to do that."

Julia looked at him again and thought he was definitely someone she could love. But that was in the future, after the mission, as she kept reminding him and herself. "John, letting those two build an army of Ratten and turning them loose on the country would not be proper. Having women and children torn apart by them would not be proper. John, I know what you are trying to do, but the mission has to come first. Are we clear, sir!"

John looked down and finally, after an obvious internal struggle, replied, "As much as I hate to say this, Julia, you are right; it is not as if any of the rest of us could do the job. But you have to be careful!"

Julia looked at him and simply replied, "I also remember the Points and the railhead, not to mention the caves. And as someone, I forget who, noted, devout cowardice seems like a reasonable and prudent course to me also, sir. No unnecessary chances, John."

Isaiah, who up to this point had been just listening quietly, suddenly asked, "Major, you still remember how to gamble from your army days?"

John and Julia turned and looked at him, trying to figure out where he was going with this. "Isaiah, this may shock you, but there is not much else to do in the evenings on a dig site in the middle of nowhere, so I have managed to stay in practice. Why?"

Isaiah scratched his chin. "Well, I was thinking that a lot of gamblers have female companions on their travels. Might be a good way to be close to Miss Julia. I was also thinking that a new tinker rolling into town in a steam wagon with his daughter would not arouse any undue suspicion. Meanwhile, a couple of gunfighters or trail=hand drifter types would just seem like part of the scenery. I mean, I was just thinking..."

Everyone looked at him.

Morton smiled. "Isaiah, that is quite some just-thinking, sir. I always wondered secretly how I would do as a steely eyed riverboat gambler—I mean, if I were not a museum professor," John finished awkwardly.

Meanwhile, Julia, Isaiah, and Peter were trying very hard not to laugh.

Isaiah smiled and said to Peter, "Father, still just- thinking here. I think it would be good if you moseyed back into town, but be careful. If a priest, one who was getting friendly with the Chinese Christians, just disappeared, it might get their suspicions up, so keep doing what you were doing, only quietly, being very inoffensive and low profile."

Peter looked at his friend in mock shock. "I am a priest, sir. How can I be other then inoffensive?"

Isaiah snorted and replied, "I remember being shackled to you all night in Saint Paul."

There were some more discussions, but Isaiah's plan did seem promising. Julia was concerned that Sarah would be heading into town into what could be danger. "Are you sure that Sarah should go along, Isaiah?"

Isaiah looked at her. "Julia, she is smart as a whip, and at least I can keep an eye on her. Besides, she is even more invisible than I am. Who is going to pay any attention to a little black girl? She will be able to see and hear things none of us could."

Julia still looked worried, but she had to agree that Isaiah was right. And if Sarah was with them, they could keep a discreet eye on her. Julia asked Isaiah if she could talk to Sarah first however.

"I think that would be a good Idea, Julia," Isaiah said, meeting her gaze. "You know, she thinks of you as her older sister. You mean an awful lot to her."

Julia actually turned a slight shade of red at this, but she nodded and went forward to their shared compartment. She opened the door and stepped in to find Sarah on her bunk reading a book. Julia was so proud of her, for she had come such a long way since John had found her in a back alley in Buffalo. She was turning into a young lady. Sarah looked at Julia with her big brown eyes and smiled.

Julia said, "Sarah, we need to talk, and it is very important that you understand what I am going to say to you."

Sarah looked a little scared because, in spite of all they had been through, she was still, inside, a very scared, insecure little girl, who was not yet sure of her family. "You are not going to send me away, are you?" she asked, almost in a whisper.

Julia looked at her. "No, Sarah, never that. I told you you are the only family I have. I will never send you away." Julia smiled, sitting down on her own bunk, she licked her lips, changed her mind got up and sat next to Sarah and put her arm around her. "Sarah, what I have to ask you is up to you, and I will not lie; it could be very dangerous, so you do not have to do it. Do you understand me? No one," Julia continued in a very firm voice, "will think any less of you or love you any less if you are too scared to do it. Do you understand?"

Sarah looked up at Julia and said, "I would not let my big sister down."

Julia hugged her and then said, "I know that, but you best hear what I have to say first, young lady. Sarah, as I told you, we are after some very bad men who want to hurt the whole country. They are very, very dangerous. Remember the railhead when you fell asleep?"

Sarah nodded.

"Sarah, you were sleepy because I gave you something to make you sleepy. I know it was not right, but you didn't know about the real reason behind the expedition at that point, and we were trying so hard to keep it from you and keep you safe. You have to believe me, Sarah, I would never ever do anything to hurt you!" Julia started to cry.

Sarah hugged her back and looked up at her. "Sister's oath?" she said with a small smile.

Julia hugged her back and smiled down at her. "Sister's oath. I love you Sarah. Anyhow, what I have been trying to say is that"—Julia wiped her eyes and her nose in a most un-Julia-like way (highly trained and tough secret agents did not cry or at least were not supposed to, she thought, unless it was part of their cover)—"we will be going into Los Angeles under cover, in secret, playing different people than who we are. Do you understand that?"

Sarah looked thoughtful for a minute. "You mean like we are playing a part in one of those musicals that the professor took you to?"

"Exactly, Sarah, but if we are caught, the consequences will be far worse than some bad reviews in the newspapers. Understand?"

"Yes, madam, I understand," Sarah replied, trying to sound grown up.

Julia smiled. "All right. The plan is that Father Peter will be returning by himself so that suspicions are not aroused, and I will be going into town as the professor's girlfriend." Sarah snickered a little at this. "Sarah, this is serious now!"

"Yes, madam, I am sorry," Sarah said quickly. "It did sound a little funny though."

"Well, maybe it did a little. But for now it is just pretend—part of the mission. Clear?" Julia chided.

Sarah, looking serious again, just nodded.

Julia went on. "Your father," for even Julia had started to think of Isaiah as Sarah's father, "is going to go in as a tinker and you as his daughter. It is our hope that you will be our eyes and ears, so you have to behave as if you are not as educated as you really are, understand?"

"Yes, ma'am," replied Sarah with a grin.

"All right, miss smarty-pants, but only till this is over. Are we clear?" Julia asked in mock horror.

Sarah laughed and smiled.

"One more thing that is very important," Julia added, "if you see any of us, unless we have been introduced while in town, you must act as if you do not know us. If we are given away, it could ruin the mission or far worse. Do you understand?"

Sarah looked very serious. "Yes, Julia. I will not let you down; sister's oath."

Julia hugged her again. "Sister's oath."

CHAPTER 26

Into Los Angeles

inner that night was a quiet affair. Father Peter had already left for Los Angeles, going back pretty much the way he had come. Isaiah and Sarah quietly went over what they would need to set up shop as a tinker. Tinsman and John Kirkland also left, since they had the farthest to go. They were able to obtain horses and were taking a route that would circle around and bring them into the town from the north—a couple of saddle tramp drifters coming down from San Francisco looking for some fun and work. The other sharpshooter would stay with the train, and he and the crew were scheduled to come into town several days later with the train itself.

John and Julia were talking quietly and making their plans. "We can get tickets on the next passenger train, John, and just show up in town. I don't see how they would be able to recognize us. We were wearing our protective masks at the time, and they were quite far away—lucky for me anyhow, or I would not be here discussing this with you," said Julia.

"I think you're right. They took off as soon as they fired at you. It was just dumb luck that the bullet hit you at such an extreme range. I doubt at that range if they could even tell you were a female, so I think our identity is safe enough for now," John replied. "I do like the idea of going in as a gambler and his girlfriend. In a way, it allows you more freedom to mingle with the other women if they think you are attached

217

to me and not out to cut in on their business, so to speak," he finished, looking quite uncomfortable and a little flustered.

Julia smiled at him and said, "Why, John Morton, I do declare; if you are not just the funniest thing around. Why you could just sweep a girl off her feet." All this was in a light southern drawl, with Julia running her hands over him and looking coy.

John swallowed again and merely said, "I believe you can pull off the part with ease, Miss Verolli."

Julia laughed and said in her regular voice, "I know I can, but can you, John? You seemed somewhat flustered there at the touch of what should be a woman you know intimately, sir."

John looked somewhat sheepish. "Sorry, Julia, I will not let it happen in town. However, Miss Verolli, rest assured that, when this mission is over, I want to find out about these, how did you just put it, these intimate aspects of yours."

"After the mission, sir, if you are still interested. But for now, John, just teammates playing a part. Are we clear, sir?" Julia looked at John sternly.

"Just teammates, Julia. Now I wonder, what is the current dress for a gambler on the West Coast?" mused John.

As they returned to their various compartments, the team members began packing for the journey into the city. Each was traveling light. Julia helped Sarah, since she was not sure what to pack. Julia reminded her not to pack any of her better clothes, since she was just a poor, itinerate tinker's daughter. Why would she have any such fineries?

As for Julia, she packed several dresses that were sure to show off her figure. Sarah, on seeing these garments, was somewhat shocked. Julia reminded her that they had to play their parts and be very convincing so that the men they were after did not suspect them. Julia told her, "Sometimes the best place to hide is right in plain sight and even by drawing attention to yourself. After all, I'm just a pretty thing, an empty-headed accessory on a gambler's arm."

Sarah looked a little shocked at this, until Julia reminded her again that they were playing parts, just like she was going to have to do.

"Remember, Sarah, no Latin or science. You're just an unlettered girl from the back alleys."

Sarah looked at Julia. "Got it, no fancy stuff. Well, at least I'm not pretending to love my father."

"I know. That part will be, easy," said Julia. "I know you care as much about him as he does about you."

Sarah smiled again and went back to packing. She stopped for a minute and looked at Julia. "What about tinkering? Am I suppose to know any of that?"

Julia looked back at her with a frown on her face. "That is a very good question, Sarah. I suppose, as a tinker's daughter, you would know some, but only about half of what you really know. After all, you are a girl and not a boy who would be good at that sort of thing."

They both chuckled at this thought.

"Definitely not the hard stuff," Julia added. "Remember, you just want to be in the background blending in, just part of the scenery. Got it?"

Sarah nodded. "Part of the scenery, just like a certain gambler's lady." This last she said with a bit of a smirk.

Julia tried to blow a wisp of hair out of her face. "Funny, young lady. Remember, some of these people may not like you because of your skin color. So be very careful, please, Sarah!"

"Miss Julia, some of the people in Buffalo did not like colored folk either. I understand," replied Sarah in a quieter voice.

Julia looked at her and could see the hurt in her eyes. "Well, you're still my sister, no matter what color you are. I cannot afford to lose my only family." She smiled at the little girl she'd grown to love in a way she'd never known as she gave her a hug.

"I know," said Sarah. "Father Peter taught me you judge people by what is in their hearts, not what is on the outside."

Sarah and Isaiah had just begun the process of unloading the steam wagon from Isaiah's special railroad car and firing up the boiler and getting it ready to travel when John and Julia stepped out to say their good-byes and catch their ride into town. Julia watched as Sarah checked the various gauges and Isaiah put another scoop of coal in the firebox and then continued loading up various tinker's tools and supplies into the wagon. John had purchased tickets for the next train into Los Angeles, and they heard the whistle in the distance.

Julia looked at Sarah and reminded her how she felt with simple words. "Be careful. You are the only family I have."

Sarah bent down from the driver's seat of the steam wagon and hugged her without any words. Then she straightened up and looked straight ahead.

Isaiah looked at John and Julia. "Figure we should roll into town late afternoon tomorrow. Good luck."

John took his friend's hand and said, "Good hunting, my friend."

Isaiah climbed on to the wagon driver's seat, and he and Sarah pulled on their goggles. Sarah opened the steam valve slowly, and the wagon began to move again, as it had during their trip to the dig site, slowly picking up speed till it seemed to snort fire and smoke like a dragon. The sound from the engine was almost like breathing, adding to the contraption's beastly and dragon-like appearance. It seemed that the wagon had barely disappeared down the road when the northbound passenger train pulled up and stopped at the low ball the station agent had set, the signal that told the engine crew the train was to make an unexpected stop.

The conductor got off and set down his little stool so they could climb aboard. John helped Julia up the stairs and then the conductor was waving to the engineer and yelling "All aboard!"

The conductor waved to the engineer and then followed the couple back on board the train. The two went down the aisle trying to find an empty pair of seats, making their way into the second car. The conductor followed and punched their tickets. They felt the train start up. They were the only folks getting on board, and the mail had been exchanged by hand since the train had stopped (as opposed to picking it up on the fly and a bag of mail tossed down). The entire process had taken less than four minutes. No one seemed to notice a mixed train sitting on the siding behind the station, looking almost abandoned. As for the new passengers—just a traveling man and a young woman, obviously some kind of hussy since she was not wearing a wedding band. *The kinds of people allowed out in public these days*, thought the older woman in the seat across from them, *just shameless!*

John and Julia could feel the train pick up speed as the engineer and fireman worked the valves and cutoffs to advantage in order to make up the time they had lost from the unscheduled stop. They had to get to Los Angeles on time—railroad policy and the crew's pride!

The Los Angeles streets were still dirt and, as the weather had been dry, dusty. As John and Julia stepped away from the station on Canal Street, they could smell the scent of the ocean in the air and hear steam locomotives and donkey engines working freight cars down on the nearby docks where schooners were tied up. Except for Peter they were the first members of the team to arrive in Los Angeles. The two sharpshooters were due in later in the day, and Isaiah and Sarah weren't set to arrive till the following day. Looking around, Julia spoke quietly to John. "Shall we see what awaits us here? Or do you have any specific ideas about where to set up shop?"

John smiled down at her, replying, "I heard from a close friend, a clergyman no less"—this with a wink at Julia—"that there is generally a game or two of draw poker at a place called the Comstock." Offering an arm to Julia and picking up their bags in the other hand, he continued, "Shall we see if we can find transportation?"

Looking around, they spotted a rickshaw pulled by a Chinese coolie at the rear corner of the station. "Shall we, Miss Julia." John gestured to the conveyance.

Julia looked wide-eyed. "Why I declare, sir; how cute. Oh dear, could we? I mean, it is just so darling!"

Morton tipped his hat, in this case a low-topped gambler style with a wide brim, to her. "Why, dear lady, now how could any gentleman resist such a request?"

The pair proceeded over to the rickshaw, John twirling his wolf's-head cane. John asked the driver how much to take them to the Comstock Saloon and Hotel. After some haggling for the sake of form, John and Julia climbed in, and before long, they were on their way to the hotel Comstock.

The Comstock was a wooden-framed building with some adobe and wood construction for the sake of style. It was several stories, and the first floor was obviously divided. On one side was a saloon and gambling hall; on the other was the hotel restaurant and desk, with rooms for rent on the upper floors. The pair went in and registered at the desk under the name John Jones, the agreed upon cover. Julia had voiced concern that the researcher John Morton might be known by name even this far west, and while the odds were against it, there was no point in taking chances. A bellboy took them up to their room on the second floor, and Julia just gushed over it when they went in.

As soon as they had tipped the boy, the door had shut, and the bellboy had headed back toward the lobby, Julia turned back into herself as if by magic "You, sir, can sleep on the couch, and I shall have the bed."

John looked at her. "I know, just teammates. Oh well, still has to be more comfortable then the dig site I suppose."

"Indeed, sir. What is our next move?" she asked.

John looked thoughtful for a moment and then replied, "I suppose that I shall go down to the saloon and see what sort of action there is after all, it is the sort of facility where a gentleman like myself conducts his business."

"All right, John. I will change and meet you down there and check out my competition, so to speak," Julia said. "One thing though, try not to win too much or lose too much. We want to blend in and not draw any undue attention to ourselves."

"All right, Julia. I will see you downstairs," John said as he started toward the door.

After he left, Julia changed out of her traveling dress and into her, as she thought of them, *working* clothes. The aforesaid clothing consisted of black fishnet stockings, black ankle boots with white pearl buttons, and a silky, bottle green dress that left her shoulders and enough of her chest bare to most assuredly catch a male's eye. What was even more daring, it scandalously showed her legs to just below the knee. Makeup, far more than she normally used or needed, and fancy costume jewelry in place, she went down to see how John was doing.

By this time, Morton, a/k/a Jones, was sitting at a table with several other men. One looked like a banker or lawyer, two like cattleman, and one like a drifter. There was some banter at the table as John tried to find out if any of the men had seen Chen or Ulrich. At first, John did not see her enter, so this gave her a chance to size him up. She decided, not, mind you, that she had been undecided beforehand but one should be sure of these things, that he cut a very fine figure. She thought to herself that, for a self-professed dull museum professor, he made a very passable rakish gambler indeed.

The game seemed friendly enough. No one was drunk, and the piles seemed fairly even; so far, just a friendly game. She also noted some of the other women in the saloon, some slightly more modestly dressed than she and most of the others far less modest. She decided that she had hit just the right level for her part. She went over to two of the women at the bar, who where giving her the eye and checking out the newcomer. She could see it in their eyes—competition!

She ordered a drink and tasted it. At least it was not watered down, which meant they'd picked a decent place based on the information Peter had given them. It seemed that the good father checked out the establishments that might attract his flock to sin, even if the parish was only temporary, so to speak.

Julia took her time getting to know the other two ladies, Kate and Rosey, after she convinced them that she was not looking for *business*, so to speak. She told them she had a steady fellow and pointed to John.

Rosey especially seemed to take her time looking him over, and Julia made it quite clear that he was off limits to anyone but her. Just so everyone understood she was not out to horn in on their action and they were to stay away from her man! Before long, the girls were chatting like old friends. Julia broached the subject she was interested in. "Would you pass the word I am looking for a Chinese man who likes white gals, and I am willing to pay for any information."

Kate cocked her head. "I thought you had a man," she said, nodding her head toward John, who still had not noticed them, intent as he was on the poker game.

Julia tried to look tough. "I have some unfinished business with him. He left a colleague of mine back in Chicago in the hospital. I just want to be able to tell him she sends her regards." Julia hoped this would throw the two off the scent.

Rosey looked at her. "Must have been some friendship to come all the way out here looking for him." She was obviously curious.

Julia replied, "I did not come this way to find him, but to be with a certain gentleman." She looked at Morton. "I heard that he might be out this way when we were up north in Frisco, and the greeting I have for him still stands. The girl in question was my cousin, so it is sort of family business, you understand?"

Both Kate and Rosey understood family, so they said they would pass the word around to the other ladies and let her know if they heard anything.

Julia took her leave of the two and went over to where Morton was sitting at the poker table. His eyes lit up when he saw her; he looked for a moment as if he was almost ready to start to drool. Julia had to cover his reaction. "I take it you like my new dress, dear" she drawled in a Virginian Southern accent that raised the temperature of all the men at the table several degrees.

Morton caught himself, thinking that he was supposed to know this woman intimately and strongly confirming his desire to know her that way after this mission. Covering himself, he replied, "Now I see why you wanted the greenbacks up in San Francisco, and if I do say, my dear, it was money exceptionally well spent!" While this came out, he slipped a hand around her waist and pulled her close. Trying, although he did not have to try too hard, actually it was rather easy, to leer, he said, "A kiss for good luck, lady?"

Julia gave him a look that could start dry kindling on fire at ten paces, ran her hands through his hair and gave him an exceptionally fine kiss. The other gentleman at the table joked about putting her in the pot for the hand. Morton, still looking into her eyes, retorted, "Gentleman, you never bet the whole farm. This is one game I plan to play out myself."

With that, Julia spun away. She said over her shoulder as she walked away with a sway of her hips that was in danger of setting off a seismic event, "Later, John." Again her voice was sweet as honey and smooth as silk.

John tried to clear his head and return to the game, not to mention the far more serious business of the hunt for Chen, Ulrich, and the Ratten. He told the other gents at the table he was going for a drink and he would sit out the next couple of hands. Having said that, he stood to go over to the bar and order a drink. There was some good-natured kidding about what he had to clear his mind of while he started for the bar.

When he got to the bar, he began talking to the bartender while ordering a glass of wine. After all, he mused, one, he liked wine, and two, there were supposed to be some new fine wines from the area— that and he did not want to become drunk. He found out the bartender was named Joe. Morton came to the point, "Joe, I am looking for a Chinaman who likes white girls. You seen him around?" Morton slipped a five-dollar gold piece over the bar.

Joe casually picked up the coin while he was wiping down the bar and it disappeared in his vest pocket. "I heard that such a fellow was in town, but I have not seen him personally, sir. If I may ask, why are you so interested him?" Joe asked this for the simple reason he did not want any trouble in the saloon—bad for business.

Morton smiled and replied, "My lady has some unfinished business with him and she got his scent up in Frisco. When she gets onto something, she's like a dog with a bone and tends to get uninterested in anything else, if you catch my drift." Morton used the agreed-on story that Julia had come up with and tried to look a little put out.

Joe had noticed Julia as she walked through the bar, as had virtually every other male in the establishment, except for the one cowpoke who was passed out drunk in the corner; it was that kind of walk indeed. "I can see why you would be annoyed, John. As I said, I have not laid eyes on the fellow, but for a friend," he said as he patted the coin in his pocket, "I will keep my eyes out. Where are you staying?"

John smiled. "Appreciate that, Joe. Actually, we are staying here in the Comstock. Got the word from a friend that it was a decent and fair place."

Joe smiled. "Indeed it is, sir, the finest in all of Los Angeles. I hope you enjoy your stay. As I said, if I hear anything about the fellow you are looking for, I will leave word at the desk for you and the lady. I got to tell you, John, I appreciate your taste in the finer things in life."

Morton smiled and replied, "Thank you, sir. She definitely is one of kind." With that, Morton sipped his wine and slowly went back to the card table.

CHAPTER 27

SARAH' TERROR

ater in the day, Julia found John still at the table, although some of the other men had been replaced with new players. This time, she wore a more modest dress, although the ladies at the church social, in almost any church, would have been shocked at her apparel. Coming up to John, she put her hand on his shoulder and, looking at the other gentlemen, said, "Excuse me, gentlemen, but I absolutely have to borrow Mr. Jones. I am simply famished and he promised me dinner, if you all do not mind."

Again, any man would have been hard put to deny her request; as before, besides how she looked, her voice and accent were enough to raise male temperatures and other male parts more than several degrees.

Since John had been careful to keep his winnings modest, there were no great objections to his leaving the table. He wished the other men good night and told them he hoped to see them at a later date. Rising, he offered Julia his arm, and they headed off to the other side of the Comstock for dinner. Over dinner, they were casual and acted quite intimate for the benefit of anyone watching them. When dinner was finished, they proceeded up to their room.

The door closed behind them, and Julia looked at him. "Well played sir. One might think you had experience on the boards."

John returned her gaze. "Madam, pretending I am in love with you is not very hard. Like you said, when the mission is over. By the way, do you get to keep the green dress? It, uh"—John fumbled for a way to put this—"brings out your color very well."

Julia smiled at him. "One of the small benefits of the position, sir, if you actually like the way I look in my frock."

Morton smiled back. "I believe you can count on it, Miss Verolli."

Again that sudden and somewhat unnerving change came over Julia, and she was all business again. "What have you found out, John?"

John took a minute to reorient himself to the dangerous young lady in front of him. "Nothing specific, only vague rumors that Chen, or at least someone matching Chen's description, has been around. I did show some of the gamblers Chen and Ulrich's sketch from Anderson. A couple thought they had seen Chen, but I am afraid Ulrich does not stand out too well—just another Anglo. What about your luck?"

"About the same, John. I talked to several of the girls, and they said they had not met him but heard from others about him. It most assuredly sounds like our man has been around. All we can do now is wait and keep our eyes and ears open."

John agreed and the two of them got ready for bed, although John was seriously wishing he could take a cold shower, as the sight of Julia in her green dress kept popping into his thoughts. As for Julia, she was also a young, healthy woman, and she was having her own dreams about a certain dull professor who looked the part of a rakish gambler. She kept reminding herself that, for now, she could brook no interference with the capture or termination of the pair of men in question and the removal of the threat of the Ratten.

The next day went much the same as the first. Julia continued making contacts among the women in the Comstock while John played cards and very carefully plied the daytime bartender with a gold coin and gently asked his fellow card players about Chen. Both had very little success.

The day was only broken by the word that a black tinker had arrived in town in a steam-powered wagon. The arrival was noted only because it had spooked a couple of horses. However, the folks were so fascinated with the idea of a steam-powered wagon that no offense was taken. John and Julia both took a break to look at the newfangled contraption, as some called it, a marvel of the age. They made quite appropriate noises about it as if the wagon were something they had never, ever seen before, nor, for that matter, even dreamed of, before returning to the Comstock.

For their part, Isaiah and Sarah were polite and quiet. Isaiah set off to find a storefront he could rent to set up his shop. Sarah stayed near the wagon and sat quietly and played with a rag doll she had found, as if she had never had a toy before. Truth be told, she did not remember ever having had a doll, so she played the part well—that and she listened without seeming to, as Julia had told her, trying to be invisible.

Some hours later, Isaiah returned, having found a man who would rent him a storefront. The price was high, but Isaiah was used to that. As a black man, he was used to getting cheated by white folk. He thought that not too many people were like his teammates, who saw him for what he was and not the color of his skin.

Before long, the steam wagon was rolling down the city street and down a wide alley to finally pull up at the rear of their new temporary home and business. With Sarah to help, Isaiah began to unload the wagon and set up shop. For her part, once Sarah had unloaded all the light items she could, she managed to find a broom and began to clean the place out. The store and living space had been left more than a little dirty by the previous tenant. This took most of the rest of the day, and then, exhausted, father and daughter settled in for the night.

By midmorning the next day, Isaiah was searching his brain for a way to contact John and Julia. He could not go himself since he was actually quite busy in his new shop. It had already become apparent that the area had been without a good tinker for a substantial amount of time. Finally, he decided to send Sarah for a bucket of beer for his lunch.

Dutifully, Sarah found a pail and headed down the street, into the Comstock, and up to the bar. She was looking very harmless when a trail hand saw her and snarled, "What are doing in here, you black bitch? This is a white man's bar!"

Sarah, without any pretense, looked scared, for it was obvious the man was somewhat drunk. "I am sorry, sir. I just came to get some beer for my father. I didn't mean no harm. I didn't know. We only just arrived in town yesterday!"

"Red, leave her alone. She's just a kid. Besides, if her money is good, I can serve her," said the bartender, trying to keep the peace.

"Mind your own business, bartender," snarled the drunk. "I think I will give her a lesson in manners she will remember for a long time." He began to take the belt out of his pants; his teeth showed, and he had a hard and evil expression on his face.

Sarah backed away in terror.

"Don't be goin' anywhere, gal. The lesson is just beginning!"

Just then, a harsh, loud, feminine voice cut through the crowd that had gathered to watch. "There you are, missy. I have been waiting for you!" Julia, who elbowed her way through the crowd, had a look on her face like a thunderhead about to break loose in a storm of epic proportions. Reaching forward, she grabbed Sarah by the arm and screeched at her, "I told you to get my things ready and paid you in advance. And what did you do but disappear. You will pay for that insolence, missy!" Turning to the trail hand she said, "Thank you kindly for finding her, sir. I can handle her from here on!" With that, she began to drag poor Sarah, who by now was terrified, out of the bar toward the hotel side.

"Please, Miss Julia, you are hurting me," cried the little girl, now in almost hysterics.

"Just you wait till I get you up to the room, missy," yelled Julia.

Red, trying to figure out what was going on through his alcohol-induced haze, yelled, "Hey, lady, you are spoiling my fun!" With that, he started for the pair.

Julia turned, and in a move so smooth she made it look like oil on glass, a derringer appeared in her hand. Looking at the cowpoke, she snarled, "This is between me and my maid. Do you have any problems with that, sir?"

Red came to a dead stop and, looking down the twin barrels of the derringer, simply said, "No ma'am; just make sure she don't come in here no more. This here bar is for white folk."

Julia looked at him; her eyes seemed to go from round pupils to snakelike slits. "Do not, sir, tell me where I can and where I cannot send my servant. Are we clear!" This time, Julia looked more like a female rattlesnake ready to strike with the double-barreled fangs in her hand than a pretty thing who should be on the arm of a gambler.

It was about this time when John showed up, having heard the commotion; in all truth, it was virtually impossible not to hear it if you were in the building or even near it outside. Tapping Red on the shoulder, he said in a low voice. "Sir, I know the lady, and when she is like this, believe me, I would not want to make her any angrier than she already is. Let me buy you a beer, and I will tell you about her temper."

Seeing the look in Julia's eyes and the way she handled the small gun, Red, being a reasonable drunk, decided this was excellent advice and turned to follow John to the bar.

After several glasses of beer later, Red and John Jones had become fast friends. Red was trying to figure out what a classy act like John Jones would see in a Texas-sized twister like Julia. This kind of thinking cemented the idea in John's mind that a) Red was none too bright, and b) he was more drunk than he thought himself to be if he could not see why a man, any man, would want Julia by his side, especially the way she looked in her green dress.

Julia continued dragging poor Sarah through the lobby of the hotel and up the stairs, all the while berating her. She opened the door to the room she shared with John and pushed Sarah into it and then followed behind and slammed the door shut.

Sarah stood there shaking and crying.

Julia got down on one knee and hugged her. "Sarah, are you all right?" she said in a scared voice, all traces of the enraged harpy gone.

Sarah sniffed. "Miss Julia, what happened? Why were you so mad?"

Julia held her out at arm's length and said, "I love you, and I also told you to be careful, did I not, young lady! I am sorry I scared you, but that man might have hurt you badly or even killed you. I could not break John's and my cover. It was the only way I could think of to get you out of there fast enough and away from that drunk." Looking at her and smiling, she added, "Silly, you're my sister, remember."

Sarah wiped her eyes and literally flew into Julia's arms. "I was so scared. I never seen you like that. I didn't know." She was crying, but the tears seemed to have turned into happy ones.

"Well, you scared me too. I could not stand to see you hurt. You are still the only family I have. And it is *saw*, young lady, not *seen*." She hugged the little girl even tighter.

Sarah looked at Julia and said, "I am sorry I doubted you. I should have known you would not hurt me."

Julia smiled at her. "In a way, I am glad you did not know. It was a very convincing show, was it not?"

With that, the two girls started to giggle together.

"Well, I guess it is easy to fool men, is it not?" said Sarah with a shy smile.

"Yes, but let us not push out luck. I cannot lose you." Julia looking down at Sarah and went on. "All right, if you cannot come here, where are you and Isaiah? We will have to come to you."

Sarah told her where she and I Isaiah had set up shop as they both settled down and got their emotions under control.

Julia looked at Sarah. "All right, missy, you are going to have to be punished."

Sarah looked shocked and fearful again.

Julia looked at her with a head cocking gesture, as if to say *silly person*. "Remember, we are playing parts, just like in the theater. Now, first we have to make it look like you have been chastised."

With that, Julia reached out and tore Sarah's dress here and there. "Now for a good whipping." With that, Julia got up and went over to her makeup. She started with some red rouge, which she streaked across Sarah's shoulders and back. Next she added some dark blue to make the marks look like bruising. She finished off by messing up the little girl's hair and adding some more dark red under her eyes to make it look like she had been crying even more than she had. "Okay, young lady, you are ready to go on stage," she said, showing Sarah what she looked like in a mirror.

Sarah was shocked at her reflection in the glass. She looked as if she had been beaten very badly.

"Okay, now this is really important. You have to look scared and hurt. Now you go running down the stairs and straight back to Isaiah, all right. Tell him we will come by tomorrow. Ready?"

Sarah looked at Julia and quite firmly said, "I will not let my sister down!"

"All right, off you go." With that, Julia opened the door, and for the benefit of anyone who might be in earshot, she yelled, "The next time I tell you to do something, girl, I expect it done right away and done right!"

At those words Sarah was off down the stairs and down the sidewalk. Even in the bar they heard Julia's voice, and Red looked up just in time to see a badly beaten Sarah come running down the stairs and into the street. This scene only convinced Red even more that his new friend, John, had been out in the sun too long to be shacking up with a rattlesnake like Julia. A man needed another beer, or perhaps two after seeing what she done to that poor little colored gal!

Sarah did not stop till she got to the store where Isaiah had set up their cover. Isaiah almost went into shock when he saw his daughter. It took a few minutes to get him calmed down and show him it was just Miss Julia's makeup and that she was not really hurt, well except for her arm where Julia had dragged her up to her room. She hugged him while he calmed down. He had been so scared that he was shaking, but eventfully his breathing became normal again. He held her and said quite forcefully "Girl, do not ever never scare me like that again!"

CHAPTER 28

A Lead at Last

By the next day, the two sharpshooters had made contact by the simple expedience of playing cards with John at the saloon. The two lost some money, and so that there were no hard feelings, John offered to buy them a drink, which allowed them to get over to a corner by themselves to talk. Julia, seeing what was going on, joined them and sat on Morton's lap to keep up the illusion for others to see. The men told John and Julia that they had heard nothing, and John told them that, as far as they knew, Chen had been in town but, so far, they'd uncovered nothing more. The drinking party broke up, and each went back to quiet snooping.

Just after lunch, John, with Julia on his arm, went for a walk, intent on seeing Isaiah in his new shop. The shop was excellent. Not only did it give Isaiah and Sarah access to quite a few members of the local populace, it also could serve as a staging area for the team. Several people were in the shop, either with items to be repaired—ranging from clocks to sewing machines—or just checking out the novelty of the new tinkerer's shop in town. For the benefit of the other patrons, Julia looking at John and said, "Remember, you promised me a new fancy clockwork, darling." Again, she spoke in that rich accent she'd adopted for her current role.

Sarah heard them and came out smiling. Julia saw her and, with a brief shake of her head, sounded stern. "I trust, young woman, we will not have to have a repeat of yesterday's lesson." She looked at the little girl with a very dark expression.

Sarah caught on quickly. "No, ma'am, I will have your things laid out proper like," she said and tilted her head toward the floor, looking very scared.

Julia and John continued to look around the store until, finally, the rest of the customers had left. Quickly, Isaiah went forward to put up a "closed for lunch" sign in the window. All four relaxed a bit, and Julia told Sarah that she had put on a fine performance and hugged her. Sarah lapped up the praise from her big sister like a kitten with a saucer of fresh cream.

Isaiah looked at Julia. "I have to tell you, lady, I almost had a heart attack yesterday when Sarah came in. But thank you for saving her from that drunk!"

Julia smiled and, holding Sarah, said, "I am sorry to have scared you so, Isaiah, but it was the only thing I could think of fast enough without breaking cover. You know, if she doesn't become a tinker or a museum professor, like someone I know, Sarah could find herself in the limelight on a stage." With this, she gave Sarah an extra hug.

Isaiah seemed somewhat shocked at this. "I am not sure if I approve of my daughter being an actress." He sounded quite concerned, as if acting were not a proper career for a young woman, which in all honesty, he did not think it was.

Julia looked at Sarah, and they both broke into giggles. John looked at Isaiah, who by now was looking somewhat stunned and remarked, "I think this giggling is starting to get out of hand."

Soon they'd all regained their composure and began to swap information. Julia told Sarah and Isaiah that, although Chen had been seen, no one had a fix on him. Isaiah, in turn, stunned them by telling the pair that he might have a lead on Ulrich. Julia gasped. "What? How did you do that?"

"It was not any too hard. I think he walked in my shop here." Isaiah smiled.

"What?" said John and Julia so close together that it sounded as if it were one voice. Julia went on, "What do you mean, he just walked in here?"

Isaiah shook his head. "Well, I cannot for sure say it was him, since I'd never really laid eyes on him. Yesterday, a man walked in who matched the description and sketch we got from Anderson, although this fellow was clean shaven and did not have a mustache. Anyhow, he opened the door and came in for some repairs on some scientific instruments he had brought with him. The fellow had a heavy German sounding accent."

John looked stunned but got out, "Did you get any information on his whereabouts or where he might be set up?"

Isaiah looked downcast. "No, cannot say I did. Shop was pretty busy; you know how it is."

Julia sputtered, "Isaiah, you had him in your grasp and you let him get away!"

Isaiah gave her a hangdog look. "Well, Miss Julia, it is a new store, my daughter got whipped real good by her mistress, and I had customers all over the place. Why, there has not been a proper tinker in these parts for ages. Seems the locals were pretty desperate for someone to repair their various mechanicals. I mean that fellow was sure upset when I had to tell him his repairs could not be done right away while he waited. In fact, he was quite upset when I said it would be the day after tomorrow before I could have them ready. I am sorry!" Julia looked stunned as Isaiah broke out into a big grin.

"Isaiah, that was brilliant." She threw her arms around him and hugged him. Turning to Sarah, she said, "Did I mention to you that your father is very smart and clever, Sarah!"

Sarah, with a smile and a curtsy, replied, "It runs in the family."

Julia smiled with a nod to Sarah. "Indeed it does, young lady."

John broke in at this point. "So he's coming back. Do you know when exactly?"

"He seemed quite put out that his equipment, including a microscope and small whirlie thing, he called it a centrifuge, among a bunch of other lab items, could not be ready that day," Isaiah replied. "I told him after ten o'clock tomorrow, so I would expect him pretty early. Just so you know, he will need a small wagon or buckboard to cart it all—there were several pieces to repair—so it should not be too hard to trail him."

Julia took up. "Wonderful. That gives us time to contact Sam and John. If we keep back, we should be able to trail him back to their lab. Did you notice which way he went?"

Isaiah shook his head. "Afraid not. He turned the corner just down the street and disappeared. He mentioned something about it was time to get more supplies. So that might not be his actual direction. In truth, it was hard to see. I did have lot of customers in the shop. And like you, I didn't want to break cover being too curious about him."

John stood there musing. "I will alert Tinsman and Kirkland so we can cover both ends of the street. I will act as a backup, but we could use another set of eyes. And while I hate to say this, Julia, from what you have told me, you are not the greatest horsewoman."

Julia looked annoyed. "You are right about that, John. I am all right but not great. However, I think I am past due for confession. Don't you think?"

John just looked at her. "What?"

Julia smiled and, looking completely remorseful, replied, "Dearest, as a man who professes interest in me, do you not worry about my immortal soul? Being a good Catholic girl, I really should go to church. After all, I have been a wanton woman of late." She looked rather guilty at this.

John smiled, finally catching on. "Oh that Catholic Church thing. That's where you have a private talk with the priest, is it not? I never can get used to that. It just seems so odd to me."

Julia smiled and put her arm in John's, and the two bid farewell to Isaiah and Sarah and walked out.

Sarah looked confused. "Poppa, what is Miss Julia talking about? She is not bad."

Isaiah smiled down at his daughter. "Sweetheart, for a Catholic to go to confession, she needs a priest to hear it. Now, who do we know who could do that?"

Sarah's eyes lit up. "She's going to see Father Peter!"

Isaiah just smiled and nodded.

John and Julia split up. John was off to find the two sharpshooters and update them on what had happened so they could begin to make plans. Julia went over several streets to find Saint Gabriel's Church, where Father Peter had taken up residence, trying to blend in. The church was pretty much empty, except for several elderly female members saying the rosary and lighting candles. Julia went to the rectory and knocked. The door was opened by a young priest, who seemed shocked to find before him an attractive young woman of questionable morals, at least based upon her dress. "Can I help you, miss?" inquired the priest.

Julia looked at him and smiled. "Yes, please, Father. I am looking for Father Harrigan. I was led to believe he is in residence here."

The young father looked concerned. "What, may I ask, is your business with him?" He was obviously still wondering what a woman like Julia, or at least a woman like the one Julia appeared to be in her disguise, would want with a visiting priest.

Julia licked her lips. "Father Peter, was my, uh, confessor when I was back east in the city, and I felt that I just needed someone to talk to!" Julia looked distraught and started to cry a bit.

"Oh, my dear young woman, please come in and be seated. I will fetch the father for you." This last came out as the poor young priest was fussing over Julia, who looked to be in a high degree of agitation. After handing her a glass of water, the young priest disappeared down the hall and shortly returned with Father Peter in tow. He was babbling to Father Peter about a fallen woman who wanted to see him and how she was so upset.

As Father Peter appeared, Julia looked at him with hopeful eyes and jumped to her feet and ran over to him. "Oh, Father, I need you to hear my confession. Please help me!"

Peter put his arm around Julia. "There, lass, I am here for you; it will be all right. Father Paul, if you do not think he will mind, I will use the monsignor's study for her confession and counseling."

Father Paul looked a bit shocked. "You do not want to go into the church and use the confessional?"

Peter looked at the younger priest, trying not to rattle him. "It is all right, son. I do know the young lady from back east, and since we are standing here, it a little late to worry about the anonymity of the confessional, do you not think?"

The young priest blinked and replied, "Well, I suppose, Father." Obviously this situation was something quite new to him, and he was more than a little confused but bowed to Peter's age and experience. "I do not think the monsignor will mind." With that, he went over and opened a door into a combination study and office and let Father Peter, his arm still around a weeping Julia, in.

As the door closed, Peter took his arm off Julia and just looked at her. "Julia, do you not think you just went a little too Buffalo Bill Cody with poor Father Paul? The lad is only just out of the seminary. This is his first posting. He does not have the experience to handle such situations yet!"

Julia looked slightly chagrined as she stared at the floor, which was definitely a nonstandard Julia look. "Sorry about that, Father. But I did not want to break our cover. I mean, why else would a priest be meeting with a fallen woman like me?" She tried to sneak in a small smile.

"Because it is my job, Julia. And you, young lady, obviously are a woman in need of confession! Dear, I ask, what has been happening between you and John?"

Julia looked shocked. "Nothing at all, Father. We are just teammates. Although I suppose that I should have a confession," she admitted as she looked at the floor. She continued as she noted Father Peter starring at her, "I have had some rather impure thoughts about him. He really does look quite handsome as a gambler, I mean, not that he did not look handsome before. But, oh dear," Julia sputtered.

Poor Father Peter, as usual around Julia, just rolled his eyes. "All right, lass, before we get to the business that undoubtedly brought you here, I believe I should hear your confession, young lady!"

Julia started her confession in all seriousness now, for at the end of the day, as one would expect with a family name like Verolli—at least that was the name sewn in her clothing—she did have memories of going to Mass, so she tried to be a good Catholic, even if she did nasty but fun things like blowing things up and removing problems or problem people on behalf of the United States government (at Anderson's direction) and even if she did not get to church very often. It was obvious that she'd tried to maintain the belief that the sanctions, as she called the assassinations, she had carried out over the last three years had involved people who no one would mourn because of their evil. When she was done, Father Peter assigned her penance. And then they started on the Ratten business.

As she finished her report on what had transpired so far, Father Peter looked serious. "Finally, we have a sound lead on these two monsters. I cannot get the looks of those men at the railhead out of my thoughts, Julia; they haunt me every night. The Church teaches us that we all have a part to do in God's plan. I can only wonder if my military experience was not part of his plan?"

"Don't worry, Peter. We will stop them." Then her voice dropped down to a whisper. "We have to!" She shook herself and seemed to find the iron for her spine again and looked up at Peter. "Can you help tomorrow? We will need everyone to cover the various routes out of town."

Peter nodded his head. "Indeed, lass. I am just a guest here, not truly assigned to the parish, so I have a lot more freedom than I normally would have. Where and when should I meet up with the rest of you?"

Julia smiled. "Can you get a horse?"

"Aye, lass. Being a priest does have some benefits. I will have no problem borrowing a mount," affirmed a smiling Peter.

"All right, Peter. Meet John and me at the Comstock about eight o'clock tomorrow morning. I know you know where it is, since you directed John there. And just how does a man of the cloth know of such an establishment, Father?" Julia chided.

"Yes, I know where it is. And a good priest, at least one who has served in the Five Points, wants to know where to look for his lost sheep when their families are worried. Just because I do not have a blue uniform on does not mean that I have no use for intelligence on the enemy, even if that enemy is Satan himself," said Peter quite forcefully. At that point he sounded a bit more like a first sergeant than a priest.

Julia smiled at him and reached over and gave him a kiss on the cheek. "Thank you for all your help and for hearing my confession, Father. It did feel good. I guess I did need it. I am having some problems I don't quite know how to explain."

"Just doing my job, ma'am," said Peter in his best imitation of a western drawl, which actually would have fooled no one, since it sounded far more Irish than western. He went on in his regular voice, "What kind of problems, Julia?"

Julia looked somewhat confused. "I've never had a family before, and I do not want to lose the one I have."

Peter smiled. "Are you talking about John?"

"No, Father," replied Julia, "although I am beginning to hope he will still be interested in me after this affair and he has a chance to reflect on the kind of woman I am. I do not know if a proper museum professor like him would want a woman like me. I guess I am not a very nice young lady. No, I was talking about Sarah. I want to live up to what she thinks of me. I told her that, in Chicago when I hurt the conductor, I was afraid she would be scared of me."

"Was she?" asked Peter.

"No, she told me she still loved me. I have tried to be honest with her. It is just—I do not know how to deal with all this. And what will I do if she is in danger and to save her I have to jeopardize the mission?"

"Julia, there are times we are all are faced with such decisions, and all we can do is pray for God to give us the wisdom to make the right choice. Simply ask yourself, would I give up Sarah's love just to make my life easier?" Peter said this in his quiet, soothing voice.

Julia looked up at him almost in shock. "No, I would never give up my sister's love, for that is how I have come to see her. I know that may seem silly. It has been the most wonderful thing! Especially helping her to heal and grow and to see her become a young lady. I never had anyone to giggle with before. It is truly the most amazing and delightful thing."

Peter just looked at her and winked and saw Julia's face light up. "Thank you, Peter, for helping me to understand my feelings."

Peter smiled. "Helping people figure out the truth is one of the best parts of my vocation, Julia. As for John, I think he feels that, as long as you do not kill any of the museum staff or blow up the building, you would make a fine wife for a proper professor. For what my opinion is worth to you, so do I. As a side note I personally would suggest no Gatling guns or baskets of explosives for wedding presents."

Julia hugged him and cried real tears this time.

As they opened the door to the study, Julia saw Father Paul standing there, obviously curious as to what had transpired.

Julia clutched her handbag and looked at Peter. "Thank you, Father, it was so comforting to know someone still cares and does not judge woman like me too harshly." Julia sniffed as she swept out the door to the rectory.

For his part, Peter just rolled his eyes again and sighed as Julia closed the door behind her. He gestured to Father Paul to indicate that he did not want to know what had gone on, merely saying, "Saloon girls, even they need saving, son. Remember, we are here to save everyone." With that, he walked back to the room he was occupying, thinking about who he could borrow a horse and tack from.

CHAPTER 29

NOT ALL PLANS GO THE WAY
THEY SHOULD, AGAIN

t eight the next morning, the sharpshooters, Peter, John, and Julia met in front of the Comstock and began heading over to Isaiah and Sarah's storefront. The men took positions down the street in both directions so that at least one of them could have a fair chance of trailing Ulrich back to the pair's laboratory. Julia, meanwhile, had gone into the store to see Isaiah and Sarah and supply backup in case any problems came up inside. Then the team settled down to wait.

At almost exactly ten o'clock, a small wagon pulled up, and a man stepped down. He was a big man with broad shoulders and a muscular build. His hair was dark, his face had a scar as if from a knife fight—or, more probably, a duel—and he walked with the firm tread of a man who was sure of himself and used to power. He tied up the horse and went into the store. While he was in the store, all the team members double-checked the copies of the sketches they had of Ulrich. His facial hair was different, and he wore a different haircut, but he was their man.

Shortly after the target went inside, Sarah came out and started sweeping the boardwalk in front of the store, the prearranged signal that Ulrich was in the store. A few minutes later, the man came out and, with Isaiah's help, started loading equipment into the wagon. Isaiah motioned Sarah back into the shop, and the man unhitched his horse, climbed into the wagon, and took up the reins.

The four men watched him start down the street right toward Father Peter who was wearing just some old clothes and looked nothing like a priest. As the wagon passed, Peter spurred his horse and followed it slowly down the street, letting it build up a lead so that it did not look as if he were tailing the wagon.

Peter kept the wagon in sight as it headed out toward the edge of the city. He was careful to hold back and blend in with the other wagons and horses in the street wherever he could. He had not seen any of the other members of the team, but he wasn't surprised. The men had been well spread out to cover all the various routes away from Isaiah's shop. He figured they would move fast to catch up, but for now, he had to assume that he was on his own.

Meanwhile, John and the other two men were dealing with problems of their own. A riot had started in the city's Chinatown, which had grown faster than expected as result of the government's urgency to build more railroads to shift troops around. Chinatown was almost adjacent to Isaiah's shop, and chaos had taken hold of the area surrounding it. The remaining team members had completely lost track of the wagon and Peter. John cursed, but it was all they could do to protect the shop and their friends from the mob. John had no idea what had sparked the troubles, but it was almost evening before order was restored. By then, the sun was low on the horizon, and they had no idea where Peter had gone.

Julia said that she would go back to the rectory to see if Peter had returned. John detailed Tinsman to go with her for safety, not knowing whether the trouble had completely burned out. Meanwhile, he and the other sharpshooter would head back to the Comstock to see if Peter had been there.

Julia knocked at the door, and it was opened by the same young priest she had met on her last visit. "Hello, Father Paul. Is Father Peter here?"

"No, Miss Verolli, was it not? He left early this morning, and I have not seen him all day. Is there anything I can help you with?"

The young priest smiled what he thought was a reassuring smile, although to Julia he looked more like a boy trying to play priest; she remembered Peter had told her this was his first posting right out of the seminary.

Julia just smiled. "No, Father. It is just that he said he would meet me for coffee, and he did not show up, and I was worried. From when I knew him back east, he was always quite prompt when he was ministering to us girls." Julia could see from the look on Father Paul's face that he was trying to digest the idea of this ministry!

Paul thought for a moment. "Well, he did borrow a horse from one of the parishioners. We can check to see if he knows something. I have to say, I am now a bit worried what with the disturbance in town this morning. I understand that it was some anti-Chinese trouble, just like the town experienced some years ago, or so I have heard!"

Julia looked worried and replied, "It was quite terrible, Father. Several men were killed. I am very worried about Father Peter, so if it would not be too much trouble, Father, I really am very concerned."

"I will get my hat," replied Paul.

Soon the three of them were walking down the street. Julia had introduced Tinsman, who'd stepped into the light when Paul returned with his hat, as a friend who had offered to accompany her while she went to check on Father Peter. The trio turned the corner and, within another block, were in front of a livery stable, where Paul banged on the door.

"What is all that noise?" sounded a gruff voice from inside. The door opened and an older woman in pants and a shirt stood there. "Father Paul, what can I do for you?" the woman asked, looking around him at Julia and then at Tinsman.

"Maggie, I was just checking. Have you seen Father Peter? He seems to be missing," was Paul's reply.

"No, but the horse he borrowed came back," said the woman. "I didn't think anything of it 'cause I told him the bay would come back here if he just turned him loose. That way, he wouldn't have to walk all the way back to the church."

"Oh dear," said Julia. "Madam, do you have any horses we can rent, for I fear the worst?"

Before long, Julia and Tinsman were heading back for John and the others. They had to walk, as Julia's green dress was not exactly suitable for riding.

As they arrived at the Comstock, Tinsman hitched his horse and went in to fetch John and the other sharpshooter.

When they came out, Julia said quickly, "John, Peter is missing. His horse came back without him!"

"Julia, go tell Isaiah. We'll get our horses and meet you at the shop," said John.

The men ran off toward the livery stable, and Julia took off for the storefront, after she'd changed into something more suitable for riding.

As she pulled up in front of the store, she yelled out, and before long, Isaiah and Sarah came out. "What's going on, Julia?" asked Isaiah.

"Peter is missing. His horse came back without him. John and the others are coming, but we are not even sure where to start!" cried Julia in obvious distress.

"All right. We know the general direction they were heading in, almost due east and into the foothills." By this time, John and the others had arrived. "We are losing light," Isaiah said. "You go ahead, and Sarah and I will join you as quick as we can."

The impromptu posse rode off, following the road they'd last seen Peter and Ulrich take.

As they left, Sarah and Isaiah went behind the store and started getting the steam wagon ready. It didn't take as long as it might have, since Isaiah had taken the precaution of firing it up when the riot started, in case he had to get Sarah out in a hurry. "Sarah, do you remember the start-up sequence?"

Sarah looked at her father. "Yes, Poppa. I know it real good."

Isaiah smiled at his daughter. "All right, keep getting the wagon ready to roll. I have some new fittings for it that I've been working on." With that, Isaiah disappeared into the back of the shop and soon reappeared carrying some large brass barrels. With speed and dexterity, he mounted these on the wagon while Sarah minded the gauges and fed the boiler firebox. Soon, they were ready to roll. Father and daughter pulled their goggles down and the wagon took off, again scaring some horses. But neither paid any attention to this; they thought only of finding their friend.

As they reached the open country outside of town, the riders began to fan out, looking for any sign of Peter. They knew they were racing against time, as the sun was on the horizon and it would be dark soon. Slowing to a canter so as not to miss anything, they rode on along the trail. Before long, they heard the steam wagon coming and saw it appear over a low hill they had just crossed, with Isaiah and Sarah on the driver's seat.

The wagon began to slow and, before long, it pulled to a halt.

Isaiah yelled. "Anything yet?"

John replied, "We have found some tracks, but we're not sure they're his. We'll have to stop soon. We're losing the light."

"Julia, tie your horse in back of the wagon and climb in," Isaiah said. "I'll need some help."

Julia wondered what Isaiah was talking about as she watched him working on some new addition to the wagon, but she knew better than to not trust him. Soon she was in the wagon and Isaiah was giving her a fast course in handling a portable lamp like that found on a warship but smaller. He showed her that by adjusting a control on the side of it, she could either throw an intense, narrow beam or more weakly light an entire area.

"Isaiah, this is brilliant. Are there no end of uses for this new steam wagon of yours?"

Isaiah smiled. "Probably, but I have not found it yet." Then an annoyed look crossed his face. "I thought the searchlights up *after* the attack on the cave. Should have come up with them sooner."

With that, the wagon and riders continued down the road, with Sarah at the controls. Julia found herself somewhat jealous of her little sister. "Sarah, you must teach me how to run the steam wagon."

Sarah, for her part, was thrilled by the idea that Julia was asking her to teach her something! "I will, Julia, if Papa lets me, that is!"

Isaiah kept moving the light on his side, looking for any clue that would lead them to Father Peter. "We will see," was his noncommittal answer.

The area was getting dark now that the sun had set, but with the beams of the lights sweeping the area, the team was able to keep searching.

Suddenly, Julia shouted, "John, over there!" She narrowed the beam and shown it on a figure staggering over the ground.

John spurred his horse and was there before the others. It was Peter, who has bleeding from a head wound. Before long, the wagon and other riders had pulled up. Julia jumped down and was helping Peter get to a sitting position, while trying to clean the wound. As soon as she could get the wagon secure, Sarah was beside her, helping her.

Julia gave her friend some water to drink and continued working on his wound.

John knelt beside him. "Peter, what happened? Did you get ambushed by Ulrich?"

Peter looked pained, and his breath was coming slowly. "No, John, nothing so dramatic. I was following him at a distance and watching him instead of where the horse was going. Stupid! There was a rattlesnake, and the horse reared and threw me to the ground. I hit my head. That is getting to be positively epidemic in this group." He patted Julia's hand on his head and tried to smile at her—without much success, as it caused him to wince in pain.

"Oh, Father Peter, are you all right?" asked Sarah. Both of the girls were now fussing over him.

"I will live, lass, but now I know what Julia felt like at the cave," replied Peter as he shifted his gaze to Julia. "At least I followed him this far. I was keeping a good distance, so I don't think he saw me or heard the horse throw me."

John asked simply, "What makes you say that Peter?"

Peter looked at him. "Because I'm still alive! Those two would kill anyone they thought a threat."

"All too true, Peter. We may as well get you back to town. There's not much we can do out here in the dark, and the steam wagon, like you said about the Congress, is none too subtle," said John as he helped Peter to his feet.

Julia gently said, "Father Peter, perhaps you should ride in the wagon. You do not seem too steady on your feet yet."

Peter looked at her. "I hate to say it, but I think you are right, Julia. My head feels like a church bell was ringing in it."

With some help from the others, Peter managed to climb up into the wagon. He sat in the driver's seat by Sarah, as it at least had some springs. "Are you sure you know how to do this Sarah?" he asked, looking at the bewildering array of valves, levers, and gauges and then at Sarah again, who seemed quite small and very young for all this.

Sarah looked at Peter, who she loved almost as much as Isaiah and Julia. "I can do it, Father Peter. Papa says I am a good steam wagon driver! I control the wagon by how much steam I give to each of the power wheels, so I do not have to turn a wheel."

Peter made the Sign of the Cross and gripped the seat tightly. Sarah pulled down her goggles and began pulling on levers and opening valves and then tapped a gauge or two. Much to Peter's astonishment at Sarah's abilities, before long the wagon was turned around and the team was headed back into Los Angeles, with Isaiah and Julia handling the lights so that everyone could see.

Tinsman and the other sharpshooter accompanied Peter to a doctor's office, while John and Julia went back to the Comstock. Isaiah and Sarah returned the steam wagon to its place behind their store and secured it.

When they got to their room, Julia and John were both mad. "Of all the times for a riot to break out. Now they got away again!" fumed Julia.

"I know; it was rotten luck, but at least we have an idea where he was headed, which narrows down our search area quite a bit. Hopefully, we can pick up something tomorrow," said John, trying to calm Julia down, though, in truth, he was fuming at the loss of their quarry too.

CHAPTER 30

SARAH MAKES A FRIEND

The next day proved to be clear, as most of the days in Los Angeles were. Julia and John went down to Isaiah's shop, only to find the sharpshooters already there.

Tinsman looked at John. "What is the plan, Major?" he asked using his rank since no one else was within hearing range.

John looked thoughtful. "We will scout the area, starting where Peter lost Ulrich's trail." Turning to Julia, he added, "Julia would you go and check on Peter? I think one of us should stay behind in case anything comes up in town, and as noted before, you are not too good a horsewoman. Nor are you used to scouting in the wilderness."

Julia looked annoyed and rather coolly replied, "Thank you for pointing out my deficiencies, Professor!"

John swallowed and noticeably paled.

"However, you are right," Julie added. "So I am off to check on the good father." She looked around at the rest of the team. "Good luck, good hunting, and do be careful. Just remember who and what we are dealing with." With a swirl of her skirts, Julia was out the door.

John looked worried. "I do not think that went any too well," he said as he watched Julia go down the walk.

Isaiah snickered behind him. "I hope they taught groveling in that fancy college of yours, Professor. I think you are gonna need it."

John replied sarcastically over his shoulder, "Thank you for the support!"

At this, all the members of the team, including Sarah, laughed.

"All right," said John, "let's get started. I suggest extra canteens and some rations. This could be a long day."

Sarah looked up at Isaiah. "I will pack us lunches, Poppa."

Isaiah looked surprised. "Hold on here, girl! What is this *us* business, girl? Who said you are going?"

Sarah looked firm. "Someone has to drive the steam wagon, Poppa—if you plan to ride a horse—and I can do it." She crossed her arms over her chest. "Besides, who will look out for you otherwise?"

"Sarah, this could be dangerous," Isaiah replied. "You do not know these men or their creations. They are pure evil."

Sarah remained just as firm. "This is just a scouting mission. We will stay back, so it will be safe."

Isaiah shook his head. "All right, but you stay out of harm's way. *Are we clear?*"

Sarah smiled, hugged Isaiah, and said, "Yes, Poppa," in a dutiful, innocent voice. Then she disappeared into the back where the living quarters where and began to pack some food.

Isaiah looked at the door Sarah had gone through and then turned to John. "Remember, John, when you told me she was learning too much from Julia?"

John just smiled and nodded.

"You were right." Isaiah snorted in the manner of fathers immemorial, whose children, especially daughters, are growing up too fast to suit them, which, throughout recorded history, has been the vast majority of the time.

Soon the team was headed out of town. Isaiah and Sarah would catch up since it took a little bit longer to fire up the steam wagon and get it ready to roll than it did to saddle up a horse. However, before long, Sarah and Isaiah were rolling out of town on the track they'd followed the day before.

They hadn't traveled far when Sarah shouted and pointed. "There they are!"

Isaiah pulled the wagon up to the riders. Looking down, he asked, "See anything yet, John?"

"Not so far, Isaiah. We've started to sweep the area, but this is a regular track, so there are a lot of prints. There is really no way to tell which are the freshest ones," replied Morton in frustration.

Isaiah looked thoughtful for a moment. "John, Sarah and I are going to take the wagon up to the top of that hill to see what we can see. I have a telescope in the wagon that is too big for horseback. It will allow me to see farther. If I spot anything, I will give you a single toot on the whistle. Otherwise, we will continue to work along the ridge line looking for vantage points."

"Sounds like a good plan, Isaiah."

With that, Morton turned his horse around and the three riders fanned out and began walking their horses, looking for any tracks or signs that could help.

Isaiah and Sarah headed off for the ridgeline with Isaiah driving. They stopped just below the crest. Isaiah climbed down off the wagon and unloaded a bulky telescope from the back. He looked up at his daughter. "Sarah, take the controls. If anything happens, you go get the major, all right?"

For her part, Sarah looked nervous. "Papa, you be careful. I cannot lose you!"

Isaiah smiled. "It will be all right. I am just going to the top to get a clear view, but plans do not always go the way you expect them to. Therefore, it is always good to have a backup, and you are the best backup I know."

Sarah still looked nervous, but she smiled. Her father trusted her, not only with the steam wagon but to watch his back. She knew she would not let him down, just as Miss Julia wouldn't.

Sarah somehow managed to watch the gauges and Isaiah at the same time. He carefully set up the telescope and slowly scanned the area. After about ten minutes of staring through the telescope, he carefully folded it up and returned. He set the telescope in the back of the steam wagon and then climbed in beside it. "Sarah, do you see that next hill over there?" he asked, pointing.

"Yes, Poppa," Sarah responded.

"If you would, please, young lady, take us over there and stop just below the crest," a smiling Isaiah said to her.

Sarah pulled down her goggles and slowly opened the main steam valve. Going easy over the rough ground, the wagon rolled along. Isaiah was proud of her. He had to admit that he could not have done better himself. Soon, they were stopping, and the earlier process repeated itself—unfortunately, with the same result.

They moved three more times, each resulting the same lack of helpful sightings.

After Isaiah reloaded the telescope, he looked ahead. "Sarah, the terrain is a little rougher up ahead. It looks like I'm going to have to hike a little farther. Do you see that jumble of boulders there at the base of the hill? I need you to head for that. You can pull up the wagon in some shade and wait for me, okay?"

Sarah was none too happy with this arrangement. Voicing her disapproval, she argued, "Poppa, I will not be able to keep an eye on you!"

Isaiah responded, "Sarah, it will be all right. Believe me, I am not the hero type. This is just some scouting."

Sarah looked somewhat dubious for she was quite positive, as daughters are wont to be, that her father was indeed the hero type. Still she would do what Poppa said to do. Again, she opened the valve and the wagon went rolling forward ever so slowly, as the terrain was getting rougher. As directed, she pulled up in a shady patch that was just about surrounded by the big rocks. As Isaiah started to get the telescope out, Sarah said, "Remember, the professor said I was responsible for your care, and I do not want to get into trouble with him." She did her best to look stern, just like Miss Julia did.

"Yes, madam. I told you, just scouting. You might want to take some time to eat. This will take me a while. I will probably be gone an hour at least."

"All right, Papa," said Sarah as she secured the steam wagon controls.

After she was done, she climbed into the back of the wagon and gave it another shovel of coal to make sure they had steam up in case there was a problem. That done, she pulled out the hamper she had prepared and fixed a small lunch for herself.

She had just about finished preparing the lunch when she heard a crying sound like an animal, maybe a kitten, from around the rocks. She climbed down and went to find whatever was making the noise. Sarah listened intently for the source of the noise, and she softly cried out, "Hello. Where are you? I can help."

The noise seemed to intensify as she continued her search. Finally, she came around a rock, and there was a creature with its leg trapped under a rock that had shifted. Sarah eyed the creature with wide-open eyes. The creature was silent and just lay there looking back at her. She noted that it was a little taller than she was and clothed in some rather colorful cloth and leather. It looked like nothing Sarah had ever seen. The creature, Sarah was not sure what to call it, was sort of human looking, with a reddish-gray skin. Its nose and mouth were more pronounced than those of anyone Sarah had ever seen. The ears stood out and were larger than any human ears, and it had a funny kind of mustache. All told, it was the oddest person—or so she decided to think of it, as there was something human to it—that she had ever seen. But whatever it was, it was obviously trapped by the rock and hurt.

Sarah ran over to it, and the thing just looked at her. She began looking for a way to free it, and as she was doing that, she talked to it soothingly. "Do not worry," she cooed. "I will not harm you. I want to help."

She obviously could not move the rock under which the creature was trapped. It was too big, and what's more, it was wedged solidly in the spot it had slid into. Sarah looked perplexed. How was she going to free the poor thing? The dilemma was, for the moment, the most important thing in her mind. Sarah had seen how some of the folks back in Buffalo had captured animals just to make them fight and to torture them, not to mention what they did to some people, especially colored folks like her. She could not stand by and do nothing while the creature was suffering.

The creature watched her with intent eyes and it made sounds that sounded like pain.

Sarah was frantic, but she was not a tinker's daughter for nothing. She looked at the creature and said, "I will be right back. I will help you." With that, Sarah ran back for the wagon. When she arrived, she immediately grabbed some tools and, lastly, a canteen.

By the time she returned, the creature looked even more pitiful and seemed shocked to see her. Sarah immediately went to work. Using a small chisel, she carefully loosened some of the dirt under one of the rocks. Next, she used the small boiler's coal shovel to remove some of the dirt. She repeated this several times, removing just a little dirt at a time and working very carefully so that the rocks would not shift and hurt the creature even more. After several minutes, she stopped to take a drink. After thinking a moment more, she offered the canteen to the creature and showed her, for it seemed that it was a female whatever it was, how to get a drink. The creature showed its teeth, rather large ones and quite unlike any Sarah had ever seen before, took the canteen and took a drink. Having taken the drink, it put the stopper back on it and handed it to Sarah.

"Thank you," said Sarah.

To Sarah's surprise, the creature responded by speaking to her. Sarah listened and thought she made out several of the words but was not completely sure. The sounds came out a bit garbled, like something that was not quite clear. Anyhow, there would be time for language lessons later. Right now, Sarah had more work to do.

About ten minutes later, she grabbed the creature's foot and slowly moved it back into the hollow she had created, and the creature pulled free. Sarah looked at the thing and smiled. "See, if you cannot raise the rock, lower the ground. That is how a tinker solves the problem."

The creature sat up and then sat on its hunches.

Sarah pointed at herself and simply said, "Sarah."

The creature blinked a couple of times, and Sarah repeated her name, pointing at herself.

The creature cocked her head, pointed at herself, and replied with what sounded like, "Cee Cee."

Sarah pointed at her and said, "Cee Cee," and then again pointed at herself. "Sarah."

Cee Cee looked quizzical and said, "Carah," pointing at Sarah.

Sarah smiled, shrugged, and said, "Close enough!"

She got up and the creature immediately stood up. Standing, it was somewhat taller than Sarah but not as heavily built. Sarah saw no reason to be scared of Cee Cee. She carefully picked up her tools and canteen. She motioned her new friend to follow her back to the steam wagon. When the unlikely pair arrived, Sarah put the tools away and offered a sandwich to her new friend; pet did not seem quite right, for Cee Cee was obviously intelligent. She was not like a dog, but she did remind Sarah of something, maybe a rat. But, in truth, Cee Cee was not like anything Sarah had ever seen before. Sarah though she must be an Indian girl; people said they were different. There were Indians around Buffalo, but she had never met one or even seen one. Maybe that was even truer out in the West. *Yes, that explains everything*, thought Sarah. Cee Cee was an Indian.

The pair sat on the ground by the wagon and tried to talk to each other. They were making some progress, as each seemed to have a smattering of the other's language. About fifteen minutes passed before Sarah heard Isaiah cry out to her, "Sarah, where are you!"

Sarah jumped up and climbed onto the wagon and then up onto the driver's seat and yelled, "We are over here, Poppa."

Isaiah responded and was soon working his way down through the rocks.

"Sorry. I got turned around in the rocks and could not see you. What do you mean *we* are here?" asked Isaiah.

Sarah smiled and climbed down. "Poppa, I made a friend. She is an Indian girl, and her name is Cee Cee."

Isaiah looked confused. "Well introduce me to your friend."

Sarah looked around, but Cee Cee was gone. "I don't know where she went, Poppa. She was here; I saved her." Sarah went on to explain how her new friend had been trapped by a rockslide, and Sarah had dug her out.

Isaiah seemed somewhat skeptical so Sarah dragged him over to where she had moved the earth.

"Well, I guess there was something here," said Isaiah. "Maybe you will meet up with her later," he added, noting Sarah's long face.

"I know, Poppa, it is just, I have not really met anyone my own age. I mean, I love Miss Julia; she's like my big sister. But it would have been nice to have someone to play with." Sarah sighed.

Isaiah put his arm around her. "I know, sweetheart. Maybe when this is all over and we can settle down, relax a bit, and put down some roots, then you will be able to make some friends your own age." Isaiah said to comfort his daughter. "So what did your new friend say?"

Sarah shrugged. "Well, we talked a lot, Papa, but we did not understand each other too good. She must have been speaking in Indian. I got some of the words although she spoke them funny, like she had a problem forming the words. That must have been why she looked so different. Maybe she had a deformity. Well, I still liked her even if she looked different!" This last was said quite firmly and made Isaiah very proud of his daughter.

He looked down at her. "As Father Peter would say, you do not judge people by the way they look on the outside but by what is in their hearts."

"Right, Poppa." As Sarah looked up at her father, she went on, "You would like Cee Cee; she had a good heart!"

Isaiah reloaded the telescope and had Sarah head over to the next ridge. This repeated the entire afternoon.

Finally, the pair caught up with the riders. "See anything, Isaiah?" asked John.

"Just a whole lot of California scenery," replied Isaiah. "We're going to have to call it a day, though. Boiler water is getting low, John; cannot go far without that." Isaiah sighed.

John nodded. "Agreed. The horses are getting tired. We will have to try again tomorrow. The train should be in tomorrow so at least we will have another pair of eyes and the rest of our equipment."

The party turned around and began to head back into Los Angeles. Isaiah took over driving from Sarah. He was proud of his daughter; not only was she an excellent hand with the steam wagon, but from what she had told him about helping the Indian girl she'd met, she was very clever. Most people would have continued to try to shift the rock, but Sarah had realized there was another solution to the problem. He was very proud indeed!

CHAPTER 31

A New Lead Appears

By the time the search party had arrived back in town, it was getting on toward evening. By unspoken agreement, they returned to Isaiah's shop. When they arrived, they found Julia and Father Peter sitting in the shop. It appeared that Julia had decided to run the shop for the day, as several items were in for repair, including several clockwork items, a watch, and a broken adjustable plow. With each item were papers telling Isaiah the name of the person and what the problem was. Luckily, Julia had dressed in a blouse and long skirt for the day and not one of her saloon-girl dresses.

Sarah beamed at her. She went over to Julia and hugged her. Whispering in her ear, she said, "I could not have done better."

Julia looking at Sarah, smiled, and whispered back, "Well, thank you. It is nice to know I came up to your standards."

Sarah giggled a bit and whispered back, "I have to. Poppa is none too great with records. He would make a terrible archivist." This last she said in a truly conspiratorial whisper, Sarah's pride in her work at the dig site clear.

Julia just pretended to look shocked. Sarah nodded her head and looked put-upon. Then both started giggling again.

John and Isaiah looked at each other and, like most sane men when confronted with such female goings-on, shrugged and went on with their business, not even trying to figure out what the female type of noise was all about.

"The train should be pulling into town in the morning," John noted. "It will be good to see our last man. Also, it will give us more equipment, although with you and the telescope, I cannot see how much more we can bring to bear on the problem."

Julia smiled. "Well, if nothing else, I will have the rest of my clothes."

"Me too," said Sarah.

"Just remember, you two, we are still undercover," chided John.

"We know! Men," they said to each other as if that explained everything.

That evening was quiet. John and Julia went back to the Comstock and changed into their working clothes, as they had both been dressed for a day in the field, even though Julia had spent the day as a shop girl. John was already in a game when Julia came down the stairs and into the saloon side of the hotel. She caught John's eye and this time had worn a dark blue dress that left very little to the imagination, although John, given the vast extent of his education and intellect, did manage to get somewhat distracted imagining some very interesting things about Julia.

A snort from the one of the other men at the table recalled him to the business at hand.

"Sorry." John sighed. "Got distracted by my lady."

Just as on the first evening, the other men at the table looked at Julia and agreed that she was indeed a rather strong distracting influence, although several put it in somewhat more colorful language. There was a round of male laughter, and then seriousness settled in again, and the poker game resumed.

Julia, for her part, started circulating and talking to the other women working the bar. It was about an hour later that she met up with Rosey, who looked at her and asked, "You still offering that reward for information on the Chinaman?"

"Indeed, Rosey," replied Julia "What have you heard?"

Rosey looked at her for a moment. "Go over to the Palace and ask for Katy. I heard she might have some information on the gent you're looking for."

Julia thanked Rosey by way of a five-dollar gold piece changing hands. She went to tell John.

As usual, he was in a poker game. Pulling him away, she told him what she had heard. Not wanting to take a chance on blowing their cover, she told him to go back to his game and she would check the lead out. Before going, she went up to their room and changed into the dress she had worn for dinner, as the dress she was wearing was a bit much, or not quite enough, for out on the street.

It was not a long walk, only several blocks, but the atmosphere had changed by the time she arrived at her destination. The Comstock was a more upscale hotel, while the Palace was strictly for a tougher and more course crowd. Julia thought Chen was straying from his usual haunts, but it had become apparent, as they tracked the pair, that Chen had enough money so that the purveyors of such pleasures noted the green of his money and ignored the color of his skin.

Julia entered the Palace, and several of the cowboys and roughnecks tried to chat her up. She just smiled and, without them quite figuring out how, smoothly left them talking to empty air. Since she felt time was of the essence, she took the most expedient route, going up to the bar and asking the bartender if Katy was around. He looked around and then said, "See the redhead over there? That's her."

Julia thanked him and started over to meet Katy. She was about halfway across the room when a drunken trail hand grabbed her and leered, trying to kiss her. Julia simply had no time for this, and the next thing the man knew, he was on his knees screaming in pain. "Really my dear, sir, your manners need significant improvement," Julia said in his ear. "Now if I let you up, do you promise to behave yourself?"

The cowboy nodded yes, but when Julia let him go, he grabbed for her again. This time when she bent his arm, there was an audible snap, which everyone in the room heard. Looking around Julia politely asked, "Are any of you gentlemen acquainted with this man? If so, could you please assist him in seeking medical attention?" Julia smiled at him and said, "I am sorry, but you did promise, and one should never break one's promises, especially to a lady."

With that, Julia let go of the man, who dropped to the floor, and continued on her way. She did note that several of the other men in the saloon went to the man's assistance and were laughing at him for being beaten up by a girl, a small one at that!

Julia finished making her way across the room and asked the redhead if she was indeed Katy. The woman, having seen the way Julia handled the cowboy, was impressed. "Yeah, I'm Katy. Who wants to know?"

Julia smiled and said, "My name is Julia, and a mutual friend suggested I talk to you. Is there anywhere we can have a more private conversation?"

Katy looked at her. This was obviously not a typical saloon girl. Not quite knowing what to make of Julia, she nodded and started over to a quiet corner of the bar, an alcove of sorts. "Well, you have my attention," said Katy. "Who sent you and what do you want?"

Not exactly a witty conversationalist, Julia thought. But the more direct and to-the-point attitude suited Julia's current mood quite nicely. "As I said, my name is Julia, and Rosey over at the Comstock said you might have information of value to me."

Katy raised an eyebrow at Julia.

Julia continued, "I am looking for a Chinaman who likes white women and pays well."

Katy looked at Julia hard. "What is it to you?" she responded.

Julia went into her prepared story. "He put my cousin in the hospital back in Chicago. I want to pass along her regards."

Katy simply responded, "He does indeed pay well. If I tell you what you want to know, it could be money out of my pocket. So why should I tell you?"

Julia looked back, her expression just as hard. "First, because I am willing to pay *exceptionally* well for the information and, second, because you really do not want to make me mad." With this last bit, she nodded at the cowboy, who was just being helped out of the saloon.

Katy looked down at Julia. She was no small woman, and even as well endowed as Julia was, she felt almost flat chested compared to Katy, that and she must have been at least five ten in her stocking feet.

Katy seemed unimpressed by the implied threat. "How exceptional?" she asked.

Julia looked at her levelly. "Fifty dollars in gold for the information." Julia was not in a mind to dicker, since each day meant more Ratten to deal with. Time was of the essence indeed.

Katy looked thoughtful. "You must want him bad for that kind of money, sister. So I can assume I will not be getting any more business from him after you've passed on your cousin's regards. Fifty now and fifty after I set him up for you."

Julia looked a little taken a back. That was a lot of money. Still, Anderson had made it clear she was to close the book on this problem as quickly as possible. Julia looked back at Katy, again matching the hardness of the larger woman's stare. "Done. When do you expect to see him?" As Julia finished, she reached in her bag, pulled out several gold pieces, and handed them over.

Katy smiled, a look of pure, happy greed on her face; she obviously had no qualms about selling out a patron. "He's supposed to see me tomorrow night. I meet him here in the bar and then we go up to my room. Since you pay so well, I will throw this bit in for free. He seemed worried the last time he was here, said something about them getting out of control. I don't know who this 'them' was or what he was talking about."

Julia was shocked. Chen must have been referring to the Ratten. From what she and the rest of them had found, the pair was on good terms with the tong. If he had been talking about the Ratten, what did it mean that they were getting out of control? Did the team have to worry about an imminent attack? The city's police force would be taken apart by the creatures; it was less than ten men strong with only two or three on duty at a time. If they were surprised, it would be even worse. Yet she could not give them a warning. Hopefully, they could get the information out of Chen or capture Ulrich too and make them talk!

Julia smiled so that Katy would not suspect anything beyond some planned violence against Chen. "All right, where is your room? And when does he usually arrive?" she asked.

Katy, clearly suspecting nothing more than a bit of revenge, replied, "Second floor, Room 23. He normally shows up just after dusk, about seven in the evening. I don't want this going down in my room, you understand. I have my reputation to keep!"

"I completely understand," replied Julia, smiling like a female tiger contemplating a meal. "Till tomorrow then."

Julia retraced her steps through the saloon; only this time, the cowboys and drifters kept their hands to themselves, not wanting to risk a broken arm or other damage. As Julia walked back to the Comstock, she kept wondering what was going on with the Ratten if their own creators could not keep them under their control. How dangerous were they? And did the team have enough firepower to handle the situation? The last thing they wanted was a fight in the city and the resultant panic and news stories!

As she walked into the Comstock, she saw John, as was becoming the norm, seated at a table with a handful of cards in front of him. Julia wasted no time and went up to the table. "Dearest, I must talk to you as soon as possible. I am terribly sorry that I have had to interrupt your game, gentlemen."

John looked at her and realized that she had something of import to discuss. Throwing in his cards and grabbing his winnings, he said, "Gentlemen, if you will kindly excuse me." Not waiting for a reply, he turned and followed Julia out of the saloon and over to the hotel side.

He was surprised when she did not make for the steps but turned and said in a whisper, "John, meet me at Isaiah's. I'll go fetch Father Peter."

John was quick enough to see that something big was up. Julia was not using her drawl and was not fussing too much to maintain their cover. "Very well, Julia. I will see you at Isaiah's." With that, he turned and went out into the street and headed for the shop.

Julia left in the opposite direction, headed for the rectory where Peter was staying.

She walked as quickly as she could and was relieved when Father Peter himself answered the door instead of Father Paul. She was beginning to run out of excuses to call on Peter—especially, she thought, dressed the way she still was, even in her more modest dress. "Peter, can you come? We need a team meeting; I have just learned some news."

Peter looked at her and could see the agitation on her face; it was as if her whole body was straining from the obvious tension. "I will get my hat, Julia, and let Father Paul know I'm going out for a while. Wait here. I will be right back."

Good as his word, Peter reappeared in less than five minutes. He and Julia began their walk to Isaiah's.

Before long, Peter was holding open the door of the shop for Julia to enter. As they walked in, Julia saw that the entire team was here—John, Isaiah, Sarah, and the three remaining sharpshooters. She was relieved that John had thought to collect them. She realized that she had not thought of it herself, which indicated just how worried she was.

"Good, you are all here." Julia breathed a sigh of relief and told them what Katy had told her, especially how Chen was worried. "What do you think it means if they cannot control the Ratten anymore? Will they attack? Should we call out the army?" asked Julia in a nervous voice. "I'm not sure we can handle them. We barely survived the attack at the cave! Even with the Gatling and the firepower from the Congress we ended up with three of us put down, and the current batch may be even more advanced than those."

John spoke. "I think the most important thing to do is capture Chen and Ulrich at this point. It is quite possible that we can get information out of the pair that will give us a better picture of what we are dealing with. Remember, we are supposed to keep this from becoming public knowledge. It looks as if we have a good chance of getting Chen tomorrow night. Let's hope we're in time, and let's not panic in the meantime."

Julia calmed herself. "John, it is just that I do not want to see those things coming into town; there's no telling how many people could lose their lives—not to mention that, there would be no way to stop the story from getting out."

"In that case, we cannot afford any mistakes," said John forcefully. "Julia, hopefully we can get a room at the Palace just down the hall. Shall we check it out, madam?"

"Why, sir, what will your colleagues at that the museum think to find out you are taking your unmarried secretary to every hotel in Los Angeles?" responded Julia in a more lighthearted and confident tone. She seemed to have recovered her poise and calmed her nerves.

"I am hoping, Miss Verolli, that if I keep besmirching your reputation in this fashion, you will have no choice but to marry me and redeem yourself." John looked more than half serious as he said this.

Julia looked somewhat pained. "That is a conversation for later, John, but it is one I do hope to have. All right, shall we see about that room, sir, so you can sully my reputation some more—even though it is in tatters already."

John smiled and held out his arm for her. "Gentlemen, I suggest you find a game of chance at the Palace and see where you can set up for our quarry." This was said as he escorted Julia out the door. He stopped for a minute. "Peter, you and Isaiah had best stay here in case we need a spot to retreat to. Isaiah, I also think that in case we need the wagon, have Sarah get a full head of steam up."

"Will do, Major," said Isaiah. "You can count on us, sir."

With that, John and Julia were out the door turning down the street toward the Palace. Shortly thereafter, the sharpshooters left also, taking a different route so that no one would think they were one group.

At the Palace desk, the couple who were still just teammates rented a room just down the hall from Katy's and went up. The room was not as nice as the one they shared at the Comstock; nor, as John noted, was the couch anywhere near as comfortable. But they did not plan to stay there long. They returned to the Comstock and packed enough of a kit for the night and then returned to settle in at the Palace.

Making contact with the sharpshooters was easy, with the simple expedience of settling down for a game of cards. The men had carefully gone over the place. A closet just down the hall opposite from the end where John and Julia's room was would make the perfect hideout, allowing them to trap Chen between the two groups. Julia gave Katy a bit of extra money to let them know when Chen showed up. It was decided to try and take him before he even got into Katy's room. The other two men would be on the stairs, one following Chen up and the other on the third floor in case he tried to escape that way. Now they settled in to wait for tomorrow.

The next day passed slowly for the team, as each tried to relax and settle in, looking like part of the woodwork.

Meanwhile, at the store, Sarah was talking to Father Peter. She spent the morning telling him about how she had met an Indian girl named Cee Cee, who had been dressed in leather and bright cloth. Sarah talked about how her new friend had talked kind of funny, like something was wrong with her voice. Peter listened and smiled as Sarah told him how she remembered that he had taught her not to judge a person by his or her appearance but by what was in the person's heart.

Peter, for his part, listened and was pleased that Sarah had absorbed the lesson so well, especially since many people judged her solely by the color of her skin. He was surprised when Sarah told him how Cee Cee was using words she didn't recognize. When Sarah repeated some of them, he told her he thought some of them might be Chinese, if you allowed for the speech problems Sarah said this little girl had.

Sarah was fascinated. She considered this suggestion. It might even explain more about her new friend, who she now guessed must be of mixed race. She had known several people like that back in Buffalo, people who were part black and part white. Mostly, they had either been born to or were themselves former slaves. And that, Sarah figured, would explain Cee Cee's odd appearance even better than if Sarah were Indian, after all, she had no real idea what people from China looked like. She asked Father Peter to teach her some Chinese.

Sarah thought it was an odd kind of language, but she picked up some of it, at least some of the more common words. Peter was truly impressed by Sarah's flare for languages. It was as if she was one of those new steam-powered or clockwork recording devices he had seen described in one of the scientific journals Julia had gotten for John to relax with. In truth, Peter thought John's idea of relaxation a bit strange, but it took all kinds. Peter, could not imagine anything more relaxing than curling up with a nice theological journal.

Just after supper, Sarah went out back and began to fire up the steam wagon's boiler, making sure all the valves and levers were in their proper position. When she'd finished, she topped off the tank with water and oiled all the mechanisms before double-checking on the buildup of steam.

All was ready, both at the shop and at the Palace. Now everyone was just waiting for Chen to show up.

The sun was just starting to slip below the horizon.

CHAPTER 32

A Capture and an Interrogation and Then Sarah to the Rescue

John waited in the room he and Julia had rented, while Tinsman hid in the closet down the hall. They had tipped the maids well to make sure they were elsewhere in the early evening. One sharpshooter waited in an alcove on the third and topmost floor of the hotel, while the last one nursed a sarsaparilla at the end of the bar nearest the stairs. Meanwhile, Julia stayed near Katy and watched for Chen.

None of the team noticed a second man come into the bar. The man, wearing a poncho and a hat pulled down partially hiding his face, took a seat near the rear. He was just another patron.

Just about seven thirty, a man matching Chen's description and the sketch came into the bar. He made a beeline for the bar and ordered a bottle of whiskey and some glasses. Getting his order from the bartender, he then headed over to where Katy was standing. On the way, he spied Julia standing there and looked at her with a leer. He finished eyeing her up and continued to Katy. He whispered something in her ear. Katy got a warm, lazy smile on her face and said, "I will talk to her."

With that, she sauntered over to Julia and, in a low tone she said, "This is just made for you. Our friend wants you to join us for the evening, he likes the idea of the long and short of it. Interested?"

Julia looked surprised and whispered back to Katy, "That could not be better, but keep talking for a moment as if we are dickering over the price."

The two women continued to talk for a few moments in low tones that could not be overheard before Julia got the same lazy, warm smile on her face that Katy had demonstrated and nodded.

Turning, they both walked back over to Chen. When they got to him, Katy introduced Julia as a friend of hers. The ladies flanked Chen as they headed for the back of the hotel and the stairs.

The man at the table noted the exchange but just shrugged and took another drink of schnapps. For that, he was glad that many of his former countrymen had settled in the wild area called Texas and then spread out across this country. Thankfully they had at least brought good booze with them instead of the poor substitute people in these parts called whiskey. As he watched out of the corner of his eye, he saw a cowboy slowly begin to follow the trio up the stairs, and he wondered.

Julia was laughing along with Katy as the threesome reached the top of the stairs and moved down the hall to Katy's room. The plan could not have worked better. She pressed against Chen and smiled, and all of a sudden, she expertly chopped him, and he fell in a pile at her feet. *Finally*, she thought, *something went right on this seemingly cursed mission*.

Both John and Tinsman heard the thud as Chen hit the floor, and they were out and moving forward to make sure he did not get away.

Chen started to come around just as the pair had finished putting shackles on his wrists and ankles. The Chinaman looked around in horror and he started to scream at them, but a rag from Julia's bag was stuffed in his mouth to quiet him.

Katy looked at her and held out her hand. Julia smiled, pulled out the rest of the bribe, and handed it over. The smile was genuine; they finally had their hands on at least one of the evil men they'd been chasing across the country.

Katy smiled and looked down at Chen. "Sorry, but she paid a lot better. I guess you shouldn't have messed with her family. Looking at Julia, she said, "Nice doing business with you." With that, she put the

271

money in her purse, turned, and went back down the stairs to resume her evening's activities.

The man at the table noted her return with a raised eyebrow.

By this time, the other two sharpshooters had arrived on the second floor, and between the four men and one woman, they moved Chen quietly down the stairs. The bartender might have noticed, but the sharpshooter who had been at the bar had paid him in advance to be looking the other way when they came down the stairs and went out the back door.

The man at the table who had been following the original trio of Chen and the two women got up and went out of the bar and around the corner toward the back of the building, keeping to the shadows as soon as he moved off the street.

The group literally carried Chen to Isaiah's shop, and going in, they threw him in a chair. Julia pulled the rag out of his mouth. She looked at him and, in spite of her dress, did not look either friendly or inviting anymore. She was smiling, but the smile was not warm or friendly. It was terrifying, like looking at a crocodile trying to smile. Chen was obviously, and quite reasonably, scared out of his mind. "All right, Chen Sun, I think it is time we had a talk," said the smiling Miss Verolli.

Chen was struggling in the chains. "Let me go. They will be coming," he cried. "I have to get away from here!"

Isaiah took Sarah and simply said, "I think both of us need to check the steam wagon."

Julia's insides turned to ice. She had not known that Sarah had come back into the store. However her body did not betray any hint at what she was feeling inside. She could not quit because of Sarah otherwise these monstrous creations would be attacking and hurting the other Sarahs of the world. They had to be stopped. "Who is coming, Chen Sun? And where is Ulrich?"

Chen was frantic, but he had stopped struggling, realizing that it was of no use; the chains were too strong. "I do not know where Ulrich is. We had a falling out; he left."

Julia just shook her head and slapped him hard across the face. "I really hate it when people lie to me, and so does my boss. I think you know him, do you not? Large man, quite powerful, used to be your paymaster." With that, she backhanded him, the blow sounding like a pistol shot as it snapped his head around.

"Anderson, you work for Anderson, do you not? That bastard shut down our project when we were on the verge of the greatest discoveries of the age! Steam is *nothing* compared to what we were perfecting— super soldiers!" Chen was beside himself with anger thinking about Anderson.

"Too bad the rest of the world sees it differently. Now back to the questions. Where is Ulrich? And where are the Ratten?" Julia slapped him again twice before she pulled out a small knife.

Chen looked at the knife and then at Julia.

Morton watched her too, and it frightened him. She was not just dangerous but very dangerous. Now he began to understand why she had said *if* he was still interested after the mission. John began to wonder about that himself.

"Chen Sun, we do not have much time, and you have even less if you do not start talking to me!" With that, Julia slammed the knife into the chair between Chen's spread legs. The knife was so close he could feel it pressing into his manhood through his pants. Then she grabbed his left hand and broke his little finger. Over Chen's scream, Julia yelled at him, "Where are the Ratten?! I am losing patience with you. Or would you prefer I work on a more personal part of your anatomy?" She broke another finger. "Before I even run out of fingers!"

Chen screamed again in pain, and the observing team could see a wet spot forming in the front of his trousers and smell where he had soiled himself. "I do not know where Ulrich is," Chen repeated. "He took off; I told you! The Rat Troopers are out northwest of the town in a hidden cave by a rock outcropping. Please no more!" He hung his head and cried.

Unknown to Julia, Chen's screams were loud enough for Sarah to hear out behind the building.

"Rat Troopers, Chen?" asked Julia.

Chen was whimpering now, "The Ratten are no more. We have advanced them far beyond the mere animals the Ratten were. Anderson should have left us alone to finish our work." By this time, Chen had passed out, either from pain or fear.

Julia took a deep breath and stepped back. She looked at John. She could see in his face that he was wondering about her. She swallowed. "Do any of you know where he might be talking about?"

John nodded. "It sounds like the area where Sarah met her friend Cee Cee. We can scout the area, but it will have to wait till dawn. Even with the lights on the steam wagon, it is just too large an area to cover."

Julia looked at John. "Like I told you, John, just teammates till after the mission and then if you are still interested. All right, we will take turns guarding him and search in the morning. The Ratten have to be the first priority. They have to be stopped. Then we have to find Ulrich. But he is a secondary priority. Any questions?"

None of the sharpshooters had any questions. They had worked for Anderson before and with Julia some; they knew the drill. John was still digesting this new Julia persona in his mind. Isaiah had come back in and left Sarah out by the steam wagon.

"So, do you want the Gatling mounted on the wagon?" he asked.

Julia looked thoughtful for a moment. "Yes, but not till we are out of town. I dare say, it would cause some serious conversation among the locals."

Julia and Morton returned to the Comstock to get some rest and change for tomorrow.

Peter meanwhile, still in Isaiah's shop, set Chen's fingers and then went off to pray about what was going on. Chen might be a heathen, but he was still human. And while Peter knew what was at stake, what they had done and, more so, what they had to do still bothered him.

As the sun reappeared over the distant horizon, the morning found Julia—who had had trouble sleeping, seeing Sarah's face in her dreams—heading down the street toward the store. She left the Comstock where John was still sleeping. They had agreed that, when he awoke, he was to go over to get their small amount of things from the Palace and settle up.

As she approached, Julia heard something from the rear of the store. Wondering what the noise was, she went down the wide alley next to the store. When she turned the corner at the rear, there was Sarah firing up the steam wagon.

Sarah saw Julia out of the corner of her eye and turned to face her; it was obvious Sarah was scared and nervous. As Sarah looked down at her from the wagon, she said, "Julia, that man, the one tied in the chair, is he really so evil that you had to hurt him like that?" Her small face was trying to make sense of all that had happened.

Julia felt more scared than she had on any of the missions she had performed for Anderson. She could well accept the idea of consequences to herself but not to Sarah—and not the loss of her love. She thought back to the question Peter had asked her, about whether she would sacrifice Sarah's love to make her own life easier, and the answer she had given him. Julia tried not to cry. "Sarah, I am truly sorry for what has happened and that you had to see some of it. I told you that I never wanted to lose your love or for you to be scared of me. You have to believe that is true! However, if we do not stop these two men and their plan to unleash the monsters they have created, there are a lot of people who could die, including other little sisters. I hope you can still love me."

Sarah looked at her. "I still love you, Julia. If you say it is so, then it is. Sister's oath, remember?"

Julia started to cry. "I remember. Sister's oath."

Sarah looked at her some more. "I heard that these monsters are out by where Cee Cee and her people live?" she finally asked.

Julia nodded. "That is what Chen told us, Sarah. I am sorry."

Sarah looked at Julia. "I have to go and warn Cee Cee, Julia, she may have a younger sister too!"

Julia looked shocked. "Sarah, you cannot go. It is too dangerous. Now come down from there at once!" Now Julia understood why Sarah was up so early getting the steam wagon ready to move.

Sarah looked like she was made of stone. "I have to go," she insisted. "I have to warn my friend! People back in Buffalo did not care if colored kids got hurt; just because Cee Cee is an Indian does not mean I do not care."

Julia looked shocked for she had seen that look before, many times in fact, when she looked in a mirror. She knew for sure this was one fight she was not going to win, for if she did, Sarah could never trust her again. Julia just thought to herself, *All right, God, this is when I need your guidance. What do I do now?*

Julia shook her head. "Sarah, it is too dangerous. You have no idea how dangerous these creatures are. You cannot go!"

Sarah still had the look. "I have to. Do you not understand? My friend is out there in danger! What would you do if it were the professor or Father Peter? I am taking the steam wagon. Will you help me? It's all set to go."

"Sarah, is there no way I can talk you out of it?" pleaded an anguished Julia. "If I have to, I can stop you, you know."

"And if Cee Cee or her sister dies, I will not be able to forgive myself, or you," said Sarah.

Julia saw herself in Sarah's face and body language. "Oh, I am never going to forgive myself if anything happens to you. Let's go then." Julia resigned herself to trying to explain all this to John and Isaiah, though she knew fighting a horde of monsters would be the easier task.

Julia climbed up onto the wagon and then up to the driver's seat. Sarah climbed up to the seat from where she had been stoking the boiler and sat next to Julia.

"Here," said Sarah. "Put these on; it gets windy up here." She handed Julia a pair of the goggles that Julia had seen her and Isaiah wear.

Once both had their goggles in place, Sarah opened up the steam valve slowly, and with just a slight hiss of steam, the pair took off as quietly as possible.

Sometime thereafter, John came into the store. He'd retrieved both his and Julia's items from the Palace and paid the bill. "All right," he said, pointing at one of the sharpshooters and Peter, "you two stay here and guard Chen. The rest of us will head out to the rock formation. Where are Julia and Sarah?"

Everyone looked around, but no one had seen the two.

Isaiah went to check out in back. He came rushing back in. "The steam wagon is gone; the girls must have taken it!"

"What are you talking about? Why would they do that?!" John was yelling now. "What do those two think they are doing?"

"I can guess," said Isaiah. "Sarah is terrified for her friend Cee Cee, the little Indian girl she met. She must have taken the steam wagon to go warn her about the monsters. And somehow, I do not know how but I plan to find out, she talked Julia into going with her."

"Great," Morton yelled. "Both females are crazy. All right, let's get the horses. We'll go after them. We can only hope we get to them before the Ratten do, especially if they are out of control!"

With that, the men, including Father Peter, ran for their horses.

John pulled Peter up. "Peter where do you think you are going?" said a frustrated Morton.

"Where I may be needed, John. Sorry, it goes with the collar," Peter replied, his tone one of utter determination.

John Morton just shook his head. "All right. It must be my day for demented people!"

Soon the men were back at the store, grabbing all the weapons they could carry on their horses. "Sorry, Sam, need you to stay here and watch Chen for us," John said. "We'll be back as soon as we can round up two crazy females, retrieve the steam wagon, warn the Indians, and whatever else comes up!"

"Got your back, Major," replied Sam. "Good luck, sir. Kind of attached to those two gals myself."

"I know," said John as he spurred his horse, along with the rest of the ad hoc search team.

CHAPTER 33

CEE CEE SAVES THE GIRLS AND VICE VERSA

Sarah and Julia sped over the track toward the rock formation where Sarah met Cee Cee. Julia was hanging on for dear life. "Sarah, can you not slow down somewhat? If we are killed getting there, who will warn your friend?"

Sarah just grunted in reply and concentrated on her driving. The miles sped by. The wagon had to be going at least seventeen miles per hour, and Julia thought she would not survive the pounding she was getting as it sped along. The sun was fully up now, and the countryside was beautiful, thought Julia between the bumps and dips. Soon, the rocks and ridges came into view.

As the terrain got rougher, Sarah began to slow the wagon down, backing off on the steam valve, much to Julia's relief. Facing a dangerous opponent was one thing; being bounced to death by your crazy younger sister was quite another. Since Julia had not been out to the location before, she asked, "Are we almost there?" She tried to sound hopeful, even though she was thinking that, if the Ratten attacked, they were as good as dead.

Sarah was still concentrating on her driving. However, she did have a little time to answer now that she had slowed down, "Almost there. Don't worry. I'm a good steam wagon driver."

Julia looked over at her. "I am not worried about your driving, Sarah, well, not much anyhow. It is just that, if we survive this, I am worried about how I am going to explain this to John and your father!" This last came out with a plaintive note.

Sarah stole a quick glance at Julia. "I am sorry I got you involved, Miss Julia. I know Poppa will be mad at me. I didn't think about him being mad at you too or about the professor." Then she turned her attention back to her driving.

"Sarah, your father will be bad enough, but I cannot imagine how John, the professor, is going to react, except that it will be bad!"

Sarah responded, "He loves you."

Julia sighed almost in tears. "I am not so sure, Sarah. After he saw what I had to do last night, I think he is wondering if he would want to spend a life with someone like me. Remember, I told you I could not let myself think or hope till after the mission is over. That is why, Sarah, because the mission has to come first."

The steam wagon finally came to a halt, in almost the exact place it had been when Sarah first met Cee Cee. Sarah jumped down and began to call out to her friend. "Miss Julia, you best stay here. I don't want Cee Cee to be scared of you. Let me get her so I can introduce you."

Julia looked very nervous. "Sarah, don't go too far. You don't know the creatures we are dealing with. They are fast and vicious." Julia just stood there looking around as Sarah continued to call to her friend.

Julia climbed up on one of the rocks, trying to get a better vantage point. Sarah had continued to call out, hoping that her friend was still all right.

Finally, Sarah heard a little chatter and went around another rock to see Cee Cee standing there in her leather and cloth garb. The two females started to talk to each other. This time, Sarah made more sense of what Cee Cee was saying; she recognized some of the Chinese words Father Peter had just taught her.

"Julia, I found Cee Cee," she called out. "She is all right! I am going to talk with her a bit more before I introduce you so she does not get frightened."

Julia breathed a sigh of relief, but she still knew they were in grave danger. "Sarah, do hurry. There is no telling when the Ratten will show up." She continued to scan the horizon for possible dangers.

For their part, Sarah and Cee Cee were making good progress with their communications. It appeared that Cee Cee's language was a mixture of Chinese, English, and something else Sarah did not recognize, although she thought there might be a Latin word or two in there. She tried to figure out where that came from.

After about half an hour, Sarah managed to convince Cee Cee to meet her sister and that her and her people were in danger. Sarah took her hand and led her out of the small sheltered area in between some of the rocks where they'd been talking. "Miss Julia, I am bringing Cee Cee out to meet you," she called out, "so do not be too surprised, all right?"

"Sarah, it's about time," replied an audibly relieved Julia. "We do not know how much time we have." With this, she turned toward the sound of Sarah's voice.

Julia was still on top of the rock when Sarah and her friend came into view. Julia turned white. Sarah's Indian friend was a Ratten, and the two were holding hands. Julia was terrified for Sarah. She licked her lips. "Sarah, let go of Cee Cee's hand and step away from her." As she was saying this, Julia pulled a small pistol from her bag.

Sarah was now terrified. "Julia, what are you doing? Why do you have your gun out? What is going on?" She was still holding Cee Cee's hand.

Julia replied, trying to keep her voice as calm and steady as possible while her heart was beating wildly. "Sarah, Cee Cee is not an Indian. She is a Ratten, one the very same creatures we are here to destroy. Now move away!"

Sarah looked at Julia and then at Cee Cee.

Cee Cee's brown eyes looked back at Sarah, and then she started to chatter to Sarah. Sarah looked at her friend and chattered back.

Julia could not make out what they were saying. "Sarah, stand clear. I cannot shoot with you that close!"

Sarah chattered some more to her friend and then, looking at Julia, took a step in front of Cee Cee. "Julia, she is my friend, and I cannot allow her to be shot." Sarah looked very firm and so grown up.

Julia was beside herself. She knew she should take the shot; the creature standing next to Sarah was a creation of evil. But Sarah would not get out of the way. What was wrong with her?

Julia prayed to know what to do, and against every bit of her training at the finishing school—*nothing* should come before the mission—she let the hammer down gently and just stood there with the gun at her side.

Sarah looked at her. "Thank you," was all she said.

She was turning to talk some more to Cee Cee when the earth heaved under their feet. All three screamed!

Sarah and Cee Cee were in the clear and had been knocked to the knees. They clutched each other. Julia had been knocked down and had rolled off the rock she had been standing on and dropped about ten feet. As the tremor died down, Sarah and her friend ran over to Julia. She was not moving, and her head was bleeding. Sarah was beside herself. What had she done to her sister? She knew she needed help, but she could not leave Julia to find it. She looked at Cee Cee and began to talk to her.

John, Peter, Isaiah, and the two sharpshooters had been riding hard, but the girls had at least a good hour-and-a-half head start on them, and Isaiah's wagon was not only somewhat faster than their horses, but it did not have to rest. Both John and Isaiah were scared out of their minds, Isaiah for his daughter. John was barely able to control his emotions. He knew that, even after he had seen her in action last night, he loved Julia. He was not sure about marriage; she had so many different personalities. None of the men wanted to envision what the Ratten could do to the pair of them. They were walking the horses for a bit to let them get their wind. As scared as they were, they knew getting to the girls would be a lot slower if their horses died under them.

After a few more minutes, they spurred the horses into a trot that was slowly eating up the distance to the rocky area. Suddenly, they felt the ground shake. They fought to keep the horse under control. There were some near falls, but eventually they had everything under control. The men looked at each other; it was the first time any of them had felt an earthquake.

"Was that an explosion?" Isaiah asked. "Could it have anything to do with the girls?"

John shook his head. "I don't think so, Isaiah. I'm not sure since I have never actually felt one, but I think that was what they call an earth tremor, natural not man-made!"

"Wonderful! Even the earth itself seems against us. What next!" bemoaned Peter.

"Come on. We won't solve any problems here." With that, John got his horse reoriented in the right direction and the posse continued their ride toward their destination.

Almost an hour later, following the distinctive tracks of the steam wagon, they were just coming into visual range of the area they thought the girls had headed for. Suddenly, John pulled up sharply, and the rest of the men followed suit. John could not believe his eyes. There on a rock sat a small Ratten, a new version but unmistakably a Ratten. The small creature was clothed in a leather and colorful cloth outfit and frantically waving a white piece of cloth on a stick. Tinsman pulled his rifle from his horse's scabbard and started to line up on the creature when Peter put his hand on the weapon and said to hold up. They looked again. There, in the creature's other hand, was a crude cross of tied sticks.

John told the others to hold up, and he slowly walked his horse forward. The creature blinked at him and furiously waved the little white flag some more. John stopped about ten feet away and just looked at it. "What are you? Who are you? What do you want? And where are the girls?" Morton was beginning to think he was losing his mind. Here he was, out in the middle of the California wilderness, having a conversation with a deadly enemy—one that happened to be a giant rat.

The creature looked at him and simply said, "Carah foffa."

John looked, if it were possible, even more puzzled. "What!" Now he was sure he was losing his mind.

The creature, obviously somewhat agitated, repeated what it had said rapidly, tapping its foot—or, the analytical part of Morton's brain thought, paw. "Carah foffa!"

John had the distinct impression that the creature was looking at him as if he were the dumbest person or creature it had ever met.

By this time, Father Peter and Isaiah had moved up. The creature looked at both of them and then back at Isaiah and hopped down from the rock it had been sitting on and went over to Isaiah. "Carah foffa?" it repeated, looking at him.

Isaiah was starting to show his worry. "Where is my daughter? Where is Sarah?"

"Carah, Carah!" The creature seemed to be excited at this, jumping up and down. Then it pointed at itself. "Cee Cee!" The creature pointed at Isaiah. "Carah foffa!" It seemed pleased that at least someone in this group of dullards was getting it.

Peter, who up till now had been silent, suddenly said, "Isaiah, I believe this is your daughter's *Indian* friend, Cee Cee. I think she wants to know if you are Sarah's father or papa."

The creature that they had identified as Cee Cee, obviously pleased, pointed at Peter and said, "Foffa foffa."

Isaiah got down off his horse. "Cee Cee, where is Sarah? I am Sarah's poppa." He tried to speak as calmly as he could when his heart was racing so as not to scare the young Ratten—not until he'd found out where Sarah was being held.

Cee Cee went up to him and sniffed him. Seemingly satisfied, she handed Isaiah her white flag and cross, dug around in her clothing, and pulled out a piece of paper. Handing it to Isaiah, she took back her flag and cross and just stood there and waited.

Isaiah blinked and opened up the paper. He read it and then, shaking his head, handed it up to John, who was still mounted. Morton read the note.

Poppa

This is Cee Cee, my friend. Please do not hurt her. She is a good person. She has a good heart. Miss Julia has been hurt. Please come. Cee Cee will guide you. I am sorry I took the steam wagon.

Love, Sarah

Morton looked stunned and handed the note to Peter.

Isaiah looked at John as he remounted. "I have to follow, Major. What choice do I have?"

Morton looked at his friends. "Indeed, Isaiah, what choice do any of us have?" Looking down at the little creature, he said, "If you would, Miss Cee Cee, please lead the way." John waved his hand and muttered under his breath, "I know it. I have been out in the sun too long. I am definitely losing my mind."

Cee Cee took off at a brisk pace across the open space toward the rocks. The band of men followed her.

When they got to the rocks, Morton slowed down. "Be careful," he warned. "It could be a trap. No firing until we know what is going on and until the women are safe."

Isaiah dismounted and yelled out for Sarah. He stopped, and then they heard it.

"Poppa, over here!" It was an alarmed Sarah's voice, and it was coming from the other side of the rocks.

The men hurried toward her, and as they rounded the rocks, they saw Sarah cradling Julia's head, and there was blood. Nearby, still as a statue, stood a Ratten; only this was no juvenile. The creature was big and clothed, for all the world, like a pirate with a wicked-looking short sword hanging off its belt.

John drew his revolver, but the Ratten just stood there.

Sarah looked up and yelled, "Professor, do not shoot. That is Cee Cee's father. He saved Miss Julia! Poppa, help. She is hurt bad!" The anguish was evident in Sarah's voice.

John, Peter, and Isaiah dismounted. The sharpshooters held back, their hands on their carbines but not drawing them.

Isaiah ran to his daughter and grabbed her. "What were you thinking? You could have been killed. I have been out of my head with worry."

Sarah was crying. "Poppa, I am so sorry. Miss Julia should not have come. She was just trying to protect me. I was trying to warn Cee Cee. You have to help her!" By now, Sarah was shuddering with sobs.

Meanwhile, John had taken over holding Julia's head while Peter looked at her wound. It was just at this point that Julia's eyes opened, and she looked up to see John's face over her. "John, what is going on? There was a Ratten, and Sarah would not get out of the way for me to get a shot off. Oh my God, John, where is Sarah?! Is she all right? I should have stopped her, John, I should have stopped her!" Julia was now crying openly.

Peter looked up. "She should be all right. Head wounds bleed like all get-out, but it doesn't look too serious. She is doing a lot of damage to rocks, though, not to mention, if she keeps getting all the lumps, it's going to be hell finding any new bonnets for her. Help me sit her up, John, so I can clean the wound and bandage it."

John helped Julia sit up. "Sarah is fine, so far," he said. He looked around. There were at least forty Ratten now visible on the rocks around them, and most were armed with various nasty-looking swords and knives. "Sarah, maybe you better fill us in on what is going on." Morton continued to look around. He knew that, if a fight started, there was very little chance they would get out alive. There were just too many of the creatures, and the range was too short. The Ratten would be on them before they could get enough shots off. He made a gesture for them all to relax and take their hands off their guns.

Isaiah looked at his daughter. "Sarah, what is going on young lady? Right about now, that convent school Father Peter mentioned once before is starting to sound pretty good!"

Sarah gulped. "I am sorry about the steam wagon, Poppa. I didn't mean for Miss Julia to get hurt. She just came along." Sarah looked at her father and wished fervently that she had a hole she could crawl into and then close over herself.

Julia was awake enough to have heard this last bit. "Sarah!" she cried. She clutched Sarah to her as the little girl came over. "You're safe. Oh God, I could never have lived with myself if you had been hurt!" Julia was crying again.

Morton looked at the two of them. "You have some serious explaining to do yourself, Agent Verolli. What were you thinking that you had to come out here by yourselves!" John realized that he had been scared out of his mind to think that he might have lost Julia. He could not imagine a future for himself without her in it.

Julia sniffed. "Sarah would not be talked out of coming out here to warn her friend. I did not know her friend was a Ratten. She would not get out of the way for a clear shot." It was at this moment that Julia looked up to see all the Ratten around them. She clutched Sarah to her. "John, what is going on?"

It was Sarah who responded. "It's all right. They won't hurt us. Cee Cee went to get help and her father"—Sarah pointed at the large Ratten standing over to the side—"pulled you to safety when more rocks started to come down."

Julia looked stunned. "What? I seem to remember that the ground shook and then nothing till I just woke up. What has been happening?"

Peter, who was still cleaning Julia's head wound, spoke up. "There was an earth tremor. You must have fallen and hit your head."

Sarah picked up the story again. "That's what happened. You were on top of the rock, and when the ground shook, you fell. I was trying to pull you clear, and Cee Cee was helping when her father came. More rocks were rolling down, and I thought you would be killed. Then he picked you up and put you over here so you would be safe. They are not evil, Miss Julia, not at all."

Julia looked confused. "But Chen Sun said they could not be controlled?"

Sarah looked at her and then at her father and finally at Father Peter. "Those men wanted them to become their slaves and follow their every order. They were afraid after some of them were beaten and chained—as a warning, they were told. They wanted their freedom. That's why they said they couldn't control them; it's not that they are dangerous." Sarah sat there looking at Julia and then at her father.

Isaiah looked back at his daughter. "I can understand wanting to be free, Major. The question is, what do we do now?"

"That, Isaiah, is a very good question. First off, will they let us go, Sarah?" John looked at Sarah.

Sarah looked a little startled at the question and then went over to talk to Cee Cee's father. She waved for John to come over by her.

Sarah looked up at him. "He wants to know what we plan to do, Professor." Sarah was obviously concerned herself. By this time, Cee Cee had come up, and her father looked down at her and started chattering.

"What was that about?" John asked Sarah.

Sarah looked a little pale or as pale as she could look and more than a little guilty. "I think he might send her to the same convent school as me for getting involved with us. He's pretty mad." This last came out in a tone just barely above a whisper.

Isaiah apparently overheard the conversation. "Well, at least we have that much in common. Tell him father to father I want to thank him, and when I get the name of the school, I will let him know!"

Sarah started to chatter to the tall Ratten, who looked somewhat surprised and then looked at Isaiah with a look that seemed to cross species boundaries; it was a look all about daughters getting into trouble.

John looked totally confused. "Sarah, tell him I honestly do not know. The possibility that they were not an evil to be destroyed was never envisioned, but tell him thank you for saving Julia and not harming you."

Sarah started to chatter some more, and Julia tipped her head. "I am getting part of it, John. There's some English and some German, but I am not getting all of it."

Peter chimed in. "I think part of it is Chinese. They must have evolved a language from Chen and Ulrich plus whatever else they heard. The pair must have developed them with the ability to speak so they could be controlled easier. I still cannot get over the clothing, though. I have no idea where that came from."

"I think as they were evolving toward humans so they could use our weapons and tools, they must have lost most of their fur, hence the clothing," John speculated, "that and mimicking Chen and Ulrich, their only role models."

Sarah turned to Cee Cee and started talking to her. Cee Cee said something back and then disappeared. "She said she would show me what gave them the idea for clothing." Sarah shrugged her shoulders and looked puzzled. Soon Cee Cee returned with a book and started to chatter to Sarah again. "She said they found the book among one of beast's things."

Sarah showed the adults the book. It was an illustrated dime novel about pirates. "So they adopted pirate dress?" said Julia.

Father Peter let out what sounded like a little laugh and shook his head while trying to control his laughter. "Oh well, that is not any stranger than what has already happened."

The Ratten leader spoke, and Sarah said, "He wants to know what your word is worth. If you give him your word that you won't harm them, what does it mean to them? He seems to want to trust you, Professor."

John looked quietly and thoughtfully at the Ratten. Finally he said, "We need to trust each other. If a fight breaks loose, none of us will get out of here, and most of them will die. Sarah, ask him if he trusts the others of his litter?"

Sarah looked confused but turned and spoke to Cee Cee's father. The tall Ratten replied. Sarah turned to John. "Yes, sir. He says they share blood."

John nodded. "I hoped that would be his answer." Having said that, he took off his jacket and rolled up his sleeve. He stepped up to the Ratten leader and slowly pulled out a small knife. There was a sound of chatter among the Ratten, and hands crept toward carbines and pistols, while elongated, tool-grasping paws crept to swords and knives.

Morton said quietly, "Stand easy." He took the knife and made a small incision on his wrist. Turning the knife around, he handed it to the Ratten leader, hilt first. The creature looked down at John, took the knife from him, and did the same.

John said to Sarah, never taking his eyes off the Ratten, "Sarah, translate this as close as you can, all right?"

Sarah nodded very seriously and said, "Yes, sir."

John spoke slowly, while Sarah translated. "Our blood is separate." Then, he slowly reached out and took the Ratten's arm. Bringing the two cuts into contact, he spoke again. "Now our blood is as one. My blood is in your veins, and your blood in my veins. Let all know that, from this time forward, you are my brother; our blood is as one."

The Ratten looked down at him and chattered. Sarah translated. "Our blood is as one."

John looked at the Ratten and held out his hand. "Sarah, tell him he has my word, the word of his brother. My team will take no action against him."

Sarah spoke to the leader, and the Ratten stuck out his hand/paw—*whatever*, thought John—and they shook.

The Ratten said something else. Sarah looked at him for a moment and then and turned to John. "Professor, he wants to know if we will punish the beasts who would enslave them."

John thought for a minute "He must mean Ulrich and Chen. When we catch both of them, they will be dealt with harshly!" John decided not to let the Ratten know about Chen back in town, in case they wanted to handle the matter themselves right away. Sarah relayed this to the leader.

As they turned to go, the leader said something. Sarah listened for a moment and, turning to her father, said, "Poppa, he said to say thank you for having a daughter that saved his." She smiled weakly at her father.

Isaiah looked at his daughter. "Tell him I am very proud of both our daughters, and as soon as I get that address for the school, I will get it to him." Sarah gulped and said something to the leader.

John thought for a moment. "Sarah, tell him to avoid other humans till we can work this out. After all this, I do not want the situation blowing up on us. Tell him we will be back as soon as we can figure out what to do." Sarah chattered to Cee Cee's father and then to her friend.

"They understand, sir," said Sarah.

John helped Julia up, then she, and Sarah climbed into the steam wagon. Isaiah climbed up and went up to the driver's seat. Looking at the pair, he said, "I will handle it, just to make sure we get back to town!"

Sarah and Julia sat in the back like two lambs being led to slaughter.

The ride back in was much slower than the ride out. The horses were tired; they had been ridden hard by the men trying to get to the girls.

"John, where did you come up with that ritual?" Julia asked in a quiet voice from the back of the steam wagon as John rode his horse near the wagon.

"South America, Julia. I was on a museum excavation in Brazil and we were having trouble with one of the native Indian tribes in the area. I saved a young boy who was drowning. He turned out to be the chief's son and they adopted me into the tribe. Any further questions, Miss Verolli?" said John, who was obviously still fuming mad.

Julia smiled weakly. "No, John," she said, looking downcast. Sarah sat next to her looking more or less the same.

The rest of the ride in went quietly. It was obvious that both of the girls were trying to make themselves invisible and, from the looks on both John and Isaiah's faces, not doing a terribly good job of it.

The party rolled into town, and the riders went off to return the horses to the livery stable, while John, Isaiah, Julia, and Sarah spotted the wagon behind the store and went in.

"Dear God," cried Julia, for there was Sam sprawled on the floor and bleeding. The chair was empty and Chen Sun was gone. She rushed to the injured man and began to check him over. Looking up at John, she said, "He's alive but badly hurt. Help me get him up."

By the time they had the man up and in a chair, he was starting to come to. "Major," he croaked, "He got away."

"It's all right, Sam. What happened?" said Morton, trying to sooth the injured man.

"Something came through the window, blew up, and startled me. Then I got jumped—white guy. I think I got a shot off and winged him—I think. Sorry, I don't remember much after that, sir." Sam was in obvious pain.

"It must have been Ulrich. They seem to want to keep outside involvement, even the tongs, to a minimum. Chen was lying about them splitting up. Ulrich must have used some kind of explosive device to free Chen," Morton theorized. "Our one lead, gone! That is just great. How are we going to explain that to Anderson!" Morton looked utterly exasperated.

Julia looked crestfallen. "Oh God, John, what have I done? If you all had not come after Sarah and me, none of this would have happened. This is my fault!" Julia was crying again.

By this time, the rest of the party returned. John gave Sam over to the other two sharpshooters and they left to take him to the doctor's office. Julia just sat there crying and Sarah stood beside her. Peter followed the men to the front of the store to keep watch.

John and Isaiah stood there looking at them. "Julia, you did not cause this. We would have been out looking for the Ratten anyhow. It just would have left Sarah and Peter in harm's way," said Morton forcefully. "You two better have some really good explanation as to what possessed you to go out toward Ratten territory by yourselves. What were you thinking, or more to the point, were you even thinking?" It was pretty obvious that both Morton and Isaiah were still steaming mad.

Both Julia and Sarah looked like small girls who had been caught by their parents, which in Sarah's case was pretty much true and in Julia's not so much. Sarah started. "It's not Miss Julia's fault, Professor! She didn't want me to go, but I said I was going anyway. She just came alone to protect me. Don't be mad at her. She loves you!"

"Sarah!" yelped Julia, obviously embarrassed by this last part of Sarah's confession.

"I am sorry, Poppa. I just wanted to warn Cee Cee. You would have done the same if it was the professor or Father Peter." Sarah was crying now.

"You, highly trained Special Agent Verolli, took a little girl into a dangerous situation and then managed to get knocked unconscious and of all things be rescued by the very creatures we were sent to destroy!" By now, the windows were shaking at the sound of Morton's voice.

"And you, young lady, I trusted you and you repay that trust by running off with the steam wagon. What were you thinking?" At this the dust was being kicked loose from the floorboards by Isaiah's voice. "I was scared half to death thinking you were already dead, and I could not bear that! Do you understand me, I could not bear to lose my family again!" Isaiah was crying now. "I think I know just what you need, young lady." With that, Isaiah stepped over, picked up Sarah, put her across his knee, and began spanking her. Sarah screamed and cried, all to no avail.

"Not a bad idea," said Morton with a dark look on his face.

"John Morton, you would not dare to—Yaaaah!" Julia wound up over Morton's knee in the same predicament as Sarah, with much the same degree of discomfort. This went on for several minutes, with Morton fuming mad, fueled by the worry and fear he had experienced during the ride out. Nonetheless, while his brain was busy being mad, certain parts of his body definitely began to respond to Julia's wiggling, and even over the pain she was feeling Julia noted his male response due to her unusual training. Before too much damage was done to their respective posteriors, the two ladies were set upright and stood on their feet.

"Now you two can stay here while we figure out how to salvage this situation."

As both Isaiah and Morton looked like thunderclouds, the girls decided it would be prudent not to protest their confinement. The two men turned and walked toward the front of the store where Peter was waiting for them.

As the men were leaving, Sarah and Julia commiserated together. "I guess I had that coming, Miss Julia," said Sarah through her tears.

"I cannot believe he did that to me." Julia winced. "Impossible, beastly man, so crude, so forceful, and so very strong. But I guess you are right. It was pretty stupid. I knew better."

Sarah looked at her. "Thank you. At least we saved Cee Cee and her family."

Julia looked even more woeful. "Do not remind me, I just do not know how I'm going to explain all this in my report."

The two of them went to clean up a little and see how bad their respective posteriors looked.

Meanwhile, Morton, Peter, and Isaiah checked out the store. "Must have been a low power explosive, more noise than power, just enough to stun Sam so he could jump him but not enough to hurt Chen. Nice touch. I will have to work on making some of those." Isaiah sounded like a man admiring a fine painting rather than someone who'd just lost a prisoner. "You know, this really was not the girls' fault. He would have just hurt them too."

"I know, Isaiah. I guess I was so mad because …" Morton took a deep breath.

"Go on John, say it", urged Peter.

"Because I thought she was dead, ripped apart by some monsters, and I could not bear the thought of my life without her in it!" Morton blew out his breath. "I love that woman."

Peter smiled. "'Bout time you admitted it, John, especially to yourself."

Isaiah smiled and then his face got serious. "Peter, were Chen's fingers bleeding?"

"No," replied Peter, "I could not see him in pain, no matter what he had done, so I gave him some field medicine and set the fingers and bandaged them. Why?"

"Take a look," said Isaiah, pointing to the floor. "Sam must have been right when he said he winged one of them, probably Ulrich."

The other two men looked down and saw what Isaiah was pointing to—a fairly thick trail of blood.

"Well, that gives us something. Peter, get Tinsman," John ordered. "The man is like a bloodhound at tracking."

All too soon, they were once again on the trail. However, Ulrich must have, somehow with Chen's help, bandaged his wound, as the trail was growing fainter. It led right down to the dock area by the harbor.

The team fanned out and asked about a pair of injured men, one of them Chinese. They found that the two men in question had hired a small coastal cargo lighter, but no one knew where it was going.

"Damn it," John swore. "We had one of them, and now they both got away!"

"Not, at least, scot-free, John," said Peter. "Both of them had some bad injuries. We might be able to pick up the trail."

The men walked back toward Isaiah's store, which had, by default, become the team headquarters. By this time, it was just the three, John, Peter, and Isaiah, as the sharpshooters had split off to do further investigations along the docks, trying to find some clues as to the direction Ulrich and Chen had taken. Peter looked at John. "I cannot say I blame you, but I cannot get over the fact you spanked Julia. As Isaiah said earlier, I do indeed hope that college of yours taught groveling. Whatever possessed you, John?"

John looked like a beaten dog. "Peter, I don't know for sure; it was just that I was so mad, crazy mad, at her for risking her life, not to mention Sarah's too. Peter, like I already said, it's just that I cannot imagine my life anymore without her in it. Now she may not want me in hers! What am I going to do?"

Isaiah looking straight ahead. "I am not going to say anything, except you got a bad case, Major."

Peter cleared his throat. "I hate to bring up another problem, gentlemen, but what are we to do about the Ratten? We cannot move against them. Aside from the fact that you gave your word and oath, sealed in blood no less, they saved Julia, did not harm Sarah, and then let us go." Peter shook his head and looked up as if for guidance "And a child shall lead them. Isaiah, Sarah was right. They have good hearts."

Isaiah looked thoughtful. "I cannot hold their wanting their freedom against them, Major. That part I understand all too well!"

Morton looked, if anything, worse. "Can this day get any more complicated? Anderson is never going to be okay with them roaming all over the country. People will ask embarrassing questions, like where they came from."

CHAPTER 34

FATHER PETER SAVES THE DAY AND THE PROFESSOR BECOMES A MASHER

eter's face suddenly got a look of inspiration. "John, what if they weren't in the country, especially if it looked like they were from someplace else?"

Isaiah and John stopped and looked at Peter. "Peter, what are you talking about?" John asked in a bewildered voice.

"Let's just say I have an idea, gentlemen, that should solve the Ratten problem, but I will need to send a telegram to a friend." Noting the look on the two faces of his comrades, Peter continued, "A fellow clergyman, and you never heard this from me. I need to swear you to secrecy!"

"Who, Peter?" said John, obviously speaking for both himself and Isaiah.

"He is a Lutheran priest. The archbishop must not find out. If he does, I may as well go find a cannibal tribe I will be in so much hot water," lamented Peter.

"I don't think I even want to know," said John. "The telegraph office is just over a couple of streets," he nodded as the three turned a corner.

Later that evening, John returned, intending to fill Julia in on what had transpired after the, uh, "incident" in the store.

Earlier, as Julia waited for him to return, she'd tried to be mad at John for what he had done to her. But in her mind, instead of anger, she kept remembering how strong and forceful he'd been—that and the fact that he had been aroused and Julia felt his arousal pressing against her even over the pain on the reverse side of her anatomy. Julia was trying her best to ignore the feelings she was having, even though they were indeed pleasant. In truth, she was not doing a good job of ignoring them, since part of her brain and her entire hormone system was reliving them much more than being mad at John.

As John entered the store, Julia looked at him, tapping her foot. Before he could even begin to explain, she said, "John Morton, how could you do that to me, spank me as if I were a little girl!"

John thought about what he knew about groveling. In all truth, it was not a subject that had been covered in college,nor, for that matter, was it one he had much knowledge of at all. John swallowed. "Julia, it was just I was so mad at you for doing what you did."

"John, I can understand about Sarah. But as for risking my own life, that is my business, sir. We are just teammates remember?"

John stepped forward and grabbed her by her arms. "No, Julia, we're not just teammates! Damn it, do you not understand I love you! I was out of my head with worry. I cannot imagine my life anymore without you in it. I need you in my life, Julia Verolli!"

"John, I told you; we can only be teammates till this mission is over. It is bad business when teammates are more than that," Julia replied, trying to break free of John's grasp, just as all her training told her to do.

John held onto her. "Julia, stop trying to hide from me; this mission is over. Ulrich and Chen have escaped; there is nothing else we can do! There is no more mission!" With that, John pulled her more tightly into his arms and, this time, was not to be denied. He kissed her with no reservations.

Julia tried to break free but obviously not too hard. "John, stop; the mission is not over," she protested. "Would you stop that, John Morton? I cannot think when you are doing that, sir."

Julia noted that all the training in the world did not seem to make her legs any stronger; they had suddenly gone weak, and she seemed to need to hang on to John to stay upright, which brought her body into contact with John, who was aroused again. A very nice arousal she could tell, even through their clothing. "John, what are we going to do about the Ratten? We cannot just kill them. You should stop that, John. This is not proper" Julia was having a hard time getting the words out or, for that matter, getting her mind to form them. Julia decided that being a young girl was definitely a nice thing. She noted too that it was also a good thing she was not a nice, proper young lady because she was quite sure nice, proper young ladies did not get wet and have these intense urges where she was getting them.

"Sorry, Julia, that is not going to help you. Peter has come up with a plan to solve the problem. Let me see now. Where was I?" Morton began to run his hands over places that a nice, proper young lady did not allow a gentleman to run his hands over, at least a gentleman who was not her husband, not to mention that his lips were engaged in some serious neck nuzzling.

Julia jerked upright. "What do you mean Peter has a plan? Now stop that this instant, Sir! What is this plan of Peter's?" All other thoughts and feelings had gone, like a haystack being hit by a passing tornado.

"I do not know, Julia," replied Morton. "But Peter seems to think it will solve all the problems. Now where were we?" John tried to pull her close again and restart his nuzzling.

"Unhand me, sir! Just teammates until this is over, John Morton, and that is final!" Julia stood bolt upright, which brought her up to the bottom of Morton's chin.

It was at this moment the door opened and Father Peter came in. Looking at the two of them he raised his eyebrow and calmly said, "Not interrupting anything, am I?"

Julia huffed. "Thank you, Father, for rescuing me from this gentleman, and I use that term very loosely indeed; this masher would be more like it!" Stepping back from John, she tried to straighten out her dress and her hair where John had been nuzzling it. "Father, John said you have a plan to solve the Ratten problem."

Peter smiled. "I am working on it, lass. And you, young man, you best curb your appetites. You are not even betrothed!"

"Yes, first sergeant." John smiled—actually leered would be more accurate—at Julia. Yes it was definitely a leer.

It was the next morning when the team met up. John looked dapper, while Julia still seemed to have some residual tenderness when she sat down. She just glared at John and muttered, "Beastly man."

Sarah had thought to bring a cushion to the table as she sat. She snuck a look at Julia, who was also obviously uncomfortable.

Peter seemed as pleased with himself as the proverbial cat who swallowed the canary. "All right, Peter, what is this plan you have figured out?" asked Julia, already in some discomfort as she sat on the hard chair.

Peter smiled. "Well, indeed my plan is coming together. Now, I need a ship with a crew that is not too curious about the cargo and, finally, can keep their mouths shut—not to mention some assorted stores and supplies."

"Father Peter, you are not going to leave them at sea are you." Julia looked worried. "They saved my life and Sarah's too!"

Sarah looked scared. "Father Peter, Cee Cee is my friend!"

Peter, as usual when dealing with Julia, just rolled his eyes. "Nobody is going to be left at sea; they will just be taking a boat ride, so to speak."

"Father, I really need to know what you have planned for the Ratten," said Julia rather forcefully.

Father Peter took another roll and began to pay particular attention to the proper application of butter to this roll, as if there was nothing else of import in the entire world.

"Father Peter!" yelled both girls in unison.

"Yes, ladies?" Peter said, looking up from his all-consuming task of butter application.

"Father Peter, Cee Cee is my friend. What is going to happen to her?" Sarah was crying now.

"Sarah, Cee Cee cannot be your friend because you never met her," replied Peter, taking a bit of the artistically buttered roll he had lavished so much attention on and savoring it as he popped it into his mouth.

Sarah looked at Peter in total confusion and then at Julia, wondering if the father had lost his mind. In truth, John, Isaiah, and Julia were beginning to wonder if maybe all this had not been too much for their friend.

"Peter," said John quietly so as not to agitate him, "what are you talking about?"

Peter smiled and said, "Sarah cannot have Cee Cee for a friend because she could not have met her yet. It is that simple." Peter was looking very pleased with himself.

"All right, Peter, let us, for the moment, pretend that I am very slow and not very bright," said John.

"That is not too hard, sir," said Julia. "Actually, it's rather all too easy; most brutes are not very bright you know."

John just gave her a hard look. "Watch your tongue, future wife!"

"What do you mean, sir, future wife," Julia sputtered. "You, sir, have not even proposed, and I certainly have not agreed. As if I would even consider marriage to such a crude, beastly man!"

"That is not what your body was saying last night," replied John.

"Father Peter, what are you talking about?" interrupted Sarah in a wail, too upset to even notice the interaction between the professor and her big sister.

John and Julia looked at each other and then at Peter. "Sorry to get distracted Father. What were you saying about the Ratten?" Julia said in an even, although obviously forced tone.

Peter took a sip of coffee and then wiped his mouth with a napkin, obviously still savoring the moment. "As I was saying, Sarah, you never met Cee Cee because she was never here. She and her people or maybe her family, anyway, are from one of the islands near Hawaii, an unpopulated one as a matter of fact. You see, no humans have met them yet. They are a previously unknown, indigenous species."

They all looked at Peter.

"Peter, that is brilliant!" exclaimed Julia, who was beside herself. "If the Ratten go along, it will solve the problem. No one will ask where they came from, as everyone will know. And William will not be able to harm them since their existence will be a great scientific discovery!"

Isaiah looked concerned. "What about people trying to enslave them, Peter?"

"Well, you see, they are going to be discovered by a Lutheran priest who will protect them and ensure that they will not be enslaved. I met him when we were both very involved with the abolitionist movement before the war. He understands and will be their shepherd."

"That was the telegram you were sending," said John. "Peter, that is wonderful! They will have their own land and be protected. Anderson cannot touch them and will not need to since they cannot be traced back to the government. They will understand that their freedom is dependent on keeping the secret of their origin."

Julia looked concerned however. "Peter, what if someone else reads the telegram and the story gets out? It will be a disastrous scandal."

Peter smiled and replied, "I doubt that it will do them much good, Julia. First I wrote it out in Latin, and second, the first two words alerted Father Paul that the following message was in the cipher we used back in our abolitionist days. We were always concerned about southern agents trying to disrupt or kill us. It was never, to our knowledge, broken. So I think the secret is safe."

Julia smiled at him. "Are you sure you did not go to a similar school to mine?"

Sarah was the only one at the table who did not seem overjoyed. Isaiah looked down at her and asked before Father Peter could retort to Julia's educational question, "What's wrong, sweetheart?"

"I will miss my friend, Poppa," she replied.

John looked over at her. "Well, I am not promising, but it certainly seems likely the museum would want to send an expedition to study these new creatures, and the expedition might need an assistant archivist."

Sarah's face lit up, and she jumped up and ran over to hug John and then Father Peter.

Julia looked at John and smiled and mouthed a silent *thank you*.

And as it happened, a small steamer was chartered by a museum to take an unspecified cargo to the Hawaiian Islands, with a short detour to pick up a clergyman in Honolulu Harbor just a little later that month.

CHAPTER 35

BACK TOWARD BUFFALO

It was several days later that a special, nonscheduled—or, as they were called, an "extra"—train pulled out of Los Angeles. The delay was to allow everyone to catch up on sleep, make shipping arrangements, arrange for a cargo pickup in a secluded cove, say some farewells, heal various cuts and bruises, and do some shopping—well, Julia shopped anyhow and, unknown to her, so did John. She would not tell anyone what she bought, with the exception of Sarah, who seemed quite pleased, although somewhat (well truthfully, quite) shocked.

The mountain passes were clear, as there had been a late season thaw. So they made better time than they had on the trip out. Before long the train was pulling into a familiar stretch of the badlands. Isaiah and Sarah unloaded the steam wagon, preparing to head to the dig site, while Julia stood nearby with a small carpetbag.

"I wish Father Peter was here," Sarah, who was monitoring the various gauges of the wagon said to Julia. "He hasn't seen the site."

"Father Peter will be joining us as soon as he returns from Hawaii. He wanted to make sure those creatures we have never met or seen or even heard about got settled in their new old home." Julia put her arm around Sarah.

Sarah just looked up at her big sister and smiled.

"Now, young lady, we have work to do," Julia sad. "Let's hope that Will hasn't made too much of a mess of the records."

"Oh dear," was all Sarah could say as she gulped and shuddered at the thought of a man doing things in what she now thought of as *her* archives and records.

After a return ride to the camp and excavation site, all four got right to work. The time went by with incredible swiftness.

For their part, Sarah and Julia worked from sunup till sundown. Sometimes they toiled well past sundown, working by the light of, thankfully for all concerned, standard lanterns. All this was to make sure everything was properly recorded, labeled, and crated. The work was exhausting, and both girls fell into their bedrolls at night without any complaints about the ground being too hard. To them, it felt like a soft and luxurious bed. Isaiah was kept busy using the steam wagon to pull strings of regular wagons to the siding where the train waited, alongside even more wagons that had been pulled by horse teams. The sheer number of discoveries was staggering, and John had to instruct the engine to go back to the junction to get several extra freight cars plus another passenger car for the dig crew.

John knew that, by now, fall was well on its way to ending for the year. While the weather had been fairly mild, storms could come up at any time in this part of the badlands, really treacherous ones. And so he hurried along the flurry of activity as the last finds were excavated, cataloged, and everything crated for shipment back to the museum.

Finally, everything was packed up, and none too soon, for the clouds rolling in were threatening. The last tents struck, stowed and the steam wagon moved out with its last wagon train in tow. Julia thought their railroad train car looked grand, and she was overjoyed at the thought of a hot bath and her cozy bunk, not to mention Chef's fine meals. She was quite convinced that beans and salt pork were getting far more than a bit old.

The last of the finds were placed in the extra freight cars, Sarah and Isaiah had the steam wagon secured in Isaiah's extra shop car, and the locomotive had steam building up. As it was, the timing couldn't have been cut any closer. A storm was starting to hit when the train pulled out, heading for the junction and back east. It was a bit of a near-run situation. The engineer was liberal with sand for the rails, since the engine was somewhat taxed with the extra cars that had been added. Luckily the train, a now much bigger train, still managed to outrun the storm. And then they were in the clear, heading home.

Dinner for five that night was a wonderful meal. As Julia had told Sarah he would, Father Peter finely joined them after several weeks. He had reported to Sarah that all went exceptionally well and that an entirely new tribe of beings would be discovered in a month or so. Sarah was quite relieved, especially when Peter brought her greetings from her friend whom she had never met and did not know and the message that she loved her new home.

Dinner was served, and shortly after desert was finished, Peter excused himself. A little later, Isaiah told Sarah he needed to talk to her up in the shop car. Sarah looked confused, but after being paddled once, she'd decided quite sensibly—she was, after all, a sensible young lady—that her father should be obeyed. She followed him out of the parlor car.

John sat across from Julia and thought she looked lovely as he built up his courage. "Julia, I was thinking that, since we are going through Buffalo, we could leave the specimens to go on ahead to the museum, and we could go to Niagara Fall for several days."

Julia looked surprised. "John Morton, what kind of a woman do you think I am? Just because we have shared a mission together does not give you license to cart me off for some amorous lusting of yours, sir!"

John smiled at her and, dropping down to one knee, took out a small box. He opened it, and inside was a small diamond ring. "I have been told, Miss Verolli, that Niagara Falls is turning into quite the honeymoon destination."

Julia looked at him. "Well, sir, as long as you are willing to protect my honor and make an honest woman out of me after dragging me to almost every hotel in Los Angeles, how can I refuse? Yes I will marry you, John Morton. But in Buffalo there is not enough time. We will need a church and the banns have to be posted and what of your family and everything else!"

When julia paused to take in a breath John smiled at her. "Father Peter telegraphed a friend of his in Buffalo, and they have been posted. He arranged for the church. I sent word to my family, such as it is—just my kid sister and her husband. He can give you away if you like."

Julia looked cross for a moment. "You presumed my acceptance, sir. You seem very sure of yourself for a dull museum professor."

"Yes, I am, Julia, because I know you love me too. At least that's what Sarah and Isaiah and Father Peter all told me," replied John with a boyish smile on his face.

Julia smiled back at him. "I love you, John Morton, but it will not be necessary for your bother-in-law to give me away. I telegraphed Uncle William over a week ago saying I would need his services. One cannot leave such important details to men you know." And then, as he slipped the ring on her finger, she kissed him very firmly.

John was struggling. "Madam, we are not yet married, and I had to promise Peter we would wait. And you, madam, are really making that promise very hard to keep!"

Julia smiled at him. "Well, I see I am making something hard. However, I certainly don't want to get the man who would marry us mad, now do I?"

John looked at her as he regained his senses, shook his head. "What do you mean you telegraphed Anderson a week ago!"

"Now, dearest, you made yourself quite clear about your feelings when you took me over your knee." She kissed him on his nose.

"Just so we understand each other, I am going to be the head of this family," said John.

"Yes, dearest," she replied as she kissed him again. She laid her head on his shoulder and smiled a true contented Cheshire cat smile.

CHAPTER 36

New Families Are Created

Julia and Sarah spent a great part of the night talking and of course giggling in their compartment, while the men enjoyed a cigar or pipe with brandy in the parlor.

Several days later, after dropping off most of the young gentlemen in Chicago so they could catch connecting trains back to their respective schools, the train pulled into Buffalo. There, the rest of the young men departed for other points.

As before, they took the same coach track near the Exchange Street station. It was the next day when a carriage pulled up and a young couple got out. Sarah was forward polishing up the brass on the steam wagon for her father who had gone to see if he could find a building for their new home and tinker's shop. Isaiah seemed quite positive about the prospects of success in this, as the Anderson Foundation had paid him a handsome salary for his work on the expedition. He told her it would be a home and shop they could buy, not rent.

She heard the commotion that announced the arrival of a carriage through the sliding loading door, which had been left open to allow extra light and air in; the fall air was cool but not cold yet, just the right temperature for burning up some elbow grease while polishing. Curious, she went out onto the end platform to see what was going on and who had arrived.

From the platform, she watched as the professor and Miss Julia came out and hugged the new people. After that, all four climbed up and then headed toward the parlor car. Being curious, Sarah went through the train to find out who these people were.

As she came into the car, she heard Julia talking. "It is wonderful to meet my sister," said Julia laughing.

Then she heard the new woman reply. "Indeed, it is like we have known each other forever."

There was more laughter, but Sarah did not hear any of it, as she ran back to the car, threw herself into the back of the steam wagon, and began to cry.

It was some time later that she heard the door open and a strange female voice calling her. "Sarah? Are you here, Sarah?"

She did not know who the voice belonged to. It certainly wasn't Miss Julia's. She was trying to be quiet, but she was still crying and sniffling when an attractive young woman, quite obviously well dressed, with blonde hair like corn silk and the bluest eyes Sarah had ever seen and popped her head over the back of the wagon. "You must be Sarah," said the young woman.

Sarah blinked at her. "Yes, madam, I am," replied Sarah in a very woeful voice as she stood up.

The young woman just cocked her head, realizing that something was wrong. "Well, I am very glad to meet you. Julia has told me so much about you. I am Susan Lewis," the young woman held out her hand in friendship and to help Sarah down out of the wagon. Sarah just stood there not moving to climb down. Sarah looked at her. "You are Julia's sister," she said, wiping a tear from her eye.

Susan laughed. "Well, not yet, not until Saturday. Now come down here. I want to see you if we are to be family. Julia said you were her little sister."

Sarah looked confused, but being a bright and talkative little girl and, under Julia's tutelage, turning into a rather refined young lady, she responded with a profound, "Huh?" She quickly followed this utterance up with a far more intellectual, "I don't understand. How could you not be her sister yet?"

Susan reached up to Sarah and finally helped her down to the floor. "My goodness, she did say you were getting bigger. I'm not her sister yet because on Saturday she's going to marry my brother. That is why I am here—to make sure that woman who has been toying with my big brother's affections is actually going to marry him and redeem his honor, the brazen hussy!" This last she said with a wink at Sarah.

"Huh," said Sarah, repeating herself and still trying to comprehend what Miss Susan had just said.

"Lewis is my married name, Sarah. Johnny," Susan continued on seeing the look of confusion on Sarah's face, "John, the professor, is my older brother. Julia is going to be my sister-in-law once she marries him. And she made it quite explicit that you were part of her family, so I guess that includes you too."

Sarah smiled and hugged Susan. "Miss Julia would never do that to your brother. She does love him, I know. Sisters share those kinds of things." Sarah looked quite firm at this, nodding in confirmation.

It was at this minute that Julia came in through the car's end door. "Oh, I see you two have met. Sarah, where have you been? I have been looking everywhere for you," said Julia tapping her foot.

Sarah ran over and hugged Julia tightly. "Do not think for one minute, young lady, that you are getting out of your duties. We have a lot of work to do!"

Sarah looked up at Julia, although in truth it was not that far up, since she had apparently had some kind of a growth spurt in the last several months, and Julia had never seemed to have one that amounted to much. "What do I have to do?"

"We have a lot of shopping to do, young lady. We both have new dresses to buy, and you need a new frock if you are going to court on Wednesday. So you best hustle your bustle, little missy." Julia smiled down at Sarah.

Sarah looked at her. "What do I need a new dress for? And why do I have to go to court?" Sarah was more than a little scared, having no idea what was happening.

"Well, for starters, Professor John Morton and I are getting married on Saturday," said Julia in a rather a haughty tone. "Sounds very romantic, does it not?" Now she was smiling and hugging herself.

"I know," Sarah said, "but I don't understand."

"Silly, you are not going to leave me by myself at my wedding, are you, after all we have been through together?" said Julia, looking shocked. "Susan will be my maid of honor," she announced. "It has to be an adult," she whispered to Sarah. "However, young lady, I will need a flower girl. And who better than my little sister?" Julia looked at Sarah with all the love a sister could have.

Sarah smiled, if possible, an even bigger smile and hugged Julia even tighter. Then, however, she seemed to get nervous again and looked up at Julia. "Why do I have to go to court?"

"That, young lady, is a very special surprise just for you, and I do not intend to wreck it by telling you. So you will just have to wait, just like the professor does for his special surprise," replied Julia, trying to look firm.

Sarah looked thoughtful for a moment. "I trust you, Miss Julia," she said. She smiled and put her hand in Julia's.

"Good. Then that is all arranged. Tomorrow, we all go shopping." Julia looked as happy as a woman who was engaged to the man of her dreams could look.

The next morning, the ladies took their leave and, climbing into a waiting carriage, went into Buffalo to find the perfect dresses and accessories for the wedding, a most arduous and serious task. It was truly an enterprise not to be taken lightly, and whether or not the gentlemen could comprehend that was highly irrelevant.

For his part, John was busy making sure the specimens were on their way to the city and the museum. He was happy that Dr. Chesterfield had wired him saying that he, his wife, and several of John's close colleagues and their wives would be arriving in time for the ceremonies on Saturday.

On Wednesday morning, a very nervous and quite dressed up Sarah, along with Father Peter, Julia, John, and Isaiah were walking into the county courthouse. Sarah, in her new dress, walked next to her father. She thought he looked quite handsome as he was in a new suit, freshly shined shoes, and a fine derby hat. They were escorted up to a judge's chambers by a policeman, but he was called a bailiff. Sarah was a little taken aback at this.

First, Isaiah went in to see the judge. He came out about a half an hour later. Next, the bailiff called Father Peter in and then Miss Julia and finally the professor. Each had his or her time in the judge's chambers.

Sarah was more than a little nervous when the bailiff called her in. The Judge seemed rather friendly but quite stern. He asked Sarah a lot of questions about how she had met Isaiah and how she had been treated. The judge went on to ask about her education. Sarah told him how Miss Julia had taught her letters and deportment, and the professor had taught her mathematics and science. She talked about how Father Peter had taught her Latin and even some Chinese. Finally, she talked about how Mr. Liman had taught her mechanicals and tinkering.

Finally, the judge asked her how she liked Mr. Liman.

"I love Poppa," she said, "even though he spanked me once."

The judge asked her to explain.

"Well, I sort of ... This will not get me in trouble again, will it?"

The judge just motioned for her to continue.

"I took the steam wagon without permission once. I mean I had to warn a friend about some danger she was in and Miss Julia came along ." She stopped, remembering what the professor and Julia had repeatedly said about not telling anyone—and they meant anyone—about Cee Cee and her family. "I guess I kind of deserved it," she finished, looking up at the judge.

The bailiff showed her out, and the five were told to wait for the judge's ruling.

A short time later, they all were shown into the judge's chambers. The judge looked very formal. "After hearing all the testimony of the two individuals in question and the witnesses regarding the character of the person applying for custody along with that of the minor person," he began, it is the opinion of this court that the minor person known as Sarah Doe, and having no known relatives, be awarded in to the custody of Mr. Isaiah B. Liman, a resident and citizen of the City of Buffalo, in the County of Erie in the State of New York, to be raised by the aforesaid as his child and that the court records shall show her to be henceforth known as Sarah Marie Liman. This child custody case is hereby closed." With that, the Judge banged his gavel.

The five friends were ushered out of the judge's chambers.

Once out in the hall, Sarah looked up at Isaiah. "Poppa?"

Isaiah looked down at his daughter with tears in his eyes and running down his face. "For now and always," he said. "Julia, we do not know how to thank you. I was told it normally took many months, sometimes years for an adoption, especially to a single man, to go through."

Julia just smiled and said, as she hugged Sarah, "If you cannot pull some strings for your sister, who should you do it for?"

Sarah hugged her back and cried buckets of happy tears.

The days flew by, and the Sunday morning *Buffalo Gazette* carried the following story in its society section:

> On Saturday morning, Miss Julia Paulette Verolli of Washington, DC, married Professor John Michael Morton of Manhattan in a Mass of holy matrimony at St. Joseph's Roman Catholic Church here in Buffalo. The bride wore a beautiful Second Empire–style white dress. She was attended by her maid of honor, Mrs. Susan Lewis of Boston, Massachusetts, the groom's younger sister. The best man was Mr. James Lewis, the groom's brother-in-law. The bride was given in

marriage by Col. William Anderson, also of Washington, the bride's uncle. Miss Sarah Liman of Buffalo was the flower girl. The service was performed by Father Peter Harrigan of New York City, a close friend of the family. The couple will be living in Manhattan after honeymooning in Niagara Falls.

Later that evening as John and Julia settled into their hotel room in Niagara Falls, Julia called out to John, who was already in bed, "I will be right there, sir!"

John just smiled.

Julia came out of the attached bathroom dressed in a silk robe with a Chinese print on it. She smiled at John and pulled out the pin holding her hair up so it came down around her shoulders. While she was loosening her hair, one leg slipped forward out of the robe, and she almost whispered, "I hope you like it, dear, but there does seem to be one flaw with it."

John, who, by this time, was having some trouble breathing, swallowed and responded, "I do not see anything wrong, my love. What is the problem?"

Julia gave John that same look she had used in Los Angeles to keep up their cover. "Well, it seems to be so smooth that, if I undo the belt, it just slides off." She proceeded to demonstrate.

Much to her surprise, John did not seem to find this to be a serious flaw at all. As predicted by Father Peter, he was very favorably impressed by his new wife as she walked toward him with her special walk in only her shoes, garters, and stockings.

Later that night, after consummating their marriage, several times and in multiple positions, John, who was totally spent, started to doze off. Mrs. Julia Morton—she really did like the sound of that, and she rolled it around in her head and savored it much like a sommelier tastes a fine wine—curled up next to her husband's back. She decided that maybe that was not a very serious flaw in that robe at all—and after she'd spent so much time in Los Angeles's Chinese quarter finding one that had that particular flaw.

Much earlier in the afternoon of that same day, Father Peter had managed to board a train headed for Albany, where he would change for one going on to New York City. As he sat there relaxing, he looked forward to not being shot at, thrown off horses, or forced to play cloak-and-dagger and, most especially, to no more riding in airships, a truly terrible way to travel indeed. All he would have to do was say Mass, hear confessions, and try to keep the peace in his parish; indeed, it sounded heavenly, even in the Five Points. He happened to sit across from Dr. Chesterfield and his wife, who was also very happy for John, although the curator smiled, remembering the warning he had given the young professor about the dangers of taking a single young woman out to a dig site in the wild, untamed west with him.

Meanwhile on a train bound for Washington, to which his private car had been attached, William Anderson fumed. Not only had he lost one of his best agents, but of all the indignities, he'd had to give her away! At least if he needed another expedition, he knew where to find a team, he thought, consoling himself.

Two weeks later, Isaiah was putting up a new sign on the new, larger shop in Buffalo, while his daughter watched approvingly:

I. Liman & Daughter
Clockworks & Mechanicals

A month later, two men, a white man and a Chinese one, got off a boat in South America and began their search for a place to set up a laboratory. Their research was proving to be quite promising.

Union Army. It should be noted that almost no unit, at any level, was ever at full strength. The numbers given are ideal, however rarely seen in the field.

- **Company**: Basic organizational unit, approximately one hundred men, commanded by a captain.
- **Battalion:** Not used during the American Civil War but used extensively during the Indian Wars, three to four companies or troops of cavalry, generally commanded by a senior captain or major.
- **Regiment:** Ten companies or one-thousand-plus men, generally commanded by a colonel.
- **Brigade:** The Basic tactical unit, three to five regiments with an attached battery of artillery (six guns), commanded by a brigadier general.
- **First sergeant:** In the Union Army of the Civil War period, the senior enlisted man of a company.
- **Sergeant Major:** The senior enlisted man of a regiment.
- **US Colored Troops**: The county's first major attempt to use African Americans in the army, units of black enlisted men with white officers; such a unit might be designated, as in this story, 2nd Regiment, C Company.
- **New York State Militia:** During the American Civil War, the United States Army was quite small and mostly posted in the

west to fight Indians; almost all troops were state militias on loan to the federal government.

General terms

Butternut: Various shades of reddish brown from homemade dyes. With the blockade in force, most Confederate uniforms were cut from homemade cloth dyed butternut, and far fewer were in the official gray.

Cow Pie: The material that is emitted from the south end of a northbound cow and left in various piles.

The Five Points: An area in New York City bounded by three streets, Anthony, Cross, and Orange, which came together to form an irregular intersection with five corners. This area was the basis for the book and movie *Gangs of New York*.

The Trent Incident: On November 8, 1861, the USS *San Jacinto*, commanded by US Navy Captain Charles Wilkes, intercepted the British mail packet RMS *Trent* and, after forcing her to heave to, sent over a boarding party to take off two Confederate agents, Mason and Slidell. No one was hurt, but in the British Parliament, there were cries for war with the United States and that Wilkes be hunted down as a pirate. In this story's version of history, the Trent was fired on, and several men were killed. There is little doubt that England would have come into the war had this happened.

Pinkertons: A private detective agency that, in many ways, served as the forerunner to today's FBI, there being no national police agency at this time in history.

Bernhardt, Sarah: Sarah Bernhardt was born in France and, later, immigrated to the United States. She was probably the most famous actress of the nineteenth century.

Gatling gun: A multibarreled gun but technically not a machine gun. External power had to be supplied to fire the next round, generally by a hand crank—until (as Isaiah demonstrated in the story) the guns were powered with steam, thus transforming them into machine guns. Modern Gatlings are powered by an electric motor, as in the U.S. Army's M-163, which achieves firing rates of up to six thousand rounds/minute.

Roman Catholic terms

Aspergil: A short-handled device with a round ball on the end, used by a priest to sprinkle holy water, most commonly seen in modern times to sprinkle a casket at a funeral Mass.

Extreme Unction: Literally, prayers for the dead or dying. The Church replaced extreme unction at the end of the twentieth century with prayer for the sick.

Railroad Terms

Drag freight train: A slow-moving train hauling a nonperishable commodity, such as coal. Generally, drag freight trains were very slow and had to give way for all other railroad traffic.

Highball: Early signals were brightly colored balls that were hoisted to the top of a pole to indicate that no stop was required; the train could "highball" through the station. If the Ball was in the lower position, the low ball, indicated a stop was required. This was an early form of "fail-safe," if the rope broke, the signal would be at the low ball.

Peddler freight trains: Local trains that switched cars at various company or privately owned sidings. In a peddler freight train, it might take all day just to move ten miles, depending on the number of switching moves the train had to make.

Wait or **stuck in the hole:** A term meaning to take a siding to allow a train of a higher class to pass or overtake.

Pump up the brakes: The Westinghouse air brake system operated on the "fail-safe" principal. Air pressure held the brakes off so that, should the train be uncoupled and the airline were to break, the brakes were automatically applied. So in order to move the train, the system had to be pumped up to release the brakes.

avid (Dave) Hornung holds a master's degree in mechanical engineering and a doctorate in environmental engineering, along with several other degrees in social and physical sciences. He is a licensed professional engineer in New York State. He has served and is still active on the boards of several technical societies.

He is retired after twenty-plus years of work for the Municipal Housing Authority and, later, the Department of Public Works for the City of Buffalo, New York, including a term as city engineer. He later served several years as an adjunct professor of engineering at Niagara County Community College.

Hornung is currently completing studies for an MA in pastoral ministry at Christ the King Seminary (cks.edu) in East Aurora, New York, which is near Buffalo.

A longtime ham radio operator (WB2SQR), miniature wargamer, model railroader and avid history buff—including many years as a Civil War reenactor (A Co. 28th NY Infantry & A Co. 15th NY Volunteer Engineers)—Hornung is happy to call Buffalo, New York, his hometown. He resides there with his wife and five cats. He notes that all the snow stories about Buffalo are mostly hype; Rochester and Syracuse get far more snow then Buffalo, but we have a better PR department.

The Ratten Expedition is Hornung's first book of fiction. Julia and John continue their adventures in the **Subterranean Expedition** out in May of 2017.

As a last note, for those of you who were wondering why you never heard of it, the Buffalo Central RR is the home railroad of the Model Railroad Club of Buffalo.

Feedback is always appreciated. E-mail at: *davehornung@verizon.net*.

Printed in the United States
By Bookmasters